In a clash of love and destiny, who pays the price?

Jackson thought he was the most powerful shifter in the world. Blessed with gifts and popularity, he's always felt bad for his brother Rush, who'd been born with the disadvantage of being normal.

But when a beautiful shifter named Bright Star appears on the scene, Jackson learns his brother is far from normal. Bright Star forces Rush to reveal unimaginable talents he's always kept hidden-talents Bright Star claims will save the world...whether Rush likes it or not.

Books by Grayson Reyes-Cole

The Builder
The Prescription Playboy
Bright Star

Lover Opalus Series
The Empire

Published by Kensington Publishing Corporation

Bright Star

Grayson Reyes-Cole

LYRICAL PRESS
Kensington Publishing Corp.
www.kensingtonbooks.com

Lyrical Press books are published by
Kensington Publishing Corp. 119 West 40th Street New York, NY 10018

First Electronic Edition: October 2008
eISBN-13: 978-0-9841132-4-8
eISBN-10: 0-9841132-4-X

First Print Edition: October 2008
ISBN-13: 978-1-61650-902-6
ISBN-10: 1-61650-902-3

Printed in the United States of America

I'd like to thank my mother for teaching me to read, how to write with a fat pencil, and for reading mounds and mounds of science books when I couldn't be convinced to. I'd also like to thank my friends and extended family for all the support.

Chapter 1

Saving: The Curse

Jacob Rush listened to the rasping, uneven breath of the skinny, wet and almost dead girl stretched out before him. He watched the girl continue to wheeze in a high-pitched plea. Her chest continued to convulse.

She should have been dead. She *was* dead. And then she wasn't.

Jacob rocked back on his knees, coming to rest on his calves. Steam rolled off his heated body. He couldn't focus his eyes. When he tried, the sweat dripped down into them, stinging and blinding him. Feeling around the cold cement in light cautious pats, his fingertips found the over-shirt he had stripped off after he'd dragged her from the fountain. Slowly, he raised it to his face. The shirt was cold relief.

He inhaled deeply and then exhaled, watching his breath crystallize and dissipate as it floated away from him in the night. He had done this many times, and knew he would do it many more. Each time it happened, it seemed to squeeze his organs tighter, to crack and reshape his bones more and to make his muscles fold over themselves and redouble. It caused that trigger, that light deep within his brain to throb and grow.

Jacob would have liked to believe it was his imagination, not his body, mind and Talent that were changing. He lied, telling himself that he had not really saved this girl. Something inside this girl had sped recovery after he'd pulled her out of the water, breathed down her throat, and pushed hard on her chest. Just performing CPR was something he could live with. But Jacob Rush knew the truth: he had done more than some rudimentary first aid technique.

He waited, knowing that soon he would experience the cold. It hit him and stung, lashing out against him. For a long moment, he let the freezing fingers of nature claw at him, willing them to dig out his anxiety and fear. How many more times would he do this? How, in the end, would it change him? When would she come and demand this thing he gave freely?

He put on the shirt. It was slightly warmer then, still heated from his face. Folding his arms and closing his eyes, Jacob Rush started to breathe slower, deeper. He started to leave this place. But before he could completely tuck himself away, a dry and low voice pulled at him. It sounded brittle, parched.

"I'm still alive?" The girl rose up on her elbows and looked around. Her damp, lank brown hair clung to her forehead and neck, to her sallow and pointed shoulders.

He'd seen her there—God knows how—still, eyes and mouth closed, at rest. Peace marked her. Completely under water, lying on the bottom of the fountain her body was pale, tinted a frigid blue and surrounded by yellow, red, and white mosaic. He'd pulled off his shirt and jumped over the lip of the pool in one motion. Then, he'd reached down and grabbed her dead weight. Her clothes, her hair, her skin all clung to the bottom so that he had to grapple with her flesh as he'd tried to peel her from the tiled bed. Her skin had become slippery like a peeled plum, and he'd lost his grip as her body attempted to adhere itself to the bottom again. But those eyes, submerged, brilliant and blue, had opened to pin him with a gaze of recognition.

Ah.

Sadly, finally, Jacob had recognized *her*. He'd been able to haul her out then, and save her.

When he should have let her die.

Jacob spotted her jacket in the fountain. It must have slid off when he dragged her out of the water. He pointed to the red, white, and gold striped material. Only a sleeve peeped from beneath a stone head and shoulder the size of a headstone.

She noticed how intently he watched her. "Why are you looking at me like that?"

"You almost died."

"What?" She sprang up and swung her head from side to side, sloshing water into the air. She blinked rapidly as she took in her surroundings. Her hands smoothed over her soaked torso. Then—Jacob could read that awkward expression anytime—she averted her gaze and rounded her shoulders in intense shame. Whatever recognition in her eyes earlier had been snuffed out.

She sighed and slowly rolled to her feet. A distance opened between them when she moved away, cutting a slice into the ready intimacy of a life saved. She seemed agitated and would not meet his gaze. Jacob stood as well, but could not stop watching her.

"Why were you in the fountain?" he asked. His voice was well modulated. His words didn't sound like a demand. He hoped they didn't sound as if the answer mattered to him.

She started to answer. Her jaw worked. In the end, she managed to explain, "I was throwing coins in. I threw one in that belonged to my mother." She chewed at chapped skin on her upper lip. Those eyes, she kept tilted downward.

Jacob knew she did not want him to study her eyes or how startling and nearly illuminated they were. She also probably didn't want him to know that she was lying, but Jacob knew. She continued, "I got in to look for it. Part of the statue must have fallen and hit me. I think I just panicked and slipped. I can't swim anyway."

She had been lying on her back. Her arms had been folded carefully over her abdomen. Her legs had been straight as well. She had not looked like a girl who had slipped, yet Jacob said nothing.

"I guess I'm thanking you for saving my life," she finished, but it did not sound like appreciation. Her voice was small, tinny and false.

Jacob Rush reached a hand out to touch the base of her skull. Her wet hair lay just over his knuckles. The wound was large and bloody and hot. It felt like an infection. *She* felt like an infection. Her blood gurgled over his fingers, seeped into his palm, and rode the veins in his arm, spreading through his circulatory system, getting into tissue, into cells. And then, the blood was gone. "How do you feel now?"

Elizabeth placed a hand over the one cradling her head. She didn't feel any pain. Outside or in. Jacob could tell. Her voluntary touch had let him inside of her. Just like that. She had become a part of him. The intimacy was back. Her thoughts mingled with his like threads in a tassel. Elizabeth was thinking then that for the first time in her life, she didn't feel any pain. She wondered briefly if her heart would stop. For the first time in her life, she didn't want to die.

He let her go. "Aren't you cold?" He asked in a voice too calm for reality. His eyes held hers, though they were clear and intense and offered nothing. He knew better than to show her too much compassion.

She hesitated. No, she wasn't cold. "Yes, I am."

"You need to change clothes." But what did compassion matter? The poison was inside him now. His hands, his skin, his heart and brain, his blood, his breath, his Energy was the curse. There was nothing left for it. "Those are wet."

She looked down at the dingy white t-shirt and worn jeans that were pulling her downward, weighted by water. Her thoughts were murky and congealed, but Jacob Rush could pick them out with ease—*He thinks I'm too skinny; He thinks I'm too dark. He thinks. I am dirty-obsessed-stained-removed crazy. He thinks my eyes and body and Energy curse him.*

Jacob knew she was hiding something. She rubbed at fine white scars on one forearm.

She was barely audible when she answered. "Well, you're right. I'm not usually around anywhere long enough to feel the cold."

He blinked. Even his vision was different now. It was as if his body was still putting out steam, and that was clouding his eyes, creating a hazy film he couldn't completely penetrate. "I live near here. You can get something out of my brother's room. You're very thin. He's broad, but he's shorter than me and he might have something."

She said nothing, just inclined her head in acceptance. She didn't think he had heard a word she'd said. At least he was still talking about clothes. She avoided his intense scrutiny and mumbled, "My name is Elizabeth."

"Jacob Rush. People call me Rush." He took her small hand into one of his own, studying it. He shook it and let it fall softly to her side.

"Were you alone?"

She followed him away, walking as if her clothing were stiff. Jacob imagined her garments were near frozen. "I don't know, I think so." Jacob felt the jumble in her head. Her memory was screwed up again. Her veins felt as if they were swelling all through her body. She winced, wanting to cry. And why was that? She was afraid that she was going to have a vision. Again.

"Why are you still here?" he asked, trying to get her attention, her focus.

"What?" She was virtually perplexed, but he was treated for once to the crystal eyes.

"Why are you still in town?" he clarified patiently. "I recognize you from the flyers. I saw them a while back."

"There was an accident about two months ago. I… I had to stay for awhile." She shrugged and Jacob thought of the emaciated cat that had taken up residence in his room when he was twelve. It had come to die, just as she had. "Doesn't matter, though. The guy who runs the gallery owns the condo, too. He wants me out."

His eyes darted into hers, sharply. Hers, that intense blue, his own, a watery, wild brown. Wet hair irritated her face as her head hung down.

She was feeling ridiculous again. The scars on her arms and inner thighs ached. This body. She would get rid of it. Jacob reached out to touch her elbow as he guided her down a side street. She forgot, for a moment, how much she had come to despise herself.

Then, suddenly, he averted his gaze. Again, eagle's eyes, bright and dark darting. "Come in." He motioned toward the door in front of them and pushed it open. It was dark inside.

Elizabeth cleared her throat. "I don't usually go into strange men's houses. It's not very safe." With a sideways smile, he turned and moved into the building. She followed him, lips slightly parted. She entered and closed the door behind her. A cloud of darkness drifted down like exploded gunpowder over her head.

She made a move to open the door. She could not. She felt him beside her and knew that he was using his weight to keep the door closed. She felt his quick breathing on her cheek and neck. Elizabeth squeezed her eyes shut and it only served to add to the darkness, to make her more isolated, to make her more aware of the length of Jacob next to her. She opened them again. It made no difference.

Jacob could feel fear lashing out of her, scratching at him. How long would it take for panic to overwhelm, to peel back the façade she didn't know she wore?

"You aren't afraid of the dark, Elizabeth." A large, gentle hand stroked a lock of hair behind her ear.

She opened her own mouth to speak but instead found herself inhaling warmth. It snaked through her nostrils, touched the back of her chilled throat, then filled her lungs and stomach with heat. Like steam, it did not stifle her.

The light came in the form of a loud crackling blaze from somewhere low on the ground. It was a fireplace. Jacob stood, losing his eyes in the flames that reached for him, licking and destroying as they strove up and out at him. He stepped closer, still out of reach. His toasted skin glowed capricious gold and orange. He stepped closer still and the flames shrank back into their cave, leaving the stone mouth still warm.

He stood up and asked, "Would you like some hot cocoa?" Elizabeth nodded. "You'll find some clothes down that hall in the last room to your right. By the time you change, it'll be ready. He watched her as she walked down the hall to his brother's room.

* * * *

Elizabeth stepped into the room. It was a world completely removed from that of the rest of the apartment. Even the comforting scent from outside did not penetrate this room. It was cold, lonely and sterile. The sun from outside pierced the windows and seared past the blue and white striped curtains. Wasn't it evening? In Jacob Rush's living room without the light of the flame, there had been complete and utter darkness. Here, her eyes hurt and she felt so exposed she was nearly overwhelmed by an illogical impulse to hide.

Ultimately, her eyes adjusted to the light and she inspected the surroundings. Her pinprick pupils missed nothing. The bed was made up as meticulously as if some Marine had been ordered to make it a hundred times to ensure he got it right. It was blue. The carpet was dark gray. The mirror mounted above caught the sunlight and bounced the white light off the stark white walls at Elizabeth. Everything was blinding white, and she could not see herself in the mirror; she couldn't see anything. It was getting hot.

The heat pressed on her shoulders and massaged her back. She wanted to sleep. Wasn't it nighttime? The bed beckoned and the light followed her as she neared it. She ran a hand over the soft downy cover, and lowered her lids with a slow smile, softening the hard and hungry angles of her face. Her limbs seemed trapped in slow motion. Her breathing was slow in her ears, but irregular to he who was listening. Yes, somehow, she knew he was there. Jacob. Rush. Listening.

The vision was starting again. Only this time, there was no beginning, middle, or end. There was only fire. She was enveloped in flames so hot they couldn't be distinguished from freezing even as they burned the flesh away from her bones. She opened her mouth to scream but only a plume of black smoke puffed out then tunneled back down her throat, turning to flame and burning her from the inside.

"Are you OK?" His voice slashed in a cool arc through her dream. Her eyes fluttered. She was still burning. Her remaining flesh was bubbling, blistering. Her eyes were tearing, and as the water streaked down her cheeks, steam arose. Her whole body was on fire. She was burning, and she couldn't understand why she was conscious through the pain. Her eyes opened, but blue light only seemed to reflect back at her. She realized she was in front of the mirror.

"I'm fine," she called, willing the after effects of the vision to end. Her eyes were open but she could not trust them anymore. She reached out. She remembered a closet. She stumbled blindly until she reached it. She felt for the door, which partly opened for her. It was dark within. She could only make out the outline of clothing inside, but it looked cool in there, safe in there.

Safe. Inside, the vision ceased abruptly. She was cooling. Still hot, but cooling. Quickly, she passed her hands over the rest of her body until the blistered skin fell away and evaporated as it was replaced with pale pink flesh. Mouse-brown hair grew back. She couldn't let Jacob see the vision on her, smell it on her.

The closet wasn't dark. It was cast in a soft blue light. Inside, there were indeed men's clothes. They hung neatly in the closet. Slacks, t-shirts, button downs. They were mostly very big and she only imagined how they would have looked on her thin, wiry body. The clothes were well-worn, well-cared for. She reached out a hand and touched a faded blue and green plaid shirt. It was so cool to the touch, cool to her heated touch. She moved further into the closet that tempted her, inviting her with a cool and fresh scent. The shirt fell around her thighs and she marveled at the size, so different from her own. She moved around in the cooling womb that had expanded for her, encasing her maternally in its obscurity.

Then suddenly, she was afraid to go out. She couldn't move again into the room with light that exposed her so much she could not see. It was a room that made her tired and told her she needed to close her eyes, to sleep a lifetime, to burn and to die.

Then she heard his voice. "Are you all right in there, Elizabeth?"

"Uhh...uhh, I'm fine." She wanted to cry out to him that she wasn't. To make him save her, but she could not. She expected his voice to move away again to leave her. It would be better than the humiliation of being stuck in a closet because she was afraid of the light.

Silence played for a moment. Then the outer door was opened, and she could barely hear the footsteps coming towards her.

He stopped outside the closet door. "Come out, Bright Star."

Slowly the door began to creep open and a small hand slipped around it. The hand was snatched, engulfed in his and she was pulled out and up. Cradled in his arms, she could see the room had dimmed with his presence. Then the darkness followed them out like a great cape that hung from Rush's shoulders.

* * * *

"Your brother," Bright Star asked as she curled up in a soft chair and sipped her cocoa. "Where is he now?"

Rush looked back at her. He was sitting in front of the fire with an arm resting on a raised knee. "Bright Star?"

"Yeah?" She forgot her own question as she felt her skin prickle under his scrutiny.

Rush remained silent for a long moment, but his face with its soft curves and hard lines was turned towards Bright Star. His gaze roamed over her features then fell to the floor and then the fire again. He was still and yet, not still. "My brother's up north for the moment."

"Vacation?"

He shook his head, closed his dark brown eyes and leaned back with his arms braced behind him, stretching out his, long, lean body. So strong and exotic. Bright Star noticed how his dark, curling hair caught autumn streaks in the firelight and how his previously dark, dark gold skin glowed hot bronze. She shifted her gaze to the flames that seemed to be dying. Again, she had a fleeting thought that they were shrinking away from him. She continued her scrutiny. With his dark eyes closed, and his head tilted back she found that his ebony lashes were long, curling, and that he had a scar above his left eye. He suddenly seemed so exhausted.

She remembered the way he carried her from that room at the end of the hall. He had pulled her into his arms and lifted her with impossible ease. He had borne her away as if he knew she hadn't the strength to move through the room to the door. She remembered that he didn't even look at her until the door had been closed safely behind them. She remembered thinking of him as her hero, her champion. And yet somehow, something was wrong. She could see it when he looked at her.

"Jacob," she called. Slowly he gave his gaze to her, though he didn't respond. "Rush? In your brother's room..."

"Don't ask me," he warned in a menacing whisper. Bright Star drew her legs up closer to her chest and studied her chocolate for a long moment. Her guess had been on the money: Jacob thought she was weak. When she glanced up at him, his features had softened as if he hadn't been able to sustain the frightening visage. He shook his head. "Just put it all out of your head for now. Just bury it."

The fear within her manifested itself in a trembling of slender fingers, a deep swallow of nothing, and a heart that felt too big for its chest. She usually talked too much when she was nervous, but now she found she could say nothing. In her own defense, she tried to retreat into herself as she had so many times in the ceaseless disquiet of the fair. Setting her mug down beside the chair, she slowly let her eyes roll back as her lids lowered. She breathed in the deep aromatic smokiness of the room. She leaned her head back expecting to feel the plush padding of the chair softly greet her head. Instead, her body continued falling back and back, and her lids became too heavy to lift. She was falling, her whole body feverish and damp with sweat as she descended. She was falling, and then, she was burning again.

"Bright Star!" The sound was loud in her ears, pulling her back. And his arms were around her, pressing her head into his chest and he was soothing her in barely more than a whisper, "Bright Star."

Abruptly, her blue, blue eyes opened, and she began to shiver. She didn't understand anything. She drew back and looked into Jacob's face. She saw something angelic there but she also saw a darkness—a shadow that was so protective and honest in the way it shielded her from the hot light of the fireplace. And she saw it when she looked at Jacob Rush. She didn't speak but held onto his arms as he anchored her. She found her voice. "Jacob? Jacob, what's happening to me? I don't know what's happening to me." He stretched long fingers over her face then, and held her with his gaze for moments. Bright Star felt his touch not only on her skin but also in her mind. She had wondered for so many years, what it was like to have someone journey through her mind the way she had with strangers for longer than she could remember. She noticed a blue glow on his nose and cheeks.

He was close enough for her to feel his breath on her face, and, all of a sudden, the light was gone from the fireplace and the house was as dark as it had been the first moment she'd come inside, save for the blue light.

"So you perform? That's what the flyers said," Jacob inquired softly. He stroked her hair.

"Psychic readings," she offered with agitation.

"Psychic readings," he repeated.

"Don't you watch TV, you know, like the hotlines? I tell you stuff about your life: past, present, future—all that crap. Except I had lights and music."

"Is that all?" he asked.

She nodded.

"Were you always right?"

"Of course, I was always right," she answered impulsively. Then with eyes cast down, she added, "It's all rigged anyway."

"Bright Star," he whispered. Had his face not remained so emotionless, she would have thought he said the name in horror.

"Why do you call me that?" she asked. He didn't answer. She wished he would say something else, wished he would offer her something to make everything real and normal again. But he offered her nothing.

Bright Star leaned closer to him and began to listen. She listened for his heartbeat, and then she listened to the very flow of his blood. Like a strong river, it sounded, strong enough for rapids. He was tense. And then, slowly, it came: *I don't know why you are as you are today, but I know you are mine, and whether I like it or not I am yours. Do you hear me, Bright Star?* Her eyes snapped upward, glistening, she watched him. He was angry, very angry.

"Jacob," Bright Star pleaded, "What are *you*?"

"Better question," his gaze was accusing. In that moment, Bright Star knew he hated her. "What are you?"

It was then that Jacob stood and clutched his hands to either side of her head. For a moment, there was a ringing in her ears so powerful that it snapped to silence as she felt hot blood trickling down either side of her neck. Her knees buckled and her body became weightless, nothing. The word *curse* repeated as an accusation in her mind. And then nothing. She was gone.

Chapter 2

The Precocial

On the morning before Jackson Rush met Bright Star, the two occupants of the small apartment on Kolter Avenue found themselves in the same room. That was a rare occurrence. Unsurprisingly, the silence between the brothers was at once intimate and awkward. Jackson, the always-favored son, leaned on one arm against the counter watching his brother Jacob eat and grunt messages. "Ronald called five million times last night."

"Randall?" Jackson corrected his brother, rolling his eyes.

"Yeah, Ronald. I was surprised you didn't answer. Oh, and once this morning."

"Huh," was all Jackson said. He pressed a button on his cell phone. He'd had it on silent all night.

His brother glanced up at him, then back down. "Glad you can be so nonchalant about it. I didn't get you up this morning because I heard you up and walking around all night. I know you didn't sleep."

"No." Jackson sighed. He closed his eyes and subtly shook his head.

Rush pushed back in his seat. "What the hell is it, Jacks?"

For a moment, there was silence. Jackson smiled. Or grimaced. Either way, he was biting the inside of his lips and flexing his hands into fists.

"What do you think?" Jackson asked into the quiet.

Jacob Rush, called Rush by all who knew him, didn't answer. Instead, he continued to eat. His shoulders were hunched over a bowl at the kitchen table. His fist was wrapped around a large spoon. He shoveled cereal into his mouth. His jaws seemed to snap, his teeth clicking on the metal spoon. Milk dribbled down his chin. Jackson watched the play in the skinny forearms protecting the bowl. His brother looked like a starved animal.

Jackson grabbed a peach from a basket on the table and flexed his fingers around it. He looked at his brother again. Rush's forearms circled the bowl as if he were guarding it. "Rush, can I ask you something?"

Rush, the brother who had a different father, the brother with dark skin and dark haunting eyes turned his attention to the golden one. He sat back, pushing the bowl away. He waited as if patience was a gift rarely granted.

"If you could… you know… do what I do, would you feel compelled to go into the Service? Or maybe not go in to the Service," he amended quickly, "but at least do something to help other people. You know, to save them."

The dark eyes that blinked at Jackson were flat, the expression blank. His brother went completely still. His chest didn't even rise and fall with breath. Jackson faltered. What had he said? Jackson swallowed. His brother frightened him. There was no explanation for it, but there was no avoiding it. When Jackson was younger, he told himself that he had just been intimidated by Rush's silence. But no, he'd gotten older, a little wiser, and now knew the only truth. Rush scared him shitless.

Physically, it made little sense. They were night and day, to Jackson's favor. Jackson knew he was handsome with his golden skin, dark blond hair, and light brown eyes. But beyond good looks, he was physically impressive, to say the least. Just shy of six feet tall and thickly muscled, he was built like the athlete and current Serviceman he was. It was part of his regimen to keep in rigorous shape through an aggressive cardio and weight-training schedule. He'd won the endurance trial each year for the past three at the Service. His body possessed an obvious strength.

Rush, on the other hand, was a sallow, sickly caramel with dark, kinky hair. That same dark hair perpetually accented his jaw, neck, forearms and legs. Even though he wore layer upon layer of clothing, Rush's tall frame appeared almost slight. Any muscle he possessed seemed to be of the lean, naturally occurring kind. Shirtless, his skin was pale and jaundiced with smudges defining each of his ribs. Similar smudges were found beneath his cheekbones. Jackson found himself urging his brother to eat more all the time, but it didn't matter. Rush ate voraciously, relentlessly, rapaciously but never seemed to gain weight. Still, instead of appearing frail or weak, Rush was like a starved leopard. Gaunt yet dangerous. Somehow, someway he gave one the impression that he was waiting to pounce, waiting to make a kill. Where Jackson eyes were soft and brown, Rush's almond-shaped eyes appeared black and absorbing. They were only made more so by the darker-tinted skin beneath them.

But even their physical differences—which were strong enough to warrant no one believing that they were even half-brothers—were the least significant reasons why Jackson should not have feared his older sibling.

There was also the fact that Rush truly cared about his little brother more than anything else in the world. Jackson knew it. Rush admitted it freely and without shame. Before their parents died, Rush had still been closest to Jackson. After Janie and Everett Rush died, he had made it part and parcel of his brotherly duty to care for Jackson as a parent would, and to support him as a best friend.

The other—perhaps most important—reason Jackson's fear of Rush should have been groundless was this: Jackson was nearly impervious to physical harm.

Jackson Anthony Rush had been the only Precocial Shifter born... ever. Since the beginning of time, they had been born one in one hundred million. Called Shifters for their ability to bend known physics laws and known reality, they had only been discovered, secreted away, categorized, honed and marshaled for a couple of centuries. The Service had come to be their destiny. But never in all recorded history had there been a Precocial, a person who possessed and could command his paranormal Talents from birth. It was taught as fact that Shifters had limitations to their powers and that Shifting could only be accomplished after the onset of puberty, making human beings completely altricial, not precocial. Shifting Talent then improved by age with no apparent peak. These were the Parameters of Shift. They governed the gifted the same way the laws of physics governed the "normal" world.

A Precocial child had been nothing more than a supposition, a complex and improbable equation endlessly disproved. It was a point to be debated amongst geniuses. It was fodder for confidential government tracts and PhD candidate theses alike. Over many years, the Precocial was—finally—a myth. Few had truly believed in a Precocial as more than a fairy tale until Jackson's birth.

Even though they tried every method known to man, Janie and Everett were unable to conceive for four years after she gave birth to her first son Jacob. Everett Rush had married her during that pregnancy. They met shortly after Janie had been deserted in her second trimester. Everett had been a customer at the market she worked. He'd been awed by her wholesome and ethereal beauty, even in her condition. He'd loved her instantaneously and planned to raise her child as his own. At least until Jacob had come along with his dark and exotic looks, and his persistently plaintive wail. Rush came with eyes the color of tar that followed Everett around the room. Rush nearly killed his mother when he pushed his way out of her womb.

Janie started trying to give Everett the baby he wanted as soon as she was healthy again. In the second year, she became pregnant, yet was devastated when the baby was lost in her third month. Janie was hospitalized for months after that tragically terminated pregnancy. Everett was forever at her side, but she knew it was only duty that kept him there. Though he tried valiantly, Everett couldn't help feeling that she was to blame. It didn't matter that she had already had one healthy son. She had not been able to have a son for *him*. And he needed that, needed it more than anything else. He needed a son that did not stare intently at him from the corner of the hospital room with those unseeing, black eyes. A son who needed a father, because it was clear that Jacob Rush—most ironically called "Rush" for short—did not. Jackson's mother had told him many times before she died how much she'd wanted him and his father had wanted him. Many times she had told him this. A year after that miscarriage, miraculously, she conceived again.

Janie and Everett struggled desperately trying not to put too much hope in this child because the pregnancy was plagued from the start with complications. She suffered gestational diabetes and hypertension, immobilizing sciatica, and bouts of severe, debilitating depression. When the time came, they'd believed this baby to be dead. But he'd breathed and cried, and as he cried, he'd called down rain that fell only on that hospital for thirteen days in a row. Immediately the phenomenon had been recorded and baby Jackson had been tested and put into a classification of his own. Precocial. Talented from birth. His power had been significant. His entire life had been spent breaking and setting Shift records. He was the most powerful Shifter on record.

Jackson fumbled for words and remembered his question. "I mean… maybe that's not the right question. If you were me, would you feel like you had to go into the Service?" Still, his older brother Rush merely peered at him. Rush said nothing. "You know… Well, I mean, I know you would have to go into the Service, really, but…"

Jackson did not press. Rush would answer in his own time as he considered the question.

But as it were, the phone was ringing and Jackson leaned over to answer it. "Hello?"

"Jackson, damn man, glad you answered."

"What is it?"

"We need you down here, like pronto. man."

We need you down here. They always needed him. That was the burden of being the Precocial.

Then he heard a voice from the table.

* * * *

"Yes." It was a lie that Rush tested on his tongue, then slipped out into the cosmos. Smaller than atoms, they floated undetectable out of his mouth. The words were of him, yet somehow did not belong to him. Rush had learned long ago how to lie and experience the serenity of removal. There was a science or art to the lack of culpability. He had perfected this science and art in the last ten years of his life as he watched the skills of his younger brother develop, as he watched his mother's love shift to Jackson the Extraordinary, while Rush longed for and achieved obscurity. "Yeah, sure." He nodded briefly. "I would help people if I could. What you're able to do is amazing, Jacks. And I totally recognize your need to put it to good use. Guess that's why you got all the power."

"Yeah." Jackson slightly furrowed his eyebrows. Then, as Rush expected, the lines smoothed, and Jackson was again at peace. "It is the right thing to do. Civil... social responsibility and everything."

Rush nodded. He watched as Jackson went into the living room. Then he pushed from the table and walked into the bathroom. He smiled into the mirror, stretching his lips as wide as he could, baring his teeth and straining muscles until even his neck tensed with the effort. He held the smile and wondered what others would feel if they were to see him smile. A smile on that face was an unnatural occurrence. He continued to hold the expression, wondering how long he could stand there that way. He had done the right thing, too. Now, Jackson wouldn't worry that he had made the wrong decisions or that he, somehow, had a monster for a brother.

* * * *

Rush fully expected his brother to leave the house then. Jackson took his responsibilities to the Service very seriously. And Rush had seen firsthand the way they revered Jackson there, the way they watched his brother in awe and with a respect that one gave to a prophet... or a rock star. That near-worship unsettled Rush.

Even though he expected his brother to go, Rush knew he was still in the apartment. For that reason, he chose safeguards. Rush traced the word *despair* into the dust on the back of his closed bedroom door. The word glowed shiny black, then vanished. He thought of testing it with his palm, but he knew the Energy was still there. He sighed heavily and faced the unremarkable room. It was green and dark gray. There was a desk and a chair. There was a TV, a game console hooked up to it on the floor, a stereo, a computer, and a long unused chess set. There was his

Grayson Reyes-Cole

bed, two mattresses on the floor with a blanket over them. His brother had complained about it half-heartedly. The walls were blank and white.

A mirror leaning over his dresser showed him his unremarkable reflection. He glanced down at his body and sighed again.

Then he changed.

His skin warmed visibly to a healthy toffee glow. His hair, dry and kinky, waved softly over his eyes. His narrow shoulders widened, his slender body strengthened, packets of flesh filled in the hollows of his bones. With a brush of his hand over his face, his strong jaw was wiped clean of stubble and his dull black eyes changed to a sherry brown. His nose was a perfect line with flared nostrils over broad lips. Rush was sure he wasn't a handsome fellow anyway. Still, people stared at him when he went around in his natural skin. Even without his unusual Talents, he could tell they were watching him. They still did, though less so with his diminished appearance. Rush would never be comfortable with that. People were smarter than even they knew. Most of them could sense there was something different within him, even if they couldn't pinpoint what.

He waved a hand and it was as if a shallow wave of dim rippled across the room. Wherever the ripple touched seemed to bend, shatter, and reshape. The white walls stretched and darkened into a shadowed slate gray. The floor shifted and opened until the carpet melted away to reveal smooth rock. The bed lowered, curved, shimmered in a cerulean blue. Eggplant and emerald colored pillows and coverlets covered the soft rise invitingly. A depression in the center of the slate deepened until it became a hot pool of scented water bubbling over dark blue tile. In the center of the pool was a long burning flame that seemed to touch the water and yet continue to burn. Similar flames attached themselves to the ceiling and walls to give the room a warm aura. Deep blue, iridescent boxes spilled soft music into the air. The ceiling dripped low and bowed into the worn stone of a subterranean cavern. This was his luxury, his heaven. A palace buried in caverns. He smiled wryly to himself: his dream home. All he needed was a dream girl. But he knew, even as she made her way to him, that Elizabeth was already dead.

Effortlessly, he snapped his fingers and a banquet appeared before him. Damn, he was always hungry, especially when he thought of her.

"How did you do that?" The voice, surprising like a beam of sunlight in dilated pupils, sliced through Rush's chest. The bones in his shoulders ached, then his collarbone and sternum. His ribs squeezed around his heart. His throat closed over and he began gulping for air and clutching at his windpipe. The muscles convulsed on the left side of his face, closing his eye then straining him so that his head began to shake. His body continued to collapse around his organs. He felt the seizing in his bladder as he struggled. He fell hard on his back.

Jackson's eyes, driven wide by the sight of his brother's act, grew tight as he went over to Rush and placed a hand over his chest. A cool charge went through to Rush's heart. For a moment, his body seemed to expand again, enough so that he could concentrate on the words flowing from Jackson's mouth.

"First you focus on your heart and lungs. Think of them being transparent, thin, so much so that air and light can pass through them." Rush followed the instruction and felt the constriction inside him begin to subside.

"Now," Jackson continued, "breathe and do the same for your mind. Imagine it empty, clear, porous. It may sound strange but try to picture fruit. A series of all the fruits you know, one after the other."

Again, Rush followed Jackson's queues. Strawberries. Apples. Grapes. Bananas. *Easy*. Oranges. He found the discomfort had almost completely subsided. Mangos. Tangerines. Peaches. *Almost*. Pineapples. Raspberries.

"All better?" Jackson inquired with a quizzical brow.

Rush nodded and looked away. That is when he remembered the Shift. The faint scent of musk on the air enhanced the exotic nature of his creation and served to remind him that this atmosphere was quite man-made, and probably beyond anything his brother had seen created so easily. He was caught—*again*—and his heart constricted—*again*. He was now going to have to convince Jackson that what he was witnessing was not real… *again*. Wearily, Rush sank down onto the side of the very normal and non-Shifted bed. He rested his elbows on his knees and waited.

"How did you do it?" Jackson asked without attempting to hide his awe. He tapped Rush excitedly on the shoulder to gain his attention.

"How did you know what was happening to me just then?" Rush countered instead of answering. He needed time to think.

"It happens." Jackson offered with a quick shrug. "Permanent Shift. Usually when you expend too much energy on any one specific Shift. You know, *Parameters of Shift 101*. What you've done here is amazing, record-breaking in the time that you accomplished it. It would have taken me days to do it. And, after I was done, I never would have been able to put it back." Jackson swept his arm toward the room that had subtly returned to its original condition.

"No," Rush mumbled absently. "This is an easy Shift." Then, as he considered Jackson's words, he asked, "Why fruit?"

"Fruit is mundane. It's the first and easiest way to train children on how to manage Perma-Shift. Something about the listing that focuses your cognitive skills and forces your Energy to center there instead of in manifestation, if that makes any sense to you. And..." Jackson paused. He measured his next words very carefully. "And they're healthy."

"Healthy?" Rush was empirically incredulous.

"Yes, healthy," Jackson assured him. "It's one of the weird phenomena of Shift. Thinking about healthy things has a significantly healthy impact on your body, including when you are in the throes of Perma-Shift."

"That's ridiculous. Why doesn't it work for heart attacks?"

"Sometimes it does," was Jackson's bashful answer.

Rush merely considered the information then nodded. He was still unsure, but chose to pursue another topic. "How did you get in?" He looked back at the door that still bore a trace of the glossy black word that should have planted the suggestion in Jackson's head that he did not want to enter the room. He should have been plagued with sadness, loneliness, insecurity, disconsolate grief. He should have been inured with the feelings of despair just by nearing the door. The further away from it he stood, the less he would feel the suggestion. Jackson had braved it anyway.

* * * *

Jackson walked over to the dusty chess set and began to study the pieces. He picked up the queen, still impressed with her heaviness. The pieces were made of solid pewter. The queen was the heaviest, the most ornate. He put her down gingerly but didn't take his eyes off her. "I would like to say that I was able to identify the suggestion from my years of training, but I didn't. In fact, the suggestion was so strong I was shaking even while I reached for the door, but I needed to talk to you."

Jackson turned to see Rush raise his eyebrows. Jackson assumed this was an indication of shock and incredulity. Though his brother looked slightly different, his lack of expression was the same. "You wanted to talk to me enough to plow through a very, very, very nasty suggestion?"

Jackson shrugged again, remembering a feeling of intense misery descending on him at the thought of going to his brother for advice. He'd started to sweat and felt bile pooling in his mouth. He also remembered the feeling that Rush was the only one in the world who could help him. When he weighed both emotions, his need to seek Rush out overrode the suggestion, the High Energy Shift used to create it. Jackson knew his brother would tell him the right thing to do.

The fact that he sought guidance from his brother more than anyone else probably had a lot to do with the fact that Rush was older by nearly five years. Boys usually looked up to their older brothers and wanted to emulate them, didn't they?

When they were little, Rush had always steered Jackson away from trouble. He taught him from an early age not to lord his extraordinary abilities over others. It was Rush who had urged Jackson to protect smaller kids, to cooperate with the incessant battery of tests to which the Service subjected Jackson. It was Rush who told Jackson constantly that their parents loved him, and that they understood and respected his unique gifts, though Jackson had never, even as a boy, completely believed it.

Rush warned him that he needed to comprehend the difference between asserting and aggressing. In all things, Rush had never failed him. He had been an unwavering and unmoving guiding star for Jackson through subtlety and nuance when necessary or relentless, persistent emotionally dealt discipline when necessary. Even despite his Talent. Amazing to Jackson, he didn't know why, but his Talent had never had an impact on Rush. He had always considered Rush to be his teacher, and Jackson had never, not once in his life, considered using his power on him. Deep down, Jackson had known in the way only a soul can know, that his Energy could not affect... could never conquer Rush. It was only at this moment, this very moment that he knew why. Rush had power of his own.

"Well," Rush prompted.

"Well what?"

"What did you want?" Rush asked patiently.

"I don't remember," Jackson admitted, sure that before Rush asked him the question, he *had* known. He ran a hand over his bristly dark blond hair and changed the subject. "You should be trained."

"I'm an adult. They don't train adults."

"They don't train adults because they get everybody when they're kids. We live in the nation's capital, not because our parents loved it here, but because they've been studying and training me since before I could walk. It's amazing you have this kind of Talent and have managed to fly under the radar. Energy has a way of making itself known to the Service. They have *satellites*, Rush, that pick up traces of High Energy. They can identify Talent from outer space. You have to be tested. You have to be protected. You have to be trained, Rush."

"No, Jackson, I don't have to be, and I won't be." His words were final. Jackson wouldn't argue. At least not then. "I can tell this isn't going to work. You and your desire to do what you think is the right thing to do... No, you won't be able to leave well enough alone. For that reason, I have to do something I don't want to do." Rush ran a hand over his face. "I'm sorry, Jackson."

* * * *

"Hey, man, I must have just zoned out. I didn't realize what time it was. You mind if I cut out early and we play some tomorrow? I gotta figure out what's going on at the center." Jackson pulled off the wireless virtual reality gloves. He briefly checked his score on the gaming console and handed the gloves to Rush.

"No problem, Jack." Rush, now transformed back into the sullen introvert, answered with a nearly believable smile. "Tell Ronald I said hi." The gloves were warm to the touch. The Shift had been precise, instantaneous, and perfect. He slid them into the console drawer.

When Jackson walked out of his room, Rush sighed and closed his eyes. That was the seventh time in as many months he had removed the knowledge of his unique Talent from his brother's memory. Seven Shifts in seven months, Rush tried to cheat destiny. Too frequently, this Talent he had been careful to hide since adolescence, seemed to want to bare itself to his brother... maybe to more than just his brother.

He did it even though he knew it was useless. Rush had always known that he could not cheat destiny.

* * * *

When Jackson Rush swiped his badge at the west lobby of the Service, he waved at the older woman in uniform behind the desk. The pleasant looking woman graced him with a huge smile. Her smooth skin was the color of fresh garlic and her eyes looked like half moons as she grinned. Her salt and pepper hair was very short and bristly. She was tall, definitely taller than he was, and plump. She wore starched navy pants and a button-down with yellow chevrons on the sleeve that looked like it could have represented any security company in the country, but of course, her uniform was not only bulletproof but also psychic-proof. All of Melita's Talent was based in self preservation. She couldn't do anything to anyone else, but they couldn't do anything to her either, including get past her. Great for security in the only place on the planet where everyone commanded High Energy of a sort.

Jackson walked through a sensor that looked strikingly like an airport security pass-through, then started down a hall. The floor was old terrazzo but gleaming clean. The walls were a governmental off-white and only interrupted by doors and windows with metal blinds blocking the view inside. He took an elevator then, down sixteen floors. Stepping out, he passed through another security booth nodding at a young, skinny man he'd never met before.

"You're new?" he asked with a smile, putting his hand out.

"Yes, Mr. Rush, sir."

"Jackson."

"Oh I don't know—"

"Nahh, it's cool. I give you permission to call me Jackson. What's your name?"

"Banks."

"Nice to meet you, Banks. You had to have done really well to be on this detail."

"Yes, sir, um… Jackson."

"And what's your…"

The young man put his hands out waist high with his palms facing downward. A bronze light, a dark brown flame almost, seemed to leap out of his palms and form a wall in front of his body. He raised his hands higher, and up the force field went. Jackson stepped closer and put a finger into the High Energy barrier. A faint buzz let him know how strong the Energy was.

"That hurts," he said with a slow smile.

"Well," Banks toed the tile at his feet, "It does for other people, y'understand. I wouldn't expect…"

"And you shouldn't. Really, I could feel how strong and controlled the field was."

The younger man beamed at that. "I have to tell you, sir. It's amazing meeting you. Amazing. We had like a whole chapter on you."

Jackson gave a faint nod of his head. He'd heard this before and was glad that no such course had existed when he was in training. Jackson proceeded through the double doors behind Banks. He took a right then entered the room to his immediate left.

There was a tall, almost sickly slim man in a white lab coat, a pale blue button-down and khakis in the room. "What is it, Ronald?" Jackson skipped a greeting.

The other man with pale yellow hair narrowed his light green eyes. "Tell your brother I said hi."

"Damn, Randall, sorry." If Jackson didn't know any better, he'd figure that a suggestion was causing him to call his co-worker by the wrong name. "What's—" Jackson didn't finish the question. For the first time he realized that the metal blinds covering the giant window dividing this room from the next were pulled up. He took a step back as a pair of huge, hot black eyes stared at him intently.

"Why is he in holding?" Jackson snapped at Randall.

"He got the rock and went ape shit."

"Nice," Jackson scowled. "Leave it to you to put it in clinical terms." He turned back to the window and looked in at the man who seemed to be staring directly at him, venom glazing his eyes. It was a man he had considered a friend, Thaddeus Okwenuba.

"Well, I could get into the details, but as I recall, you're not much interested in those."

"Sometimes," Jackson conceded with a shrug as he continued to watch Thad, who seemed to be watching him back. He shouldn't have been able to see Jackson through the glass. Jackson was quite sure that he could, though. High Energy sight was just one of Thaddeus' Talents.

"We need you to get the rock." There was almost a play of a smile across Randall's thin lips.

Of course they needed Jackson to get the rock. Thad wasn't even dangerous without it. He wasn't typically dangerous with it either, but that was only after an initial release of stored High Energy. An astonishingly violent release.

"Wasn't it in containment?"

"Yeah," Randall answered. "It's not now."

Jackson gritted his teeth then demanded, "Did you ask him for it?"

"Um, no." Randall responded with derision.

"You can reason with him, you know."

"Um, no." Randall repeated. "What I know is that you can't reason with him, at least not yet." Before Jackson could interject, he went on to explain, "Sure you can reason with him and everything's fine once he releases that initial bout of aggression. He hasn't done that yet. He was about to do that. Don't know how he even made it all the way here."

That was indeed a feat.

What amazed everyone at the Service was that Thaddeus couldn't seem to access his High Energy at all without the pebble. There had been no other cases, truly, where High Energy could only be tapped by use of an inanimate object. There had been plenty of cases where Shifters used inanimate objects—prisms, pools of water, seeds, even other people—as a focal point to enhance their Talents. Some naturally occurring objects had been found to have special properties that helped in that aspect. Yet hematite had not been established as one of those materials. There was absolutely nothing special about it. Nothing at all. That's why it and its owner had been transferred into Dr. Sandoval's care. The lab had tested it with every method they could and found nothing out of the ordinary. Heat, cold, elemental interactions, impact testing, microscopes and particle beams. Later in life, Thad, a Doctor of Physics in his own right, had even recommended half the tests. He had been as eager as anyone to discover the power the rock held over him. They'd even given it the ultimate test. They'd given it to the Precocial—Jackson had stopped just short of sleeping with the damn thing under his pillow—but nothing happened. The rock was nothing more than a piece of hematite that fit easily into the palm. Not even a subsonic hum. Still, without it, Thad—an untried teenager at the time—professed to be unable to use his Talent. So they tested him.

Mental and physical stress trials represented the mission for the R&D division of the Service. They were structured to test all of the known types of Talent manifestations. Pyrokinesis, telekinesis, clairvoyance, regeneration, replication, the list went on and on. *Parameters of Shift 101*. They had a thousand tests to evaluate the 223 categorized Talents. These tests had shown no High Energy in the man without it. It didn't make any sense, because the one thing they all knew for sure was that Thad was a dangerous man with the object and he was not even 50% assured to be able to control the strength of the Energy.

"How'd he get it back?" Jackson asked, taking off his jacket. He pulled his shirt out of his pants and loosened his belt. He breathed deeply, letting his muscles relax, his arms went limp at his sides and his legs were parted. His head rolled around clockwise then counterclockwise on his neck. He took the stance of a fighter as he faced the man standing in a similar fashion on the other side of the glass. "I thought we decided he didn't get the rock back until we figured out how to help him control it."

Randall Sandoval shook his head. "That's the thing. We aren't exactly sure how he got it back. It would be easy to think he reached out for it in a Shift, but we both know he has never in all these years exhibited any High Energy without the thing."

"Hmm," Jackson frowned. He turned to leave the room but noticed two other doctors had come in. Medical doctors. He smiled ruefully. They were there not to treat him for the injuries he was bound to sustain. They were there to study how he healed from them. So many things yet to learn about the Precocial. He walked over to where they stood and waited patiently as they gave him a series of injections. Into his arms, his hands, his feet, his legs, four in his chest (heart, liver, lungs), one for each kidney, seven on different vertebrae, two at the base of his skull. Sensors. In less than half an hour, Jackson's body would expel the foreign objects, but until then, readings would be taken and transmitted.

He walked out of the room and turned left. The next door was locked in triplicate: mechanics, electronics, and Shift. A small atrium was on the other side, and another door with another series of locks. Even some of the older Servicemen would have trouble opening it while keeping the occupant inside. This task was not difficult for Jackson. What was difficult was preparing himself to go into this room remembering that Thad would kill him if he could. *God*, he was so happy-go-lucky under normal circumstances. He was an intelligent man, a funny man, a good man. A best friend.

Thaddeus was very dark skinned, he wore dark clothes, and the room was dimly lit. He lurked in a corner and Jackson could barely see him, even though he could sense black eyes peering at him. Thad's loose limbs swayed a little, almost as if brushed by a breeze. High Energy buzzed and crackled in the air. Thaddeus lunged at him with preternatural speed and furor. Jackson barely had enough time to see that the rock was in Thad's mouth. That way he could use both hands to rip Jackson open.

Jackson had trouble describing it. He could see the skin on his arms being shredded, feel the blood drip down. The grating sensation of nails and teeth scraping his bones was visceral, intense, but no more painful than a baby's scratch. When he fought on, the popping noise sounded in his ears as both arms were pulled, one then the other, out of the joints. Distended, disconnected shoulders snapped back in place, jarring, but Jackson didn't even wince. Like a fly lighting on his flesh.

Even the mental push meant to liquefy his organs, the push that ate at his insides like acid. He was completely cognizant of what was happening to him yet totally removed from it. Jackson should have been in pain. He should have fainted with it. Instead, his wounds felt more like someone touching a foot that had gone to sleep. And besides, every rip, every tear, every melting organ, regenerated nearly at the same rate that it was destroyed. Each bit of blood or flesh that left his body reversed its path, returning to him. Vials of blood somewhere deep in the bowels of the Services yearned to return to him even then.

"Get it out of your system already!" Jackson shouted, feeling annoyed that Thad, even in this state, would be foolish enough to think he could hurt him. *No one could hurt him.* He had just lunged at Jackson, wildly slashing again and hurling so much High Energy that it pulsed in almost imperceptible violet waves from his body. Anyone else, it might have killed, but his resilience was another strange attribute to Thad's Talent.

Jackson could make this stop, but he didn't want to hurt a man who had become his friend. He also knew that in only a few moments, Thad wouldn't be able to expend any more Energy. Perma-Shift would finally set in. He would need the doctors and Jackson to keep him alive through it. And, as soon as he thought it, Thad started to scream. His body doubled over and he crumpled to the ground. The convulsions started, Thad cracked his head on the cement floor with a sickening thud and vomit bubbled out of his lips.

Jackson rushed to kneel beside him and swept his finger into Thad's mouth to clear out both vomit and the rock. He checked the pulse and when he realized that it was strong and that Thad was breathing, he rolled the unconscious man over onto his side in case he vomited again. He dried the rock with a handkerchief pulled from his pocket. He pressed a hand to Thad's forehead and checked quickly. All residual Energy. Nothing that could hurt anybody. He gave the thumbs up to the window and the three doctors joined him shortly.

After checking to see that Jackson had no damage to examine, they all started to work on Thad, including Sandoval. Jackson just stood and watched. He was exhausted and Perma-Shift—the only thing that brought him pain—made his brain feel like it was splitting in two. Catching a glimpse at his watch told him he had only been at work for 20 minutes. Sandoval looked up at him then. Always the empath. "Go ahead, Jackson. You may want to lie down for a few minutes in the dormitory."

Jackson turned to go, but hesitated even as the sensors made pinging noises when they dropped to the floor around him. He needed to give Randall the rock.

"For God's sake, Jackson," Randall said, reading his intent. "Take the rock with you. Put it somewhere only you can find it for now."

Chapter 3

Saving: The Return

Jackson Rush was tired when he left work. So very tired. The encounter with Thad had drained him physically and emotionally. Although, that experience wasn't what he would remember later about that day. Instead, he would remember the events about to change the course of his life. As it were, destiny was about to start. Exhausted or not. Ready or not.

Jackson walked into his apartment that evening and slipped in something slick. His shins bumped against a hard object and he fell forward. He tried to brace himself with his hands but they slipped in the dark, thick liquid on the pavement. He fell further forward until the side of his face hit the ground. Realizing that his legs were still lying on whatever he had tripped on, he flipped over onto his backside and scooted back, staying low. His eyes widened as he took in the dead red haired girl. Something dripped into his eye then onto his lips from the tip of his nose. When he raised a hand automatically to wipe it away, he saw that it was smeared crimson. Blood.

She was lying on her back. Her legs were closed and bent, her knees pointed to the East. Her arms curled gracefully at her sides. In the bright fluorescent light of the full moon, her skin was translucent and pale. The coppery red of her straw-straight hair emphasized the delicacy of her skin and small bones. He could make out green-blue veins in her jaw. She wore a white dress with glossy white boots. She lay in an oval of dark blood, almost black in the night. A smaller oval soaked her dress surrounding the hilt of a knife sticking straight up out of her stomach. Her fingertips and eyelids twitched. They were on a rooftop.

Jackson scuttled back even further away from her. Shaking his head slowly, he tried to deny the scene before him. He backed into a low wall at the edge of the roof. Quickly, he looked over his shoulder to see the twinkling skyline of his city. They were at least thirty floors up. He turned back to her. Her head lolled toward him. Her eyes were rolled into the back of her head, just slits of milky white. Then, as if from force of will, bright blue eyes snapped to attention and pinned him where he sat. Jackson swallowed. He tried to ask her who she was. He tried to ask her who did this to her. He tried to ask anything, but he couldn't. Those eyes were on him. They held him and assessed him. When she blinked, tears streaked her cheeks, and her eyelids flickered convulsively again, he was able to ask her, "What happened to you?"

"My name is Bright Star." She answered in a rasp. Forming words caused her to pant in grating wheezes as she struggled to breathe. Her eyes were wide. Blood trickled from the corner of her lips with each violent gasp. She swallowed and her auburn lashes fluttered as she stared upward. "I'll be dead soon."

"No!" Jackson rasped. Somehow, he found control of his limbs and rose up onto his knees at her side. He could handle this. He had been trained to handle this. He reached out to touch her hand with its endlessly working fingers. She was ice cold to the touch. He held those fingers still in his own, willing them to warm.

"You have great Talent," she stated in a deeper voice than she'd used before. Her eyes that had been a clear aquamarine, blazed bright and turquoise. They were so bright that Jackson imagined her lids were tinted blue as she blinked.

Jackson shook his head. He needed to be clear. "Who are you, Bright Star? Please tell me."

She started to speak but only managed a painstaking swallow. She opened her mouth again but only gurgled blood. Jackson pinched her nose with his left hand then used the fingers of his other to swipe excess liquid from her mouth, thinking that it was the second time in the day he had performed this technique. He pressed her tongue down then turned her head to the side to clear the last of the fluid. In the back of her throat, he could see a thick, bloody bubble. Her breath was sweet, salty and metallic. He blew into her lips and she swallowed again, this time less painfully and her airway seemed to be no longer blocked. "Talk to me," he commanded again, shaking her wrist. He watched her hand flop at its end.

"I...I—"

"Come on," Jackson coaxed.

"I'm dying," she told him again.

"You're not," he told her forcefully, rubbing her fingers more briskly between his palms. But she shook her head silently, refuting his words. "Just keep talking to me. Keep talking. Tell me who you are."

"I am a Shifter, like you," she told him, though her words were slow and measured. She swallowed freely. "I am going to die in seven minutes. The Shift I used to bring you here required too much of me, more than I have to give. The Perma-Shift sped up the bleeding. I... I..."

Jackson considered her words. She was a Shifter. Not a Serviceman. Amazing. Impossible. Children with Talent never managed to avoid the Service. None with any real power as far as he knew had ever done it. The only Shifters who didn't get fully assimilated were those whose Energy was so insignificant that they could pass for instinct, intuition, good luck even. But the Service still watched them, looking for the power to blossom into something more. This woman was powerful, maybe more than he was, but she was not a Serviceman.

An image of his brother Rush flashed in his mind. Jackson shook his head again. "How long have you been here?" He asked as he searched his pockets for his key ring. He didn't have it, but located it on the ground, having dropped it when he fell. The mini flashlight on it beamed light in each of her eyes. Her eyes—God, they were incredibly blue—followed him intensely, but her pupils did not respond. He killed the light and her eyes drifted closed. Her fingers went limp in his hand, and he patted her cheek firmly to bring her back. Then he started talking to her again: "If you could call me—bring me here—you may have been able to save your own life. Why would you Shift to bring me here?" he asked roughly, though his voice sounded desperate.

Her eyes blazed brighter like a fire that had been stoked. "Save me," She whispered in a full-hearted plea.

He would not tell her that he couldn't save her, that he wasn't sure he possessed the power to do so. "Why did you bring me here? Why won't you save yourself?"

"I couldn't. I can't. I haven't the Energy," she answered, bringing one forearm up to cover her eyes. "Please," she begged in an agonized croak. "You have to save me."

Jackson considered her words then cast his gaze around the rooftop looking for something, anything that would help him save her. He turned back. "Bright Star," her eyes were closed. "Bright Star!" he called again, clapping his hands over her face. Blood spattered on her milky skin and her eyes came open gradually.

"Bright Star, I need you to keep your eyes open," he told her in strong clear words. "Can you do that for me?"

There was barely a nod, but there was one just the same. Jackson leaned over to look her in the eye even while his hands eased up to her abdomen. "Please just keep your eyes open. Please. And keep talking to me."

Her eyes widened and they snapped to the hand at her waist. She started to shake her head violently. Her chest rose and fell quickly with her increasingly rapid breathing. "Don't." she told him. "Don't!"

"I'm not going to do anything," he told her, stroking hair from her face. He grimaced when he realized he had smoothed more blood into her skin. It was a red crescent over her forehead and cheek. "I just need to check your wound."

"Don't!" She pleaded again. Clear drops began to collect in the corners of her eyes. They balanced precariously on her cheeks then melted down her face. "Don't," she begged raggedly.

Jackson stopped gazing into those tortured eyes. He couldn't do this if he had to see her looking at him like that. Slowly he slipped his hands up to the tender, opened flesh around the knife. He tested the thick syrup around the wound. It was clotting already. That was good. Clotting was good. He checked the knife: tapered, edges smooth, not serrated.

He leaned toward her again. His face nearly pressed against hers again. This time he tried to hold her mesmeric gaze. He would have to distract her from what he was about to do. He would have to see if the knife came out freely, without causing any more damage. Ever so careful, he eased his fingers up the black, plastic handle, barely touching it. Then, just as slowly, he wrapped his fingers around it.

"Please stop," she cried. Her eyes were luminescent, drowning pools. "Please stop."

"Look at me," he softly urged. She didn't. "Look at me," he commanded more firmly. Her blazing blue eyes turned back to him and he found himself lost in them again. Only for a second. Jackson knew what he had to do. He firmly took hold of the handle and pulled. He sickened at the sound of the knife cutting away at her insides. He looked down and his pulse quickened as he realized the bleeding had started again and now her entire abdomen was soaked in blood. It was flowing from her as if her body was a scarlet fountain.

"Oh no," he heard himself say. "Oh God, no." The blood was so fast and so abundant. Hot and sticky, it bathed his hands when, on impulse, Jackson pressed his fingertips to the wound, applying pressure. He hoped the pressure would stop the blood, but he also needed to touch her to release as much power as he could stand into her at full strength. He closed his eyes and shook his shoulders loosely, trying to relax, to block everything but the wound and repairing it.

For a moment, he could feel it. He stopped the blood as his own veins started to burn and his muscles, all of them, started to strain. His neck tightened his back, his arms and legs, his buttocks. He could feel the tissue rethreading itself as something in his head began to rip apart. Pain. His flesh, his cells were searing from the inside out. His eyes were bulging from their sockets. His teeth were grinding painfully as if there was a vice around his skull. The pain within him was so strong that his bones seemed like they were being stretched and bowed to the point of cracking. For a man who rarely experienced pain, it was too much, and yet it was fascinating. His lungs refused breath. Blackness started to cover his vision and blanket his thoughts, but his years of training wouldn't let him. He cut the Shift and started pounding his palm against his forehead and tears started in his eyes. He couldn't save her.

"Please, Bright Star." He turned to her, an ache in his voice. "Please. If you have any strength left, then maybe we can do this together. Maybe together."

Jackson knew in his soul that he could not prevent her death alone. The Perma-Shift would kill him before he repaired her enough to keep her alive. Jackson knew if he persisted, they would both die. There was never anything more certain.

"I can't," she wheezed. Her head started rolling from side to side as if the movement would shake away the cloud of death. "I'm not strong enough. We aren't…" Her breath started coming faster and in the silence, the rasp was equivalent to mental friction. Jackson ran a hand across the stubble on the top of his head. It was an additional scrape to the strained cacophony. She was going to die in less than a minute. He lashed out with his mind and called to the only person he could.

The warmth, the pattern, and the glow that was Rush flowed over Jackson. The light collected in his open heart. He felt it slipping over his fingers and filling the gaping hole in her stomach. A low, barely visible gold light burrowed inside of her. Her mouth fell open and her wide eyes seemed to beam blue light into the night sky. Her chest arced into the air. Her head tossed back, and her jugulars strained. Her fingers curled into claws. Her teeth clenched.

Rush was saving this girl. He was saving her life and—Jackson realized—his life as well. Jackson tried to breathe but inhaled too sharply and started to cough violently because the rush of oxygen into his lungs was too much. Then, there was relief. Every muscle in his body loosened, and he buckled. Jackson turned his head as vomit rushed through his throat, filled his mouth and poured from his lips. Training had taught him to give into this. His body was righting itself from the excess of High Energy.

As he emptied his body, Jackson started focusing on facts. Something had to anchor him before the Perma-Shift really did kill him. *Parameters of Shift 101.* He could see the text behind his eyelids: *The brightest recorded light manifestation of Shift was approximately .96 watts, about as much as can be powered by twenty-four volts. A single Christmas tree light. The longest recorded distance for a Shift was five kilometers, just over three miles.* He looked at the skyline. If he judged correctly, he was about ten miles from the apartment. And his brother was doing this from long distance. Even Jackson had only been able to affect a Shift from ten miles away. Rush was at their apartment more than ten miles away. Jackson swallowed, trying to push that thought from his mind. *The youngest recorded age for someone to Shift was eleven.* Well, that had been true before Jackson was born. But Jackson was the anomaly, the outlier always excluded from statistical measures. Precocial.

Jackson shuddered and rocked. He had to focus. *The average age for someone to be able to manifest a Shift was thirteen and a half months. The phrase, Permanent Shift, was derived from a permanent magnet. A permanent magnet retained its magnetism after removal of the magnetizing force. Perma-Shift was what happened when the High Energy used to create a Shift was out of balance with the High Energy required for the Shift. When there was too little Energy, the strain started to tear the Shifter apart, inside out. When the High Energy was more than required and left unrestrained, it had nowhere to apply itself but back to its source. The average time it took to recover from minor Perma-Shift was 176 seconds. The average time it took to recover from major Perma-Shift was never.* He wiped his mouth with the back of his sleeve and turned around.

Bright Star breathed normally beside him. There was no deep rush of air, no coughing as if she had drowned. Nothing. She simply started to breathe. The blood that had pooled around her slowly turned clear then evaporated up into the air in transparent flakes. Even her skin began to grow thick, opalescent. The veins disappeared, turning her skin from alabaster to porcelain. Bright Star had not been healed, she had been returned.

The Shifter sat up. Her shiny, copper hair fell just behind her ears. She blinked. Her eyes were slowly returning to a natural, earthly blue as she pinned them to Jackson. Her first words in this rewound life were accusatory. "You didn't save me."

Jackson felt the shame but was not sure if he showed it. He had been trained to hide such things, and his training had come back to him once she was safe. Her gaze fluttered to the ground at his feet and he knew she had seen.

"It was my brother," Jackson offered, scratching the back of his head. *His brother.* Funny. Jackson had not known before those moments that his brother possessed Talent, yet he had known to reach out to him. He hadn't been the least surprised at the strength his brother had exhibited. He shook his head.

"Is he dead?" she asked, her eyes coming to his again, startlingly clear. He was beginning to recognize the incandescence as a signal of her High Energy. Brighter than a Christmas tree light.

"No. No, he's not. I would know if he were." Though he hadn't once thought about it before, Jackson knew his words to be true. "To be honest, I'm not sure he can experience it." Jackson pushed off from the wall and took a step toward her. Not another. He was too cautious for that. He shook his head. "I'm not sure of anything."

"Is he here?" Her Bright Star eyes searched around the dark recesses of the rooftops. A faint blue tint illuminated any and every thing she studied.

"No." Jackson replied.

"But he is close?" she persisted.

"No," Jackson answered warily. He knew her next question.

"Then how could he have—"

Impulsively, Jackson told her, "I can Shift from ten miles away."

The blue gaze fell on him and stilled. Her eyes seemed to dim. "So can I." In a soft voice she added, "I brought you here."

Jackson said nothing. Five minutes ago, he had been the One, the Precocial. He had broken records. He was the most Talented, most special of *anyone* on Earth. And yet, here was a Shifter who claimed to match his Talent. He had a brother somewhere whose power he had not known before that night. It was a power, a High Energy, he felt that could not be measured or weighed.

In a swift and graceful roll, Bright Star came up to her feet and stood before him. She was rounder and shorter than she had looked lying down. The top of her head just barely reached his chin and he was less than six feet tall. Her face was a perfect pale apple with defined cheekbones, a broad brow, and with a shallow indention in her chin. Her lips were pink and her lashes russet.

"You nearly killed yourself bringing me here," Jackson mumbled.

"Well, if you were who and what I believed you to be, that wasn't much of a risk. You would have saved me. I realize, however, you are not who we thought you to be at all. It's your brother we need." Her eyes rolled upward and Jackson could almost see twin blue ribbons of light reach toward the moonless sky.

Jackson did not deny her conclusion. He knew at that moment, and had maybe always known, that his power was nothing when compared to that of his big brother Rush. Now he wasn't the only one who suspected his brother's deific skill. He was nothing, and Bright Star knew it.

Without thought, he reached out to her, his hand leaving his side like metal drawn to a magnetic force. For a moment, she studied it then allowed him to take her hand.

"We have to get out of here." His words seemed late. Maybe the threat was gone; maybe it wasn't. He was doing this all wrong.

She asked him, "Where do you live?"

"Not far from here," he answered. His voice had been quick, high, and wavering. He sounded eager even to his own ears. Maybe there was a chance.

She tilted her head up a little and their eyes met. Her rod-straight red locks hung back. Dark pink lips parted slightly before she licked them. The move had been natural, without artifice. Bright Star had nearly died. Of course, she was not trying to seduce him. Still, Jackson felt a sharp pressure on his sternum. Jackson couldn't breathe for a heartbeat, and then when he could, he noticed she smelled like freesia. She stepped closer to him. Her body radiated heat. Her scent was even stronger and seemed to wend its way inside of him. Though she didn't touch him, he knew her body was soft. "Does your brother live there, too?"

Chapter 4

I Know You

When the couple came through the door, Jacob Rush raised his head from the kitchen table where he'd been waiting for his brother. Before Rush had heard the call, Jackson had been overdue by at least half an hour. His brother, the consummate good boy, rarely got home late unless he was going out with friends on the weekends. This was a Wednesday, and even if it hadn't been, Jackson always told Rush where he would be and generally for how long. On those rare occasions Jackson was delayed unexpectedly, he called to let Rush know he wasn't coming home. Jackson was forever conscientious. Sensitive. Righteous. But he'd been late. Tawny, short-cropped hair, tanned skin, and a giant white smile coupled with an eagerness to please bordering on compulsive made Jackson a star. He was golden.

But he was also Rush's little brother, and he was late.

Then the call had come like a thin piercing hum. It was a Shift. Nothing more than manipulated waves, frequencies, moving demi-atoms. His brother's distressed and frantic state contacted him even before Jackson consciously thought to reach out. It had started out as a tickling buzz in his ears then graduated to a grating in his teeth. Then it had traveled, the current, through his body. Rush had felt the urgency, and then... Well then... Well, no one ever had a choice really, did they?

Rush, of course, knew before the door opened that Jackson was not alone. Another first. Rush knew his brother to be quite successful with women. A Serviceman would have to try very hard not to be. They were physically perfect specimens, mysterious by nature and necessity. And then, there was that damned sensitivity.

Boy Scouts without the saccharine and the pre-pubescent bodies— Jackson was the epitome of them, the mould. Still, he never brought women home. Rush discerned long ago that this wasn't out of deference, not even respect. No. It was that Shifter sensitivity. Jackson didn't want Rush to feel bad. The sincere and wholly unnecessary discretion never ceased to bring a wry smile to Rush's lips. Just because he didn't bring them home, didn't make Rush any less aware of the number of women by whom his brother had become irrevocably yet temporarily fascinated. With a rising of gooseflesh on his arms, Rush grew painfully aware that this woman would be more than a strong but passing fancy. She was going to be the death of him.

At first, just before he saved her, Rush didn't know who she was. For a split second—he had to calculate it—his world was safe from her. He could breathe. He could see. He could eat, drink, walk, piss, spit and grin. He could go about his solitary business. But, Rush reasoned, that had been less than a second, and he had never really been safe.

"Bright Star," he breathed.

She had made herself into a fantasy. His fantasy. When he'd first seen her so long ago, she'd been skinny, bearing no womanly curves. Elizabeth's chest had been flat. Elizabeth's lips had been thin and cracked and pale, making her look nothing less than dead. Elizabeth's dingy white skin had had the same effect. Her smiles had been toothless and unsure. Her hair had been limp, brown and unhealthy, nearly always covering her eyes. Elizabeth had possessed no features worth remarking on, save for those eyes. They were so blue and startling he had seen the end of the earth in them.

Now, as Bright Star walked through his door, her skin was creamy peach all over. Bright Star's lips were full and a light, earthen red. Silken copper strands of her thick hair fell over her forehead into those amazing eyes. Bright Star's body was all that was soft, rounded and womanly. She had none of the skinny angles and points of before. Her waist was narrow but her breasts were full as were her hips and bottom. He could tell Bright Star's legs were long and shapely.

Rush's first thought was that she looked like everything he had ever imagined he wanted in a woman. His next thought was that there had never been a crueler illusion.

When she saw him, her mouth fell open in a smile so brilliant he had to look away from it. Her bright blue eyes sparkled and beamed. Her joy caused blood to pound behind his eyes. So much pain. Her voice slipped like a slow snake into his ears and into his brain as she uttered his name reverently. He ignored her, but her arms came open as if she waited for him to embrace her. When he did not, she shook her head as if to castigate herself then dropped to her knees in a dejected wilt. She didn't look at him. She just quietly admitted her surprise. "You know me." Then, twisting her hands in her lap, she muttered, "Of course you know me."

Rush remained silent. There was nothing to say. For nearly four years, he had managed to escape her. He had known the situation wouldn't be permanent when he sent her away. Now he knew he would never be rid of her again. "What happened to Elizabeth?" he asked more to himself than any other.

"I don't know who you mean. It is Bright Star you saved," was the damning answer.

"You two have met?" Jackson questioned, then bit his lip.

Silly question.

"You have to go," Rush told her through clenched teeth.

"You know I won't." Bright Star shook her head slowly with a determined set to her jaw. She appeared proud, regal even, as she remained on her knees before him, kneeling and defiant at once. "I've spent the last four years looking for you."

"Where have you been?" Rush breathed automatically. He hadn't wanted to ask, but couldn't seem to help it. He'd sent her to the other side of the earth. She'd been on a remote, nearly deserted island that had been occupied by a violent indigenous tribe that believed white flesh to be a sign of evil and women to be the bane of man, constantly trying to hold him from heaven. The nearest occupied land mass was three days away by boat. He'd left her there with nothing, not even clothing. She should have died. Yet here she was.

She offered her hand to him. "See where I've been. See how I've come to be here." she dared solemnly. Rush didn't take it. Instead, he turned his back on her and worked to control a shudder.

"Jackson, we need to talk," Rush urged his brother.

"But, Rush—"

"Now."

Jackson knew the shock showed on his face. His quiet, introverted, sallow brother rarely spoke to him let alone commanded him to do something. But that voice, that voice had been forceful and brooked no argument. He turned a tight smile on Bright Star silently begging her forgiveness. She continued to sit broken on the floor. Jackson followed Rush out of the living room and into the small, half-bathroom in the hall. Rush closed the door behind them, locked it, and started to run water in the sink—as if to stop her from listening.

Jackson prepared himself for the lecture from his brother on why the girl couldn't stay. She hadn't asked and Jackson hadn't offered, but anyone who could breathe could sense the path her mind had taken. Jackson knew she had nowhere to go. He also knew there was something compelling about her, something that almost forced him to help her. Something that would make him argue just as strongly to keep her as his brother would argue to make her leave.

To Jackson's surprise though, Rush did not wage a verbal argument up front. Instead, his brother tilted his head and studied him pensively for a moment. Then, Rush stepped close and laid a cool, wet hand against his forehead. The blow from the power in that hand nearly knocked Jackson off his feet. He stumbled then caught himself against the sink.

Instantaneously, painlessly, without the usual pomp and circumstance that accompanies life-changing events, Jackson had all of his long-suppressed memories back. Everything.

* * * *

Jackson vaulted from his very birth into the future through a tight bundle of memories. He remembered catching Rush holding thunderclouds in his hands when they were boys in the backyard. He remembered Rush touching his own broken leg after a nasty fall from his bike and standing up to ride again. More Shifts came to him, and more. He saw the seven Shifts in the last seven months he'd managed to witness and Rush had taken away from him.

In a matter of seconds, Jackson Rush discovered his brother Jacob Rush.

His throat tightened, his tongue thickened. He knew *his* brother, and suddenly life made sense. It frightened him, but finally made so much sense. One expects for the day the sun finally shines light on all of life's mysteries to be a good day.

"You..." Jackson rasped as he searched his brother's face. He knew this face, had always known it. But now...

Rush didn't say anything right off. Instead, he started to sit down on the edge of roof. He ran a hand over his face. In seconds, the brothers had been transported. They were standing on the roof of their building. Rush stared out at the night sky still illuminated by a giant moon.

"You do this so effortlessly. How have you managed to keep this a secret for so long?" Jackson intoned astonishment in his voice.

Rush frowned and closed his eyes. It was as if he was concentrating on an answer. Nothing came.

"How did you manage to avoid the Service? No. Forget the Service for now. Mom... Dad?" Rush didn't answer. "And what is it Rush? Where does it end? How much High Energy do you have? What you've done...

what I've seen you do... Rush, no one can do that. No one. Not even me. *No one.*"

Rush still seemed unable to find the words to answer. Instead, he looked at his brother and stated plainly, with fatigue, "I gave you back your memories for one reason and one reason only."

"Why?" Jackson was barely audible. His brother sat on the ledge, the electrified sky behind him.

"So you will believe what I have to tell you about her."

Jackson didn't understand, but he certainly knew who "her" was. "Bright Star?"

"That name," Rush mumbled, shaking his head. He rubbed hard at his eyes.

"I know. Isn't it a little funny?"

"No, Jackson, it isn't. She... she..." Rush's face crumpled. He appeared to struggle for an adequate explanation but ended completely inarticulate. "She's bad. I mean, not bad. But... bad."

Jackson chuckled for a moment. Then he sobered. Rush wasn't kidding. "You mean like the Devil bad?"

"No," Rush answered.

"You mean like she sleeps around bad?"

"No," Rush repeated.

"What? I mean, she cheats on her taxes, she steals, she murdered someone? What kind of bad?"

"None of those things. All of those things. Worse." Rush returned.

"Or did she do something as fucked up as spend her whole life stealing the memories from those closest to her?"

Rush did not respond, but neither did he cower or apologize. He just seemed to wait for Jackson to reign in his anger.

"How could you do this to me?" Jackson's voice quaked.

"I had to." Rush told him.

"You didn't. I know now. I know everything now, and the world hasn't come to an end. You could have told me. You could have left my head alone. I would never have done this to you."

"I know," Rush dipped his chin and spoke quietly, "You are a good person, Jackson. I know you wouldn't do what I did, but I only wanted to protect you."

"From what?"

"From me," Rush responded, his voice so quiet.

"Show me." Jackson breathed. When Rush only shook his head, he made a new request. "Then show me Bright Star." If Rush wanted him to know exactly what it was that made Bright Star bad, he could use his power to show him.

"No," Rush shook his head again. "You don't need to see what I see."

"Rush, you've done this to me since I was a kid. I'm an adult. I'm a member of the Service. I'm precocial. What could you possibly be protecting me from?"

Rush gave a lopsided smile. It was at once benevolent, sad and condescending. Jackson knew then that his brother would still try to protect him. Rush was stubborn to the end and would never allow Jackson to know what he knew.

Suddenly, another memory burrowed its way back inside his mind. It was of his mother. Jackson paused. He'd thought that none of those were left. She stood in the kitchen carefully cutting through a foam board. Rush was sitting at the kitchen table drawing. Jackson had been standing next to her studiously taking direction but leaning in too close. His full-scale model of the solar system was due the next day. Janie hummed and laughed, telling him stories about the planets, as she worked with the knife until it slipped and nearly sliced Jackson on the arm. At first, he didn't understand why Rush would have bothered to take away that memory. Then, comprehension dawned on him. Rush hadn't taken it, only given it back.

That knife would have cut him very badly had he been a regular little boy. But at that point, before he'd started training for the Service, his mother hadn't understood how far his Talent ran. She hadn't known that she couldn't hurt him. No. In the last minute, she had used a Shift to deflect the knife. Rush had never even looked up from what he'd been doing. Rush hadn't saved him that time. His mother had.

"Did you know?" Jackson demanded.

"Know what?" Rush asked truly bewildered.

"Know about Mom?"

Rush had started to turn away but he slowed his movements. His eyes focused on Jackson's as he grasped for his brother's memory. "I had a good idea."

"You never said anything."

"No." Rush leaned back against the wall. There were dark smudges under his eyes. Stubble shadowed his jaw. There were beads of perspiration on his upper lip. He slid down the wall to the floor with his knees bent in front of him.

"What's wrong with you?"

"Please make her leave."

For an instant, the new memory still fresh, Jackson believed Rush to be talking about their mother. But he wasn't. Jackson took in the sight of his brother who wore fatigue and frustration like a badge. Rush's appearance was as he saw it normally, but Jackson remembered what he really looked like. He was again amazed by what he had missed over the years. He couldn't process it. He couldn't. Instead, he focused again on the issue at hand.

"Please tell me why."

The woman of discussion appeared in the doorway to the roof. Her bright blue eyes glowed and she smelled like fresh gardenias as she walked past Jackson. She squatted in front of Rush with her arms around her knees. They were eye to eye. "I've searched the world over and now I've found you, love," she sang softly. Rush said nothing but returned her unwavering gaze. "Jacob Rush, I am your servant."

"Really?" Rush asked dryly. Jackson almost identified a smirk on his lips. "Then tell my brother why you're here and why I want you gone."

Bright Star stood and approached Jackson with careful steps. She followed Rush's direction. "Your brother has been given a very beautiful gift."

"Yes," Jackson stated just as dryly in a voice much like his brother's. "I know. He reminded me of it just moments ago."

"Yes," she agreed with a soft nod. "You saw what he has done in this world so far. His Talent is more than just the power you have seen. Silly little Shifts that change a room, light a match, bend a spoon. He has the power of life. But it's much, much more than that."

"Again, I say, I'm aware."

"No, Jackson, I'm afraid you don't understand."

"But—"

"Leave it alone, Jackson," Rush said, standing. "Leave it alone. I thought I wanted her to tell you, but I don't. I didn't realize how… Never mind. I'm going to bed. You can sit out here all night if you want, Jacks, but I'm going to bed." At the doorway, he added, "And, Jackson, I want her gone in the morning."

He went back into the building. Jackson noticed that his brother did not look the same as he had just moments before: he had reverted to his natural form. Gone were the bags under his eyes, the washed out complexion, and the emaciated physique. They were replaced by a lean yet muscled body with its tall frame, toasted bronze skin, and those entrancing black eyes. Apparently, there was no point in hiding now or ever again.

Chapter 5

Resident

When Rush woke up the next morning, there was a pain between his shoulder blades. The pain was sharp and cleared the fog in his brain. Without concern for hiding his High Energy, he growled. *Why is she still here?* He inserted the question directly into Jackson's dreams and woke him up.

"She wouldn't leave." Even to his own ears, Jackson's silently uttered reason sounded pathetic.

Make her leave, Rush demanded.

"Why won't you?" Jackson shot back. Then abruptly, the mental path was cut. Only with it gone did Jackson realize that he and Rush had always used a mental path to talk to each other. Never before had he thought anything of it. It hadn't occurred to him that this indicated Talent in Rush. He had only accepted it. It was a part of the manipulation he learned of the night before.

Jackson couldn't think of that anymore. Perhaps, if his memories had shown his brother being anything but honorable, or if he had seen even one act of aggression, one indulgence in vice or one time when his brother had not worked to protect their family, then Jackson would have been able to give rise to his anger. But he couldn't because Rush had done nothing; nothing short of protect him his entire life. His brother had demonstrated a care and concern for him that was even stronger than the care and concern Jackson had displayed for others in the Service. Jackson's brother was noble. There was not and would never be an argument to the contrary.

Jackson reached for the mental link again, but this time the mental path had been cut neatly. His brother had shut him out just like that. Jackson tried to open the line of communication again, but found he could not. He tried harder. His brow creased, his heart raced, the hair at his nape stood on end. His nose started to bleed. He stopped.

The door to his room opened and Rush entered carrying a towel. He threw it at his brother who pressed the soft material to his face. "You shouldn't have done that," Rush told him.

Jackson offered silence as he tilted his head back and applied pressure to his nose.

Finally, after he was sure the bleeding was subsiding, Rush told him, "You have to put her out."

"Why?"

"Because she has to go," Rush answered as if that was explanation enough.

"Rush." Jackson sat, checked the towel, and pressed it back to his face. "Why?

"You don't understand."

"And I won't understand if you don't answer the damn question!" Jackson returned. He didn't like puzzles. He had never liked puzzles. He didn't like delays. He didn't like for the people around him to keep secrets. It was rare that anyone could keep anything from him, but when they did... Talking around this subject was only making his patience wear thin. "Why does she have to go? And when you answer, try not to be cryptic."

"I can't tell you why," Rush told him with muscles straining in his neck. "But I can tell you that she is trouble."

"You don't even know her."

"Jackson, trust me when I tell you *I know her*," Rush argued. Then in a softer tone, he added. "You know about me now. You have your memories back. You know I have certain... Talent... and..."

"Then you do it!" Jackson spat angrily. He wanted Bright Star to stay, but even more, he wanted to thwart the brother who had kept such an important secret from him. Rush certainly had the power to do it. And Jackson had no desire for her to leave. He didn't completely understand why, but at that moment, he truly couldn't say he cared. Rush should get rid of her. "This is part my place, too. And, I want her here."

"You have to do it," Rush explained, raking his hands over his face. He sat down in the recliner in the corner. "It's not you she's after. You don't know why she was on that roof. You won't hurt her, and... Jackson... I might. It has to be you."

Jackson challenged. "Rush, if you trust me. If you would just tell me... then I..."

Rush didn't answer. Jackson knew that he wouldn't. He knew his brother wouldn't tell him anything that hinted at his link to Bright Star.

Even if it meant she remained in the home to torment him. Determined to protect him to the end, Rush wouldn't tell him.

Jackson knew who would. He backed out of his room and headed down the hallway to the guest room. His whole body could feel the disapproval seeping out Rush's pores into the universe. This time, Jackson didn't listen.

Rush fell into pace just behind him.

"Do you know why Randall was calling me the other night?"

Rush shook his head.

"He was calling me because Thad was back in holding."

Rush's eyes widened. "He got the rock?"

"Yes," Jackson answered. He saw the question in his brother's eyes. "Nobody got hurt, thank goodness. I don't even know how they got him in there."

"But how did he get the rock back?"

"We don't know. No fucking idea." Jackson rarely swore, but this situation was ripe for it. "He got it back and we were lucky he didn't kill someone."

"You had to get it from him?" Rush's eyebrows furrowed. It was as much a look of concern as Jackson had ever seen from him.

"Yeah," he responded. "You can't imagine the levels of High Energy he puts out when he first gets that thing." Then with a sarcastic sneer he appended, "Actually, I'm sure you can."

Rush ignored that statement. "Is he OK?"

"I don't know. I was going to go see him today."

"Do you think they'll let him out?"

Jackson considered that. "Probably. If they figure out how he got it and are able to neutralize the source."

"Why not just let him keep it? He gets the one violent surge out and then no more stored up Energy. He's calm."

Before he could answer, Jackson felt the hairs on the nape of his neck rise. He felt his breathing rush and his skin tingle. He looked up and Bright Star was standing in the door.

"There's no food in the kitchen." It was hard to tell whom she addressed. Her gaze flashed back and forth from the ground to Rush, but her body was turned to Jackson. "I was going to get something. I want to contribute, you know. Say thank you. Anything special you want for dinner tonight?"

Chapter 6

Old Times

"Bright Star?" Jackson started pushing his vegetables around on his plate. "You haven't told me how you ended up on that roof. I mean, maybe we should call the police." She made a face. "If you don't want to do that, I'm sure I can get someone from the Service to investigate discreetly. Really, no one will know what they find but us."

"I don't think that will be necessary," she said in a docile tone. She gave him a comforting smile and her blue eyes seemed to glow under the shining fringe of red hair.

For a moment, Jackson softened. In the end, she had come away from this fine. Whole. Jackson's face clouded as the image of this woman in a puddle of the glistening blood, her face stained red, imposed itself on the moment. "Bright Star, you almost died up there!" Jackson declared. "You can't let them get away with it. There is no reason to protect someone who could have killed you."

"I'm not protecting anyone," she argued. Funny how she could argue forcefully and at the same time convey the vulnerability that had led Jackson to try to save her in the first place. Her eyes were down as she continued, "I'm just telling you there's no need for the police. What happened, happened. Besides, I may not have died."

"If you didn't think you would die—and I assure you that you would have—then why did you call out to me?" Jackson asked. Bright Star kept her eyes on her plate and was silent.

"Great question. Why don't you answer him?" Rush interjected as he strode into the room.

Jackson took note that his brother, who normally walked with his shoulders hunched and his head down, directly addressed the newcomer as he neared the table. He still wore his dreary layers. A faded black long-sleeved knit shirt. A dark, army green t-shirt over it. Baggy faded black jeans. But somehow, he looked larger, stronger. He sat down and reached for the bowls at the center of the table. Jackson couldn't remember the last time he'd seen Rush eat something besides cereal or burritos.

"I called for help, you just... you just answered." She explained reluctantly. Jackson noticed that she looked at him but never directly at his brother. Jackson wished Rush would stop making the poor thing so uncomfortable. Jackson had seen his brother intimidate people plenty of times, but this time he obviously did it on purpose.

"Jackson," Rush started even as he continued to scoop food onto his plate. "Did she call you by name?"

"I don't remember," Jackson answered truthfully with a frown. "I'm sure she didn't. How would she know my name?"

"Yes, Bright Star," Rush tilted his head and questioned her. "How would you know his name?" The girl didn't answer. He turned his attention back to his brother. "Jackson, with all of your Service trained skills of observation, you don't remember whether she said your name or not when you were whisked away to that rooftop?"

Jackson did not have a ready answer.

"At the end of the day, you're an officer, Jacks. Why didn't it occur to you to ask who did it? To call for help? To file a report, *anything*? Follow the path backwards. See for yourself."

Jackson furrowed his brow. He thought back. He brought a hand up to cover his eyes and shut out anything but the memory of that rooftop. What had happened there? He began to concentrate, breathing slowly. In. Out. He breathed in and breathed out. Worrying his bottom lip with his teeth, he felt his body get heavy. He focused on physics laws. Somehow, they made these Shifts easier. It hadn't been explained in his parameters but... His body got even heavier. More and more weight seemed added to his chest until his heart was a boulder and gravity was in excess. Weighted down and down and down, Jackson expected to hit the floor and to have the breath pressed out of him, but that didn't happen. Instead, he found his skin tingling as his soul peeled itself away.

He had admitted it to no one, but he loved this sensation. It felt like butterflies and his knees getting weak. Only it wasn't just his stomach and it wasn't just his knees. All of his joints, his body just seemed to melt into a languid tingle. Like floating in warm salted water. High; he imagined this is what it was like to be high. Then, he was hovering over the roof of that building several hours ago.

Slowly, the scene unfurled before him in his mind. There he was, crouched over her. There she was, a white and untouched angel lying in a deep ruby pool of her own making. Then he was gone. She was lying there broken and alone. Her lips were moving but no sound was coming out of them. He couldn't tell what she was saying. Then, he heard his name like a soft sigh on the wind. His name. She called his name. *Jackson Rush.*

Jackson brought his hands down from his eyes, though the cloud of Shift made the room and its inhabitants dim. Bright Star was even darker, her brilliant white skin dim like honey. Everything was hazy but the eyes. Her blue eyes were more pronounced, as they were the only things to truly penetrate the fog. "Do you know me?" he asked her in surprise.

Bright Star put down her fork and steepled her hands in front of her. She was still and careful as she said to him, "I did not."

"Then why did you call to me for help?" Then he answered his own question: "Because you knew about me being the Precocial. You called me because you thought I could save you." It hadn't occurred to him, but it had happened before. Many times in the field, he'd fought alongside men with varying preternatural Talents. Some had called to him when they were in trouble because he was the strongest. Jackson wondered why he hadn't thought of it before. He was the Precocial. She didn't say anything. Jackson continued, "You believed that I was the only one who could save you. You knew of me the way every other Shifter knows of me."

"Yes," Bright Star chirped with a firm nod.

"No," Rush provided at the same time.

Jackson looked from one to the other and back again, "Bright Star, you called to me because you wanted to be saved."

"Yes," she answered with a more fervent nod.

"But not by you, Jackson," Rush interjected. He pierced Bright Star with his gaze, but she still refused to look directly at him.

"Then who..." Jackson queried slowly, just milliseconds before the answer dawned on him. He wasn't the person in the end who had saved her. Precocial or not, Jackson didn't have the Talent. But Rush did. "How could she have known?"

Rush replied solemnly, "I told you. We've met before."

"I did know Rush and I knew that he had a brother, Jackson," Bright Star added.

Jackson thought on this for a moment, then questions started to flood from him. "If that was the case, then why would she call me and not you, Rush?"

"She was afraid I wouldn't come." Rush stated pointedly. "Isn't that right, Bright Star?"

The creamy-skinned, red-haired girl remained mute. She cast her eyes downward this time, not looking at either of them.

"But how could she know that even if you were my brother, you would come? I didn't even know about your Talent, Rush, before yesterday. How could she know you would come?"

"She's a very, very clever girl, our Bright Star," was Rush's only answer.

"Is this true?" Jackson turned to her. She didn't answer. Her hands rested folded in her lap and she studied her plate. "You just used me to get to my brother?"

"I was dying," Bright Star reminded the younger brother as she tested the thickness of her mashed potatoes with her spoon.

Jackson swallowed. That was true. Did it matter when you were dying who saved you or how you got them to do it? He didn't voice the question aloud.

"Don't stop your questions now," Rush encouraged. "You're getting to the heart of the matter. Don't stop."

Jackson listened to his brother but his eyes were captured by the large blue ones that were—now he was certain—glowing. "What are you?"

"The same as you!" she declared. Her eyes went brighter. "You can Shift, and so can I."

"But you were dying and you managed to bring me all the way to you. You managed to do it in time for me to call my brother."

"I am blessed."

Rush scoffed audibly and bit into a piece of chicken. Jackson didn't believe it either. "How did you get up there? Who attacked you?"

"I told you, Jackson." She didn't raise her voice, but he could tell her patience was wearing thin. "It doesn't matter."

Jackson thumped his fists against the table in frustration. He didn't like puzzles. He didn't like that this beautiful woman was keeping a secret from him or his brother's cryptic smirk. He pushed back from the table and covered his eyes with his hands again. Gradually, he was able to slow his breathing and his heart rate. Gradually, he was able to make out that scene on the top of that building. He saw her lying there. He saw himself at her side. He began tapping his forehead with his fingertips unconsciously as he tried to force the images to go in reverse. It didn't happen as readily as he wanted, and already he tasted bile. He hadn't done that good of a job preparing himself.

He felt an intrusion and a jolt that he knew to be Rush. Rush was easing his path as he struggled. The images behind his eyelids jumpstarted and he saw Bright Star with her arms out, leaning over the rail of the roof into the frigid, wet wind. She smiled as if she had just found home. Jackson was struck with how perfect she looked.

Then she leaned back and turned around. She picked something up out of a bag on the ground. She leaned down again and came up with a glinting, black-handled chef's knife and a thermos. Jackson recognized the knife as the one he'd pulled from her near lifeless body. Bright Star twisted the cap on the thermos until it came free. She tossed it into the bag. Then she poured some of the contents into the hand holding the knife. At first, Jackson could only see that it was water. Then she turned and went to the edge of the roof again. She held one hand over the mouth of the thermos as she poured with the other. Water dribbled out from the cracks in her fingers. She made a small, tight fist. When she opened her hand once again, it was littered with tiny red blossoms. Blood.

Before Jackson could begin to guess, Bright Star turned up the glass to her lips and drank the whole mixture of water, acid, glass, and chamomile. When she was done, she staggered, but still managed to put the thermos away in her bag. Then she gripped the knife in both hands, holding it high, the blade pointed inward. She smiled wide, rapture on her lips, then plunged the blade into her gut, just below her sternum. It sank in to the hilt. This time she fell. She lay there for more moments than Jackson cared to count, then the bag disappeared and he saw himself standing in front of her.

Jackson shook his head to come back from the memory and stood up. Unfortunately, he took part of the tablecloth with him and all the items on top of the table spilled off. Bright Star dropped to her knees and began cleaning up the mess.

Jackson backed away and kept backing away until his back came against the wall. He couldn't take his eyes off the girl whose russet head was bent over the busy task of cleaning up his mess.

"You tried to commit suicide," he accused.

With that, her glowing eyes actually beamed hot blue light at him. She stood, drawing herself up impressively even though she was a good deal shorter than he was. "I didn't."

"But, I saw you," Jackson yelled pointing at her.

"I know what you saw," she agreed. "And it is true that what happened on that roof I did to myself. But I didn't commit suicide, nor was I trying."

Finally, she looked over at Rush and her eyes found his, directly. "Rush didn't let me die."

"Jackson didn't want you to die," Rush replied as if that answered all questions.

"You saved me," Bright Star spoke to him in a forceful tone. "Jackson, I would not kill myself. I did it for Rush. I did it because… I just wanted your brother to understand."

"To understand what?" Jackson asked horrified. "What could hurting yourself possibly make him understand?"

Bright Star opened her mouth to speak but nothing came out. No words. She tried again to the same outcome. For a moment, her eyes looked mutinous. Then she was docile again. The bright blue dimmed. She dropped to her knees and went back to cleaning up the mess on the floor.

"Why won't you let her tell me why she did it?" Jackson came to stand eye to eye with his brother.

"You don't want to know."

"That's not your fucking decision, Rush!" Jackson growled. "I don't care what she said. That girl tried to kill herself last night and I demand to know why."

Bright Star raised her head and, this time, Rush did not stop her words. "Jackson, I'm not suicidal. I never appreciated life until I met your brother, and now I think I appreciate it more than anyone else does in the universe. No, I didn't try to kill myself, I only gave Rush an opportunity to save me."

"You what?" Jackson gasped, brushing his palm over his head.

"Because that's his destiny."

Had the answer been less dramatic, Jackson would have been inclined to believe it. But this he couldn't handle. Here was a girl who had chewed poisoned glass and plunged a knife into her delicate body trying to tell him about destiny. He started to laugh. She was crazy.

"I'm not crazy," she argued, picking the thought directly from his mind. "I'm not." She looked at Rush again, who remained painfully silent as she pleaded with Jackson. "Please listen. If you believe in Shift and you believe in High Energy, then you know there are some things greater in this world than what we can see, taste, hear, smell, or touch."

"Of course I know that."

"Then if you know it, you must know that sometimes we can overcome time and space."

"*Parameters of Shift 101*," Jackson retorted with condescension. "I know that as well."

"Then how can you not understand or at the very least entertain the thought that there may be a destiny for all of us. That it already exists. There, perfect, waiting, and that we might be able to see it ahead of time?"

"I'm not denying that," Jackson argued. "But are you telling me that Rush's destiny was to save you on a friggin' rooftop last night?"

Rush swallowed audibly. He watched them both intently.

"Yes and no," Bright Star offered. She put out a hand in entreaty. "What happened last night was fate. That was like a beginning, though it wasn't. Destiny does not start or stop. It culminates. Manifests. Events lead up to it. *All events* lead up to it. This was just one such event."

"You don't believe this."

"I believe it." She came around the table and grabbed his forearm in a firm grip. "I believe it, and you will believe it.

Jackson rolled his eyes and puffed his cheeks out. She stepped away from him.

"Okay, fine." He halted her. "Where does Rush's destiny culminate?"

"Jacob Rush will save the world!" Bright Star proclaimed with a joy so strong that she laughed and clasped her hands together.

Jackson started laughing for an entirely different reason. This had to be a joke, a preposterous one at best, but a joke just the same. He laughed so hard tears started in his eyes and he sank bank into his chair holding his stomach.

"How long did you think this could go on?" he asked his brother, who had never once, not even when they were children, played a practical joke on him.

"It's not a joke, Jackson," Rush said. "And for the record, I don't believe any of it either. It's preposterous, just like you think, but she's not kidding. That's why I told you to leave her alone. She really believes what she's saying. She does. And there's no telling what she's willing to do to prove it."

Jackson sobered. His brother, in his own expressionless way, looked petrified. There was something about his demeanor, the way he sat on the edge of his chair. The way he had finally stopped eating. This was no joke.

"Why does she have to prove it?" he questioned hesitantly. "If it's your destiny to save the world, then why can't she just wait until you do it?"

"Jackson," Rush returned. "Sometimes you're brilliant. Bright Star, if it's my destiny, then won't the deed be its own proof?"

Bright Star did not address either brother. She succeeded in getting all of the debris off the floor and back onto the table where she folded the ends of the tablecloth over the mess and tied it up so she could take the bundle to the kitchen closet. She was dressed in all white again. A pair of white slacks. A white sweater with a low neck. White shoes. He didn't get any of this.

"Are you crazy?" He posed the question as if it were a question that ever elicited more than one answer.

"No." She shook her head with its silken red locks, took her bundle, and left the room.

Of course, she would say no. When she was gone, Jackson and Rush faced each other. "Now do you understand why she has to go?"

"No," was Jackson's answer. "Now I see why she needs our help. She's obviously a danger to herself, Rush. You and I both know that. If we turn her out now, there's no telling what she might do to herself."

"Jackson, we are not psychiatrists. We can't help her. Don't you think she belongs somewhere where people really know how to help?"

Jackson's mouth came open in shock. What Rush had just suggested was unthinkable. *Where people really know how to help?*

"Jackson," Rush attempted to soothe the effect of his last words. "It won't be the same."

"People in institutions do not understand how to handle Shifters. Most of the world still doesn't even believe High Energy exists. I was lucky to go into the Service. At least they knew what it was. They understood how to handle it. They trained me to use it to…" Jackson choked off those last words as he felt the old emotions wash over him.

"Then take her to the Service." Rush leapt on his brother's words. "You were quick to suggest it for me."

"You're stronger than she is—"

Rush ignored that comment. "You're the one who said I had to be trained. You can take her there. Take her to Ronald—"

"Randall—"

"Whatever. He won't be able to resist getting his hands on someone like her. He'll monitor her twenty-four hours a day. You can't do that. Leave it to someone who can."

The option had not occurred to Jackson. Still, as quickly as he considered it, he disposed of that as an option. "She won't go there."

"But, Jackson, you just said—"

"You should see the way they hold Thad."

"Thad goes voluntarily."

"Thad realizes he's a threat to others."

Rush started to say something but Jackson interrupted. "*She* is only a danger to herself."

"You don't know that—"

"And, I don't think they will understand how to help her. She's unstable, but all they will care about is her Talent. They'll keep her physically alive, but they won't take care of her mental health."

"That's not true, and you know it. You've told me so many times how they help Shifters deal with their Talents. As you well know, Shifters have a higher incidence of emotional and behavioral problems." Rush was regurgitating everything Jackson had told him over the years.

"This is different. Bright Star is different. She is vulnerable," Jackson's voice broke, betraying his attempt to sway his brother.

"Not as vulnerable as you think."

"You might have saved her, Rush, but you weren't there."

"Why didn't you call the police, Jackson?"

"What?"

"Why didn't you go after her 'attackers,' Jackson?"

"I don't—"

"Why did it never occur to you to take her to her own home, Jackson?"

Rush's little brother had no answers.

"Vulnerable?" Rush gave a nasty chuckle. "Vulnerable, Jackson? She's not fucking vulnerable. She played you like a goddamned piano, man. That woman in there is not Mom." Rush stated soulfully. "She's not being persecuted or ostracized for being different. We are not casting judgment on her without all the facts. She is not broken the way our mother was broken. You know Randall Sandoval. He might be an asshole, but he would make sure she was treated well. And she truly is dangerous. You've seen it with your own eyes. Our mother was not crazy. She was unhappy, very unhappy, but not crazy. Please," he begged, "don't get the two of them confused. Bright Star will hurt people."

"She only hurt herself."

"She will hurt others," Rush declared.

"So what? You can see the future, too?" Jackson snarled this with sarcasm. He nearly bit his tongue when his brother only glared his affirmation at him.

"Please send her away or at least get your Service to take her, Jacks. You know Sandoval won't turn her away once they see what she can do."

Jackson thought about that long hidden memory. He thought about his mother saving him from the knife and the way she had stripped him of that memory for his own protection. She didn't want her own special, precious child to look on her with the disdain she'd felt her whole life. He considered Bright Star and her fragile nature. He thought of her lying near dead on a rooftop from self-inflicted wounds. Then, he thought of the rock that was in his pocket at that very moment. He had taken that rock from a man he considered a friend. A man who was now strongly sedated, whose only words from time to time were "my rock."

Jackson knew what would happen. They would test her, hold her, study her the way they had when he was boy, the way they still wanted to now. They would hurt her and not even know it and expect him to help like he had with Thad. He couldn't do that to her. He couldn't. "I can't do that," he told his older brother. But, Rush was no longer there.

Chapter 7

Electricity

Bright Star had been in their home more than a month before it happened again. She had a bedroom. She was there for meals that she sometimes prepared. She watched TV with them from time to time. She was learning all of the shortcuts in the virtual racing game they played. Her clothes were there, though Jackson was not sure when that happened. Hell, he didn't even remember them having a third bedroom. Jackson saw her when he left for work in the morning and found himself looking forward to seeing her when he came home. Jackson found himself talking to her about his day. He would tell her what he had seen at the Service, what he'd been asked to do, and the new things he had learned about High Energy.

Bright Star didn't pay rent or utilities as far as he knew, but somehow that didn't matter, either. Her presence had become so much a part of their lives that Jackson could barely remember the time without her. She was like the water in the pipes, the signal in the radio, the electricity in the wires.

Rush had become more of a recluse than ever. Jackson barely saw him. But Bright Star was there when he left for work, and there when he came home. She sat with him and ate with him. She laughed with him and, Jackson believed, was happy with him. Perpetually in action, she cleaned and cooked and followed Rush around whenever he deigned to come out of his room. And she always took time to practice newer and more difficult Shifts with Jackson as a witness.

Sometimes, Jackson liked to practice with her. It was at those times that he was more and more amazed with her significant Talent. For a civilian, she had amazing control over her High Energy. From birth, Jackson had always known his power to be great; greater than anyone that had ever walked the earth. That was due to being Precocial, they theorized at the Service. He'd had the gift from birth so it had more time to grow and develop. As with all other aspects of a child's formative years, the potential to grow was exponentially greater than in a teenager or adult. It was the reigning theory, but Jackson was beginning to doubt that was the only reason.

In his own family he had discovered two other Shifters who seemed to have greater ability than he. Amazing. When he was young and his Talent had been first recognized, Jackson remembered that the Service had tested his entire family. Everett, Janie, and Jacob. None of them had shown the slightest signs of having the power to Shift. But that had been nearly twenty-five years before, and the technology—traditional and Shift-enhanced—had been nowhere near as advanced. He wondered how they would all fair today.

Bright Star, he already knew, would test off the charts. As they practiced, they would focus on a single item and start with light shifts. One day, they each began with a plastic cup with their signatures on them. Bright Star stood casually barefoot in faded jeans, a white shirt, and giant white hoops in her ears. She raised only an eyebrow and the cup with her signature levitated from the table into thin air. Jackson did the same with his own cup.

Bright Star's cup wiggled a little from side to side. Jackson's cup did the same. He couldn't suppress the smile caused by the hum of controlled High Energy coursing through his body. Bright Star's cup went up and down, so did Jackson's. Bright Star walked over to her levitating cup and slipped off the shiny white band she always wore on her left ring finger. She put it in the cup marked Bright Star, then the cup disappeared. Jackson slipped off his watch then put it in his cup and that one disappeared at Bright Star's will as well.

"Now bring it back," Bright Star ordered, exposing a dimpled cheek.

Jackson grinned at her then closed his eyes. He slowed his breathing then held up one hand as he searched for the distinct Energy frequency that was the cup. Like a deep red thread, so dark it was almost invisible, Jackson read the link to the cup. Ah. She hid it in Rush's closet. How expected, Jackson thought sardonically.

"OK," he said brandishing the cup and giving her ring back. "Bring mine back."

Then, with a slight bit of more visible effort, she closed her eyes and held her hands up as if she were being robbed. Then she reached one out and plucked the cup from the air. She dumped Jackson's watch out in his palm. Jackson chuckled until he realized she wasn't done. With her other hand, she plucked another cup with his signature on it from the air and dumped that watch in his hand as well. It was the same one with an *identical* energy. It was real, not a suggestion with identical Energy. Impossible. Bright Star produced a third cup, and a fourth and fifth. All frighteningly, *exactly* the same. She was reaching for another before Jackson's hand clamped around her wrist. He didn't mean to hurt her, but this wasn't right. That was not the way High Energy worked. He swallowed deep and his heart thumped aggressively in his chest.

"Stop," he rasped. "Stop!"

Bright Star did stop and snapped the fingers of her free hand to make all of the cups and watches except for the original go away.

The speed and effectiveness of that Shift without even so much as a blink told Jackson more than anything that she had not even begun to show him her Talent. She'd been humoring him, teasing him. She hadn't experienced the ill effects of Perma-Shift once and already, Jackson felt a low throb in his head, a pulse deep in his cheekbones, behind his eyes. He was lucky in that no matter how severe the Perma-Shift, it never affected him much more than that. Except for the times he tried to save her on that rooftop and the time Rush shut him out.

"I didn't mean to scare you." Bright Star apologized.

Jackson stepped away from her. He'd be lying if he said those words had not been an attack on his pride.

"It's nothing to be ashamed of," Bright Star offered, only making it worse.

Jackson couldn't speak. His heart had started pounding when he'd inspected that second watch, and it was still racing. He couldn't talk about it. Not then. He couldn't take the hand she offered, and started to leave the room. *Parameters of Shift 101*, he thought in amazement. One could not make something from nothing. That's why it was called Shift in the first place. Something could change to imitate something else, as long as it already existed. One could take an object and bend it, invert it, convert it, but one could not create something that had not existed in one form or another.

Every object had its own identifying Energy, even the set of sixteen physically identical plastic cups in a convenience store. Everything. Each and every one of the cups possessed a unique natural signature. But Bright Star, somehow, managed to create something from nothing and give it the exact Energy as the original item. According to what he'd been taught, it was impossible.

A hand appeared on his shoulder. It was small and feminine with blunt nails. "It's nothing compared to what Rush can do," her low voice came from behind him. The last thing Jackson wanted to hear, but he accepted that she couldn't stop herself from saying it anyway. He didn't turn around. The warm hand slid down to his bicep as she stepped around him and faced him again. "I'm sorry, Jackson," she said honestly. "I know this is hard for you especially."

"I've always been... I don't know..."

"Special?"

"Yes." He nodded slowly, deliberately. "Special. And now, it's almost as if everything that has made me special...doesn't even exist anymore. And it's all happened so incredibly fast."

Bright Star nodded sympathetically.

"I always knew, deep down, that Rush was hiding his strength. Even when we were kids, I looked up to him in a way that went beyond a younger brother's awe of his older brother. I always knew it, but I never knew how Talented he was."

"I know why you're worried," Bright Star soothed. "But you don't have to be. You are still the most important thing in this world to Rush."

"He told you that?" Jackson whispered.

"No." Bright Star shook her head slowly. She sighed, and it sounded like sadness. "I'd have to be a fool not to know it, though. And you are a fool, Jackson, to believe that what is happening is any less important than it is. I know you think I'm crazy—"

"I don't—"

"Fine," she conceded. "You think I'm disturbed. A danger to myself. But, even still, I know that you and I have something in common."

"What's that?"

"We believe in your brother equally. I can't let my personal worries or fears get in the way of what I know. Neither can you."

"Bright Star, this has nothing to do with me. All of this tension is between you and Rush."

"We all have our parts to play," she answered cryptically.

Jackson stood there staring at the watch still in his hands. Bright Star dropped something round and smooth into his palm next to it. She left the room before Jackson realized it was a shiny hematite rock. He followed her and reached for her arm. "How did you get this?"

Bright Star did not answer. She didn't say a word. Jackson grabbed her arms, shook her. "How did you get this?"

She said nothing for a moment. Jackson could feel the frustration mounting to extreme levels inside of him. The tendons in his hands strained.

"You keep it on your nightstand, Jackson. I took it from there."

Her voice was small, vulnerable. Jackson let her go and she nearly ran away from him while he stood in the hallway trying desperately to control the pounding of his heart.

* * * *

It happened the next morning.

Rush was still in bed... or at least in his room. Jackson had just finished getting ready for work.

As with every day, he and Bright Star met each other in the kitchen. She usually woke up just before he left. This day, she stumbled in as he poured himself some coffee. She fished in the refrigerator for juice. After finding a carton, she leaned against the closed door. Jackson leaned against the counter across from her that held the coffee pot. They sized each other up in silence. Then, like always, Jackson gave it a shot.

"You do know how much we care about you," Jackson opened.

"You mean how much *you* care," she returned, tilting her head to the side with a sleepy but patient smile.

"Rush cares, too. I think he's just worried. I'm worried, too." He added that last quickly. "But I think he's worried that this can't be fixed. I think it can."

"What?"

"What what?"

"What do you think can be fixed?" she clarified.

"I think that you can—"

"I can be fixed?" This time, she full out grinned. She was playful in the mornings: her body slow and languid, her mind quick and teasing.

"That's not what I mean, Bright Star, and you know it." Jackson was half exasperated half amused. "Fine, then. I care about you. I believe that you are smart, beautiful and Talented." Bright Star looked directly at him. But mentally, he could tell, she was rolling her eyes. He plowed ahead. "You don't deserve to be hurt, even by yourself."

Her smile slowly evaporated until it was as if it had never been there, as if it were desert rain. She turned away from him and put the juice back into the refrigerator. Jackson thought of saying something else to her, but he wouldn't. He would let his words soak in, because over time, she had to believe it. That was the recommendation Randall Sandoval gave him when Jackson questioned him about the high incidence of suicidal tendencies during the developmental stages of Shift. Some of them also showed homicidal tendencies. Powerful nine-to fourteen-year-olds were frequently sent to "Summer Camp." The facility was only a floor above where they kept Thad Okwenuba.

Randall proved worth his salt by asking slow and subtly probing questions, using his own particular Talents to discover if Jackson was speaking of himself. Once he realized that Jackson had a very real fear for someone else, he'd done his level best to persuade Jackson to tell him who. Jackson had done his level best to avoid telling him and to block the image of Bright Star from his mind. Sandoval was, after all, a Serviceman first. If he figured out who, he would do his duty and have their best team bring her in whether she was cooperative or not. As long as he could not read her identity from Jackson, he would be limited to offering his knowledge. He offered Jackson the words of support that usually started the slow process of acceptance for what they termed Class D Shifters.

Jackson had spoken these brief words to her. An encouraging phrase or two with a hint of suggestion to keep her safe this day. Every morning he tried to leave her peaceful, her mind and heart still. If she were anxious or agitated, according to Dr. Sandoval, she might be more prone to engage in "erratic" behavior. At Jackson's rolled eyes, Sandoval assured him that it wasn't rocket science.

After those words, Jackson reached out and lamely patted her on the shoulder. She smiled at him still with sleepy eyes and a lazy yawn, assured him that all would be well, and told him she was going to clean the kitchen. Jackson stepped out into chilly December air.

* * * *

In the kitchen, Bright Star took a deep breath. She reached into the refrigerator again, this time removing a pitcher of water. She cast her gaze around and also took hold of the spoon Jackson had used to stir his coffee. She carried them both over by the table and sat cross-legged on the floor in the corner. She took another deep breath and thought of Jackson's words. She was smart, beautiful now, and talented. Smart. Beautiful. Talented. And strong. She was strong, too. She could do this.

Bright Star lifted the pitcher and poured all of its water into her lap. The water wet her and her nightgown from the waist down. It ran in rivulets over her crossed legs and onto the floor. She Shifted a little, and the water formed a standing, two-inch deep puddle around her. She sat the pitcher down on the floor then took the spoon in her hand and rammed the handle into the electrical socket.

Suddenly the electricity coursed through her like tiny glass shards abrading her veins. She stung all over and her ears were ringing. She couldn't let go of the spoon if she tried, and did not try. She allowed herself to be magnetized at that very spot; allowed her skin to tense and her hair to smoke. Her body started to convulse and her teeth chattered as she tried to speak. She didn't know what she would say. She didn't call for Jackson this time. Instead, she sent her distress call directly to Rush.

That is how Jackson found her. Something in her final, guarded gaze before he left had given her away. He knew something was terribly wrong. That feeling drove him back into the house and found her on the floor involuntarily bending and snapping like a fresh caught fish. Service training kicked in. He shouldn't approach within 10 feet until he was certain that nothing else including the air around her had been charged with harmful electricity. Rushing across the room anyway, he reached down to jerk her away from the wall.

"Don't touch her!" Rush commanded as he walked into the room and with a mental push, he stopped Jackson in his tracks. "You're not grounded," Rush explained before closing his eyes.

"It can't hurt me."

Jackson pulled away from his brother's suggestion, and dropped down to his knees beside her. His pant legs were wet and he could still feel the tingle of the current. He knew that if he could feel it, it was still affecting her. Her muscles were still constricted. Tearing her from the wall, he watched as blue electricity arced out to her in threads from the socket like starved tentacles. He lifted her stiff body in his arms and took her into the living room where he laid her on the floor. He started to check her vital signs. She wasn't breathing, and he couldn't find a pulse. Her body was still taut, every muscle strained. He started CPR.

Before he could lean down to place his lips over hers, she sat up. Her eyes opened, shooting blue lasers across the room. In seconds they dimmed again and she threw herself off the couch. She ran back into the kitchen and fell to the floor in front of Rush, her knees making an awful timpani note on the tile.

"You saved me," Bright Star gasped and crawled to Rush. She threw her arms around his legs and wept.

"Get her. Get her off of me!" Rush yelled as he tried to extract himself from her grip without actually touching her. The contorted scowl on his face spoke volumes. If Rush did touch her or use Shift, Jackson thought, he was much more likely to stick her back to the wall plugging her right back into the current. "Right now, Jackson!"

Jackson knelt and began to pry Bright Star's arms from his brother. After Jackson physically lifted her from the ground into his arms, Rush quickly left them, the muscle in his jaw ticking wildly.

"Jackson did you see it?" she mused, turning in his arms. The wide grin stretched her round cheeks. A dimple formed in the side of her chin. She was happy. Happy even as there were sparks in her eyes still and her skin had turned thicker, darker.

Slowly, Jackson eased her to the ground. "I saw that you stuck your finger in a socket and nearly killed yourself. Again."

Bright Star's smile turned into a grimace. "No. Don't be blind. Did you see that he saved me? He rescued me."

"Yes," Jackson placated her. His throat nearly closed over the word. "Yes, I saw it. But don't you understand? Rush is just a man. He has Talents, but so do I. We are just men. It's like doing CPR for a normal person, Bright Star. It's what we should all do. We should save someone in need if we can. There's nothing more to it."

"There is," she snapped. "There is. I could *see* him, *smell* him. I could *feel* him, Jackson. All there was in his mind was my coursing life current, that High Energy thread that's me and me only. Rush reached out to that current redirecting it into my body even as it tried to escape. He repaired skin and bones and blood and nerves as he went to rebuild what I—"

"What you had impulsively and stupidly sought to destroy."

She looked as if she had been physically wounded. She wiped at her eyes. Her voice became hurried and zealous. "Amazing though it was, what he did for me, Jackson, is nothing. At your Service, didn't they teach you about Perma-Shift?"

"Of course, Bright Star," he answered exasperated. "That's just *Parameters of Shift 101*. The bigger the Shift the more likely you are to experience severe Perma-Shift."

"But he didn't."

"I've seen him experience it before." Jackson recalled the time he had surprised his brother in his bedroom.

"Maybe, but not this time. Saving a life is the one most difficult, unstable, complicated, and strenuous Shift of all. Jackson, you know it. It's huge. And he didn't even blink." She held tightly to Jackson's shirt as she tried to communicate her message. "You don't recognize his power for what it is. He's not some EMT who saves one or two people on his shift. He's not some random Serviceman fumbling around with his budding Talent. Rush can save us all."

"From what, Bright Star?" Jackson asked and for once she didn't have an answer readily available. She paused long enough for Jackson to calm down. He untangled her from his shirtfront and set her back from him. He tipped her face back to look at the blue eyes, soft creamy skin, perfect, supple pink lips. She looked a strange mix of passion and vulnerability and Jackson wanted nothing more than to kiss her.

At that thought, he firmly took a step back, farther away from her. What the hell was he thinking? He couldn't let his mind travel that path. No matter how intrigued he was by her. No matter how strong the attraction. No matter that his brother wouldn't come near her with a ten-foot pole. Jackson knew there was a stronger bond between Rush and Bright Star than he could ever have with her. She only ever watched Rush, had just literally been pulled off of him. Jackson knew, somehow, that if he were to seek her out, it would be a betrayal Rush would not likely forgive.

She answered his question finally. "From ourselves."

"Jackson," Rush called firmly from his room. "Do *not* let her in your head. Remember what she just did. Remember that you just saw her convulsing in a puddle she made on the floor. Remember that just a minute ago, you were trying to save her damned life! She's suicidal. She's crazy."

"If you believed I was suicidal and crazy, you could have stopped me before I did it," she countered without shouting. Of course, Rush could still hear her. "You would have stopped me."

"I didn't think you would go through with it." Rush volleyed.

"A suicidal crazy person would have."

Jackson knew she had made her point. He was surprised to see her face crumple in hurt. Something he hadn't been privy to had happened. Bright Star and Rush's final psychic exchange had not left her as confident. Jackson slid down into a chair at the table and studied the hands that had *not* been instrumental in rescuing her.

"I believe in you," she declared to Rush out loud. "Of course you must understand. I believe in you. I believe in you!" She started to scream it hoarsely as tears coursed down her eyes. "I won't stop believing in you! I won't stop! I won't stop! I won't stop! I believe!"

She and Jackson were left alone in the room both physically and mentally. Before he said the words, her eyes flared and snapped to him. Her tears dried and her mouth parted in a little snarl. Jackson started to speak. His lips even moved, but no words came out. It was more than a suggestion, it was a full on Shift. Bright Star tilted her head to the side. Jackson's eyes widened as he realized that it wasn't his brother, but

Bright Star who had ruthlessly, cruelly taken his voice. She snatched her attention away from him suddenly. Jackson's words came back. He said to her: "You can't stay here unless you talk to someone."

Bright Star was silent, the set to her jaw mutinous as the seconds ticked by slowly. Jackson rubbed his throat, still not quite believing she had attacked him although, he reasoned, she was very upset, had nearly died moments before. He had to remember that she needed his help. It wasn't so hard when he studied her face.

"I know someone." Jackson plunged forward, "He's a doctor and he's sort of a friend at the Service. He can help you." When there was no response, not so much as a change in expression, he continued. "I can make sure he leaves you alone for the time being. You don't have to show him the extent of your powers. You know how to mask them. I've seen you do it. If you do that, then he won't feel like he has to keep you there."

Bright Star said nothing, but her expression did change this time. It was resigned. It was sad.

She nodded.

Chapter 8

Getting to Know You

When Jackson found Bright Star, she was stuffing whites into the washer and looking incredibly normal. He crossed his arms over his chest and leaned against the dryer to watch. She wore white track pants and a white tank top. Her arms were long and white and taut with smooth muscle. They complemented a well-built torso. She still looked soft, but Jackson noted that she looked strong as well. Her collarbones were both prominent and delicate. The swell of her breasts was undeniable, and her waist tapered from a broad and sinewy back. Her stomach was just slightly rounded. Her track pants rode low on flaring hips. For some reason, he wondered if she was wearing shoes or socks. The pants were a little too long for her, so he couldn't see her feet. His own feet danced and he couldn't figure out whether to stand or continue leaning.

"Hey," he croaked.

"Hey," she returned his greeting as she started picking through a basket looking for small items. She came up with socks, which she also tucked into the machine.

"I don't think you can get the clothes clean that way," he joked.

"Why?" Her rounded cheeks and lush, earthen lips curved invitingly.

"You've got about three loads too many packed in there as it is."

Bright Star stood back and looked in the machine. A lock of sweat-dampened copper hair fell into her eyes. Her hair was softly curling this day. "I hate laundry," was her answer.

"Then why are you doing it?"

"It's good for me," she answered. When she said nothing further, Jackson crossed his arms in front of him. "And your brother." As if there could have been any other reason. Jackson mentally rolled his eyes. "I don't know why," she continued, "but he has this great respect for people who do laundry. I've never particularly liked it, but I have to respect people who do it, too." She laughed and even though he didn't understand, even though he chafed at the fact she was glorifying the act of doing laundry, he laughed too. He couldn't help it.

Then, he held his hands over the open mouth of the washer and put them together. He wringed them as if he were washing them. Below, the clothing seemed to Shift as well. Once he was done, he stretched his hands out again then flipped them up quickly. The clothes came out of the washer in a steady stream and folded themselves back into an empty basket. When Bright Star looked around, the other baskets held clean clothes as well.

For a moment, Jackson worried that she would reject his Shift and wash the clothes anyway, but she didn't. "I won't tell if you won't," she grinned.

"A Service Man knows how to keep a secret," Jackson vowed.

"Jackson?" When she said his name, it was always as if she were going to asking him something profound, something earth shattering. It was enough to suspend his breath and jolt his heart. "Were you looking for me?"

"Yes," he replied automatically. For a moment, he let himself bathe in the blue of her eyes. "It's... ah... time. Well, not really, you've got just under two hours. I thought I'd take you. There's nothing to eat in the house, so I was going out to get something anyway. Do you want to go?"

Bright Star paused as she thought about the offer. Then with a quick nod, she agreed, "Sure, I don't think Rush will mind. I need to get changed first. After we eat and if there's time we can go by the grocery store as well and pick up some things for the house."

"Good. I'll meet you outside in ten minutes?"

"That works."

Jackson felt like an idiot as he rushed upstairs to change clothes. He didn't have to do it. This wasn't a date. He knew that very well. But, the idea of spending time with her outside of that house... well. He changed into nice jeans and a button-down. He wore a light leather jacket, some nice shoes, and designer aftershave. He'd raced down the stairs trying to ensure he made it out and to the car before she did. He didn't want her to believe he had gone to any great lengths.

Bright Star was less than a minute behind him. Jackson remarked that she hadn't really changed clothes at all. Instead she'd put on a dark mustard-colored jacket and a white baseball cap with a bill of the same dark yellow color. White sneakers were peeking out from beneath the hem of the track pants. She probably had ten of those twenty minutes to spare. "Where we going to eat?" she asked casually as she went round to the passenger side of the car.

Jackson missed a beat but quickly rounded the car to open the door for her. "I don't care."

"Peter's?" she asked.

"Sure," Jackson returned wondering how his reservations had turned into an afternoon at a hot dog stand.

* * * *

She convinced him to sit outside. The air was piercing with its chill, but Bright Star found them a spot near the rattling space heater suspended from the metal rafter supporting the awning. She sat cross-legged on top of a flaking picnic table. She had two chilidogs and a giant cola. Jackson had the same. He sat on the edge of the table next to her with his feet up on the bench.

"A woman after my own heart." He whistled as she pushed the sleeves of her jacket up on her forearms and took a large bite from her dog.

"I adore chilidogs," she offered with a grin. "I used to be a performance artist. I think liking chili dogs comes with the job."

"Really?"

"Yeah. At least, that's what I liked to call myself. Performance artist. I travelled with my troupe—so to speak—though everyone else called it a circus. I was a side show… hence the hot dog fetish" She paused. Jackson didn't press her because it was the first time since he'd met her that she'd actually talked about herself without talking about Rush. "Anyway, I started when my Energy started to show itself. My first job was guessing things about people. You know, their heights, their weights, age, name of their childhood ferret…" They both chuckled. "You name it, I was guessing it. Then, as I got stronger, I started to make small predictions, ones that could be proven before the show was over. It wasn't long before I was billed for private readings. Usually whole groups at a time. Individuals rarely wanted to book me. I guess they thought I was too intense. For legal purposes I had to give them the entertainment spiel up front and continue to call myself a performance artist, but it didn't take long for people to start ignoring that, even. Sometimes it felt like they were swarming on me, you know. It felt like they wanted both more and less from me all at the same time. They wanted everything, and I didn't have the strength then…" She didn't finish.

Jackson nodded, patiently waiting for her to continue. Bright Star sighed.

"Anyway," she chirped too brightly, "when I started out, in true circus fashion, we had a hot dog guy who made the best coneys ever."

Jackson was disappointed that she'd cut off her story so quickly. Then he caught sight of something that Bright Star quickly tried to hide. She was pulling down her sleeves when Jackson said, "Stop."

She did stop and she was there, a fallen angel frozen in time. He reached out a hand to grab her wrist and pull it toward him. There were three horizontal marks starting at the tender place where her hand met her arm and graduating in length and depth as they disappeared into her jacket. The last one that nearly wrapped around her arm had merited seventy-five stitches. Jackson caught a flash of her lying in a hospital bed picking at the tape covering the bandage. For a moment, he absently massaged her flesh with the pad of his thumb.

"I want to help you," he told her softly.

"There is only one way to help me."

"Anything."

She leaned close to him. She pressed her lips so near to his ear that he could feel them move against his flesh. "Get your brother to see that if he doesn't start to care soon, I *will* die, because the world as we know it will end."

Jackson pulled back from her. For a moment he was speechless. His jaw worked but he said nothing. Finally he was able to get out, "I know you've got this idea, this theory, or whatever you want to call it, but you're a smart woman, Bright Star. You know that's just an excuse to hurt yourself."

"It's not."

"You scared me, you know," Jackson told her somberly.

"I know," she answered almost apologetic.

"We have to find out why you keep doing this—"

"That's not a mystery, Jackson."

Jackson ignored that feeling, the quick tension that occurred every single solitary time she said his name. He tried to focus on the fact that her voice was no longer apologetic. It was now bordering on impatient, but his body's reaction only strengthened as he watched her. "If we understand it, we can stop it. You can stop it."

"I'll go see your doctor, but it won't matter. I can't stop. I won't stop. One day you'll see," she argued with a mutinous set to her jaw and an electric luster to her eyes. And then she was calm again, her voice dry and monotone. "Your chilidogs are getting cold, and we only have forty-five minutes."

Jackson cast around in his mind for a way to make peace. He shoved his hands in his pockets. His right hand found something small, smooth, and cool. His fingers closed around it and he found himself saying, "There's something I want to give you."

She looked up at him and waited with strained patience.

"Open your hand."

She did so.

Jackson placed his hand over hers and dropped the glinting hematite rock back into her palm. He'd forgotten that he brought it, then in one moment, he'd realized that he needed to give it to her.

Her expression was quizzical.

"You took it from my nightstand that day... It belonged to a friend of mine. It was dangerous for him, but despite the havoc it wreaked on his life, the rock always brought him comfort in the end. Why don't you hold on to it?"

* * * *

Peter's was adjacent to the grocery store parking lot. After they finished eating—Jackson spent the rest of their meal trying desperately and failing miserably to engage her in conversation—they walked across the lot and went inside to shop.

Some of the tension left them as they pushed a buggy up and down the aisles picking up normal items for a normal household. Sometimes, Bright Star would even hold up things for Jackson's approval and he'd nod or shake his head. Jackson noticed as they carried on that men were looking at him with envy. Bright Star was not gorgeous. She was mesmerizing. And she was obviously deferent. He looked like a strong, tall, masculine man who'd picked his small, fragile wife up after work and brought her shopping. They looked like a happy couple.

Jackson couldn't help making the comparison. He knew if she were there with Rush, they would not look like a happy couple. Instead, people would be looking at her with pity and shaking their heads. They would see Rush as swarthy and menacing. They would see him hang back and away from her, watching furtively and with an unexplained control. They would see her deference and attempts to please and understand that she could *never* please him. It was a cruel thought, but Jackson didn't care. His brother didn't want her.

God help him, Jackson did.

As they packed bags into the car, Jackson asked casually: "Are you ready?"

"If you are," she responded noncommittally. Then she cast her eyes fleetingly at the trunk. Jackson laid a hand on top of it for a moment to cool the groceries. Jackson smiled at the thought of being her personal refrigerator. "If you're up to it after your session, there's a place I'd like to show you."

"I'm game," Bright Star answered and let him take her hand then tuck her into the passenger seat.

"Do you have ID with you?"

"Yeah, will I need it?"

"Not sure," was his only answer. Jackson tamped down the urge to ask her to see it. He wanted to know what name was listed on her government-issued identification. "Depends on how much High Energy you emit when they read you at the gate."

"How much should I emit?" She asked.

Jackson started to laugh but realized that she was serious. Of course, she was serious; he already knew that she was a pro at masking her High Energy. What he didn't know was how much control she had over it.

"OK," she answered audibly reading the gauge in his mind. They drove in silence for the next ten minutes. Their destination was just off the interstate.

Service Headquarters sat on 100 acres. Completely circular, the building lay bracketed by a series of white pillars that went from base to roof. The columns gave the impression that the building, while elegant, while beautiful, was behind bars. Lit well from the ground up, the building acted as a beacon on any clear day or dark night. Close up, the famous structure was obscured by a thick white wall rising to twelve feet.

Jackson drove up to the complex and the thick white wall seemed to pull right back and open for him. Upon closer inspection, one could see it was an arcing gate only designed to look like a portion of the wall. He stopped at the entrance of the gate At first glance, it didn't look as if there was anything beyond the gate but a long cobblestone driveway. Jackson rolled down his window and leaned out. Bright Star peered around him as he talked with the security guard leaning out of a dark green guard booth that blended smoothing into the foliage behind. The guard was not close enough for Jackson to reach him from his car. However, a wand slid out of the side of the guard house and Jackson swiped a badge against it. The wand retracted and Jackson eased his car forward about ten feet. It was at that point he reached out of the window and held his hand in the air. The touch screen appeared out of what seemed like thin air. Jackson pressed his entire hand against it. He introduced Bright Star as his guest to no one in particular. He indicated that she roll her window down and hold out her hand. The touch screen appeared next to her hand and she also pressed her hand as it prompted. The heavy gate slid open and they drove inside.

"Very nice," Bright Star breathed.

"Yes, but I have to tell you, though, this entrance has the least security of any of them. It's not the employee entrance. There are a couple thousand people who work inside and most come in from east and west underground entrances. This public entrance is where tours come through, et cetera. They don't get the full treatment because they don't get access to ninety percent of the building. Most don't even know the rest exists."

Bright Star listened but her eyes grew wide as they neared the massive white structure.

"Oh, if you think the outside is impressive, you'll definitely love the surprise I have in store."

Jackson drove round to the west of the building, ensuring Bright Star had the opportunity to see the impressive flora that surrounded it. Positioned all around the porch, rocking chairs gave the image of being very quaint but not nearly as deceptive as they needed to be. Jackson got out of the car then went around to Bright Star's side to open the door for her. She accepted his hand to help her out though they both knew she didn't need it. He led her into the west lobby and through another security checkpoint. He waved to a tall woman and chatted with her as he signed Bright Star in.

"Can you just bring anybody you want in here?"

"There are certain perks to being one in a trillion."

"Precocial?" she offered, letting the word roll slowly off her tongue.

"Yes," Jackson gave a cocky smirk. "Hey, we have to stop by my office for a minute first."

"OK," she said and followed him to a room with an expansive glass window. Inside, there were bookcases, file cabinets, a desk and a computer, a baseball trophy, and a picture turned toward the seat at the desk. Bright Star went over to it and turned it around. There was a flaxen-haired Jackson probably no more than four years old being held with his fingers fussing intently with the top button on the woman's—obviously their mother—blouse. She was holding him with one arm and pressing a kiss to his forehead. Her other hand was tangled in Rush's who seemed, even then, dark and brooding. He looked foreign and unrelated to the other two. He stared right into the camera. Bright Star ran a tapered finger over his face. Jackson was glad she only touched cool glass.

He cleared his throat, "Let me call Sandoval and make sure he's ready for you," he said, then made the call. "He wants us to give him fifteen minutes. We'll take the scenic route to his office."

Bright Star started to follow him out of the office. Jackson could feel her disapproval as she could probably sense his discomfort with the way she looked at that picture of his brother.

Jackson led her to a set of double doors and swiped his badge again to allow them access. With the sound of cicadas and the feel of humid air on her skin, Bright Star knew they were outside again, this time at the center of the building. There were compact metal tables and chairs dotting the perimeter of what looked to Bright Star like a sawed off lighthouse. She said as much.

"What is it?" she asked as they went up to the door of the round building in the center of the courtyard.

"The observatory," Jackson answered, then reached for her hand again.

Inside, there were just two other people in the darkened room. They were sitting one seat apart in seats that looked very much like those in a movie theater and discussing something related to hot gases and Energy. Jackson didn't know either of them, but they apparently knew him. They didn't ask if he had permission to be there—Jackson had permission to be anywhere. No, they just watched him as if they were watching a rock star. That's how people saw him at the Service. He was a celebrity amongst Shifters. He was the most powerful and unique of all the Shifters. He was precocial.

He was nothing in comparison to his brother.

Hell, Jackson already suspected he was no comparison even to the woman standing beside him. Suddenly, there was thudding in his chest and goose bumps shot along his arms. "The sensors," he rasped.

"Don't worry," Bright Star smiled. "I figured you'd have sensors here."

"But if they find you..."

"I said don't worry," she whispered with a finger to his lips to quiet him. "I dimmed my Energy when we drove up, remember? They won't pick me up."

"If they do—"

"If they do, then they will know I'm an unregistered Shifter and you'll tell them that's why I'm here. Dr. Sandoval will confirm you were bringing me to him so that I could be documented. My Energy won't be high enough for them to truly care about me, knowing that I am, have been, and always will be in your care." Jackson clamped down hard on the inside of his cheek upon hearing those words. She didn't mean them the way he wanted, but just hearing them… "I'm telling you, they won't pick me up."

"How do you do that?" Jackson asked when she moved her hand.

Bright Star didn't answer.

"Look up," he said to her finally.

Bright Star had been glancing around the room uneasily but she hadn't looked at the ceiling. When she did, she gasped.

"Oh…" She brought a hand up to cover her mouth.

"Amazing, isn't it?" Jackson asked.

"Yes," she nodded her head in awe.

Above them was the night sky, but apparently not the night sky as Bright Star had ever seen it. Her mouth lolled open as she took in the view.

They were silent for long minutes until Jackson stepped closer to her and asked, "What are you looking at?"

"That place there," Bright Star pointed.

"What about it?" Jackson struggled to see what she saw.

"It's empty," she stated simply.

Jackson followed her slender finger and scratched his head. There was a spot. A spot he could probably block out with his thumb. A spot that was nothing short of blank. "So?" There were many blank spots. It was, after all, space.

"Nothing," she choked out.

Startled by her voice, Jackson glanced down at her. She looked vulnerable and he could barely see her eyes.

"How do you do that?" He felt compelled to ask for the second time of the night.

Bright Star didn't pretend not to know what he meant. "I can dim my eyes when necessary. Most times it isn't even necessary because they just don't burn as brightly if I'm not expending Energy."

"But you dim more than your eyes," he pressed.

"Yes. I mask my Energy as well."

"How?" he asked. No one at the Service even believed it to be possible. "I am amazed every time I see you do it."

"I'm not as good as you at explaining things. Maybe one day I'll try to show you."

Jackson thought for a moment then asked, "Does it hurt?"

"What? When my eyes are bright?" she laughed. "No, not at all. Doesn't even sting. I can only tell they are doing it when everything in the world turns blue."

"Oh."

"Yeah."

"Bright Star?" Jackson started. "I need to know what will make you stop hurting yourself."

"Why?"

"Why?" Jackson barked. "Because no one should spend all of their days trying to end them, that's why. Because no one should hurt the way you hurt especially at your own free will. Because I care about you. Because watching you dying *twice* is the hardest thing I've ever done. God, I don't know how the hell to get through to you! You just can't go around hurting yourself, for any reason. You could *die*. You don't seem to comprehend the fact that you could permanently hurt yourself or *die*. You need help, that's why. And, like I said I… I care about you," he ended helplessly.

"Jackson, I have given you my reasoning over and over again. I don't believe I will die, because I do not believe he will let me die. And, Jackson, he hasn't. He is so much more than you can comprehend. Jackson, all you do is tell me that what I say can't be true. You don't want it to be true. You don't want to believe I have done these things to get through to Rush. But that's the reason. And you can never understand why I would hurt myself because—"

Jackson turned his back on her knowing full well what she was going to say. He didn't want to hear it.

"Because you can't hurt."

Jackson said nothing. Finally, he turned back. He just stood there not looking at her. But even though he couldn't see her, her scent penetrated his wall of defense anyway. Finally, he felt her little hand slide over the bulky muscles of his back and arm as she came around to face him. He raised his chin an inch to look beyond her. She tilted her head to the side.

"You want me."

Jackson's mouth popped open but he didn't say anything.

"We both know it, Jackson," she pressed. "Your Energy smells of it, and I'm—"

"Do not," he commanded through a tight jaw. "Do not tell me you're flattered."

She smiled patiently, "I won't say it, but you have to know that Rush and I…" She stuttered uncharacteristically, "That's to say Rush—"

Jackson shook his head bitterly. "It didn't appear Rush wanted anything to do with you at all."

Bright Star's cheeks and neck stained crimson. She averted her gaze and said quickly, "No. Rush tries hard every day to pretend I'm not even there."

"Then why?" Jackson's hand clamped around her upper arms.

"You won't understand. Rush and I are meant to orbit each other and there is nothing in this world or the next that can change that."

"That's bullshit."

"That's truth, Jackson," she bit out.

"But, Bright Star," Jackson breathed desperately. "He doesn't even care about you. He doesn't want you. How can you bear it?"

"It is fate," was her exasperating answer. "It will happen. Like New Year's Day will happen. It will happen."

"Bright Star!" Jackson yelled and clapped his hands forcefully in front of her face. It was almost as if he was trying to wake her from a powerful trance. Then he lowered his voice immediately as the two other stargazers turned their way. "What is wrong with you?"

Neither his action nor his tone so much as startled Bright Star. She merely blinked at him. "There's nothing wrong with me. I just believe something you don't. You don't believe in fate and yet you brought me here, here to an observatory of all places."

Jackson was confused. "What's wrong with bringing you to an observatory? I thought you would like it."

"Why on Earth would you think that?" Her voice rose an octave. She truly sounded horrified at the very idea.

"Why wouldn't I?" Jackson threw back sarcastically. "Look at the name you chose for yourself."

"I didn't choose it," she said catching him off guard.

"What?"

"I didn't choose Bright Star as my name. Your brother gave it to me," she paused and looked up again at the blank space where a twinkling star ought to have been. "I won't refuse or disrespect any of his gifts." She shook her head. "Not like you have."

"What do you mean?"

"Just what I said," she returned with a spark in her muted eyes. There was a confidence about her that came whenever she spoke of Rush. There was a defiance and devotion that Jackson wanted only to smash.

"He doesn't love you," Jackson declared stonily. He wanted to break her heart.

"He doesn't have to," was her stoic answer. Then, "I'd like to get this over with. Lead me to your doctor."

Jackson did take her then, down to the sixteenth floor. He led her to Dr. Sandoval's office, hesitating as she slowed down in a hallway of locked rooms.

"Patients," Jackson explained.

Bright Star nodded. Outside of one of the rooms, she paused, clutching the pebble tight in her hands. It was a soft hesitation Jackson barely noticed as he pulled her into an office.

Chapter 9

Hiding Knives

Jackson had never spent New Year's Eve hiding knives before. He didn't really care for the fact that he was doing it this year. *And* he wasn't just hiding the knives. Cleaning agents. Flammables. Aerosols. Small solid objects and glass. They all had to go. He was also creating small suggestions on each item he touched to make them less noticeable… cosmically. They would stay where they were, but they would only exude a much minimized Energy, so as not to call attention to themselves. He'd finally learned the trick from Bright Star herself.

Granted, he knew there was no way to get rid of all risks. Still, he could certainly minimize as much as possible. Nearly a month wasn't enough time to make him forget. She'd said it to him as plain as day: "It will happen. Just like New Year's Day. It will happen." Jackson hadn't thought much of it then, but something about those words, or perhaps the way she said them played on his mind. She hadn't tried to kill herself for weeks. She would try that night. He knew it. And Jackson was going to do whatever he could to stop her. Maybe if he managed to prevent her from doing this, just this once, she would give up all this nonsense about fate and destiny. Maybe she would just…stop.

"What you're doing doesn't make a whole lot of sense," Rush admonished slowly. Caution marking his words, Rush watched his brother work through his bag of locks.

"You don't want me to help her," Jackson replied, continuing to sift through the metal loops. None of them seemed stronger than the ones he'd used when he tied her up. "I get that. But I won't just stand by and watch her kill herself."

Rush leaned forward. His forearms rested against the counter and he cradled his face in his hands.

"Don't look at me like that." Jackson raised a brow at him. "Don't look at me like I'm your foolish little brother. You didn't see her."

"I did," Rush contradicted softly.

"You weren't there," Jackson challenged.

"I didn't have to be." Rush sighed. "I saw her the first time when she tried to drown herself. I saw her lying on that roof, the blood bubbling up out of her mouth. I saw the beams of light shooting up like flares into the sky. I saw her use enough electricity to power the city to fry herself stuck to a wall in this kitchen. You should leave her alone."

"Why?"

Rush answered that question with a question. "What did the good doctor say?"

Jackson ground his teeth together. He wouldn't respond.

"Maybe you didn't hear me," Rush goaded him. "She's seen Ronald—"

"Randall."

"Dr. Sandoval six times since you had that conversation with her. Twice every week she goes. That's the deal to keep her on the outside. If he's working with her, what gives you the impression she will go through with this?"

"To be honest with you…" Jackson didn't finish his sentence.

"To be honest with me?" Rush prodded.

Jackson rolled his eyes. "I don't know why you even ask me questions."

"Respect?" Rush's response sounded more like a cheeky query.

"I don't know where you got this new sense of humor from, but I hate it."

Rush gave an easy chuckle. "Well, if you are inviting me to tell you what you're thinking rather than ask you, I will. You think she'll go through with it because Sandoval seems to think she's as sane as the day is long. In fact, you're worried that rather than influencing Bright Star to be normal, these sessions are working in the reverse. You think she's influencing Sandoval to be a little crazy." This last was said with a somber tone.

"I'm going to help her." Jackson ignored his brother's incredibly perceptive remark.

"She doesn't want your help."

"Well, she's going to get it."

"Maybe I should put it another way," Rush stood and came round to look his brother in the eye. "You can't help her. That doctor can't help her. You don't understand everything at work here. You don't understand half of it."

"And you won't tell me," Jackson pushed.

Sadly, Rush shook his head. Creases appeared around his mouth as he chewed his lower lip. "I can't, Jacks. You'll want me to do it. You'll want me to fix everything, but I can't help her either. If I interfere with the path. If I allow *you* to interfere with the path to save Bright Star, then—"

"Then what?"

"Then we'll never get the real..."

"The real what?"

"I'm not who she thinks I am," Jacob blurted in defeat. "I can't talk about this now. I can't."

Jackson started to say something but thought the better of it. For now, he could leave it. He had something much more important to do.

There hadn't been an episode in a month. Bright Star had been calm, lovely. She was always there when Jackson came home from work. She took care of everything... "That reminds me," Jackson halted his hands for a moment. He was diverted by a question that had been nagging him since his memory was retrieved. "Do you have a job?"

Rush chuckled even though he'd been dead serious just a moment earlier. That was a funny question. He posed his answer in the form of a question. "Sort of?"

"What the hell does that mean?"

"It means I have a job. I get a paycheck direct deposited into my checking account every month. I pay taxes that are used to pay your salary. I pay my half of the rent and the utilities. I don't pay the phone 'cause I don't use it."

"But do you *go* to work?" Jackson persisted.

"No," Rush answered with a lopsided, bashful grin that turned his dark and perpetually haunted face into a handsome, charming and almost sunny visage. Quickly, he was solemn again, his expression cloudy. "How did you manage to get her tied to the bed?"

Jackson had been trying not to think about that. One could think it had been too easy. "She didn't fight me."

Rush raised one eyebrow at that but said nothing about it. "How long will you keep her tied up?" he asked.

"As long as it takes to get her to stop doing this. She needs help, Rush."

"I believe I told you that months ago when you brought her here but you didn't care." Rush reminded him. "I gave you an ultimatum that hasn't really done the trick either. 'Get her in counseling for as long as she stays here.' But, she's now seeing someone and making him just as crazy as she is. She barely leaves the house otherwise."

"I gave up on Sandoval. I'm not stupid, no matter what you think. I started to go see someone for her. I've been—"

"Listen to yourself, Jackson. You can't *go* to a shrink on behalf of someone else. And here's a newsflash, she's not getting any better. If she were, then she wouldn't be tied up in her bedroom right now and you wouldn't be hiding knives."

"She hasn't done anything in a long time."

"You're *hiding* knives!"

"She needs help but you know that people like us don't do well with regular treatment." Jackson didn't like saying it, but he had to get his brother to see his point.

Rush grimaced at the reminder. "I know that as well as you do, but you can't stop her from doing this. I ask you again: How long can you keep her locked up?"

Jackson didn't answer. Instead he picked up his bag and started tucking knives into places he thought she wouldn't look.

"How long?" Rush asked again.

"Until January second," Jackson called over his shoulder as he left the room.

Rush followed him until he saw Jackson disappear into Bright Star's bedroom. Rush could see her mentally. She was tied at her wrists and ankles with leather ties to locks made like metal rings that had been attached with posts to her bed. There were mittens on her hands and a mouth guard taped into her mouth. She was wearing her favorite white night gown and no shoes. Rush considered going in there but thought better of it. After all, what if it worked? It wasn't going to... but what if it did?

* * * *

Jackson removed his hammer and nails from the bag, he picked up a sheet of wood he'd brought that morning and started to board up the windows. He banged hard to make as much noise as possible. He wanted to think of the job, not the woman even though he knew she was trying to work the mouth guard out of her mouth.

Still, her muffled words reached him. He knew she was just trying to beg him to let her go. He knew he should ignore her and continue his work. All he had to do was make it twenty-four hours and thirteen minutes. It was only thirteen minutes to midnight. She was trying even harder to get the makeshift gag out of her mouth. He went over and sat beside her on the bed. Slowly, trying not to hurt her, he pulled the plastic from her skin and the guard from her mouth.

"Jackson," she called. Her voice was a soft, plaintive stream. A lost child calling to a parent to save her. "It's time now. Untie me."

He shook his head and turned away. He wouldn't look at her. He knew that if he did, he would be lost.

"Jackson," she called again. Her voice caressed his arms, his back, his neck. He still didn't turn around. Instead, he stood and went back to work. He banged louder with his hammer as he covered the windows in plywood. After he finished one, he worked on another. He continued until he realized that he had used eight sheets of the plywood that had been cut specifically to fit the windows, and she had only three windows. He turned then hurled the hammer... at the door. He watched her whole body jump satisfyingly. At least her reflexes still recognized danger. His jaw clenched and his breathing labored as he watched her.

"My hands hurt," she said softly. At that, Jackson turned around. Like a milky moon on a foggy night, she radiated a dark light barely discernable from the rest of the room, though her eyes still sparkled indigo. "My hands hurt," she repeated.

He neared her. He really couldn't help it, and reached up to massage the ties loose on her hands. Just a little. She wouldn't be able to slip out of them if he loosened them a little bit.

But no. He shook his head. He resisted what he knew logically had been a suggestion. He withdrew.

"Untie me, Jackson," she ordered gently.

"Can't you untie yourself?" Jackson asked, hoping his voice had not betrayed his frustration. His ability to subdue her surprised him. That surprise was only surpassed by the knowledge that his bindings had actually held her. He'd accepted she was stronger than he, but he'd been willing to take the risk. Still he suspected Rush had something to do with his ability to restrain her that night. He wondered if he could even release her now.

But he knew Rush was trying to trust him. Jackson needed, more than anything, to be worthy of that trust. Letting her go after he'd gone through all of this trouble to keep her bound would make him look like a fool.

"You have to do it. Untie me," She pleaded. She begged. Her eyes were now a warming clear blue—the color of a tropical sea. They did not burn through him as they did when she was allowed to use her High Energy. Without the surreal glow, she looked young and vulnerable. Her burnished locks fell against her apple blossom cheeks. Her breasts shined as pale half moons over her white bodice.

Bright Star followed his gaze down to her chest and quickly covered herself. A rustle like wind pressed material up on her chest. Then she seemed to affix a smile to her face and looked up at him again. She willed her clothes away.

The Shift, minor though it was, sapped what Energy she had left. She sagged against her restraints. Her body was a cream white, rounded pastry presented for Jackson's slow consumption.

"Untie me," Her lips barely moved, pink and supple, they opened like watered petals over the words. "Please."

Jackson's resolve was shaken by the naïve sigh or the broken slant of her head on her slender neck. He couldn't hold himself firm against the dim but fighting light in her eye. He stepped toward her again and instantly felt a crackle like a feeding flame. It was a warning. The universe was telling him not to let her go. Jackson was not heeding the warning. He began undoing the enchanted leather straps at her ankles. After they were unbound, he stood close to her as he unfastened the straps at each of her wrists. Her lips parted and he could feel her breath brush his cheek.

Jackson took a step back to give her room. Regretfully, he found she didn't need it. As soon as her bonds were released her eyes blazed turquoise heat at him and her feet left the ground. It was as if she were a fairy or a pixie hovering naked before him and smiling an otherworldly smile. Her High Energy radiated powerfully from her body, and Jackson was a fool. Jackson's mouth went dry. He could do little more than blink.

"Thank you," she said with a girlish giggle then disappeared.

Jackson heard the giggle down the hall. He rushed out. There she was, floating down the foyer, and placing divine fingertips to the petals of devout flowers with white and yellow blossoms lined against the walls. Jackson had never seen the flowers before; he couldn't reason through the fact that each seemed to have a displaced Energy inside and that they offered her deference. Flowers. Followers.

He trailed her gliding form. Her body was masked to him by what looked like either thin material or smoke swirling around her. Jackson was hypnotized by the substance until he realized with horror that each time she passed one of the places he had hidden a knife, it found itself free and levitating. The blades gleamed as the followed her like heat seeking missiles. Jackson felt his stomach start to flutter in anticipation, then drop as it would if he had fallen a great distance. He started to run.

Bright Star floated into the den where each knife, with the force of a cannon, shot through the air, mounting her against a bare wall.

Chapter 10

Object

"What is it going to take?" Jackson demanded.

"What do you mean?" Her large eyes blinked patiently at him.

"What is it going to take for you to stop doing this, Bright Star?"

"Rush will have to accept his fate." She said this as if those were the most natural words to ever come out of a person's mouth. She said it in such a way—with a maternal and patient glance—that Jackson almost felt silly and childish for not knowing the answer already.

"Yes," he yelled, shaking the insecurity from his mind; focusing. "You've said as much, but what does that mean? What will he have to do to assure you that he has done something as lofty as 'accept his fate?' He's saved *you* time and time again."

Bright Star didn't answer readily. Instead, she leaned back against the counter and closed her eyes. When she opened them again, it was as if Jackson had opened his eyes as well. He looked around him. They were both seated on the shallow ledge of a cliff. Really, it was a small shelf in the rock face. Their perch overlooked crystal blue waters to the right that stretched out as far as the eye could see. As he remarked on the view to his left, Jackson gasped once more. They could almost see the entire luminous green island. The pristine sugar sand beach was lightly sprinkled with people and speedboats. There were shops and open-air restaurants lined on the shore. Obviously wealthy vacationers slowly strolled on the sand with wide brimmed hats, sunglasses, and vibrantly hued swimsuits.

The sun and wind touched his face in a warm caress. A sky that had been the only thing he'd ever seen bluer than Bright Star's eyes presented a backdrop to the breathtaking scene. The sound of cawing birds, the smell of fresh salt and surf told him he had truly been transported.

"Paradise." Bright Star reflected his thoughts in her word.

"Yes," Jackson could only agree.

"Only one mile inland... just there," she raised a slender arm and pointed beyond the stretch of small, tidy and expensive boutique restaurants and bars to a verdant forest sprinkled with white, yellow and red blossoms. "You see?"

Jackson saw the tops of hills cluttered with dry and brittle thatch roofs. He couldn't see any people, but it was certain that was where the indigenous lived. Not the sleek and carefree set of supermodels with their wealthy sycophants promenading carefully along the beachfront.

"Look at this beach," her voice betrayed a sad serenity. "I had never in life seen anything so beautiful. But look up there, in the mountains and in the thick, primal jungle. That is where he left me. Up there, white skin is equated with evil. Red hair—mine had changed from brown to red after Rush laid his hands on my head—was considered a reason to smother the life from newborns. Up there, women accept their lots as the bringers of destruction. When crops fail, they are blamed. When storms ravage the island they believe it's because of a female's sin. The women cut themselves and curse Her name. They slice their cheeks and arms and thighs. Some slice their stomachs, expecting and welcoming the suffering."

"This is where Rush sent you." Jackson's voice was disembodied.

She responded only with a curt nod.

"How long were you here?" he breathed, wanting more than anything for her to tell him of her experience in the years before he found her on that rooftop.

"Two years," she answered with a slow and sad smile. She repeated it as if she couldn't believe it herself, "Two years."

"He told me that... that he left you in this place without any money, any identification, any clothes even. He left you here to die."

"He did," Bright Star agreed. "But, though this island is small and remote, even the interior has been touched by our brand of civilization. It didn't matter what they believed about me or my kind. They didn't apply their rules to me because I was obviously foreign. All they could see was that there would be trouble if harm came to me. They wouldn't touch me. Instead, the men fashioned gloves for their women before they allowed them put their hands on me. Then they wrapped me in a rough fabric made of dried leaves, and dropped me in the entrance to the Magnussand Golf and Racket Club." She gestured with her head and Jackson made out a white, Grecian building that appeared to be right on the northern shore of the island.

"There's one of those everywhere," Jackson kidded although his voice seemed awkward even to his own ears.

"Yep," she returned. "I was given clothes and questioned as to how I got there."

"What did you tell them?" Jackson asked, transfixed by the calm she exuded as she told this tale.

"Nothing," she answered, gradually turning to him to possess him with her eyes.

"Nothing?" he swallowed.

"Nothing," she repeated. "Instead, I remembered where Jacob left me. I remembered that spot and I knew—knew with all my heart—that he left me there for a reason. They couldn't talk to me. They couldn't cajole me. They couldn't force me. They couldn't do anything that would make me give him up. Jackson," she said his name to make sure he was listening though there had never been a chance that he would not have listened. "Jackson, I was so caught up in worry that he would find out I had gone, that I wasn't where he left me. I… I…"

"What did you do?" Jackson prodded gently, knowing that she wanted to share this story with him.

"I asked them to take me back to the village."

"But they wouldn't," he guessed.

"No," she shook her head. "No, they wouldn't. I could have had a plane ticket or yacht ride to any destination in the world, but no one would take me two miles back up that mountain. I had to make my way there on my own." She squinted her eyes and peered up at the cloudless sky. "What do you think the villagers did when I went back?"

"Accepted you with open arms?" Jackson responded with some cheek.

She looked down at her hands, small and white, playing over each other in her lap. "They thought I had come back to bring death to them. The men cursed their own cowardice in ever allowing me to go down the mountain alive the first time. The women tried to make me leave. They worried and fretted over me. They even showed me a picture carved into an opalescent ancient stone of a goddess who, amazingly, looked as I should have. They showed me the person Rush had seen when he looked at me. Jackson, she *was* me. She was their Goddess of Destruction. But…" she choked on her words.

Jackson reached out an arm to hang inelegantly over her shoulders.

"But I am not Destruction. And I told them," she continued. "I was not destruction. I was nothing but… a devotee. I wouldn't leave, Jackson.

The need to make them see overwhelmed all else. They did awful things to me, but I would not leave.

"Some wanted to sacrifice me, but none could muster the courage. They feared me and I could not understand why. All I knew was that their fear had been steeped in their religion, in this belief. So I did the only thing I could. I asked them to teach me this prophecy they feared. I asked them to speak of their gods to me and to tell me of that alabaster figure with burning blue eyes and bright red hair.

"They dressed me as she." Bright Star stood on the ledge then and raised her palms to the sky at her side. In milliseconds she was naked, then garbed in something Jackson could only describe as tribal. Much of her pale legs, arms and torso were exposed. Her hair was covered with a three foot tall headdress of palm and mango leaves, sharp gray feathers, and spring blooms. Her eyes were startling, even more unnatural looking as they were outlined in black—charred bark. Flexible olive and orange fronds were woven together into a flaming bodice that curved over her breasts and unfurled towards her hips, but did not cover her back. It was held in place by a sweet smelling sap. The same woven leaves folded up and over her soft mound and behind her to cover her plump bottom, adhered there by the same sap, as they did not cover her hips. Blossoms were linked and twined around her wrists and ankles. "Then they told me her story.

"They told me that she was the goddess Burn. Burn had been born as a gift to the god Guard who had spent an eternity protecting the island. Because she had been born for him and of him, Burn longed for Guard with an intensity that transcended lust and even love. He held a part of her soul within him. Burn spent that life from childhood to womanhood working to make herself into all that Guard wanted. She watched him with women and changed her hair to that which he liked. She changed her childish body to that which he liked. She changed her eyes and nose and lips, to all of those to which he had shown partiality. After years of work, she knew herself to embody every physical desire Guard had ever harbored. Still, he showed no interest in her.

"Others fell in love with her. They begged for a glance, a touch of her hand. They offered their lives, which she greedily accepted, for a mere taste of her lips. They willingly damned themselves at her request to lie with her once. You see, Burn could not stand the touch of another on her conscience when she was made for Guard, so she murdered them all. And yet, Guard despised her for it, and he still did not want her.

"One night, Burn grew bold and slipped into Guard's bed. She presented herself to him in an earnest and sincere sacrifice. Guard turned away from her without a word and left her alone.

"The next day, Burn lured one of her young lovers out on to a cliff. The one you're sitting on, actually, the tribesmen believed," she gestured to the narrow outcropping. "The young man thought they were coming there to make love, but Burn had long since become bored, angry and disillusioned from lying with anyone but Guard. No, instead, she brought him to the place where Guard spent the majority of his time. This is the one place that overlooks the entire island. The one place where he could both be alone and keep everyone close and safe. Burn wanted Guard to find her with her lover and become jealous. Instead, her lover became angry and humiliated. His betrayal of Guard was a living, palpable thing. And so the young man jumped over the ledge, dragging her with him."

"Guard saved them…" Jackson mumbled absently.

"Yes," Bright Star confirmed, nodding excitedly. "Yes, he saved them both. It was his duty and yet it was more than his duty. It was the one time Burn had ever seen him feel passion. And that passion had been for her."

"Not her." Jackson contradicted firmly.

"You didn't let me finish. The passion was for Burn *and* for her lover. The passion was for life. It was his only passion.

"But that passion didn't last. Nothing happened in this sleepy little village. Nothing."

"If nothing ever happened," Jackson asked considering her words. "Then why did they need Guard?"

Bright Star did not answer this question. In fact, she continued as if she had not heard him. "Because the village was sedate, tranquil, at peace, Guard was uninspired. Burn never saw him gaze at her with anything more than acknowledgement that she was present. Burn was no longer the recipient of Guard's passion. But, as was her nature—at least the nature these people believed in—she was destructive and she craved Guard's attention. She started covertly endangering the lives of all of those around Guard, one by one, so that she was always with them as he saved them. She wanted to bask in his glory even if it wasn't directed at her. As became her namesake, the beautiful goddess finally burned the entire village, the entire island in an ultimate bid for Guard's attention." Her voice had gone deep and hoarse. She floated before him, an ancient goddess limned by waning sunlight.

Jackson called to her. He barely believed her to be more than an apparition, "What did Guard do?"

"Guard did as his nature dictated." Bright Star finally smiled. Her eyes finally dimmed. Her hands finally came to rest and she was in her own clothes again, sitting beside him once more. "He saved the village. He saved the island. But then he locked her away in a place on which the villagers never dared speculate. Then, he followed her, locking himself away as well, leaving the village forever unguarded."

"Why?" Jackson asked, amazed at his truly visceral reaction. Amazed that he was physically horrified by Guard's action. Bright Star cocked her head gently toward him in a question. Jackson asked the question again, "Why did he lock himself away, too?"

"It can only be because he had, in truth, loved her."

"But that's not what the villagers said?"

"No," Bright Star glanced away from him and her fingers began to work again. "The villagers say that he followed her because, had he stayed, she would have only found a way to come back to him and destroy them all over again. It was more than her will. It was what she was created for: to be with him in all worlds, this one and the next."

Jackson asked her, "Why did they allow you to leave alive?" *Because they weren't strong enough to stop you* instantaneously emblazoned itself on Jackson's mind.

Bright Star's eyes sparked for a moment, then she responded. "I assured them, Jackson, that I would never, ever be responsible for the devastation of this world. I assured them that they had merely misunderstood this tale and had misunderstood it since the beginning of their recorded history. They didn't comprehend that I was not a bringer of destruction, but a soul of devotion and determination. I did not argue against their prophecy because it was at least partially true. I knew who their God was. I knew who would bring an end to their suffering. It was Rush. Jackson, you have to believe my sight," she held his face between her palms. "I would give it to you. I would give it to you freely right now if you would but accept it and he would but allow it. But even if you will accept it, he won't let me give it to you."

"It doesn't matter, Bright Star. It doesn't matter," Jackson studied the horizon. "Without Burn's actions, the village would have continued to be at peace."

"Jackson, you don't understand. What is peace? What is happiness? What is tranquility? They are all wonderful things, but they do not urge innovation, change, improvement of the... the..."

"Human condition?"

"Human condition," she agreed. "If only you could see it, could see how much *more* everyone and everything can be."

She grew silent and Jackson was lost in the blazing aquamarine eyes that held him so intently.

"Why did they believe you?" Jackson asked, wanting this zeal, this intensity to end, wanting to think of nothing less mundane than the cocktails and henna tattoos being served on the very beach they hovered over.

"Why would they argue?" she demanded defiantly. "I showed them my power. I showed them who I was at the heart of me. I became her before their very eyes. How could they deny me?"

"You became…"

"I became the woman Rush wanted from the start. That woman happened to be the same woman these people had wrongly feared and persecuted for thousands of years."

"He didn't know, Bright Star," Jackson told her, wanting, pressing, pushing the words into her mind. He didn't have the strength for a full suggestion, but he subtly added High Energy to his words. "He didn't know what would happen when he sent you here. You know that he sent you here to die."

"If he didn't know, Jackson, then think of the Providence that led him to bring me to this place of all places in the world."

Jackson did think of it, then stopped thinking of it. This he couldn't handle. Not now. Instead, he asked, "And they let you leave with only that as an explanation?"

"You were right when you thought that, quite simply, they couldn't stop me. And, you were right to wonder why they would believe my declaration of faith and innocence."

Jackson tried desperately to ignore the way his stomach dropped at her statement. *When you thought…* not when you said.

She grinned quickly and licked her lips. Cocking her head to one side, she seemed to be framing the words in her mind. "They still believed I would bring destruction. Even in the end… But, I promised them something they would never be able to pass up."

"What's that?"

"I promised to bring Guard to them. I promised to bring him back one day so that he could be their salvation."

"What makes you think you can deliver that?" Jackson demanded.

Bright Star didn't answer. She merely smiled again and tapped her temple next to her eye. *I can see.* Those were the words, in her voice, that rocketed through Jackson's mind. *I can see.*

* * * *

He did not need to seek Rush out when Bright Star returned him to their home. Rush was already waiting for him in his room as had become the custom. His brother did not spare even the slightest glance for Bright Star.

To Jackson, Rush appeared tired. There was a taut crease between his brows. There were lines around his mouth. His dark garnet lips were compressed and his jaw ticked. There were dark puffy circles beneath his eyes. He looked like a different person from the man who had joked and mocked Jackson the night before. Jackson didn't readily understand why Rush was so different, and he didn't ask.

"You know what she showed me today?" Jackson asked, though it wasn't, in truth, a question.

"I don't," Rush surprised him by answering. He leaned his head back against the wall and closed his eyes with a sigh.

"But you have to know what she experienced in the time she was on that island you banished her to," Jackson pressed.

"Banished?" Rush exhaled roughly. "Jeez Jacks, you're starting to sound like her."

Unconsciously, Jackson shook his head as if attempting to rid himself of what might have been undue influence. Rush would never put it past Bright Star to use her Talents on his brother.

"Looked like I wouldn't be able to convince you on my own," Bright Star explained without shame as she hovered in the doorway.

"My brother will not be a part of this game," Rush told her without opening his eyes, raising his head.

"This is no game, my world," Bright Star countered.

"Even though I wish it weren't so, you are right, Bright Star." Rush sighed heavily, then rose from his seat. He started out of the room needing to get away from the both of them. There was no luck for him this day, because the both of them followed.

"Rush," Jackson pleaded, chasing after him. "Please, can we talk about this?"

"No," was the blunt response as Rush rounded the corner to his room.

"We have to," Jackson insisted. "I have to tell you what she went through when you sent her away."

Rush turned around so fast that Jackson stopped in his tracks. The exhaustion was gone. The only thing left was an animal, a predator unleashed. Rush's coal black eyes flashed with fury. He was so tightly wound that muscles bulged in the sides of his neck. His voice was a deadly whisper. "You don't have to tell me anything! I know what happened on that island. Do you think I could have sent her away and not kept track of whether she would be saved or not?"

"But she was saved," Jackson pounced on the opening. "And if you monitored her, then you know what she has come to believe and why."

"If you listened to that story, Jackson, then you should have believed, as I did, that nothing good could come of any of this. As an intelligent, reasonable adult you would understand that none of this could end well. Bright Star came away from it ignoring the outcome, not giving a damn about it, wanting to actually perpetuate it."

Bright Star shook her head violently but remained mute.

Rush ignored her.

"Then why don't you do something?" Jackson breathed.

"Do what?" Rush's hands fisted at his sides. Bright Star's eyes focused on them and they were washed in an aqua glow. It was as if she waited for him to strike. "What makes you believe I can *do* anything?" he roared, then stormed out of the room.

"Rush," Jackson forged ahead, following despite his brother's incredulity and obvious anger. "Rush, she believes what she has told me. She's shown it to me. Please know that if I could chalk this up to a hoax or someone making up stories, I would. But these kinds of coincidences do not happen normally. Not when we are all in balance."

"Jackson, there is no such thing as a coincidence. I believe as strongly as she does. Still, how we choose to interpret the things we know is extraordinarily variable. What she sees and what I see are the same. They are exactly and without fail the same. However—and it is important that you understand this—the way we interpret and act based on that interpretation are different. I don't know how to explain this to you."

"Try," Jackson pressed. They had come to the kitchen and Rush had given up escaping them. Instead, he paced around the room as Jackson and Bright Star looked on.

Rush cast around for an explanation. "Think about wearing sunglasses. You wear ones tinted green, and I wear glasses tinted blue. Even if we look at the same object, we see it differently. Still, that object is, in its nature, only one object."

"I'm trying to follow you."

"I don't think I can explain it any better."

Jackson squinted his eyes. He was all of a sudden tired. His head was splitting. He didn't understand, even after all that Bright Star had shown him. He just couldn't get it all straight. More than anything, he didn't understand why his brother, who was obviously at the center of this, who could—at least according to Bright Star—stop this, didn't do just that. "I know you can stop her. Why don't you stop her from doing this?"

"She won't stop. It's a part of her nature," Rush explained as he had what felt like a thousand times before.

"Why don't you send her away? At least then—"

"You spent the whole day learning the beginning, and yet, you think sending her away will work. That's crazy, Jacks. I sent her away once, she came back. No matter where I send her, unless I *kill* her she will come back."

At that last, Jackson was stunned. The fact his brother had even mentioned it meant that he had thought about killing her or rather, letting her die.

"Unless you want that," Rush pressed on, "Unless you want me to let her die the next time she does this. Because, let's face it, we both know she will do it again." Jackson said nothing. But Rush brought his face close to his brother's and pressed further. "Will you be able to forgive me if the next time I just let her die? Will you be able to stop yourself from trying to save her yourself, first with your Service first aid, then with Shift? And when you can't save her and the Perma-Shift starts to kick in will you let go of the Shift or will you kill yourself right along with her?" Rush's voice rose passionately and his words came faster and faster. "I wouldn't let you, Jackson. I wouldn't let you die. But would you be able to cope with the knowledge that I didn't save her and you *couldn't* save her?"

Jackson didn't answer him.

Rush then turned his angry gaze to Bright Star. "What do you think, Bright Star?"

Bright Star's mouth fell open in alarm.

"What do you think will happen if I just let you die next time?"

She brought a hand up to her throat as if she were strangling.

Rush turned away from her. "Stop the histrionics. We both know how selfish I am. We both know we have a long way to go before we die." Rush then left the couple standing there. Jackson watched Bright Star closely.

Chapter 11

Follower

Frankie Monnish stood at the front entrance of the Magnussand Convention Center. She was the coffee-skinned woman in the tailored navy suit and smart low heels with her thick black hair pulled back from her face. She was the one wearing small silver loops in her ears; the one who smiled softly and ushered her partners away with reassuring smiles and nods. She patted their backs, squeezed their hands, hugged their necks, and kissed their cheeks. She assured them the seminar had been a success and that their research would be fully funded for the next five and a half years. They had investors and "friends" aplenty with pockets that ran incredibly deep. Some of these friends at that very moment were hopefully observing, waiting to be needed. She assured them all would be well. Then, she reminded them of their next meeting and of the objectives on their aggressive timeline. That was her job, and she was good at it. She was their leader.

As the bellmen secured taxis for the group of seven physicists and eight very wealthy physics aficionados, Frankie stood back a little and grinned openly when any of them glanced her way. When the youngest of the consultants turned a hopeful and somewhat unsure smile her way, she couldn't help but run her fingers over her cufflinks. She was wearing the platinum ones with an etched blue star on each. She didn't know why she'd bought them in the airport. Maybe the layover. Still, Frankie had been drawn to them. So drawn that she bought them even though she didn't own a shirt that needed them. She'd bought a shirt, electric blue with a fine white stripe, shortly after she landed. The young physicist had been asking for the cufflinks since that morning when he'd first spotted them. Frankie suspected it wasn't the little gleaming metal buttons that prompted him. She shook her head every time she tried to figure out why his attraction didn't extend to someone younger, more lively.

Frankie stroked the links again and waved vibrantly as her peers and friends started to pile into the cabs. When Kate, the oldest and most disheveled of the group started to ask her again to join them, Frankie put up a quick hand in farewell. She dug the nails of her other hand into her palm. The acute, piercing pain served as a focal point for her thoughts, and helped her mask the horrible tangle of emotions twisting her insides. She could never make it through dinner. Even now, she wouldn't return to the hotel. Instead, Frankie would go for a walk.

When the tears were shed, she did not want to risk someone seeing as she made her way to her room. She didn't want to continue the pretense or maintain her plastic smile as she suffered in silence. Starting away slowly, Frankie took a look back to watch them make a decision about where they would eat, then pile into taxis. The cabs lumbered away in the heavy, wet traffic.

As if it had been waiting for the perfect moment, a ragged sob tore from her throat though her eyes were dry. She walked quicker, wishing she could just be home in that moment. Another sob ripped through her and she found herself slumping against the aging building, holding her arms over her stomach. She wished more than ever that she had had a baby. Never had she wanted anything more than she wanted a child. Now, she would not have one.

"Hi," a young woman whispered softly to her. Frankie didn't respond. She couldn't if she'd tried. "Hi," she whispered again. Frankie stumbled. The young redhead eased closer to her. Frankie stumbled again and the other woman flew to her side and supported her with a shoulder beneath one of the Frankie's arms.

"Hey," the girl with red hair breathed. She moved her fingers in front of the Frankie's eyes trying to get her attention. But Frankie's eyes did not focus. She brushed at the hand before her.

"Hey," the girl with the opalescent skin called one more time, continuing to hold on to the older Frankie's heavier frame. "Are you OK?" The girl obviously didn't expect an answer. She didn't get one. Instead, in an exaggerated movement the woman threw the arm off her shoulder and shuffled forward. Before she took five steps, she stumbled again.

The girl rushed to her side again. Frankie didn't move, but the stranger whose eyes were a glowing blue could tell that she was crying. "What's wrong, Point?"

"Nothing."

"Something's wrong or you wouldn't be crying," the newcomer argued sensibly. The other woman just shook her head.

The young woman leaned against the building. Her shoulder was just a couple inches below that of the other woman. She huffed a big sigh then crossed her arms over her breasts.

"What are you doing?" Frankie asked.

"Waiting," she answered in a pleasant tone. "You wouldn't believe how patient I am."

"How patient?" Frankie couldn't help asking. She wanted to smile but it only came across, she was sure, as a pained grimace.

"I waited four years to find…" she screwed up her face. "To find my true love?" That was close enough and probably palatable.

"That's patient," Frankie agreed, this time truly managing a watery smile. Then she switched gears. "I don't know you from Adam. You're a total stranger. I don't think I should or could talk to you."

"Sometimes it's easier to talk to a perfect stranger. No expectations, you know. No judgments. Or rather no judgments you have to concern yourself with."

"I see you've given this stranger thing a lot of thought." Frankie pushed herself away from the building and started walking again. This time she was determined to go back to the hotel. At least there, if she could make it up to her room, she would be able to have a couple hours alone until her crew started back from dinner.

"I have." The woman nodded and fell into step beside her. "Would it help if I told you something?"

"Probably not," Frankie answered.

"What if I tell you something that you may find impossible to believe?" Frankie shrugged as if saying 'give it a shot.' "My life was saved once by a stranger. He's been saving me ever since."

Frankie thought about how poetic that sounded. And idealistic. The girl must have been younger than she appeared. "Are you in a cult?" Frankie grinned, though she was only half kidding. "I have to warn you that I'm a pretty rational lady. I'm a physicist."

"My name is Bright Star." The girl put out a small hand. "And I am not a member of a cult. I've got just two friends in the whole wide world, and unfortunately they are both men."

"Frankie," she returned, taking the hand with a smile. "Bright Star? That's an odd name."

"Better than the one I was born with," she kidded. "Here," Bright Star instructed, holding her arms out. "Hold on to me."

"What?" The other woman asked, backing away warily. She bit down on her lower lip, and appeared quite horrified.

"Hug me," Bright Star told her again and waited. "I can tell that you don't usually touch people, especially strangers. I know how much I ask when beg you to believe me, trust me. You need to be held. You need what he can offer you."

Frankie felt dubious. She also felt—without sound reason—hopeful. Bright Star waited. Frankie rubbed the palms of her hands together. She didn't truly understand what the young woman was offering. She did understand that whatever it was had to be monumental. She could feel the air around them sparking. Sometimes, she could feel things like that. Frankie thought that was why she was good at her job. She didn't just know Energy. She felt Energy. She commanded Energy in her own small way.

Sure, she'd been tested when she was a kid but she had been rejected. She hadn't been as strong as the other Shifters. But she had been strong enough to draw the attention of the Service. She was strong enough that if she ever found herself without a job or resources, she would be accepted back into the fold no questions asked. But she had never felt the High Energy as strong as she did in that moment. It was a living, pulsing force, drawing her into the smaller woman's arms.

Point immediately collapsed inside. Amazingly strong, Bright Star anchored her so that she did not crumble physically in her succumbing. She could have never prepared herself for the force of that jolt. As the arms had closed around her. Light and Energy and Sound and Touch were all present and absent at once. It was an instantaneous immersion. Baptismal.

When it was done. Frankie felt free of the cancer that ravaged her body. She felt as if she had died and come back, been reborn without it.

"How did you…"

"I didn't, Point. I am merely working through the Energy that has been left in me by Rush. For me, it has its limits but…" She sighed and shook her head. "This change you feel is not permanent. Even now, the cancer is growing again. I have only given you the gift of time, not of life."

"But I feel so… so…"

Bright Star nodded, feeling the pride swelling up inside of her. Rush had given her a gift, and now someone else was beginning to understand its strength.

"It's not me. I couldn't have even done this much for you if not for him." Bright Star held her firmly by the hands. "Rush can finish this. Rush can take this from you forever."

"Who is he?"

"He is Rush." Bright Star answered reverently. Then her eyes sparked blue. For the first time, Frankie noticed them. They were so blue they almost...almost seemed to shine; to beam light. And then, Bright Star had a vision. "Point," she called to the former Frankie, "Would you like to meet him?"

* * * *

"Why do you call me Point?" the woman who had once been Frankie Monnish asked. She smoothed her hands down over her body. She felt new. Ten years younger. She looked it, too. She didn't know why. Was it the Shift? Was it the fact that she did not have to carry the burden of her disease anymore? Even though Bright Star had told her this transformation was only temporary, she couldn't count this as anything less than a miracle. Even though Bright Star had told her of Rush and had vehemently contradicted her when she suggested it, Point knew the blue-eyed woman had been the one to save her.

Bright Star did not answer the question. Instead, she shook her head as if she'd been preoccupied by something. She took a deep, cleansing breath then opened the wooden box drawer by the refrigerator, the one with worn polish and a dark brass knob. Inside was a knife. It had a yellow clear plastic handle and a glinting blade. At Bright Star's nod, Point came over to stand next to her. Bright Star waited. Then she removed the knife and went to sit at the kitchen table.

They sat at the table that way for hours. There had been long, stretching silent moments. There had been moments when Point had been compelled to confide in Bright Star in a way she had never confided in anyone. And of course, Bright Star had taken moments to speak reverently of Rush. There was always the knife nestled there in her lap.

She could already feel this change inside of her. She knew that Bright Star's Shift had started it, but she didn't know what was propelling it forward faster than the speed of light. This was a transformation from skeptic into believer? From fatalistic despair to overwhelming hope, to the knowledge that she had received a confirmation she didn't even comprehend. Where did these answers come from, the answers that explained so much of her life? The one hundred percent confidence with which Bright Star could tell her that all would be well if she only chose this path. All would be well. Everything in her life would be good if only she surrendered herself to this new truth. Point was willing, and Point believed.

She swallowed, then gave a reassuring look to Bright Star. She didn't want to appear more nervous or afraid than Bright Star expected. She wanted to ignore the quivering in her stomach. She wanted Bright Star to know that she believed. But there was the pain. Point had never been one to tolerate much pain. As a child, she had screamed for hours until her throat went raw and her muscles ached from skinning her knee after she took a tumble from a bike. She'd never in life ridden a bike since. She couldn't take the pain. She kept telling herself this was worth it. Besides, she kept telling herself she was going to die anyway. What did this matter? What did this one little cut matter? She swallowed again. She didn't know if she could do it.

In the end, she couldn't. "Bright Star," Point pleaded, "please don't hate me. Please don't send me away. I believe! I do! Just don't send me away."

"Why would I hate you or send you away?" the smaller woman inquired.

"I don't know if… Can you do it for me?"

Bright Star scooted back and away from Point, shaking her head. She pressed a hand over her heart and her mouth opened. No words came out. She just kept shaking her head.

"Please," Point begged.

"No!" Bright Star piped abruptly. "I couldn't. He may see it is as my doing, not your willing sacrifice, not your faith. No. I can't."

"But…"

"I can't, Point," she reiterated with a firm tone.

For a moment, the older woman just sat at the table with the knife in hand. Then, in a quavering voice she asked, "Will it hurt?"

Bright Star didn't say anything. "It will. I know from time and time again that it will hurt. But, I have grown to welcome the pain. It is my sacrifice, my appreciation for a gift that always reaps a reward that is incomprehensible to one who has not experienced it. There are no words to describe how you will feel, the good that you will be doing, the global importance of this one assignment."

"It will hurt," Point nodded, pressing the tip of the knife to her finger and twirled it. She focused on the tiny spot of crimson, the pain. That tiny discomfort could be reasoned away when she concentrated. It wouldn't be like that if she were dying. But, a wry and bitter smirk settled on her lips, she had already been dying before she was saved. She sat up quickly and started to suggest—

Bright Star abruptly interrupted her. "If you are not conscious when he saves you, you won't feel your rebirth. You won't know it like I know it. It will be there, but you won't recognize it for what it is. You won't believe in it. It won't be like last time."

"I believe—"

"You won't believe in it," Bright Star insisted. "You must experience the destruction of your rebellion and pride, then the revolution within as you are—"

"Rebuilt," Point finished.

"Reborn," Bright Star corrected. Then after studying Point's face, she sighed doggedly. "You don't have to do it. There is another way. We have a mutual friend, you and I. You will have your time later." She patted Point on the back of her hand supportively.

Chapter 12

The Cleric

Thaddeus Okwenuba stayed home from work on Thursday. He told Katie Ann, his boss's administrative assistant he was sick. She'd giggled at him and said something fatuous about playing hooky. Of course, he'd probably never told a more obvious lie. He smiled to himself wryly. Thad rarely missed work because he was physically ill. There were plenty enough other times when he had to miss for other reasons, so he couldn't waste the days. He never even called in sick. He was proud to announce to anybody in the firm that he had contaminated the office with the flu every year for the past six. Nope, his last hospital stay had been in a locked cell about 175 feet below ground. Now *that* had taken him off work a couple months ago, but the episode had been the only one in almost three years, and it had—luckily—happened during a planned two weeks of vacation. He really wanted his deposit from that cruise back.

True enough, Thad had lied to Katie Ann, but he hadn't known what else to say. He had been at a complete and total loss. Was he supposed to tell her that he couldn't come to work because Frankie wasn't there? Nope, he couldn't say that. After all, he did have his pride. Everybody in that building knew Frankie Monnish was not interested. The other problem was that no one else seemed to be worried about Frankie's absence in the least. He'd made mention of her absence and Katie Ann had just raised one eyebrow as if he was only worried because of his futile and obvious crush. Granted, she'd told them all that she was going to take some time off, and as the boss she had that right. However, Frankie had planned time off more instances than Thad could count, but she had never, not once, actually stayed out of the office.

He saw her last at the investors' meeting. Frankie had seen them all off at the hotel three nights before. She'd left a message at the hotel telling them that she was going out of town for a few days, and later, she'd left word with Katie Ann about her impromptu vacation. Rather than be concerned, they—idiots all of them—thought this was good. Katie Ann speculated that Frankie's doctor had recommended she get away from the stress for a while. The fact she had even seen a doctor caused Thad to have mild palpitations. But he knew a doctor's recommendation would not have stopped her from coming in, either. Not with the new money they'd generated. She'd be all over planning its disbursement. Other people might have seen the investment as a time to celebrate and relax before getting down to business. Frankie saw it as the most important time for strategic planning. Frankie *did not* take time off work. According to Katie Ann, their fearless leader wasn't expected back into the office until that following Monday. Thaddeus knew he wouldn't return to work before that day.

So why did he sense something was terribly wrong? That something was completely out of whack in the cosmos? In truth, he didn't know how staying home from work was going to help unless he went out searching for her. But he wouldn't do that, either. No matter what was wrong, Frankie would not appreciate him seeking her out like some love-starved kid with the excuse of verifying her well-being. Instead, she would smile at him and patronize him the way that always seemed to get him hard. What the hell kind of reaction was that? Frankie was probably fine. Frankie was always fine. Thad desperately needed to believe that Frankie was fine. He really didn't know what he'd do if she wasn't. Really. No... *really*. He didn't know what he'd do, because he'd always been a bit... erratic. He made a fist, then opened his hand and looked at his palm. There was a small, oval-shaped indention in the middle. He exhaled heavily.

Around six in the evening, already dark outside, Thaddeus considered the project waiting for him at work. Last week, yesterday even, it had seemed important. It didn't anymore. There was something happening, something coming soon that made work unimportant. He didn't know what that something was, but it was near, and it had something to do with Frankie Monnish. He knew it because every time he thought of her, his palm started to itch and he could feel his hair stand on end, his body grow hot and his hearing become hypersensitive. It was like electricity everywhere, assaulting every one of his senses. It was a feeling he rarely felt, but when he did, it usually foreshadowed catastrophic events in his life. It was a feeling he had told Sandoval he never got without that damn rock. And it had been true, until Frankie left. It was the hum of High Energy.

He needed to know where she was. Since the day he'd met her, he'd needed to be near her. He'd accepted a middle of the road offer with her company right out of his PhD program for that reason alone. There had been plenty of companies that would have paid more, but he stayed. Thaddeus had stayed with the company and made every move possible to get into her department. He'd been working at a desk in the same lab with her for the past eighteen months.

Schroedinger's cat told him that he wouldn't be at his desk that next day. He either would, or he wouldn't. He wasn't there then, but tomorrow… He wouldn't be there. His quantum state would cease to be a mixture. He smiled at that thought. Stupid physics experiment. It wasn't Schroedinger's cat, an experiment that naively challenged fate; it was intuition, plain and simple. He'd learned long ago not to deny his intuition when it was this strong.

The center of his palm began to itch again. It always did when he felt the call of High Energy. He craved the small, smooth rock the way heroin addicts craved their next fix. He had never been considered a strong Shifter. Actually, he wasn't even sure if they considered him a Shifter at all, since he had such little control over his High Energy. What had he seen on that orientation film? It had mentioned human focal points, or some such nonsense. But those were only people who could harness High Energy to be used by others. That wasn't exactly his situation. He could use it, he just couldn't control it. And he couldn't use it without that damn rock. God, how he hated that thing even as his hand flexed again and he desired it almost more than he did the woman he loved.

Thad had never exhibited any predisposition towards High Energy until he was about fifteen, when he found the rock while hiking on a class field trip. In retrospect, it had been the worst day of his life. The defining moment that changed him into the man he was. Just like that, he had found the rock, and attacked. He hadn't had a moment to process what was happening to him or to even get a grip on what he was feeling. No. The High Energy exploded through him, through veins and pores, it raged through him. The elemental reaction blinded him, deafened him, choked him, then burst from him in a brutal force that took control over everything. Violence spawned from rage greater than he had ever felt before in life. His body seemed to recall every slight, every moment in which he had felt cowardice stifle his words and actions. Every time in life when he watched something he wanted go to someone else flashed in his mind. Every time when he had been ignored, forgotten, or discounted, every time he'd felt someone take a look at him and come to the wrong conclusion, everything fueled his primal fury.

He didn't kill Matthew. Matthew told him afterward that he wished Thad had. He would never be able to walk or see properly again. He would never be able to function independently again.

Thaddeus hadn't even gotten into trouble, although he didn't find that out until later. It took six grown men to wrestle his small, wiry body to the ground and sedate him. When he came to, his mother was peering at him and silently weeping as she held his hand in hers. His wrists had been pinned down at his sides by chrome fastenings with a company name embedded in them in white enamel. For the life of him, he couldn't remember the name of the manufacturer and couldn't figure out why it even mattered to him.

"Is Matthew mad at me?" Thad asked. He already felt like he knew the answer. Matthew didn't even like to be touched. He cried like a girl when he was hit. Matthew hated him.

"No," his mother told him as she sat at his side and stroked his hair. It wasn't until later that Thad understood the extent of what he had done to Matthew. It wasn't that he didn't remember the episode. No, it played in his mind over and over and over again. He couldn't get it to stop. But somehow, his brain could not accept that he had done those things. He could not reconcile the violence with his desire to please people and his true faith in harmony. He had always been a mild-mannered, calm boy. He hated to hear people yell. He couldn't imagine that he had done extreme violence to his friend. Even as he struggled with it, though, he remembered all the malicious feelings that had taken hold of him. Those were things he had truly felt, but the mechanism that reasoned through those feelings and kept them from overcoming him had been dismantled by the little winking rock he found on that trail.

Not long after he woke, a doctor came in and released him. The man was tall and blond with thin features. He didn't talk much, but he watched Thaddeus in a way that made him uncomfortable. It wasn't that the doctor seemed rude, cruel or dishonest. Thaddeus just had a feeling that Dr. Randall Sandoval was a man who had already accepted his own death. An odd thought for a child, but he felt it nonetheless.

His mother hesitated for a moment before grabbing him and squeezing too hard.

"Where does he have to go now?" she asked.

"You can take him home, Ms. Okwenuba."

"Home?" she repeated in disbelief. She didn't even move, she just watched the doctor in her wary émigrée fashion.

"Yes, home," the doctor told her. "We'll come by to pick him up tomorrow."

"Pick him up?"

They tested him and tested him and tested him. For months, they had tested Thad and found nothing. No residual High Energy, not even the smallest trace of Talent. His eyes crossed and he got a headache every time they tried to force him to Shift. They had been very near to calling what had happened on that field trip a fluke. That is until they decided to sign his belongings back over to him. They'd been confiscated for testing right after the incident.

By the time the staff was able to sedate him again, the boy had nearly ripped out the heart of the nurse holding his bag. Again, he had to be subdued. Again, they put him through test after test after test. He failed all of them. He felt like a bee. They weren't supposed to be able to fly, but they could. He had no High Energy of his own, but he could Shift. Dr. Sandoval himself came to check Thad every single day and was nice, however, most of the comfort he got during that unsure time was from his mother's near ubiquitous presence. He knew she had to work, and he asked about it. Dr. Sandoval had been the one to assure him that they would find a way to take care of his mother even though Thaddeus was not a part of the Service family. That knowledge had frightened him. They wouldn't take care of him forever if he couldn't do any of the things they asked. For that reason, he demanded the rock again. He needed them to take care of his hardworking mother as promised.

Thaddeus had felt the presence of the thing when they brought it in locked in a box. He couldn't reach for it with his mind as he had been instructed to do time and time again, but he knew it was there. It took a huge effort to rip his attention from the box and realize the scientists were leaving him in the locked room, again. But he did lift his gaze when he realized there was another kid about his age, maybe younger, in the room. He was shorter than Thad, but certainly more muscular and fit. He had blond hair and eyes that were light brown. He was fresh faced and he seemed friendly.

"What are you doing here?" Thaddeus asked him.

"I'm about to give you the rock in this box."

Thad's eyes widened as they focused on the child waiting quietly to the side. He heard his own panicked voice, "No!"

"Hey." The other boy held up a hand. "It's okay."

"It's not okay! You don't know what it makes me do."

"Sure, I do. They let me see footage." The kid had the nerve to smile at him. "I'm telling you it's okay. My name is Jackson, and I'm a part of the test."

"What part?"

"I'm here to tire you out." The boy grinned again. "Randall will probably want to record things like how long and how much it takes for your High Energy to diminish." Then he took the rock out. With another grin, he said, "It's okay. I'm Precocial."

After the attendants and Dr. Sandoval left the room. Without a shadow of hesitation, Jackson gave Thad the rock.

When Thad was lying on the ground breathing so hard it made his chest hurt, he said, "I don't know if my mother knows what I've done. I don't know if she would understand this."

"My mother would not be happy if she knew what I just did, either." Jackson laughed out loud.

They did not become best friends, or maybe they did. It was strange. For sure, they had something in common. They were both the rules and the exceptions of the Parameters of Shift. They would also both be experiments for Randall Sandoval.

Over the years, Sandoval and his team would conceive and test theories about why Thad's High Energy manifested itself through violence, but none of them would be conclusive. He would continue to cross paths with Jackson, but unlike Jackson, he was allowed to live a normal life outside of the Service. He changed schools and cities. No one knew him or what he had done. As long as he was without the rock he was normal. But every now and then, the Service would contact him and they would give it back, and the nightmare would start all over again.

Still, this time, even without it, Thaddeus knew something was coming. He didn't know if it had anything to do with the rock or not. They'd asked him how he got it that last time, but he couldn't honestly say. He'd been home at the time, packing for his vacation. He'd reached into a dresser drawer and there it was. When he touched it, it was like a static shock magnified to a point where he felt as if his ear canals were sparking. After Jackson had taken it from him this time, though, he found that he continued to have some of the residual High Energy. High Energy that warned him something was coming. Something that let him know it was Frankie Monnish.

He wouldn't be at work tomorrow, the reason why… Well, he would leave that to the principle of determinism. He opened his refrigerator to think of more lofty questions: those that he felt he could actually impact. Beer or wine? Beer always seemed to win when he was alone. He grabbed two, actually, then made his way to the sliding door of his fifth floor balcony. He put his beers on the table then stretched out the plastic and aluminum chaise that provided the only seating. He opened a beer.

Then he saw her. Unsure and unsteady, he said her name. "Frankie—"

"My name is Point," she interrupted gently, but stepped forward anyway. "I have something for you." She held out her hand, and in the palm were the platinum cuff links he'd admired just days before. Her thick black hair, which she normally kept pulled back in a tight pony tail, caressed her shoulders as it blew in the subtle wind.

For a moment, he'd thought about not taking them. Just a quick doubt. A pinprick. He'd learned long ago to listen to his instincts, the intuition his mother had bragged about when he was small. But he found something stronger than his intuition this time. He found that he had to have those cuff links. So he took them and put them into his pocket.

"Frankie, I—"

"Point," she corrected him again.

"OK," he whispered, finding himself willing to agree with anything she said or wanted. "Point. Are you okay?"

"Better," she answered with a warm grin. Her teeth were white and straight. Her lips luscious. His body started to stir. Yep, this was his woman, all right.

"Where have you been?" he asked.

"Here in town," she answered, sitting down on the rickety chaise and pulling her arms around her body. "Not very far away at all."

"Cold?" he asked. Point nodded. Thaddeus reached inside the door to pull a throw off his sofa. He handed it to her. She wrapped the material around her shoulders and gazed up at him. She looked tousled, her pretty brown eyes languid. Thad wasn't quite sure how to react. It seemed so unreal, a fantasy.

"What is it?" he questioned.

"Nothing." She chuckled. Her dark brown eyes seemed to sparkle at him, then. "Funny, if you'd asked me that last week, we'd have probably had much more to talk about. But nothing's wrong."

"I don't understand." Thaddeus slowly shook his head. He wasn't completely sure he needed to understand. He already knew it felt as if he'd been given new life when he saw her. He hadn't known until that moment how much he needed her. He'd suspected, but never really known.

"You will," she responded, then stood, throwing off the blanket. She stepped close to him and into a ready embrace. Thad was startled, but held her anyway. He would never have missed the opportunity to do so. She spoke to him, "I have something wonderful to tell you."

"That you love me?" he asked, trying to laugh, but grimacing instead. He had meant for it to be a joke, but his throat closed over the words. He wanted her to love him. God knew he'd loved her from the moment he'd met her. It had been too much to expect that she reciprocate.

"I do love you." She nodded. She said it so easy. As if weren't cataclysmic. "More than I could ever show you." Before he could adjust to that revelation, she spoke again. "But there is something else."

And even as she told him there was something else, Monk could see the woman standing in the shadow of his balcony watching them, her blue eyes startling as they shined in the dark. She tilted her chin up and down as if in approval. Then, Point's slender, feminine fingers pressed something tightly into his palm, something he knew very well.

* * * *

The back door slammed open. Jackson jumped to his feet and swung around. His jaw dropped when he saw the man entering his home.

"Oh my god! What the hell are you doing here, Thad?" Jackson demanded. The taller, slim man passed through the back door and the kitchen with two duffle bags. He nodded at Jackson in a nonchalant greeting. Jackson noticed his friend was being followed closely by Bright Star and Point.

"Thaddeus," Jackson called. The other man kept walking. "Thaddeus!"

Thaddeus slowed. He stopped. Then he turned. He didn't say anything but he acknowledged Jackson with his eyes as Jackson approached.

Bright Star stepped in front of him. "Monk," she corrected. "His name is Monk, now."

"What?" Jackson breathed. "No, his name is Thaddeus Okwenuba."

"Monk," Bright Star repeated sternly. She drew out the word as though Jackson needed time to process it.

"But why is he here? Bright Star, how do you know him?" She didn't answer. He turned back to Monk and demanded, "Why are you here?"

"I'm here because Point brought me here," he answered. As if he realized how cryptic that sounded, he added, "At the end of the day, I'm here because I have to be."

"Don't get me wrong, I love you like a brother, man," Jackson said, "but you can't stay here. Does Sandoval know you're out?"

Monk shrugged his shoulders, a nonchalance that bugged Jackson.

"Doesn't matter about Randall, Jackson. Monk has to stay here," Bright Star explained.

"But he's dangerous."

"Jackson." Bright Star laughed. "Honey, we're all dangerous. You know that."

"Yes, but we haven't all nearly killed someone," Jackson argued.

Bright Star didn't answer, but her silence was enough to remind Jackson that may not have been true.

"Rush?" Bright Star asked the older brother, who had only observed.

"He can stay," Rush told them. He lounged in the doorway.

Jackson jerked around and scowled at his brother. "You said *she* couldn't stay, but you're completely fine with this guy living in the house?"

"Exactly," Rush answered with a surly and challenging smile. "You kept a guest. Now, I guess I'm keeping a guest."

"But can't you smell it?" Jackson persisted. "I can *smell* the violence on him. I can."

"The violence has passed," Monk informed Jackson. "Rush saved me from it."

"So, he's moving in, too," Rush stated casually.

Jackson was glad to see his brother taking it so well. He'd like to know how many more people were going to be squeezed in the tiny... two... four... five bedroom? When had they gotten five bedrooms? He went in to follow the trio as they started into the heart of the house.

"Don't you have to go to work?" Rush stopped him. Jackson looked at his watch. He had to get out of the house. It was morning already and he felt he'd been standing around in that kitchen all night. Maybe he had. He didn't remember ever going to bed. What day was it? They were running together. No beginning, no end. Always changing, and yet, he was accepting it all as if it were not monumental.

"Wait a minute." He narrowed his eyes suspiciously.

"Nobody's been tampering with you," his brother assured him. "You just plain lost track of time. Easy to do with the hours these people keep."

Jackson was in no mood for Rush's laconic wisdom.

"Go on, Jacks. I'll deal with this here. And, Jacks?"

"What?" Jackson's irritation was growing by leaps and bounds.

"Don't tell Randall he's here."

Jackson stared at his brother for a long moment before reluctantly agreeing. He searched for his jacket, for his bag, for his keys then left the home he barely knew anymore.

Rush, however, followed his new guests. When he found the new room Bright Star had obviously added, he saw something he did not expect. Propped upright against the wall, Bright Star hung with her arms limp at her side. The new man, Monk, had his hands clenched around her throat. She gasped but did nothing to stop him. Neither did Point.

Rush had to stop him before she was really and truly dying. He reached out and pried Monk's hands from Bright Star with pure brute strength. He didn't use any High Energy, only physical muscle. Bright Star started to cough convulsively, but her eyes shot daggers into Rush. He hadn't truly saved her life. Not as he was destined.

"Damn, man. I thought we determined the violence was gone," Rush stated plainly. He tried to relax. "You can't hurt her that way."

"Don't you know what she's going to do?" Monk yelled as he reached for her again. His eyes were wide with desperation. Sweat was beading on his forehead. Bright Star threw her head back and leaned towards him. She welcomed the onslaught.

Rush pulled them apart again. This time, he placed a hand on Monk's chest that jolted him backwards and knocked him into a wall. He glared silently at Bright Star who didn't bother to massage her throat where heavy red welts were appearing.

"Don't you know?" Monk asked again in a deflated rasp as he slumped against the wall. "I saw it. I *just* saw it."

"Yes! Of course, I know," Rush responded with more passion than he was accustomed to showing. "And don't you know what I have to do if you actually start to kill her?"

That brought Monk back to his senses. *Yes*, Rush thought, *he knew*. It was at that moment that Monk's almond shaped eyes widened. Then he sank to his knees in front of Rush.

"Get up," Rush commanded with shock in his voice.

Monk didn't comply immediately. Instead, he just continued to peer up at Rush for a painful moment.

"I won't kneel if you don't want me to," Monk told him. "But know that I am not a man who typically gets on his knees in front of another man. Understand that I know who you are and what will happen. Know that I am only trying to do what you want."

"Why?" Rush asked exasperated. "Hell, I should be kneeling to you."

"It's hard to explain," Monk answered.

At that, Rush found himself laughing. "I live every day in 'hard to explain.' Try."

"I feel things. Or rather I know them. I always have, but haven't been able to express my Talent without this," he held up the rock for Rush to see, then handed it to him. "And, I feel who you are. I feel your *Energy*."

"Who do you think I am?" Rush asked. His hawk's eyes pierced the other man's.

Monk looked over at Bright Star. "I agree with her."

"I am not a noble man," Rush stated.

"Sadly, I agree with you."

The man called Monk stood in front of Rush. "You nearly killed Point tonight," Rush stated. The woman in question did not address the statement. In fact, she turned away from them.

"I know," came the hollow response. "I will always be indebted to you for saving her life. And for saving mine. I wouldn't have wanted to live without her. I couldn't let myself live if I had…"

Rush held up a hand. He opened it, and Monk's eyes widened to see that Rush held the rock he had just pressed close in his palm. The small hematite rock that Jackson wrestled from Thaddeus Okwenuba only a few months before, the same one that had just caused him to rip apart the woman he loved. Even then, both Monk and Rush could sense the increased heart rate, the adrenaline, the corporal obsession Monk experienced just from looking at it. But he didn't reach for it. No. He stood still, his eyes affixed to the pebble. As the man watched, the pebble floated high above Rush's hand.

The explosion was loud enough to cause both Point and Bright Star to bend over clutching their ears. The hematite shattered into glinting dust that froze like ice crystals suspended in air for mere milliseconds before exploding again, this time into dust. "Now," Rush told him, "Your rock is with you forever. You don't have to worry about it anymore. You just need to learn to focus your High Energy and to control it." As a command, it was a strong one. But the monk still had doubts.

"I don't have High Energy without it," Monk told Rush. He was astonished that Rush had destroyed the thing that had haunted him for nearly two decades. "I can't believe you destroyed it!"

"Listen, Monk, I am not a part of the Service. I don't know why that rock activated your High Energy or why you became so violent with it, and I don't care. All I know is that you used it to focus your Talent. I can tell it's inside you even if Randall can't. You just need a focal point. And now you have another one," he nodded to Point. "I know you won't hurt her again."

Monk turned and reached out to Point. As soon as Rush said it, he could tell the man knew it to be true. Point would lead Monk to his Talent.

Monk shook his head, "When she came to me…" He was reluctant to continue. Point still wore a haunted expression as she watched him, but she held on to him anyway. "She came to me and I already wanted her so much. Then she gave it to me: the rock. I couldn't control my urges when I had it."

"You don't only have violent urges. And you noticed you have some use of your Talent when you're with her."

The monk smiled bashfully and lowered his head. But then, as if he had been reminded of a horror, he said to Rush: "You know what she's going to do. To us. To you. To the world."

"Knowing what she's going to do and stopping her are two very different things." Rush hedged.

"But you know. You know and you can stop her!" Monk accused.

"Yes," Rush agreed. "I do know, but I can't stop her."

"You *can* stop her. Stop her now!"

Bright Star looked on and nodded in support of Monk's words. Point joined in, pleading with Rush as well.

"I can't," was his only reply. Then he turned and left the room.

The disappointment was tangible. It sapped the other three of their energy. It left them morose, depleted, and aggrieved. It left Bright Star with a new plan.

* * * *

In the South bedroom, the two newest souls stood facing each other.

"I killed you," Monk told Point. His eyes were wet.

"You nearly killed me," she corrected him with a smile.

His whole body shook with a sob he felt he had been holding for decades. His eyes started to burn and the tears came without permission. His shoulders quivered. He bit down on his lip, but another sob escaped. She didn't have a scratch on her. There wasn't even a blood stain on her clothes. Nothing. But he could still feel it. Could still smell the fresh blood and opened flesh. Could still see inside her. Could still imagine the pain he had caused her. In his head, there was a refrain: *I should kill myself. I should kill myself. I hurt her. I could hurt her again unless I end this. I love her, but I hurt her. I should just end it all.*

Point swayed into his body and reached up to drape her arms over his shoulders. She kissed his eyes and stroked his cheek. She told him it was okay.

"I was dying already," she explained in a soft voice. "My mother and her mother both died this way. I was dying already. I barely felt it. Then again, I barely felt alive except when you were near, and now I'm all better, sweetheart. You helped him save me."

"I didn't," he rasped in a broken voice and shook his head.

"You did." She held his face between her hands and looked directly into his eyes. "You did. Without you, Rush would not have saved me, repaired me, delivered me. I couldn't do it myself. Bright Star wanted me to, but I couldn't. I was a coward. Without you and Bright Star, I never would have known what he has been put here to do. You have to help, Monk. You have to help us make him recognize his destiny."

Monk's eyes dried. "He knows his destiny."

Chapter 13

Blossom

Bright Star was alone in her room sitting cross-legged on her bed. It was either late in the night, or impossibly early in the morning. She didn't know which.

The large bay windows in her room were open. Icy rain slipped in from the heavy blue sky. Wind caused it to swirl and assault. She didn't care.

She raised her hands high above her head and breathed deeply. She exhaled. She did it again and again. She didn't stop.

She caught her reflection in the mirror. A pale white body bathed in muted moonlight shown ethereal, otherworldly and alluring. Above the body were glowing blue eyes. Even to herself, she looked like a specter. Like a succubus. She ran her hands over her body. Her new body. It was newer even from when she had first made it over. Every time. Every time she was new again. She was stronger, faster, smarter, more Talented than she had ever imagined she could be.

Rush. She called to him knowing he wouldn't respond. That was okay. As long as she knew he was there. And he always was. He was only a flicker of consciousness away. She felt warm, safe and secure whenever their minds touched. She flooded him with those feelings. She wanted him to know what he had done for her. She wanted him to know what he could do for everyone.

At that last thought, he shut her out. The mental link between them was cut. Still, she knew that was only a ruse. Rush would never truly abandon her. She smiled.

In the mirror, she watched her reflection. Slowly, though she remained the same, it changed. Waxy green leaves covered her breasts and the apex between her thighs. Green and blue leaves laced together to circle her head. Peacock feathers and tall fronds sprouted, creating a glorious headdress. Her arms raised and she grinned. Bright Star shuddered at the image of herself. Then she felt sharp pain shooting through her toes and up her calves. The image was on fire. Blue flames licked their way up the image. The flames became so intense that all Bright Star could see was a giant, brilliant blue ball of flaming gas. She wanted to scream, but she wouldn't. She would face it. She would face what she had to do. She would not waver. She would never falter. She was who she was. The image disappeared.

Chapter 14

Breaking Bread with Phantoms

This time, she was dead for two minutes. Jackson had felt her pull and knew it to be weaker than the first time. He knew why. She was calling to them both at the same time. She was only calling to him in case he was the key to getting to his brother. She was also farther away.

Jackson forced his eyes and his body to remain open and strong against Perma-Shift as he crossed a distance greater than he ever had. He brought a hand to the back of his neck to rub at the pinching beneath the skin there. She was lying on a bed. There were others with her, circling her. They were dressed alike and holding hands. Through a Perma-Shift fog, Jackson could see Point, Monk, and some others he'd never met before.

Bright Star's eyes were open and wearing a blue blaze into the ceiling. Her hair fell back from her delicate brow. The white dress she wore flattened against her skin shaped by her thick thighs and breasts. She could have been an opalescent goddess carved into the front of a ship. A thick leather belt was cinched around her throat. It was one of those he'd used to secure her on New Year's. He tried to tamp down the guilt that suddenly, physically came over him. He had to force it away if he was to help her.

Bright Star's face should have been red. It probably had been, but now, now it was an opaque, pristine white. She had no pulse. Her body was growing cold.

"What have you done to her?" Jackson railed. He turned to the group all garbed in white standing around her. Some of them shifted from one foot to the other with anxiety. Others closed their eyes and wept. Who were they? It didn't matter.

They had done this. He unleashed his anger and fed it to his High Energy. He may not be able to save her but he would certainly be able to destroy the ones who had done this to her.

Never had fury taken so completely over his being. *Parameters of Shift 101*: Feel nothing in excess. That way led to imprecision. Servicemen could not afford imprecision. That way led to excess leakage. Servicemen avoided leakage at all costs. Jackson didn't give a damn.

The anger raged inside of him. With one psychic heave, Jackson hurtled pure Energy at the group. Enough High Energy to kill them all. Blinding pain sliced through his head at the effort but still he could easily see his Energy did not reach them. Instead, it slammed against an invisible barrier then found its way back inside of him. As the Energy poured back into him, the Perma-Shift subsided until there was nothing left but the knowledge that he had failed. A force protected them from his violence.

Breathing heavily, Jackson turned his attention to the one who had summoned him. Jackson neared her without any sense of his feet or legs. He was drawn like a moth to a flame. He reached down to touch her. She was still so goddamned beautiful. His chest hurt.

Suddenly, a cool, steel hand circled his wrist. He stepped back as Rush took his place next to the bed. With efficient and gentle fingers, he eased the strap from the buckle. White and red marks crisscrossed angrily beneath it. Both of his hands clenched around her neck. And for a moment… nothing.

Then, she was alive. She was alive! Her skin was warm, and her eyes were as bright as ever. She was up on her knees in the bed, laughing as fat tears rolled over her cheeks. She reached out to embrace Rush, but he peeled her arms from him and backed away.

Jackson couldn't believe she was alive. Alive and perfect. He could barely tear his eyes away from her to watch his brother's retreat. Rush stood back, then turned to the watchers. Rush did not address the assembly. Instead he started to walk out. The assembled group, with the exclusion of Jackson and Monk, fell to their knees before him. One of his eyes blinked. That one, uncontrolled flutter explained the effort of the Shift, the albatross of responsibility being lowered around his neck just as the belt had been tightened around hers.

He could have easily Shifted himself away but he did not. Followers caught at his pant legs. Still, he walked out of the room with little expression. Jackson did not know whether to follow him or tend the delicate woman who had just been returned from the brink of death.

Quickly, he focused his High Energy and located his brother. He reached out to him. Rush returned a mental wave that indicated that Jackson should not come after him.

Jackson watched the girl who had just been saved. She was awake and calm.

"Why?" Jackson questioned.

"Jackson," she called his name. It was sweet like candy on her lips. "He's saved me every time. Every time. Imagine. If he saved everyone in this room, in this city, the way he has saved me…"

"You can't save everyone." Jackson challenged, using words that sounded contrived even to his own ears.

"Rush can," she answered in a hollow voice. Then her eyes rolled back. She dropped back on the bed. Jackson hurried to her side but not before her chest arched up off the bed. She was taut like a bow and her eyes burst open with blue light so intense the ceiling started to burn. Then she slumped quiet again.

Jackson stood with his jaw dropped. He had never seen anything like it. He didn't know what to do.

When she opened her eyes again and sat up, she smoothed her hair with one hand and let him help her up with the other. Jackson didn't have to ask for an explanation. Monk provided one.

"You understand leakage, right?" Monk asked. "Of course, you do. It's all in that damn Service orientation film."

"*Parameters of Shift 101*. I know all about it."

"Well, you just saw what Rush's residual High Energy does after a Shift. It doesn't affect him with Perma-Shift like other Shifters. But he does have immense leakage, so instead of returning to him, his High Energy affects the person who experiences the Shift." Jackson waited. "Look at her."

Jackson did, and immediately he knew. He had to have been blind, deaf and dumb to have missed it before. Bright Star's entire being was fairly glowing. She hadn't just been saved. She'd been enhanced. At once, Jackson understood. It explained her amazing level of Talent. To be saved by Rush was to become more than you were before. It was to become just a little like him.

Monk nodded, reading his mind. "Every time it happens we become more and more like him."

* * * *

There were ten places set for dinner that night, though only eight were occupied. Rush and Monk had both decided not to come. Jackson didn't even know why he was there other than to make sure Bright Star was really and truly okay after what had happened that afternoon.

When he sat down, Bright Star immediately began to introduce him to all of the people around the table, all of whom now lived in that same residence on Kolter Street. Granted, they had more than enough room between the three floors—when had they gotten three floors? But Jackson still wasn't sure he was comfortable with their presence.

There was a young woman who looked like Bright Star, only skinny. Her name was Myrto. There was Point. There were Xavier and Megumi. Then there were the scrawny lank-haired teenagers Bright Star introduced as Destroy and Harm.

Even though the bedraggled pair looked completely as if their names suited them, Jackson joked, "I hope your parents didn't name you that."

"Don't matter what they named us," the girl, Destroy, answered. "We got the names the world gave us."

Jackson started to say something but decided against it. There was something wrong with both of them and the way they stared at him with their red-rimmed eyes.

"Jackson, leave them alone," Bright Star admonished. "They believe and that's all we should be concerned about."

"That's right," Harm piped in as he speared a chunk of meat on his plate. "We believe. You should leave us alone."

Jackson thought to get up from the table and go, because the wave of nausea and disgust that hit him then was so strong. But he didn't. He would overcome this suggestion. As long as Bright Star stayed, he would stay. He stared at his plate as he ate and tried only to talk to Bright Star as much as possible and to avoid the repellent gazes of the youngest two.

That's why he was shocked when dinner was over and he found himself left sitting alone with them both.

"We're special," Destroy announced to him without guile.

"I'm sure you are," Jackson returned, not knowing what else to say. "Everyone here is."

"Do you want us to show you?" Harm asked. He sniffed a little but held Jackson's gaze.

"No," Jackson answered truthfully. He didn't care if he sounded like a coward. He had never felt the kind of High Energy that streamed off of them. It was horrible and he wanted no part of it. "What I do want to know is how she found you."

"Bright Star?" Destroy clarified. "She didn't find us. We found her."

"You did?"

"Yes," Harm answered. "Easy for me." Then, as Jackson watched, the boy's eyes began to wobble, bubble and crawl. Slowly they came alive until they were a mass of swirling, swelling, squirming gray. Jackson knocked his chair over as he jumped up out of it.

"Calm down, Cowboy," Destroy put a surprisingly strong hand on Jackson's arm. Surprisingly strong. He could barely move out of her grip. "He just sees in Energy like that."

"What?" Jackson demanded.

"He sees in Energy and we were following the Energy for two years until we were able to find the center of it. Now we live in it." She smiled, and Jackson noticed her eyes were also crawling. It was like looking into a pit of oily, swarming, sodden gray worms.

Destroy and Harm both stood then, with their mercury eyes roiling. They held hands and spoke in unison. "You have Energy, too, Jackson."

Jackson said nothing. He could feel his heart rate speeding up and the inside of his mouth turning to cotton. He tried to tell himself there was nothing to be afraid of. Hell, he even told himself he wasn't afraid. But no matter what he told himself, the truth was a different story.

"You have Energy," they continued clasping hands, speaking in a haunted harmony. "But it isn't the Energy we need. Your light does not burn as bright." They took a step toward him. "You needn't worry, Jackson. We can't hurt you."

Jackson continued to be silent and to slowly back away from the advancing pair.

"You're protected by him," Destroy said. And as she said it, Harm put his nose in the air and sniffed. He sniffed again, pointedly in Jackson's direction.

"You've always been protected by him," Harm stated, then sniffed again. "Destroy!"

"Yes, brother," she snapped her attention to the other.

"We have come to our doom here."

"Of course, brother," Destroy agreed.

"Let's not interfere with fate," he said.

Then, they were gone. Jackson started to gulp air desperately. He'd only been half aware that he had not been breathing before.

He went to find Rush.

* * * *

Jackson didn't know what made him stand outside the door instead of walking right in, but he knew what kept him there. It was the conversation—or half conversation—he heard on the other side of the door.

"Don't ask me that. Please, God, don't," his brother was saying with a cracking voice. Never in his life had he ever heard Rush sound so vulnerable and broken. It gave him pause and he felt an empathetic pain that made him tremble. He couldn't stop trembling. Waves and waves of anxiety coursed through his body. It was as if he was falling.

"I can't let you die. I can't. I don't know what I would do. I want to. I want to so badly, but I can't find it inside me to do it. I don't know what it would do to me. Just wait, please wait. We'll find another way. I just need more time."

Then, somehow, Jackson heard a voice, or rather an Energy—a pure Energy—that sounded inside him like a sad, feminine voice. "You have to let me go, my wonderful, beautiful, shining star. You should have let me go then, but it's not too late." A sob, then a stuttering sigh. "You can let me go the very next time, the very next."

"What if she won't let you go?"

"The very next time, my world."

Jackson didn't know if he should go in or not. This was all too much. And suddenly, he felt like his head was going to explode. It seemed to be splitting with Perma-Shift and he hadn't even expended any High Energy. He didn't know what the fuck to do.

He stormed into the room, and as soon as he was inside, the pain dissipated; almost as if it had never been.

Rush was seated on his bed facing the window. Jackson could only see his back. He slumped over and cradled his head in his hands. Jackson took a quick scan of his surroundings, both with his eyes and with his Energy. He could feel the subtle but aching buzz of abused Energy. There was no one else in the room. There wasn't even any other Energy in the room. Not a trace. "Hey," he called hesitantly.

"Hey." Rush returned. He didn't sound guilty to Jackson. He didn't even turn around to face him. He sounded tired, though, as he continued to stare out of the window.

"Were you just talking to someone?"

Rush looked at him then and shook his head slowly.

"Can I talk to you?" Jackson asked, taking a step into the threshold.

Rush turned and Jackson could see his strained expression in profile: tense lines around his mouth, smudges like those he used to wear all the time. "Jackson, I can't right now. I'm sorry, man, I just can't."

Jackson didn't argue. He just walked out of the room with a shake of his head. There were so many things wrong in his world right then, so many things he didn't understand. He couldn't handle anymore.

After Jackson was long gone, Rush looked at the girl who had moved to stand in front of the window. Her shoulders were rounded in a sad slump and her hands were clasped in front of her. Rush didn't want to be in love with her, knew that the world would be a better place if he wasn't.

"You have to let me go," she urged him sadly. Then she faded into the sunlight and the room went dark.

Chapter 15

First, Second and Third Degree Burn

This time was for Jackson. She dressed in a diaphanous gown. The sheer white layers fluttered and settled on her like netting over a trapped tarpon. She chose the gown for its color—Rush liked her in white—but also for the ease at which the material would burn. The dress clung to her soft and primitive curves. It, like her skin, had been rubbed down by elderly women and blinded men with a thick, sandalwood-scented oil. The oil's aroma would blossom on her skin when heated by the flames. The oil itself would cause her to burn faster. The Followers had bound her hands and feet with dried vines, then attached her to a wooden pyre in the center of the ancient ballroom. They'd restrained her so the natural human instinct of self-preservation would not prevail. It had never had any chance of prevailing. Bright Star would never try to save herself.

She waited patiently for Point to return. She'd gone to get Monk who had been absent from the congregation much of the morning. He would have to do the honors. Bright Star didn't care to explore why. She just accepted that this was the role. He was progress and somehow at the same time record.

Point entered the room. She wore neat gray slacks and a cream blouse. Her hair was up in a bun and she wore short heels. She looked like the professional that she was. She looked like the leader that she was. She was carrying a lit torch and a clipboard. Behind her, following slowly, was Monk.

He wore a white t-shirt, white pants, and a yellow armband. He was tall and had the aggressive gait of a military man. He came and stood before Bright Star. With a minor Shift, she reached out to him with her mind and touched his cheek.

His disengaged glare turned soft. He believed.

"Take this." Point handed him the torch. "And please, say the Energy."

This had become his role. Before that last time, he had been compelled to say something to them all. He'd retold the story of Bright Star's first rescue. He talked about her vision. He talked about her sacrifice. Then he touched the lit torch to the flowing fabric near her feet and with a whoosh she was consumed in flames.

Forty seconds passed. In the first ten her skin bubbled, her hair shriveled, and her ears began to melt away from her skull. At twenty seconds, she opened her mouth to scream but inhaled smoke instead. At thirty seconds, her blue eyes were turning black, as was her charred and flaking skin. Amazingly enough, she only started to die at thirty-five seconds.

That's when Rush appeared.

When he entered the room, many of the Followers sat down. They knew he hated the kneeling, but some couldn't bring themselves to stand in his presence. Some were physically incapable.

He walked in and his jaw dropped when he witnessed the burning pyre in the center of the ballroom. He'd known the time was near for her to make another attempt. The world could feel her High Energy gearing up over the past several weeks. He had even known that this time, this time there would be fire. Still, he couldn't have been prepared for the acrid smell of burning flesh. The disfigured but living soul melting in a ball of orange and blue flame in the center of the room even dipped its head in deference to him and he felt his mouth pool with bile. He was going to be sick.

"Save her," Monk prodded.

"Don't you dare speak to him!" Point whispered harshly. She was shocked at Monk's audacity. "It is his choice to save or not. He must make it, or all that we work for is lost."

Monk ignored her. He had to, as they all felt the life slipping from them. The sudden wash of grief that came over him was overwhelming. Something hard pressed into his back, he couldn't breathe. Bright Star was sharing her pain. And her pain wasn't the fire or the flames, or physical in any way. Her pain came from the knowledge that Rush was truly considering not saving her.

The Shift did not take forty seconds. The fire was out. The pyre was gone. Again, there were no amazing flashing lights or booming claps of thunder. Bright Star's flames did not reverse until they subsided, nor did her wounds. No, the state of the universe merely changed from one to another, a world where Bright Star had not burned. But she had. There remained the acrid smell of smoke and her fiery auburn locks were still seared to the quick in patches on her smooth and melting skull.

Rush turned to leave.

"You saved me," he heard from behind him. Then there was an awed and subdued cheering. The Followers were embracing Bright Star and hailing Rush.

* * * *

"Wake up."

Jackson rolled to a sitting position in his bed. He squinted against the near blinding sunbeams streaming through the window.

"What did she do?" he asked groggily. His voice was raspy.

"She had those fucking Followers of hers set her on fire in the ballroom!" Rush answered. "A ballroom we didn't have two weeks ago. Do you understand?"

"What?" Jackson asked attempting desperately to shake the cobwebs from his brain. Then, the words registered. His eyes snapped wide. "What?"

"You were there, Jackson!" Rush answered slowly through his teeth. "You saw her soak herself in oil and have Monk light her up with a burning torch. She was only one and a half minutes from death at my estimation and not the kind you come back from. She couldn't even call to me. She had Monk do it instead."

That woke Jackson. Truly, truly she could have died. What if Monk had not been strong enough to call to Rush?

"I would have known anyway," Rush responded to the unasked question.

Jackson scowled at him, irritated at the mind intrusion. Then he swung his legs off of the bed and stood, heading toward the bathroom. "What are you going to do?" he questioned his brother.

"Do?" Rush shrugged coming to lean against the door frame. "I'm not going to do anything. In fact, I think I'm going to go away for awhile." He brought up a hand to massage the back of his neck.

"Go away?" Jackson asked, hoping he didn't sound like an overly dependent little brother as he splashed water on his face.

"Yes. I haven't decided where, but I think that I may be able to relax some if I leave for awhile."

"That's ridiculous," Jackson argued as he toweled himself off.

"Maybe she won't do it if I'm not here," Rush offered finally and Jackson met his gaze in the bathroom mirror. He said nothing.

Rush gave a derisive grin, then turned to leave. He knew hope was futile. He knew she would always, *always*, be able to find him. The pain in his back started again.

"You should go see Dr. Sandoval." Jackson watched his brother wince.

"I thought we'd established that Randall was useless," Rush answered dryly. He wasn't going to see anybody. The problem in his back was purely and simply stress-related, and it was never ever going to go away. It would only get worse until, well… the pain wouldn't matter anymore then.

"Where is she?" Jackson asked.

"In the kitchen," was Rush's response. "She's waiting for you. Even if she seems as if she is not. She is."

"Not Bright Star."

Rush looked at him sharply. "Who?" his voice was gruff.

"Never mind," Jackson answered softly and left the room.

* * * *

When Jackson entered the kitchen, it was to see Bright Star curled into a window seat eating a bowl of fruit. She gazed outside wistfully. Badly bruised all over her body, she smelled like burning tar. Her lips were cracked and raw. She had very little hair and her scalp looked at if it were still melting. It was shiny and smooth like plastic. Still, her face remained the same. Beautiful.

"Why do you allow it to remain that way?"

"What?" she asked turning to him. "My hair?"

Jackson nodded.

"I can't change it," she answered without pain. She obviously considered the loss of her hair insignificant. And—Jackson was convinced—she chose not to dwell on her inability to reverse what was a minor consequence of the fire.

Jackson reached out to her abused skull. Where his hand smoothed over the brittle stubble, bright, burnished copper locks fell straight and familiarly. As he touched her with his hand and his smile, her crowning glory was returned. She reached up. Her hand mingled with his as she touched the soft strands. He rubbed a thumb over her lips. Her rosy lips made a soft O. Still, she was silent.

"Don't forget: I am still the Precocial." He stood back from her. If he had remained close to her, still smelling the musky scent of burned wood and oil on her skin…

Bright Star smiled warmly. The sight stirred that longing inside of him until he realized she looked beyond him. He turned.

Rush entered the kitchen wearing only pajama bottoms. While his body had grown thicker in the past few months, he grew only muscle. The ropy cords of ligaments, the smooth egg of muscle on his biceps and another connecting his shoulders to his neck, frowning angrily on his shoulder blades. His waist was narrow, his stomach hard and ridged. Even his feet were broad and sinewy. His physique was enhanced by the velvety, glowing brown skin covering him. He looked like the heathen Jackson's father had always called him. Rush had always been powerful, now he allowed his physical presence to show it. No need to hide anymore. Everything about him gleamed with health. Jackson didn't know what to make of it. He considered asking his brother why he'd hidden himself for so long, but he wouldn't dare. He was just as afraid of the answer as he was of posing the question.

Rush reached into the refrigerator and produced a bottle of water. The one sweeping move captivated the woman at the table. Her eyes blared aqua. Jackson could hear her breathing deepen. He could hear her throat's reflexive swallow as she watched the movement of Rush's Adam's apple. This was disgusting. Jackson started out of the kitchen. Bright Star wanted Rush. She would always want Rush.

"Don't go," they both commanded. Jackson turned around. They had both spoken the same words for obviously diametrically opposite reasons. Rush because he wanted Jackson to understand that there was no strength of bond between him and Bright Star. Bright Star so that Jackson could witness that bond.

He looked to his brother, but Rush spoke to Bright Star. "I see that your appearance has improved."

Bright Star cast her eyes down and bit her lips together. If Jackson did not know better, he would think that she hung her head in shame, but he did know better. She would never be ashamed of what she had done in that old ruined ballroom.

"I did not change myself, my world. I was unable to do so. I was embarrassed by my vanity when I realized you had stripped me of the ability."

Ah, Jackson realized now that Bright Star was not ashamed of her actions the night before. She was ashamed she had allowed Jackson to repair the damage that had been done.

Rush studied her for a long while. "I was wrong."

"My world?" She asked.

"I assumed that letting you stay here would make it easier to keep an eye on you, to prevent you from bringing harm to yourself and others.

I thought I could change all of this. So stupid, when I've been telling Jackson all along that there was nothing to be done. So arrogant." His lip curled and his eyes narrowed as if he ached. "I was wrong."

Her pale white cheeks flamed red and she lowered her eyes. "My world, I only do what I must. I can't stop until you acknowledge who you are."

"*Burn,*" he breathed through his teeth.

Her mouth opened and her hands tensed until her nails dug into her palms. So tense, she began to shake. "I...I'm not," she stuttered.

"I acknowledge who I am," Rush inserted. A rare show of irritation creased his brow. "You are asking me for a whole lot more than that."

"You must be responsible, my world," Bright Star argued. Jackson had never witnessed her argue with Rush.

In a sudden change of conversation, Rush asked Jackson, "Have you noticed how our apartment isn't an apartment anymore?"

Jackson chewed the inside of his jaw. Rush had asked him a similar question earlier that morning. He had noticed. This had once been a two-bedroom apartment with an eat-in kitchen and small living room. It had become veritable mansion. There were twenty bedrooms now. There was a formal dining room and an informal one. There were two wings and a courtyard. There was a nursery. There were buttresses and gargoyles. And no one seemed to notice that it had been a fundamental change in the scenery of the city. What had once been a block of old re-purposed government buildings and residences, was now all one unit. It was all undisputedly Rush's home, and now there were at least 50 occupants.

Rush shook his head then, and left the room.

Jackson remembered his conversation with his brother. He went and joined Bright Star on the window seat. He took one of her hands in his.

"Bright Star," he began.

"Yes, Jackson."

"You don't know what you've done this time," he urged wearily.

"What is it?"

"Today, Rush talked about leaving."

"What?" she straightened and her eyes started to glow.

"He talked about leaving and not letting anyone know where he's going. I think he means through a very serious Shift. I think he intends to block you out. You won't be able to call to him."

Her lower lip quivered as she struggled to breathe. She blinked rapidly and turned her gaze anywhere but on Jackson.

"Bright Star," Jackson called and captured her head in his hands. He turned her to face him. For a moment he was captured in the soothing light of her water eyes. "He left you burned as a warning. He won't save you again. "

Jackson could see it in her eyes. She wanted to argue. She wanted to give him some spiritual lecture explaining why his words couldn't be true. But she'd seen it when Rush left the room. Finality.

Chapter 16

Crash

Bright Star hadn't wanted to believe it. Jackson could tell. Rush had been gone for six days already and the entire house and its inhabitants seemed to buckle under the strain. They cried and they sought Bright Star for explanation. For the first time, she was silent. She only communicated through telepathy and only then to say she would not speak or eat or sleep or drink until she had the answer. The assumed question was "where is Rush?", but it that wasn't what she wanted to know. Bright Star would not tell them the question. Instead, she left them to work through their despair alone, and like new orphans, the Followers were lost.

When they failed to get their reassurance from Bright Star, they went to the Monk who put them at ease before invariably leading them to Jackson. Jackson didn't understand it, but Monk for some reason felt that Jackson was the key to communicating with Rush. The Followers came to the Precocial and made offerings of mundane items, items of significance to them and them alone. Teddy bears and gold watches, old coins and colorful scarves. And even though Jackson rejected their gifts outright, they peered at him with cloying and needy eyes. Clearly, they made him uncomfortable. Jackson tried to avoid them. He had nothing to offer.

Even so, he had come to spend nearly a hundred percent of his time at home in the kitchen. There was something about that one room, the one unchanged room in their home that made him feel near to his brother. Safe. The rest of the time, he sleepwalked through his shift at the SHQ. The only reason he continued to go to the site was that every other day, though silent, Bright Star went with him for her sessions with Dr. Sandoval. Jackson told her shortly after she began her visits that she could end them. Her time with Sandoval had changed nothing. He would not admit it to Rush, but Jackson agreed that Bright Star seemed to be influencing Randall rather than the other way around.

On the seventh day of Rush's absence, Jackson shut down his computer, gave a longing stare to his mother's picture, then locked his office. He went to the observatory to wait for Bright Star. She never liked when he came to her sessions, and he hadn't wanted to exacerbate her despondency by interrupting.

This day, the domed ceiling was rolled back, and he was staring at the sky when she came to find him. As she neared him, he gave her a tentative smile. Her lips moved and he thought she would return the expression. She didn't. Instead, Jackson realized she was talking to herself, and though she neared him, she didn't seem to see him.

"Bright Star?" Jackson queried. There was no response.

"Bright Star?" he tried again. This time she acknowledged him with little more than a subtle tilt of her head towards him. "What's wrong?"

"Hmm?"

"What's wrong?" Jackson asked again, this time with more force.

"Nothing," she answered and continued to watch the trees move past them as the car seemed to stand still.

Jackson did not ask how the sky had gone dark and why he was now driving the car home. These things he didn't spend much time on anymore. Shifts in space and time were inconsequential these days.

"You seem distracted," Jackson pressed.

"I do?" was the wan and noncommittal response.

"Yes, you do. And not just distracted, disturbed."

"It's nothing," she said and leaned back, resting a hand over her eyes. The subject was closed.

When they arrived home, Jackson came around to open her door. Slowly, she stepped out of the car and seemed to look past him again. She didn't start for the house. He followed her into the statuary. Her lips began to work again, and Jackson was at a loss.

"What happened when you went to see Randall today?" he asked.

At first, Jackson didn't expect her to answer. But after a long pause, she did. "Nothing. Nothing ever happens when I see him. I talk and he listens. He says very little, but he listens very well. Today was no different. But I asked him, Jackson." And there was a catch in her small voice. "I asked him to help me, this time."

Jackson held his breath. Maybe this time...

"I asked him to help me but... but..." There was another catch. "He couldn't. Do you know what his Talent is, Jackson?" Jackson shook his head. "Well I won't tell you. I won't."

That's when Jackson stood in front of her. Tears were flowing freely down her face. Jackson wanted to touch her, to console her. But he knew she wouldn't have any of it. And he knew that Rush, however far away, would know that he had touched her. Rush would know that he had wanted to support her... He couldn't do it.

"Why?" she pleaded with him. "Why won't he just accept his fate? Why does he fight me?" Her leg seemed to be aching. Jackson had no idea where she had gotten the injury or if she had, in fact, been injured at all. When he scanned her, he could sense no trauma, though to her body the pain was undeniable. She kept putting weight on it. Jackson could barely admit to himself the dark fact that he was fascinated by this. So rare was his ability to even feel a morsel of what she did. As it finally gave out, she slowly sank to the ground.

She picked a crystal goblet from the air. There was what appeared to be red wine inside. She took a small sip. The crystal goblet lolled listlessly in her hand until its burgundy liquid dribbled on to the ground and its lip kissed the smoothed stones of the walkway. It was then that in a fit of rage she smashed the bell of the glass against a limestone cherub, shattering it so the stem she held in her hand was capped by a ragged glass crown. She wrapped her whole fist around the upside down stem and ground the sharpest, most angled edges into the inside of her wrist. The brittle tips crumbled but eventually cut through her skin and into her meaty flesh. She twisted it. The only sounds were a sharp sigh and a dull—near silent—thump of fat drops of blood landing on the ground.

Jackson ran over to her to pull the glass from her wrist, but she wouldn't let him. She wailed and she fought. She swung the glass at him, grating it across his cheek. A mild, thin pink slash appeared on his face, then just as quickly disappeared. When he pulled the glass free and clamped his hand over her wound, she screamed. She brought up her knee and planted her foot in the center of his chest, trying to get him off her. Jackson moved back in concert with her movement and twisted to the side. Her foot slid past him and he was back, grappling for her hand.

Bright Star balled up the fist of her good hand and swung hard until she connected with his face again. After, she dug her nails in. She reached back to swing again, but he caught her other hand, tried to hold her still. Then she started to kick again. She kicked and kicked until he was forced to let go of her hands. Then she levered herself up until she was on her feet and ran in the back door directly to the counter in the kitchen where the knives were. She reached for a large chef's knife. She took an unsuccessful swipe at an already mending wound.

It was then that she looked down. There was no more break in her skin. The blood was even dissipating. It was as if she had done nothing. She raised the knife then drove it directly into the front of her throat. Only a sharp cough escaped her as she fell to the floor once more and blood sputtered out of her mouth and from the wound. Not seconds later, though, the knife appeared to free itself, levitating until it set itself back on the counter.

Jackson heard a hoarse wheezing and realized that she was crying again, this time in great painful wracking sobs. There was no wound, no more blood. He knelt down beside her, not knowing what to do. "Bright Star," he whispered, stroking her hair.

She took deep gulps of air and coughed as she tried to stop the tears. She jerked her hand away as he tried to grab it.

"Bright Star," Jackson started again. "He saved you. Isn't that what you wanted? Isn't that what he always does?"

She shuddered. Then her body went dead. She was still when she answered in a sharp, gruff tone. "He didn't save me." She didn't give Jackson a chance to ask the obvious question. "It was automatic. A side effect from the last time. It won't last. I didn't even *feel* him," she spat. "He didn't even come for me. It's just… just secondary Perma-Shift, or leakage, whatever you people call it."

Jackson was silent. He had been there. He would always be there. But she didn't care. Rush hadn't come.

"I need to go to bed," she stated abruptly. She stood and walked away, veritably melting through the walls to her room.

"He won't save you again," Jackson couldn't help but mutter as she left. And though he said it softly, he knew that she heard.

* * * *

They were going to wreck the train.

The day was bright and blustery. The sun had not shown in three days. But that morning, it caused the streets to glitter with the precipitation of the night before. Puddles of melting ice showed signs of the burgeoning warmth from that lone star in the sky. And yet, the wind whipped through the people with a frigid whistle. It cut to the quick, forcing muscles to tense, hands to clench in pockets, bodies to strain toward solid in a brace against it. And yet it was still so very bright out.

Birds circled and cawed above them in a near white sky. Cars and pedestrians went by, barely noticing the heightened Energy pulsing to life around them.

They looked like a tour group.

They—all fifty-five Followers—stood together but clumped into smaller groups. They laughed and talked about their day's events. Few talked about their night's plans. That was an insult. Some held steaming coffee cups. Some carried nondescript, small leather journals. Destroy and Harm took turns punching each other as hard as they could in the arm. The stronger, the louder each blow landed, the louder they laughed. Monk stood chatting with someone while holding Point, an arm loose around her shoulders. He stood in the way of the wind for her and let his hands tangle in her thick, free-flowing hair. All of the Followers were dressed in comfortable clothes and carried minimal baggage. Few of them were tense. Few of them were nervous. Most waited as patiently as anybody would at a stop for a train.

They were waiting for the next train. They'd already passed up one that was already filled with passengers. They preferred to ride in a single car together. The next one would be arriving in three minutes.

Darting in and out of the group in uneven but hurried strides was a copper haired woman bundled in a white jacket with a gold and white scarf. She wore very dark sunglasses. She checked with each of them. She made sure they had their tickets. She asked if they needed anything. She gave an encouraging squeeze to trembling hands though those were few and far between. When the train arrived, she called them together, appearing only as a guide for them. She spoke softly for a moment and then the entire group went silent and still.

Passersby who had paid minimal attention to the assembly, stopped to watch. Some of them even lowered their heads as well, as if in prayer. The long moment, only a minute in truth, ended and the group filed into the train. Though it took time to get them all in, the doors did not begin to close. Instead, they waited until all were inside the car. Then the car lurched gently forward.

After they had been in motion for nearly fifteen minutes, Bright Star reached out and touched Point's shoulder. "It's a little late for me to ask…"

"What is it?" Point questioned. She briefly covered Bright Star's hand with her own. It was rare that she had to lend strength to the woman who had become her leader, but she felt honored that Bright Star allowed it.

"I know your…" The red-haired woman paused. "your issue…"

"With pain?" Point questioned with a tilt of her head.

"Yes," Bright Star told her. "With pain."

"The second time I was born, I was born with no fear of pain." It was the first time she had shared this with Bright Star.

Bright Star nodded slowly then her blue eyes ignited and she smiled. She placed both of her hands on the taller woman's arms.

In turn, Point grabbed Monk's hand. He looked down at their entwined fingers briefly, then leaned against Ban, whose elbow bumped Destroy, who stepped on Harm's foot, who tangled his fingers in Mix's braid. And so on, and on, and on, until they were all connected and one's Energy could not be distinguished from another.

It was then that Monk said the words. He hadn't planned for them, but couldn't stop them from spilling forth from his lips. The softly spoken words reminded them all of where they had come from and why they were there. These words entreated the universe to recognize their plight and to help Rush either deliver them or destroy them. It was at once a prayer and a curse. An ode and a eulogy. And on the final stanza, the High Energy in the car seemed to swell, intensifying as it grew at an exponential pace.

The metal room began to hum. The sound of snapping and whipping wires joined it. The whir of broken wheels enhanced the noise and then the train peeled off its path and crashed over the elevated track. The first indicator of the car folding in on itself was a metal spike that plunged down from the roof of the train. It sheared through Bright Star's collarbone, shattering it, tearing through her lungs and liver, breaking her hipbone, impaling her, affixing her to the floor. And then there was only the roar. A loud, ear-splitting roar that sounded like Rush.

Chapter 17

Souvenir

"How did you get that scar?" Jackson asked, raising a fingertip to her face. Against his own better judgment, he traced the angry, jagged pink scar that marked her from her widow's peak down between her copper brows and under her gently rounded cheek. The injury's puckered ridge, both raw and dark, punctuated the softness, delicacy of her pale skin. His fingertips tingled at the touch. The feel of her was pure High Energy. Addictive. He put his hand in his pocket.

"Rush left it for me," Bright Star answered with a flippant shrug of her shoulders. Her red hair rustled and settled with the movement. Her eyes were heating up, casting blue light everywhere they touched. No blue light warmed Jackson: she would not look at him. He knew she was hiding a bashful and enchanted smile.

Jackson touched her face again in an attempt to erase the mark. He failed. In fact as he touched it this time, he could feel Rush's pattern in his fingertips. Rush would not allow him to repair her this time. And, obviously, she did not want to be repaired.

Jackson tried to stop his hackles from rising. That was before he saw her get up and walk to the sink, dragging the blanket she'd been cocooned in with her. She was dragging her right leg as well. The same leg he had been sure she injured before the train wreck. "What happened, Bright Star?" he demanded, coming to stand in front of her.

She only gave him a sunny smile then averted her eyes. She washed her hands slowly. Jackson stood there crowding her space. Silly of him to think he could intimidate her into answering his question. Even realizing that she would not succumb, he didn't budge. She smelled like tropical flowers. For the first time in months, Jackson was reminded of that isolated island, the beliefs of its people, and the promise that Bright Star had made them.

Finally, she turned toward him, her face tilted up and waiting. Jackson reached a trembling hand into the warmth underneath her blanket and laid his hand on her hip. With a mental flex, he read that her leg was broken from hip to ankle in three places. He could sense the mending injury to her lung. Her hip had sustained the worst of the injury. He swallowed and his heart began to beat rapidly, his chest started to constrict, but before Perma-Shift could take place, he realized his efforts were for nothing. He wasn't repairing her.

Her small hand came down and lay over his briefly before she grasped his hand and pushed it away from her.

Jackson felt a spark of anger. Violent and visceral, that spark flared but he quickly tamped it down with long-practiced discipline. His anger was tempered by well-honed logic. He would reason through this... this state of affairs that didn't seem to make sense. Bright Star didn't want to be fixed. This, she had, in effect, done to herself. She had caused the train wreck, the wreck that had the Followers give themselves to Rush as sacrifices as well. She had stood in the valley intending to cheat death that day. She intended to cheat death every day. The train crashing had merely been the most recent and most cataclysmic of her attempts. Jackson had heard her explain many times, "I'm not suicidal." No, she wasn't suicidal. She thought she was saving the world.

And somehow, she managed to draw Rush out each time. He saved her each time. This last, he had shown his anger, his emotion, by leaving her the scar on her face and the apparently serious injury to her leg. But Bright Star did not appear to mind. In fact, she seemed proud of the mark. *Rush left it for me.* It was as if she were a child finding a gift beneath her pillow. She had said it with reverence, with love. Jackson's anger thundered again like the aftershock of an earthquake.

The urge to grab her was powerful. It consumed him. He shook with it. The only thing that stopped him was the fact he didn't know what he would do if he did. Hit her? Kiss her? Equally damning.

She turned to him, shifting her weight onto her good leg. One sleeve of the white tank top she wore slipped over her shoulder. He realized that the oversized garment only stopped when it caught precariously over her breast. She wasn't wearing anything underneath it. He could see the soft slope to the dark peach halo, but even when he strained, he couldn't see the tip. Unconsciously, his hand moved toward his sharp, quick, and painful erection. Before it was too late, he moved his hand to a dish instead. He closed his hand over the cool hard glass and threw it at the wall. It shattered into countless pieces. Bright Star jumped and the shirt slipped beneath one heavy, cream globe. She hurriedly pulled the sleeve back up on her shoulder and rewrapped the blanket around her.

Jackson walked away from her. He couldn't do this. Damn, he couldn't do this.

In the doorway he paused, but did not face her. "Bright Star, how could you have led those people to die?"

"None of them died," she contradicted. Her expression was one without remorse. She had already slipped down to the floor to clean up the mess he had made.

"You made them sacrifices," Jackson accused her.

"They made themselves sacrifices, Jackson." She slid a waste bin close to her and began to dump pieces of the plate into it. "And I'll tell you again—*None of them died.*"

"God," Jackson gritted. "Do you have to do that right now? We are talking." His voice broke. "Do you have to do this now?"

"Yes, Jackson," She looked up at him briefly, "Yes, I do. "

"They could have died."

"No, they couldn't have," she debated. She wrung her hands and sat back on her heels. Jackson could tell she had reached the point of exasperation. "Rush wouldn't let all of them die. You don't understand, Jackson. He couldn't."

"What makes you think so?" Jackson finally faced her as she said that. He thanked God that she had pulled her blanket up to even cover her shoulders. "He's been gone for six days, Bright Star. We don't know everything he can do. What if he wasn't able to save all of them?"

"He was."

"What if he hadn't come?"

"He hasn't gone anywhere, Jackson," she said, shaking her head. "I'm surprised you didn't know that."

"What?"

"He never left the house." Bright Star explained. "The others understandably believed he was gone. And if he wanted them to believe it, I wouldn't tell. I was hurt that he sought to hide from even me, but that is his prerogative."

Jackson could barely focus.

"He never left," she repeated. "He just cloaked himself. Like I do."

In truth, she didn't have to repeat the words. Jackson knew them to be true just as he knew himself to be a fool. He'd grieved just like those other poor souls when he should have known that his brother was right there in the house with him.

He squeezed his hand and pounded himself on the forehead. "Stupid, stupid." He castigated himself. Never in life had he felt as inadequate as he had in these past months.

"Stop it," Rush appeared, grabbing Jackson's hand. "You haven't done that since you were a kid."

"How can you stomach me?"

Rush was perplexed, and his face showed it. "You're my brother. And you shouldn't beat yourself up for not knowing I was here. No one should have known. I don't know how she knew. I swear to you I don't. I just couldn't go without keeping an eye on things here. I felt something was going to happen even if I didn't see exactly what it was."

"You see," Bright Star said, alerting them that she was still there. "You see, Jackson. He's starting to give in. He's starting to accept what he has to do."

"Bright Star," Rush warned. "Don't start this. And please do not interrupt this conversation I'm having with my brother."

Bright Star said nothing else, but Jackson, for the first time, could feel a growing animosity inside of her all directed at him. Bright Star was starting to hate him.

"Please," he entreated, holding his palms out to her. He didn't know what he was asking for, but he knew he had to try.

"This wouldn't have happened if you had made her leave."

"She's not safe out there alone."

"She's even less safe in here. Or rather, everyone else is less safe with her in here. Because remember, she's not alone. She has her own personal little army of fanatics. Isn't that right, Bright Star?" Rush turned an accusing eye to her. "Your own *growing* army of fanatics."

"Who have no meaning without you," Bright Star offered. Though her words were submissive enough, and her demeanor no less, there was a challenge.

"Bright Star," Jackson reached out to her.

She didn't answer, merely raised her hot gaze.

"What will it take for you to stop this?" How many times had he asked this question?

"Stop what?"

"Stop... this."

"There is no 'this' to stop, Jackson. This is our way of life until Rush delivers us."

"But what does that *mean*?" Jackson's frustration was palpable.

She shook her head. She puffed out her bottom lip. She shifted where she stood on her bad leg.

"What does he have to do?" Jackson demanded again. Still she said nothing. "Why isn't the fact that he saved you—that he continues to save you—enough?"

"You don't understand," she said finally.

"*That* I won't argue. Today, you led a group of people onto a packed train. You and that same group of people crashed the train and called out just in time according to some estimate or equation I *don't* want to even know about for Rush to save you. And, he did. He saved you. Every last one of you and all of the other people you endangered when you did this. What else do you want?"

Again, she said nothing, and her bottom lip began to quiver. Jackson wanted to stop asking her questions. He wanted to go back the way he'd come and avoid bringing her to tears. But he didn't have a choice. If he were going to help her, he needed to know exactly what he was up against. "What else could you possibly want from him?"

"You already have it," she answered cryptically, angrily. "So even if I told you, you would never understand what we want or why we want it."

Chapter 18

Gang

They entered in slow motion. Bright Star stepped aggressively even with her pronounced limp. One brilliant blue eye was covered by a lock of melting fire. Flanked by Point and Monk, she wore her standard white fare. A fuzzy white pullover. White pants. White, shiny heels. A white, plastic ring around her middle finger. Her luscious lips were even a translucent white. She had one yellow satin ribbon tied around her delicate wrist. Her broad face was bracketed by impossibly large white hoops in her ears. She didn't even look at him. None of them did.

They kept coming and started up the stairs to the front door. When, finally, they reached the door, Bright Star turned. Monk and Point stopped short. Then, upon a non-verbal, non-observable cue, they both nodded their heads and continued inside. Bright Star tossed her hair back and bathed Jackson in the full unadulterated light of her mystic blue eyes. Just her neck. Nothing else. She turned to him.

Scheherazade, Bathsheba, Jezebel, Helen, Ceres, none of them could have produced that fascinating yet slightly condescending look that curved her lips. "Remember," she told him in a deep and sultry voice. "I belong to him."

"I—"

She cut him off before he could begin the lie. "Rush doesn't want me. We both know that, Jackson. But I won't betray him."

"I don't know what you're talking about," Jackson countered. Too late. The hungry gaze had already traveled up and down the length of her.

"You know," she threw back, then squatted before him.

"What happens now is bigger than the both of us," she told him as she grasped his face between her hands and stared at him gravely. His face was bathed in warm blue.

"I wish you would let me help you," he said helplessly.

Bright Star scoffed and stood. The moment they shared was now over. "Help, help, *help*. It's all you ever talk about. You can't help me. Jackson, I think you know that. Furthermore, I don't need any help." She was quiet for a moment. The blaze from her magnificent blue eyes, cut in half by the persistent scar, stroked his body. "What I need from you is your faith."

"Faith in what?"

"Faith in him, of course."

"He's my brother, Bright Star. Of course I have faith in him."

"He's not your brother," she argued, reaching a warm and slender hand out to him again. "Okay, well, he is. Yes. He is your brother. But he is so much more. So much more. He belongs to the Earth, not just to you."

"Or you," Jackson dared. He watched that hand in anticipation. Would she touch him?

"Or me," Bright Star agreed, ruefully pulling her hand back. She never hid her wants and desires when they came to Jacob Rush. She stood and started back into the compound.

"You never leave the house unless it's to the SHQ. Where have you been?" Jackson asked, wanting to end that perilous thread of conversation.

"We have a lot to do today," she winked at him.

"Bright Star," Jackson entreated, "Whatever you're planning… whatever it is, please tell me that it…" He didn't finish.

"I won't tell you what it is at all. That, apparently, is the only way you will be able to sleep at night." And with those words, she started after Point and Monk into the building.

Before she made it inside, Jackson stopped her once more. "Then tell me who she is."

Bright Star turned back to him and she fixed him with a cold and ruthless stare. She had never looked at him that way. In fact, he had never seen that expression at all on her face before. "Who?" Her voice was like a scratch in his ear.

Unfortunately, Jackson didn't know who. All he had was the memory of his brother talking to a phantom girl once before and offhand references to someone by the Monk. There was nothing else. Bright Star narrowed her eyes just so, then turned and entered the building.

Jackson sat for a moment, but found himself restless. After the train, there had been a growing tension in the house. The tension wasn't just emotional or a "feeling." It was pure unadulterated High Energy. It had shown up on the satellite images and sensors at SHQ. Jackson had not been able to cover the fact the Energy was directly from his home. But, amazingly, he hadn't had to. Every scientist, doctor, military advisor at

SHQ seemed to believe this Energy field was completely normal and unworthy of investigation. Jackson did not agree but did not want them storming his home. His home, which over six months ago had been a two bedroom and was now a veritable compound housing more people than when it had been a regular apartment complex.

Bright Star was planning something huge. Something huge enough for her to expend Energy to put up a barrier for the minds of every one of the Followers living in their home. Jackson found it impossible, thus frustrating that he couldn't break through the wall. He couldn't stop something he couldn't foresee.

Rush had been around more than normal, too. As if he, too, knew it was coming. Of course, Jackson thought, Rush knew. Of course he did. Rush knew everything. Rush was the fucking all powerful! Jackson threw the tennis ball he'd been hitting against the side of the building. Rather than bouncing back, it wedged itself into the brick wall. Then the wall seemed to wobble and accept the ball into it. Jackson grunted in frustration. Nothing was normal anymore.

"Ta dah!" Jackson heard from behind him. He turned to see the twins. His skin crawled at the very sight.

Regardless of the fact that they shared a beautiful room with its own bathroom. Regardless of the fact that they had access to whatever they wanted including clothes. Destroy and Harm persisted in looking like thrown away children, like filthy panhandling street urchins.

"What do you two want?" There was no love lost between them and Jackson.

"We thought *you* wanted something, Cowboy," they said in unison.

"What could I possibly want from either of you?"

"We thought you wanted the wall to go down." Destroy smirked. A dimple creased her dirty cheek.

"What wall?" Jackson asked glancing around. He felt like a criminal for just standing there with them. He also couldn't deny the unease he felt at the High Energy that throbbed around them like an infected wound.

"The Energy wall, of course, Cowboy," Harm told him. He sidled close to Jackson and looked up at him. His gray eyes were already starting to churn in the way that made Jackson want to vomit.

"Let's forget about the wall," he managed. "Why don't you just tell me what they're planning?"

"Unh unh unh," Destroy tsked, shaking her head. "There's a way, Cowboy. You know that. A way these things get done."

Jackson didn't say anything. He just stared at the two who were barely more than children. And yet, with their clammy skin and roiling mercury eyes, they were dangerous. He considered, was considering, what they were offering. The pair knew for certain what Bright Star was up to, but—as was now tradition when it came to Jackson—they wouldn't tell him. They were going to make him use their Energy to infiltrate the wall. He would have to become a part of them. He looked around again. There was no one there to witness this. In the sky, stars winked at him.

"Okay," he muttered.

"I'm sorry. We didn't hear you," Destroy prodded.

"Come on. Let's get this over with." Then he started around to the back of the grounds. He couldn't go inside. Rush and Bright Star would know what he was up to if he went into the house. They might know anyway, but he thought to lessen the chance. Destroy and Harm followed him, holding hands.

They went into the utility shed. There was an old tub inside filled with landscaping supplies. Jackson considered briefly that five minutes ago they hadn't had a utility shed. He didn't remember anybody ever doing any landscaping.

"We'll need to use that," Destroy said of the tub. She began to levitate boxes and containers out of the tub with a wave of her hand. Jackson tried not to be amazed. He hadn't the kind of control she possessed at that age. Both she and her brother's Talent had increased exponentially since coming to the compound. He wasn't sure why, but he was sure it had something to do with Bright Star. Or his brother.

"For what?" Jackson asked.

"Guess, Service Man. You were trained in all of this anyway, weren't you?" Harm stated with a surly curl to his lip. "We're going to fill it with water, too."

Jackson did know what they were doing. Sometimes with certain Shifts, water sharpened the skill, heightened the Talent. The Shift would be more prone to work with at least one of them submerged in water.

"That will be you, Jackson," Destroy said.

"You'll need to be in the water. We don't have anything to learn." As she said it, she waved her hand again and the dingy tub started to fill with water.

"We have something like this at the SHQ." Jackson's nervousness was making him chatter, "But this is a long way away from the Sense Dep tank."

"You won't think that once you're in it," Harm grinned. "Now, get in the tub." It was a harsh, dark command.

Jackson did as instructed. He stepped into the tub and sat down.

"Now lie back, relax." Destroy gave him the instruction with a coy yet chillingly childlike smirk.

"What are you going to do?" Jackson asked with his teeth clinking together. He was amazed at how cold the water was. Every inch of his skin felt hard. Ice formed in his veins. He started to shake. He started to convulse. He asked again, as best he could through an uncontrollable stutter, "W-w-w-what are you g-g-going t-to do?"

"We're already doing it," the twins stated in unison, their eyes whirling.

Jackson closed his eyes against the sickening image. His blindness amplified their voices which were sibilant, grating, just as terrifying. They chanted in words that were foreign, words that snaked into his ears and spread like acid vines through his skull. Forcing his eyes open again, Jackson found himself bound to a post, the islanders circling him and circling. He was accused and found guilty. He had interfered and he would be sacrificed. The chanting natives assured themselves of prosperity once the traitor was hurled from the mountain. And over the cliff he went, bracing himself to be dashed against jagged rocks.

The world went black then, frosted and drowning. Under water, blue spheres shot past him. Jackson realized he wasn't breathing. Instinctively trying to rectify that, he took a deep breath and all the water rushed in. It went down his throat into his lungs and stomach. It burned his insides and the blue souls became aggressive, swarming around him, stirring the waters and... bleeding.

More than freezing, more than drowning. He thrashed and thrashed, but that sent the water deeper and deeper into his lungs. And inside, his chest was burning.

Then everything became tart and metallic. Syrupy. He was covered in blood. Her blood. He tried to keep his mouth closed, but it clotted and forced its way into his mouth, thickly filling and stretching his lungs and stomach. Who was she? Who was she? Not Bright Star. Who?

Then Rush was there. His hands were wrapped around Jackson's arms, and he was pulling him up from the tub. Jackson sputtered and thrashed. He wiped at the blood that was now only water. When he could stand, he blinked water furiously from his eyes as he coughed and spit on the ground. "What the fuck did you do to me?" Jackson he yelled hoarsely at the two that were watching in horror.

Jackson went over and grabbed them both by the hair. He lifted them from the ground.

"Put them down, Jackson," Rush ordered. "They didn't know what they were doing."

"They knew *exactly* what they were doing, and you know it!"

"They didn't. But it doesn't matter anyway," Rush urged. "Just forget this and go back up to the house."

"How can I forget?" Jackson's eyes were haunted.

"I can help you," Rush offered softly.

"No!" Jackson barked. "There's been enough fucking with my head for one day! I'm done!"

Destroy and Harm laughed. They laughed so hard that their mouths distended and their jaws unhinged. Horrified, Jackson watched as they laughed more and dropped to the ground. They moved awkwardly. Destroy on her belly; Harm on his side. Jackson recoiled in horror.

Rush walked over to them and dropped to the ground beside their writhing, unnaturally coiling bodies. Immediately, they stilled, and for the first time, their eyes stopped squirming. They swallowed in unison. Rush kissed his fingertip and pressed it to each of their foreheads.

When he stood, they were both unconscious. Jackson noted that this was not a normal comatose state, either. No, their High Energy had been totally drained. They were complete vegetables, at least temporarily.

"You know what she's planning?" Jackson asked eyes riveted to the unconscious pair.

"I do," Rush answered. He looked back at the twins and they both disappeared into thin air. Then he walked to the house.

"It's ridiculous that after all this time, after everything, I need someone to save me," Jackson yelled after him.

"It's ridiculous, Jackson, that you're the only one who doesn't understand that no one needs saving. Not you, not Bright Star," Rush retorted. "No one."

He left his brother to think about that.

Chapter 19

Burning Mermaids

Jackson noticed immediately that the house was empty. Impossible not to. There were at least seventy-five people living inside the house and another hundred that lived encamped around the premises. But today, no one. And he knew what that meant.

He ran to the Monk's room. The temple, they had started calling it. He knew better than to believe that there was anything special about the place, however, Jackson needed all the help he could get. He needed to focus and find them before they did something irreversible this time. They hadn't seen Rush last night and Bright Star hadn't listened. She never listened. Rush wasn't going to save anyone this time. He'd said it and he meant it. They were all going to die.

Jackson knelt down before a gleaming yellow ball at the altar. He breathed deeply. In and out. In and out. He held his hands up in the air and closed his eyes. Gingerly he began feeling around in the air. It was a trick he'd learned in the Service. He'd use his whole body as a divining rod. He would find the strongest wave of Energy and follow it like a raveling thread until it lead him to that pulsing surge that could only mean Bright Star and the energy of the Followers feeding into her.

He worked at it and worked at it until everything went black. For a moment, he thought he was passing out, but no. There was a glimmer of wavering blue light, another and another. He had a faded sense of déjà vu.

* * * *

Bright Star pressed a kiss to each of their foreheads. And when she did, a thin, golden bubble of light surrounded them. They rose and floated out over the ocean, then plunged below. One after the other. One after the other. This way they would easily be able to follow each other to the depths, to the underlying cave. The one of blues and grays. The one where the water periodically rose to the top, consuming all space, leaving none for air or topside life.

Monk was the last to go. The first had been Point, of course. She could lead them anywhere, and she had refused to listen when he asked her to wait. But Monk, who had a charisma of his own, had waited. "This is the second time I've met you on the side of a cliff."

Bright Star smiled with a teasing dimple. "I know. But last time, I lost faith and you were there to restore it to me. This time, I will restore yours."

Monk swallowed. How did she know that he had been having doubts about their mission?

Before Bright Star could kiss his forehead, he interrupted, "You know he won't come this time."

Bright Star smiled and nodded. "He will." She leaned towards Monk again.

Monk backed away. "He won't."

"Monk," she intoned, focusing on him intently. "I won't let you lose your faith now."

Almost hysterically, Monk took a step away from the slight mental push and piped, "I haven't lost my faith, Bright Star. On the contrary, I believe more now than I ever have, because I know. I know. Do you understand? I *know*. He won't save me or any of them. And you will barely escape with your own life."

"I don't believe that," Bright Star declared. Even as she argued, she pushed him harder. "He will save us. He will come to believe in himself. He will recognize his responsibility. It would destroy him to allow innocents to die this way. He will save us, and he will save us all."

"No he won't," Monk countered forcefully. He reached out his hands as if to shake her, but instead he fisted them at his sides. Touching her would be folly for sure. "And I'm not going to do this. I refuse to betray him with you again."

Bright Star recoiled. Her face crunched into an ugly and menacing visage. She rose into the air. Her fingers curled into claws. "You will go, Monk. If you don't—"

"If I don't?" he challenged, finding the courage of certainty. She was stronger than he and the fear inside of him was palpable, but he found courage. "If you waste your Energy on me, who will say the Energy and Keep Time?"

Time. It had become one of the most important tenets of the Followers from the first time he'd used it. Without someone to keep time, Bright

Star would have burned that day in the ballroom. *Yes*, sardonically he thought, *time was all-important when cheating death*. If Rush was called into action too soon, he would save them before there was truly danger. There would be little effort and little Shift. If they called him too late, well, there would be no calling at all, they would all simply die. Keeping Time to ensure zero loss took all the Energy one could muster when dying. Bright Star knew it. Without him, she would have to be the Timekeeper, and she needed her strength.

"You will not come?" she asked finally.

"No," Monk answered and blinked wildly in his own amazement. It was the first time he had ever openly defied her. He gave silent thanks that no one else had witnessed it. He didn't know what she would do if she perceived that he threatened the faith of others. And, while his insolence was freeing, he knew it to be damning as well. His heart was still beating like bat wings in his chest. He stepped back from the edge of the cliff as she spun into a blue ball then lengthened like a spearhead and stabbed into the roiling gray waves. He turned his back to the ocean.

As his legs pumped wildly beneath him, he reached out with his mind. He called to Rush, the only time outside of Keeping Time when he had dared. But there was no answer. Rush was not listening. He didn't want to hear the sounds of their screams.

Monk stopped short. He just... stopped. He had almost made it to the bus. Almost. But he stopped. It hadn't even been a full-fledged vision. He didn't know if it had been supernatural at all. All he knew was that while the Followers still would not be saved, *Point* would not be saved, Bright Star would be. Maybe there was something he needed to do after all. Slowly, he turned around and headed back to the cliff, counting in his head.

Chapter 20

Bright Star's Children Are Dying

Directly, Rush had not interfered. Directly, he had left the entire order trapped below a half-mile stretch of craggy outcropping beneath the ocean. The protective bubbles Bright Star had given them burst with explosive force as she joined them in the water. But, Rush did not come. Instead, Monk had come. Monk, whose power was nothing in comparison to hers, thus inconsequential when compared to Rush's, had come back to save them. He stood in the same place she'd occupied on the cliff with his arms outstretched. He harnessed his High Energy and focused it on everyone below. Wildly, the Energy traveled beneath the water, searching for those souls. Fish had come to the surface working their slick mouths in hopes that the Energy would find them, but Monk continued.

One by one, the bodies started to emerge from the sea. One by one, they rose with their eyes closed and their hands folded over their chests. He had expected them to be bloated with water and grasping for life. Instead, they were surreal in their beauty, and they were all dead. Monk almost faltered, he did, as he saw them coming, one after the other, one after the other, and he realized that he had not saved anyone. A strange pain in his chest started, it pressed his lungs and his heart to the point where they were too small inside of him to support his life. But he didn't stop. Monk continued to bring the dead from the depths. It was only when he brought Bright Star forth, that he realized he had at least one save. And then, he reached for the last of them, and they all came forward, injured, nearly dead, but alive.

With Perma-Shift cracking his brain and organs into fifty million pieces, Monk brought all forty-seven back to the compound. The five survivors were sent to sleep in their rooms to recover. The forty-two that died lay face up, six feet in the air in a tidy six by seven levitating grid in the courtyard. A cloud hung over them and bathed them in cleansing waters. The ground opened up into forty-two plots beneath them and the grass lifted up to bind their bodies. Monk lowered them into the ground slowly and prayed as the earth sealed itself over them. Monk realized from his second ascent of that cliff that the only reason the Shift was not killing him was that Rush was sharing his burden. This was something he could never have achieved on his own. But only he knew that, and he would never, never tell the others.

He breathed a long and belabored sigh of relief when his task was completed. Then, he saw a vision of a soft, thin, pale, dark-haired angel and the darkness took him.

* * * *

This time they didn't all come back. Forty-seven had gone. Only five had returned. Besides Bright Star, there was Point, Destroy, Harm, and Mix. Bright Star had felt him waiting. He had waited and waited hoping that he could wait until they all perished beneath the sea. She had even felt Monk turning back to come for them, no, not to come for them, to ensure Rush's will was done. Still, to Bright Star, none of it had mattered. Forty-seven had gone and only five had come back. Bright Star thanked Rush she was in that number. He had proven how important she would be to securing the future.

Bright Star lay on her back in the center of her bed. Her room, which she liked drenched in light at all times, was dark. Her arms were spread straight out in right angles from her sides. Her legs were straight. Sweat made her whole body gleam an unhealthy white, even in the dark. Her hair was matted to her skull and her silken apple-green nightgown had turned forest with her perspiring. Pools of crimson blood, black in the night, collected beneath her fists as she dug her nails into the flesh of her palms.

Her eyes were open, but not blue. They were clear and dull. She shouldn't be able to see anything. But what she did see...

First was Myrto. Myrto had piercing blue eyes and red hair like her own. She'd been born to a family on a Greek island where hair like hers never resulted of natural circumstances. That's how she'd been recognized, even though she was barely eleven. Bright Star tried to picture Myrto's face but all she could see was ash, all she could feel, could smell was ash. Ash stung her eyes and made its way into her mouth. She squeezed even harder at her fists trying to allay the sense of horror. But she was not to find release.

Next was an image of Lila. Lila, dark and seductive, was calling to her from inexplicable blackness. Bright Star strove to find her but her efforts were in vain. She tossed in her bed. Somewhere her beautiful daughter was still trapped beneath rock and water, dying slowly even though her body had been buried. And then there was a vision of Deluge beckoning to her with water swollen limbs each time she closed her eyes. There was Sunrise and Sunset, the bound twins, whose souls had been led together into the sun; she had felt them drown, then burn. She felt them hurtling from the sky to the ground, dead again, dead forever this time. And then more, more, and even more of her children fading away.

When all of her children were slain again in her mind, she watched it over again, the images coming faster and faster making her scream uncontrollably in the night. "Jacob!"

* * * *

The slim, dark-haired girl walked into the Service Infirmary barely noticed. The body was clad in an ink-black sweater that looked soft as angora over a long flowing satin skirt the color of pitch. She wore soft leather boots that laced up her trim ankles and calves. She held a small, black change purse in one gloved hand, and as she marched through the halls smiling at the loud clacks her boots made on the floor, the sterile chlorine and lemon hospital smell filled her lungs and she started to whistle. It was late. There weren't many people in the hospital. The door had been locked when she'd arrived. It had even had these interesting electromagnetic strips on either side of the door meant to prevent the use of High Energy. She guessed it was past visiting hours. Good.

She arrived at the elevators and started to push the round button with the up arrow. Instead, she grinned a little. The girl's natural light blue eyes were flat and uninteresting. Not a single, telling, flicker of a glow. She held up a hand. Her palm faced the elevator door and she felt the slightest tingle in her palm which traveled all the way through to her shoulder. Presently, the up-button beamed bright green. And only moments later the elevator doors opened. She looked over her shoulder to see if she'd been spied. An elderly woman in a worn blue robe stood with a gleaming metal cane. Her ashen skin rippled in folds around her mouth as it quivered. The girl's lips pulled back from her teeth in a feral smile as her bright eyes trapped those of the older-looking woman. As fast as she could, the rickety woman skittered around the corner and the elevator door closed. The girl tittered as the silver box began to rise.

"That was unkind of you," she heard from the empty elevator.

"Go away, Jackson" she sneered. "I don't understand why you of all people can't see The Purpose."

"I will never see the purpose," he returned, then added, "Besides, I thought you were finished... you know... after." She focused on the fact that this stung. She crumpled a little against the chrome wall behind her.

"Stop looking through my eyes, brother," she answered in a soft, wilting voice. She was tired and in pain. She wanted to get rid of him but she knew that if he were to find enlightenment, if ever her Purpose were to be fulfilled, she was powerless to push him from her mind, so she waited until she could feel him withdrawing his presence. She started down the hallway of the intensive care unit.

A nurse in a white coat with red, green, and blue flowers printed on it stepped in front of her. "Do you know it's past visiting hours?" She asked.

"Yesss," was the response, barely more audible than a whisper. As she listened to the sound, the nurse's eyes rolled back as her head and body became heavy and she slid to the floor in a deep sleep. Was it sleep? Another nurse coming from a patient's room touched a hand to her throat as she tried to make sense of what she was seeing. When she turned to run, another soft whisper sailed on the air and kissed her hair. She, too, slipped to the ground.

The girl bit down on her lip, feeling a little tired, and marched forward until she found the room she was searching for. She pushed open the door and was more than perturbed. "Another one," she muttered and rolled her eyes.

The nurse's head snapped toward her. "What are you—"

"Join your friends."

The nurse slumped in the chair she'd been sitting in. Her hand was still folded over that of the unconscious patient she'd been tending.

The nurse didn't even have time to use the minimal amount of Talent she had. The girl noted the hands and smiled a little, thinking of his ability to seduce a woman, apparently even while he slept. Pride somehow took a close second to more hostile feelings. Her eyebrows crinkled and a small crease appeared between them. She was thinking of Point. She pursed her lips and blew out a little. Like a dried leaf in the autumn wind, the nurse's hand drifted over and off of her patient's. Satisfied, the girl neared the bed and leaned over it, resting her forearms on the side rails. She shook her head, wondering why he couldn't just wake up, get out of the bed and walk away with her. At any other time, he would.

After a moment of studying his perfect features: cleanly sheared black hair, long-lashed eyes, his dark, brown skin and aquiline nose, she straightened and laid her change purse down on the bed beside him. She understood why Point had refused to come.

Slowly, she pinched at her fingertips one by one to take off the glove on her right hand. She didn't want it to interfere. When the glove came off, she softly laid it on top of the little black purse. With measured control, she touched the hem of the sleeve of that same arm, and pulled until she tore the sleeve right from its seam. She laid that over her glove. Then, she lifted up her hand, palm out, like she had earlier. She closed her eyes and breathed in deeply until his scent was all she knew. She breathed in even deeper, using his scent as her vehicle to take him in. Then she felt him being drawn out of himself and into the core of her. She breathed in deeper, still feeling herself become light headed with her efforts as she took in as much as she could. And then she let her own power mingle with this foreign presence within her that made her cold as it drew from her the very heat that gave her life.

Bright Star gave as only a mother could give to her child. Then, with mounting power, the presence began to ball up into a hard, hot sphere in her chest. Warm tears trickled from her eyes as she tried to hold on and not let him take too much of her. Her body shook ferociously. Her head lolled back and she could see a pale blue light illuminating the ceiling. Finally, the ball began to move from her chest through her shoulder and down, pressing small through her elbow then wrist and out of her palm. It was only perceptible as a mild violet light glowing in her hand, though the power was immense. Then it floated through the air to land on the man's chest where it disappeared. She bent over him and laid her hand and arm across his chest as if to enhance her work through physical connection. Her arm was a slender white arc against his darkened complexion.

She felt faint. She was glad she was seated as her knees tingled and wobbled. Monk stirred beneath her. Bright Star yawned and rubbed her eyes, knowing it would take some time for her to regain her strength. How long was it 'til sunrise?

"Thank you," Monk said, smiling hesitantly as he opened his black eyes to her and sat up in the bed.

"Let's go," she ordered stonily.

"Ahhh," he said knowingly. "You're tired...and worried, yes?"

She turned away from him and waited as he donned the black jeans, T-shirt, and leather jacket hanging in his closet. He headed towards the door and she started after him. As soon as she stepped away from the bed, she heard her footsteps as they crunched down on gravel. Gravel? Ash, hard ash. She looked down, it was creeping up her leg; her boots were covered in it. It billowed in powdery puffs up to her thighs, her waist. She smelled burning flesh, her own burning flesh. She felt dizzy and clutched her head as she stumbled. She fell against Monk and began to quake uncontrollably. She stared up at him but only saw an exploding yellow ball in an impossibly white sky. Her breathing came in heavy, unchecked gasps.

"Rush won't like you taking someone else's body." Monk's brows furrowed in concern.

"I didn't," Bright Star smiled, shaking off the suggestion that had affected her so strongly. She motioned down towards herself. "This is mine."

Monk did not pursue her. Instead, he took a long moment to study her. This was the face, he thought. This was the one. He drank in the sight of her. He was unlikely to see this one again. "You shouldn't have bothered with the nurses and the elevator," he said with an apologetic grimace and fell into step just a pace behind her. "I wouldn't have taken so much of your High Energy if I didn't need it. You know it's impossible to stop until you're full."

"Imagine if you were dying and not just broken."

Monk narrowed his eyebrows at the subtle admonishment.

"It isn't that," she rasped and looked up at him.

Monk put his hands around her upper arms and stared hard into her eyes. For moments they stood that way. "When's the last time you ate?"

"I can't," she answered in barely more than a whisper.

"You can't?" She shook her head slowly. He brought her into his arms, holding her tightly. He thought of how rarely anyone touched her. He thought about who she once was. "Then tomorrow, tomorrow when the sun comes up..."

"Yes," she agreed as they left the room. They stepped into the elevator.

"You know now? You know that Rush is—"

"He's not!" she lashed out. An arc of blue fire slashed against him, searing his jacket.

"I wasn't going to say abandoning us," Monk assured her. He did not even put a hand to the flesh that had also been seared by the burst of temper. "Rush is fighting us. Harder than he ever has. You know why I couldn't heal myself. Why you can't eat. Why your leg won't heal. Why Ban and Myrto and the rest?" These were not questions and she didn't respond. "Because it is almost time." She turned intensely angry eyes upon him. Soon she would not be able to hold back the blue. "The time is almost here, Bright Star. You know it. And you know what he's doing and you know why he's doing it." A hand shot out fast in the night, a pale white flash against his skin. He didn't smile like so many other times. His expression only grew graver. There was a tick in his clenched jaw. Her angry brown brows ground together in frustration. "He's stronger than he has ever been. He's more determined to deny us than he has ever been. I can only wait for the last."

"I won't let you die," Bright Star whispered gravely. "*Rush* won't let you die. Not again."

"What will you do, Bright Star?" he asked her in a soft voice. She couldn't tell whether his tone was mournful or accusing. "What will you do, Burn?"

Chapter 21

Discere Vivendo

"You killed those people," Jackson's throat was sore, even as he accused. He felt as though he had been screaming for days. His voice was hoarse and pained. His muscles ached from the constant tension of grief, sorrow, and guilt. "I thought I knew you. You are my brother. I've always known you, but this... Oh my God, Rush. You *killed* them."

"I didn't," Rush retorted listlessly with an almost imperceptible shake of his head. Jackson had to strain to hear him. Rush was lying on his side on his bed. Even though he was fully clothed with shoes on, a blanket was drawn over him. His dark eyes were open and searching the endless sky with its setting sun out of the window. The frame and pane had stretched wide and gaping, offering both a panoramic and dismal view of a red and violet horizon. His hands were clasped together as if in prayer and pressed to his mouth. He shook violently as if a fierce chill overtook him.

"You did!" Jackson accused. He snatched at the blanket, and Rush didn't move. "You let them die. You knew what they were going to do and just like always, you *let* them do it. Then you just... you just let them die. How can you lie there? How can you live with it, live with knowing what you've done? How?"

"I didn't" Rush said again. His brother was broken. "Jackson," and Jackson heard what sounded like a bone-deep sigh. "I'll never be able to explain—"

"And that's not the worst part." Jackson forced the words out even as he felt the bile rising again in his mouth. Rush covered his eyes and face with his hands. He continued to lie on his side, looking out of the window. "That's not the worst of it, Rush. You brought *her* back. Why? Why not just end it all right then and there? Why not just let her die and end all this? God knows I couldn't have let her go, but you... Rush, please, please, God please. I'm begging you. Tell me why. Tell me how."

"I can't. I didn't let them die, Jackson," Rush rasped from behind his palms. "She did."

"Don't you blame her for this! Don't you dare blame her for this," And then his voice broke. "You had the power to save them. I couldn't. No one else could. You had the power to save them, all of them. People that we knew. People that cared about us. You could have saved them but you didn't."

"She didn't—"

"No, Rush, *you* didn't. *You* didn't."

"I'm not going to argue anymore. It's pointless. I know you won't forgive me."

"They won't forgive you, Rush. They're dead." Jackson said and found his knees collapsing under him. He reached out and steadied himself as he slid into a chair. "You let them die but you saved her."

"You can't understand what this feels like for me. You can't understand the guilt, the pain. They aren't inside of you the way they've crawled up inside of me. It's like someone opened me up and put hot bricks inside of me; like someone burned their faces into my brain. You don't see them every time you close your eyes."

"I don't. But you know what, Rush? I'm glad you do. I hope you see them forever."

The words were out before Jackson could stop them, even if he had wanted to. Rush's face seemed to crumple. His eyes darkened and he started to chew the inside of his cheek. Before Jackson left the room, Rush stopped him. "What if I had let her die?" he asked his brother.

"Doesn't matter. You didn't."

"But, what if I did? Would you forgive me?"

Jackson thought about it. Her face appeared. Her voice. Her will. He wouldn't answer the question. It didn't matter. "Don't make this about me. This time, I know it's not about me."

Jackson left the room, slamming the door behind him.

"I don't know if I can keep on with this. I don't know if I even want to live through this anymore."

"Shhh… Don't say that. He didn't know what he was saying to you. He just wanted to hurt you. He doesn't know that you're already suffering."

Rush didn't respond.

"You should have let me go," the dark haired girl whispered. She had been lying beside him for days and materialized there, still lying at his side. She reached up and stroked his brow with a feather light touch.

"He wouldn't have forgiven me." Rush told her. He lay on his back and stared at the ceiling.

"He won't forgive you for those people buried six feet below the ground in our backyard."

"I won't forgive myself for that." Rush answered her.

She was silent for a moment. Then she told him, "I know you won't. I see them, too, you know."

"I know," he answered, trying to shut out the souls for them both. He settled his arm over her shoulders as she nestled into his body.

"Do you think it's my fault, too?" she asked softly. He could barely hear her.

"No. I don't think you could have stopped her." And then, she started to cry. Large wet and hot drops fell from her eyes onto his chest. "You're warm," Rush told her. "Warm like you're real."

"Remember," Elizabeth told him with a shudder. "I'm not real."

"I'll remember," he promised before he squeezed her hard and began to shake with sobs.

* * * *

Three days later

"You're back," Jackson said dumbly as he found Monk standing in the kitchen holding a bottle of beer.

"Yep," was the flat reply. Monk cracked open the beer.

"You're having a beer?" Jackson asked Monk.

"Yep," he answered quickly. "And why in the hell wouldn't I have a beer? My doctor didn't say I couldn't have a beer." Then he mumbled under his breath, "as if *that* could stop me anyway."

"None of..." Jackson paused. "Well, none of the rest of them drink."

"You know," Monk started, handing Jackson the beer he'd opened and opening another for Rush who walked into the room. He opened a third for himself. "I don't know why they don't drink. It's not as if we are some strange religious cult."

Jackson raised a brow as he looked at the man who was draped in a white sheet with a yellow sash around it.

"Would you believe a toga party? No? How about: I didn't have any clean clothes?" Monk grinned. "Anyway, we were talking about drinking."

"Yes," Rush replied dryly as he eyed the "robes" Monk wore. The man looked like he'd just rolled out of bed dragging the sheets to cover himself while he had every intent of going back to the warmth waiting for him. In fact, he smiled to himself, that was exactly what Monk had done, even if he'd been wearing the honorary colors.

"Anyway," Monk continued, snubbing the all-seeing Rush. "Rush himself drinks a beer or two, so I really don't see anything wrong with it. Besides, what's the point of embracing life without... well... embracing life?"

"Here, here," Rush raised his beer in a mocking toast and took a sip. Jackson followed suit. Monk hitched up one sagging side of his sheet.

"So, I'm curious," Jackson began leaning against the counter. "How does one keep the faith when the savior cuts the ranks in half whenever the hell he wants to?"

Silence. No one had spoke of the dead in weeks. Now the words were out there, like poisonous darts shooting through the air in search of a target.

"One keeps the faith, Jackson, when one accepts that the path is what it is."

"So no free will in the Followers of Jacob Rush religion?"

Monk smiled benignly. "We are not a religion, and I believe whole-heartedly in free will. I also believe in human nature. We are who we are. We do what we do. There's only one path."

"Sounds like bullshit to me," Jackson mumbled. He looked over at his brother who had gone quiet. Then he turned back to the holy man. "What is the significance of the yellow?" Jackson asked.

"This?" Monk motioned to the sash at his waist.

"Yeah," Jackson returned. He looked over and noticed the hard set his brother's face had taken. Something had just put severe tension there. "Why not blue?" he pressed.

Monk looked over at Rush, always conscious of what the idol felt. "Why would it be blue?" the Monk returned.

Jackson thought about discarding the question. He didn't like the Monk's habit of answering a question with a question. Monk had told him many times that a holy man had to be properly Socratic. Instead, though, he thought about it. Why would he have assumed they would have chosen blue as their color? Ah.

"You are right, Monk," Jackson had conceded, though the Monk had not offered a verbal argument. "There is no reason for you to have chosen blue. It still doesn't explain the yellow. Rush isn't keen on yellow."

Rush gave a half-grin at that and took a swig of his beer.

Jackson was glad to see his brother relax. So was the self-proclaimed holy man.

"He's not self-proclaimed," Rush contradicted Jackson's mental note.

"Stop doing that!" Jackson yelled though there was no longer anger in his voice.

Rush laughed out loud this time. "Tell him, Monk. Jackson thinks of you as a self-proclaimed holy man."

"Oh hell no!" Monk answered. "I didn't proclaim anything. Bright Star and Point are at the bottom of this. They did it to me. You know me, Jacks. My name was Thaddeus. I was a physicist. A very, very bad physicist, mind you. I couldn't get beyond determinism... never mind. That's why I was in consulting and sales. I worked with Point who was then called Frankie Monnish."

"Frankie Monnish?" Jackson chuckled at the name. Something about that name and their severe, devout Point didn't mesh.

"Yeah. Anyway, we were at a conference rubbing elbows, pimping out our skills. When we decided to leave one night for a big celebratory dinner, Point decided not to go with us. She said we should enjoy ourselves but there were some loose ends to tie up with our newly won contract with a Department of Defense sub-contractor. So we left and had a grand old time. We didn't know that—" He swallowed. "We didn't know Point was very, very sick. She didn't go out with us that night because she had just found out she was dying from cancer compounded by a rare blood infection. She disappeared that evening."

It was difficult for Jackson to digest. Again he thought of the woman who was the field marshal of the group of Followers. She organized. She directed. She coordinated. She was the backbone for them: the leader of a movement. She was Bright Star's right hand and had probably been second most successful at bringing new Followers into the fold after Bright Star herself.

"Well," Monk went on. "The next time I saw Frankie, she wasn't Frankie Monnish. She was Point. At first, I thought she was a ghost. Not that she looked it. She looked great. Younger, more vibrant, happier. Still the same but so much more that I thought it had to be supernatural. And I had been so worried. She'd been gone for three days. I couldn't remember a time when I hadn't seen her or talked to her for three days since I met her. But then she was there. She came back and showed up in my apartment... and I was so happy—"

"You're in love with her?" Jackson uttered, awed.

"Yes," Monk said with a quick shake of his head as if to admonish Jackson for not noticing earlier.

"How does she feel about you?" Jackson asked, knowing that he would hear the sad truth. Point's devotion was unshakable, thus uncontested.

She ate, drank, breathed, lived to perpetuate this movement, to second Bright Star in her push to make Rush recognize his responsibility. There was nothing else in her life that she would put before that duty.

"I figure she must like me okay since she let me get her pregnant." Monk smiled wide, barely able to contain his happiness.

"Oh," was all Jackson could muster. Then, a flagging, "Congratulations."

"Just because she is devoted to that one…" Monk motioned to Rush. "Does not mean she can't love me or have desires other than forcing him to see the light."

Rush rolled his eyes. "And on that note…" Rush pushed himself away from the refrigerator and started out of the room.

Rush stopped in the doorway to offer what sounded like a damnably genuine, enthusiastic, "Congratulations to the both of you."

"He runs from me," Monk grinned. "I don't understand it. He doesn't like the Followers. Not one bit. And they show him the proper respect and deference. He doesn't like Bright Star and she has placed her soul beneath his feet. Me, I treat him like my next door neighbor, and he doesn't like me, either. But he likes you." He pointed at Jackson. "And that I'll never figure out."

Both brothers barked laughter at that outrageous statement. Monk had a way about him that made everyone laugh. He could release some of the tension by making them all, even Rush, take themselves a little less seriously. And yet, he always asked the profound questions, forcing them to think about their actions. Jackson could never see him as Thaddeus again. Not the good natured physicist. Not the man who could be turned into a violent beast just from exposure to an unimpressive, insubstantial pebble. He had always been Monk.

Jackson's smile settled, though, and he watched his brother. It had only been three months since the day the Followers died. In that time, their number had tripled in the compound which had also grown exponentially in the same amount of time. They all knew of the deaths. Jackson knew that they would all willingly die as well. It was a matter of Rush's will.

Bright Star's will, Rush's voice resonated from inside his head. Then, Jackson's brother left the room.

Chapter 22

Justice

Bright Star felt the horror before she heard it. It was a malicious, oily feeling that seemed to push its way down her throat. She sat up in bed and held her head in her hands. Her skin felt like it was eating her alive. She was freezing. She was on fire. Her brain was coming out of her skull. Something was terribly wrong.

She slowly, silently rolled from the bed to her feet. Not actually to her feet. They hurt in the mornings and the pressure worried her hip. Instead, she hovered just slightly above the ground, gliding across the room and through the door. She summoned gossamer white robes from the air that covered her, and a circlet to hold back her hair. She let High Energy guide her to the disturbance.

When Bright Star arrived at the source of the destruction, she cloaked herself. She needed to go unnoticed. Easing her way through the group with Shift and finesse, she neared the center of the crowd of Followers and lost her cloak as she stumbled in horror.

Pigs. There were growling, spitting wild boars snarling at each other, goring and biting each other. They circled and circled. Then, they went in. The male's jaws snapped like jagged vices over a neck, a front leg. The gashes, cavernous wounds spewing blood and serrated flesh, closed as quickly as they opened. Then the female moved in, trampling with hooves and holding the other down as her jaws snapped his throat, biting and rending its muzzle and ears.

The Followers stood back, gasping in surprise and clinging to each other. They didn't dare get in the center of the violent display. The animals would not be torn from their sport. They didn't attempt Shifts. Bright Star knew it wouldn't do any good. These two animals were more than capable of continuing this gruesome detail and holding off a Shift at the same time.

As she looked on, one of the pigs was tackled and rolled onto its back by the other. The pig scrambled to get up but before it could, its sister ripped open its abdomen. Ropy, slick intestines erupted from the belly, and a bloated, purple liver gushed fluid onto the floor,

Everything turned blue.

Bright Star shook. Her whole body began to quake and her teeth chattered angrily together with the force. The ligaments and tendons in her hands drew up until her fingers curled like claws. Her eyes, which had been itching, now stung intensely and she knew that the light from them was beaming stronger than it ever had. These ones did not deserve to be. These ones had rejected the gift they had been given. These ones gloried in the hurt; they were not transcended by it. These ones did not deserve... did not deserve... did not deserve. These ones could destroy all that she and the others had come to build. These ones would push Rush even farther away. She could feel her blood in her veins, every cell, atom, particle. *This is why he let the others die. This is why. I won't let it happen again, she thought.* These ones would *fuck... up... everything.* They did not deserve to be saved. They had not even deserved their first lives. They would not be saved again. This time, they would not be saved again.

The Followers felt the Energy. It crackled like electricity in the air. They could feel their hair standing on edge. They could feel a buzzing jarring their clenched teeth. The Energy was not being allowed to escape the room. Bright Star couldn't afford to let it out just yet. The Followers began to part the way for her. They slid into the periphery as she glided forward. But the spectacle did not end.

The twins changed back into human form. Their faces were mangled beyond recognition, though they had already started to heal. Harm's eyes and stomach had been *cut* open. Destroy's pretty nose was broken and her shoulder had been unhinged from its socket. Their bodies glistened with a pungent mixture of sweat, spit, bile and blood. But still, they repaired. Soon, before her eyes and those of the assembly, they were restored. They looked as they always looked. Dirty, pale, and frightening. Their eyes started to swirl.

Bright Star allowed the fury to well up within her. Her eyes blared blue and her hair began to whip around her head. The High Energy began causing the lights to flicker and the air to thicken.

She rubbed her hands together then put her palms over her eyes. When she removed them the whole room was washed in blue. Her voice rang deep and hollow, "You do not deserve his grace."

The pair broke apart and turned in unison to face her. "Bright Star?" Harm yelped, then winced as his split lips cracked and bled.

"You do not deserve his grace," the floating woman in white repeated. "He is not saving the world for you." Her hands started to rise from her sides. And though her palms were up, there was no appeal being made. Instead, there were small violet balls building in each until they burned blue and grew to the size of oranges.

"We know her. He might save us just because we do." Destroy countered with an irreverence born from a mix of desperation, repression and adolescent overconfidence.

Bright Star's burning blue eyes narrowed and her mouth fell open. "You don't know anything. He won't save you. He won't know and he won't see. He won't save you." Then, both of their necks snapped until their heads drooped against their backs like wilted lilies. They were dead before there was time for anyone to do anything about it.

It was in that moment that Rush appeared, floating just above the two bodies. In a full body sigh, he wilted to the floor and laid a hand on each fragile chest. There was nothing he could do. Bright Star had managed to blur what she was doing in space and time so it was difficult to pinpoint or act upon the situation until it was far too late.

"They didn't understand, my world," Bright Star offered hurriedly.

Quietly he stroked the hair from their battered faces until at least their countenances were repaired. "Finally you admit to deciding who should be saved and who should not, Bright Star? How can you be the judge over their souls?"

"I certainly do not presume to be that which you are." Bright Star's eyes widened. She was truly shocked at what he was implying. "I am hurt by what happened to our flock beneath the water. With every living breath I am hurt by it." She ducked her head in deference and apology. "Rush, I am trying to tell you that they were not like Destroy and Harm." Bright Star defended her actions. "Those two were destructive and bred nothing but ill-will among us all."

"They were children." Rush countered angrily though softly as he repaired their wire-thin, young bodies. At the end of his labor, they appeared as sleeping angels.

"They... They only used your power to increase their own in order to wreak even more havoc. Look at them, my world!" She gestured to their bodies. She hadn't paid attention to his work. But as she did, she found their wounds were gone. Their bodies had been cleaned and anointed. They lay there naked of clothing and free of discord. They appeared young and guileless. "It doesn't matter what they look like now," Bright Star shrieked. She began to weep. "It doesn't matter." She reached out a hand to touch Rush but found that he was forever out of reach.

"Who are you saving the world for, Bright Star?" Rush asked her finally. He knew she wouldn't answer.

He raised his hands and the children rose from the ground. Followers started forward and began wrapping the children together in white cloth.

Bright Star stared, horrified. Rush was having them buried as the other Followers had been buried. He was having their bodies treated with honor. After they were dressed, Rush started out of the room, the bodies followed, and the Followers fell in line with the grieving procession. The powerful suggestion Destroy and Harm had used to spark their interest had passed and they were now stricken with horror and pain.

Bright Star pushed ahead of them all and laid a hand to Rush's cheek. "Why do you care about them? Why do they inspire you to do what you were born to do? What is it about these two—two who don't deserve you—that make you care this way?"

"What is it about any of you?" Rush asked, then stepped through her, literally. The rest of the procession followed, all of them moving through her as she stood her ground calling to them. They could no longer hear nor see her. Rush had made her insubstantial.

Twenty-four hours later, Bright Star was still invisible to much of the household. Even when Point called out to her and stood queerly in the exactly same space she occupied, Bright Star did not try to contact her. She stood in the foyer her eyes still on the ballroom where the spectacle had taken place. In the hours she stood there, the room had changed. Now it was a temple. Though dark and cool, the room was filled with white and gold. The gold altar up front was unadorned. Bright Star slowly neared it, then knelt to meditate. Monk, who had watched the entire spectacle unfold, came to kneel beside her and hold her hand.

* * * *

"I haven't seen Bright Star all day," Jackson mentioned casually as he settled on the sofa in the back den. He had found Rush there watching television.

"She killed Destroy and Harm today," was the candid reply. "She snapped their little necks in two and they died. They are buried in the backyard with the group from Tuesday."

Jackson sucked in a deep breath. He didn't know how to process this. He didn't know what to feel. Those people gambled with death every day of their existences. Anything to get Rush's attention. But even when Rush had failed to save them all from drowning at the bottom of the ocean, Jackson had not believed his brother to be so affected. Granted, he was sitting on the sofa eating nachos and watching television, but that in and of itself spelled trouble. Jackson couldn't remember the last time he'd seen his brother watch television. For that matter, Rush had what could only be considered as a cultivated or contrived demeanor. He was hiding how he truly felt about the deaths of these two. Then there was his choice of words.

"Destroy and Harm, Rush," Jackson retorted with a quick and dismissive sneer. He opted for incredulity. "They probably thought it would be funny to prolong the Shift longer than necessary or to tamper with Keeping Time." God, did he know their practices so well that they just came out of his mouth as if they were normal? "They probably—"

"Do you know how many gruesome acts, how much destruction, death and pain she's brought to our house? And it's like we've just gotten used to it. It's like it's okay in this house to mutilate, torture, murder another soul." Rush stopped him. "She killed them on purpose. She fogged up the Energy so that I couldn't pinpoint where she was or her intent immediately. She's never done that before, so I wasn't expecting it. Just that alone told me that she was up to something. She killed them."

Jackson swallowed. That was murder. Maybe he had been unclear about what to call the other incidents, but this was not unclear. Bright Star had committed murder. He didn't understand. Even as his stomach churned, he could only reach out to defend her. "They've done nothing but intimidate, sabotage, create distrust. They were evil."

Rush winced as he turned to his brother. "It's not up to you to decide that, just as much as it was not up to her."

"Tell me that they weren't."

"They were kids," Rush answered. But he didn't argue with Jackson's assessment. They both knew the twins had been angry and destructive. They had been destined from birth to inflict cruelty and violence on themselves and others. But where Jackson may call them evil, Rush had to ask himself what the difference was between them and Bright Star. She led people to their deaths every day.

Not to die. Her voice was stamped into his mind. It cut like a flashlight through the dark. *I don't want any of them to die.*

Rush ignored the voice. Impossible to acknowledge when it had been such an incredible lie. If she thought the deaths would bring him around, she would use them. She killed two people, and somehow, she had prevented Rush from intervening. She killed two people.

"Jackson, get out," Rush ordered with a lethal edge to his tone.

"What?" Jackson asked even as he stood looking around the room.

"Jackson get out, now," Rush ordered again. Jackson left the room briskly, wondering if that had been his own will or a powerful suggestion.

My world, I said nothing when you allowed your Followers to drown beneath the ocean.

They aren't mine and I didn't put them there, Rush thought though his throat began to close and the pain between his shoulder blades became more pronounced.

And yet, you agonized over it. If you could have saved someone's life and you chose not to, did you not murder them just the same?

"You led them there!" Rush roared. "You convinced them to endanger themselves."

Bright Star materialized quickly before him. "I didn't convince them, my world. You did."

"I didn't!"

"You did!" her voice went higher as she argued. Her eyes lit up the entire room. "Without their faith in you, the faith you have given them, without that would they have gone to the bottom of the sea with me? I am merely a Follower."

Frustration pulsing through him, Rush contested, "You are not a Follower Bright Star, and what you have done is unforgivable."

Her eyes went dim. Instead of hovering, she stood before him. She was still. "What do you mean?"

"I mean that what you've done has changed everything. You are right. Me allowing people to die could be considered the same as you murdering Destroy and Harm."

Bright Star nodded warily.

"I'm already damned."

"No!" A sharp protest bubbled from her lips.

"I'm already damned so I can forget saving my soul or anyone else's." The words were uttered calmly but they meant something profound. The gauntlet had been thrown and Rush knew that his anger, his proclamation could easily be ushering in the doom he had sought to avoid.

She reached out her hands and fisted them in his shirt. "You can't do this."

"It's done," he replied with a shrug of his shoulders.

"You can't!" she gasped, and leaned up to press her lips firmly to his.

With broad hands, he forcefully pushed her away. Her bad leg gave and her hip connected painfully with the edge of a table. Rush vanished and left no Energy trail behind for her to follow. Quickly, she lifted herself into the air and sped from the room. She had to find Point.

* * * *

"Jackson, what I have to say to you is very important."

Jackson didn't argue. He just sat down in one of the four chairs in the small gray room. There were no windows and… no door. They were inside a Shift.

"Amazing," Jackson whistled. He had been able to maintain a place inside of a Shift before, but it had been the size of a small closet, completely non-descript and had lasted for less than ten seconds. The Spartan quality of the room identified it as a Shift, however, he knew it to be a major feat.

"It won't last very long," Rush told him. "And this is the only way we will be able to talk safely."

That sharpened Jackson's wits. There was something Rush had to tell him. Whatever it was was of utmost importance.

"Bright Star will destroy you, Jackson,"

"Is that it?" Jackson asked incredulously.

Rush hurled a loosely formed Energy ball at the wall. Nothing happened. Like just absorbed like. "You have to promise that you will stay as far away from her as possible."

"Rush, you should know better than anyone," Jackson stated deadly serious, "I can't be hurt."

"Not physically, no," Rush agreed. "But there are other ways, and she won't hesitate to use them."

Jackson did nothing to deny the implication that Bright Star had the ability or capacity to hurt him emotionally. "She has no interest in me," was his bitter counter.

"She has an interest in everything I care about!" Rush returned in a frustrated shout. It wasn't what Jackson wanted to hear. He knew that his and Bright Star's relationship was only a bi-product of her relationship with Rush. "You have to be able to take care of everything after. You have to be steady and sane the way you have always been steady and sane. This thing is about to come to a head and I have to be able to depend on you. Stay away from her, I'm begging you."

Then the Shift ended and they were back in Jackson's bedroom

"Then why do you let her continue to do this? Why not let her die like you let the others die?"

Rush balled up his fist and with all of his physical strength he slammed that fist into Jackson's jaw. His brother staggered, but that was it. He was stunned, and he stayed stunned longer than he felt the effects of the blow. He had only felt the sharp sting, then the pain was gone. But, though he no longer felt the pain, he felt a release. Something inside of him swelled, then popped and he had swung at Rush before he knew it. Rush jumped back in time to avoid the blow. But Jackson, in a smooth movement, lowered his shoulder and rammed his brother in the stomach, taking him down to the ground. Once Rush was on his back, Jackson drew back his fist to hit him, but found that he could not. As much as he struggled to bring his fist down, he couldn't hit him.

"Let him go!" Rush boomed, his voice carrying down the hall.

Immediately, Jackson felt the grip on his arm release. As soon as it did, Rush put his palms flat against Jackson's chest and pushed him over. He followed with a swift roll to raise his hand and punch Jackson again.

"You can't hurt me!" Jackson yelled as he grabbed his brother by the throat and rolled over on top of him.

Then Rush went still. He just lay there beneath Jackson's hands. Jackson's rage took a moment to subside. It took a moment for what was happening to register. There was no pulse under his fingers. Shocked eyes fell to his brother's face which had gone pasty in pallor.

A great wail went up in the walls and everywhere around him, in him, Jackson felt pain. It made his lungs and heart seize. It knocked him over until his mouth came open and he tried to wretch but found that nothing would come out. He had never, even when his parents died, felt the level of grief he felt at that one distinct moment. He rolled from side to side, holding his eyes and willing the sob to come out, but it never did.

And then, just as quickly, the suggestion lifted. It lifted from the whole house until even the walls and ceilings sagged in relief. Rush wasn't dead.

Jackson's brother stood up and looked down at him. "Bright Star can hurt you."

Chapter 23

Anguish; Pall

The grieving wouldn't stop.

Black flags hung from every window. Every hall, every room went dim. The walls were damp and rapidly darkening with mildew. The air was stale and sour. Bowed heads. Hunched bodies in black cloaks shuffled silently through the halls. Usually in groups, the Followers cleaved to each other, giving support even as they struggled to make it from dusk to dawn. Sometimes, they would pass each other, acknowledge the red rimmed eyes, then feel their chapped cheeks stinging with new tears. Their hearts were broken, and they grieved without denial, without nuance, without pride.

The anguish bled into the world beyond the compound. The air outside for miles was both cold and heavy. It lodged like ice in the lungs. The sky was worn gray splotched with sooty clouds. The streets were lethargic with cars moving in slow processions. Bars, coffee shops, newsstands, subway cars, arenas even: silent. Silent. Silent. As if speech was a vulgar and unforgivable sacrilege. All of this, all of this even though the Followers knew, the *cosmos* knew, that in truth Rush was not dead.

Jackson felt it. A dull thud made his ribs too tight and too delicate to stop his lungs and heart from bursting out. His whole chest was sore from it. He hadn't slept soundly in what felt like months. Every time he'd tried those first couple of days had just ended in him waking up to sheets that were dripping wet with perspiration. He was also aware that he had been sobbing uncontrollably. His throat was always dry and he found himself swallowing convulsively. His eyes always burned. They burned until moisture collected in the corners and spilled down his cheeks.

In his waking hours, Jackson hadn't had the energy to report to the Service. His only desire had been to stare out of the window from his bed and watch the black clouds' slow roll. When he didn't report, they'd sent some men around to evaluate him. They had always monitored him closely. This change in his behavior would definitely put them on alert. Before, Jackson had not considered their perpetual presence and perpetual studies as invasive. Now, he hated them. He hated that they did not understand Shift any more than he could. He hated the humiliation he felt at their inability to truly comprehend the context of their own questions. He hated their limitations and the fact that they would never understand what was happening around them. Uncharacteristically and with anger, Jackson had used a Shift beyond any they'd known—one he wouldn't have thought possible before the last few months—to ensure that their report would be satisfactory. He'd never used his Talents on those from the Service before. This time, he just didn't care. He couldn't go back. The pain wouldn't let him.

Instead, he spent most of his time out of bed wandering aimlessly through the labyrinth halls of his home. Jackson noticed the change in the environment. The entire compound which had usually been sunny and warm appeared to have been washed in gray. Everything looked dull and neglected, listless. Sometimes there was no color. Jackson considered that it may have been some collective and subconscious Shift, but he hadn't cared enough to investigate the phenomena. It suited his mood.

* * * *

Rush had not intended for his Shift to have such a profound effect on this household. He had only wanted to show his brother the danger. Instead, he could not move through his own home without someone falling to their knees and clasping him around the waist. The extreme relief was in their eyes. It was in their words. It was in the strength of their holds and they worked both physically and psychically to hold him close, to reassure themselves that he had not been lost.

He still could not get used to the way they continuously reached out to him, even in their subconscious, just to be certain that he was there. Alive. Well. Alive.

Rush hadn't wanted that, but here it was. He'd been trying to prove a point to his baby brother. It didn't take him long to decide that the motive had not been worth the residual effects. He didn't want this. God knew he didn't want this.

"If you don't want this," Jackson interrupted Rush's reverie as he sat at the kitchen table. "If you truly don't want this world that has been created for you, then you know all you have to do is tell them to leave. All you have to do is tell them to stop killing themselves every day just to gain your notice, and they will do it. Rush, why won't you do the small thing that could end this?"

"He can't," Monk answered for him as he entered the room. Rush rolled his eyes. "He can't. If he tells us to leave, if he gives such a... a... lofty edict, then he has to accept his power."

Rush was silent save for a ragged sigh of frustration. Jackson contemplated Monk's words. Both of the brothers recognized the wisdom they held.

"Where is Bright Star?" Jackson asked.

Monk and Rush exchanged a glance, the meaning of which Jackson could not begin to guess. Jackson was surprised at the realization that he had not seen Bright Star for more than a month. Not since that day.

* * * *

Bright Star sat in the chair next to the window in the dark room illuminated only by the light of the moon. She held four large, shiny silver coins in her hands. She tried to maintain the silent uninterrupted peace of the night but could not. She found she could not arrest the cough that started deep in her chest though she clamped her mouth shut and squeezed her arms in closer to her body to control it. When the attack subsided and she'd wiped hot tears from her bloodless cheek, she held her palm open, focusing on the glow of the coins. As she concentrated, the cicadas and the crickets came to life outside her window. She could hear all sorts of things crushing brittle leaves and twigs as they rushed through her woods. The lights flashed on, then off again. She couldn't stop the spillover of energy no matter how hard she tried to focus. The crease in her brow sharpened and sweat beaded in the small of her back and at her temples. The tears slipped out again, even hotter.

The coins wobbled in her palm until they became precariously balanced on their sides. She sucked in her breath, ignoring the light's incessant flicker. She sucked in her upper lip, catching it in her front teeth. The coins then started to roll against her skin, circling the upraised hand. Her brow relaxed only slightly as she watched the coins orbit her hand only lightly brushing her skin. And as she watched the quarters moved slower and made indentations in her flesh as they circled. Then they turned even slower as they bore even deeper into her skin, leaving redness in their wake. The coins made four identical trails of blood on her hand. Her hold on her lip tightened as she watched in horror as those same trails paled, then disappeared as if she had never been cut.

She barely noticed the door opening and a shadow quickly enveloping her room, even usurping the moonlight. The coins fell to the ground.

Blood evaporated before it dripped from her raised hand and her lips. Vacant eyes found bright ones in the night.

"Everything I do is tainted with her. Everything. Look at my hand. She's stalking me. Even when I am vulnerable, quiet, she is ruthless and stalks me." Jackson blinked at her. "Jackson, don't you see, I die when he is not with me. I die. She finds a way to be with him. She's killing me."

"Who?"

"Elizabeth," she answered in a plaintive whisper.

And though he could feel Bright Star fading away, his heart finally found resolution, and though he had never met her, he wanted Elizabeth back. He wanted to see her, to touch her, to stop her from hurting Bright Star.

He came to her side and knelt down. He lifted her slight weight and laid her gently on the bed. Then he took her hand in his and pressed her palm to his lips. Lovingly, he bestowed kisses on each crimson path cutting her lifeline, her love line, and restored each one of them. Finally, he just held her hand in both of his and looked down at it. He raised his gaze to hers.

Her skin was tinged with yellow. Her bones pushed violently against her flesh, giving her the look of a thinly veiled skeleton. She was all teeth and brittle bone; a skull perched on caving shoulders. Jackson could not deny that death lie beside her in the bed stroking cold unto her brow. He couldn't help it. He couldn't stop himself. He called for Rush as he always had.

Suddenly, he looked up. A sound. A sound that couldn't convince him that it was a sound. Jackson knew it came from within him. And then again that sound. He felt the hand in his hand grow rigid and looked down at Bright Star. She had heard, too. The bones in her face squeezed to wrinkle the skin above her brows. She jerked on her bed and he realized that she was sliding off it. She crumpled on the floor in front of him like a discarded dress and wrapped her arms around her head as she rocked back and forth like timorous child.

The laughter in Rush's voice startled Jackson. His eyes moved from the fragile Bright Star to locate the voice.

Rush was perched in the window. He was smiling and somehow his wide, strong mouth had stretched even wider as he bore his teeth in a horrific smile.

"Bright Star, you're back," Rush stated plainly.

"Understatement," she replied with her brows drawn together. The bravado was undercut by the moisture in her stark blue eyes and the way she had slipped to floor.

Rush hopped off of the sill and to the ground. He neared the bed, brown eyes turned golden. He stopped at the rocking heap on the floor before him. Bright Star had not moved from the ground.

He reached out a hand to smooth Bright Star's hair. Bright Star shrank back, still covering her eyes. Laughter bubbled up from deep within Rush, then erupted like a geyser. He laughed so hard he wrapped his arms around his waist and fell backwards on the ground. He kicked his feet and thrashed violently on the floor. Then, abruptly, he stopped laughing and rose. He stood soberly then let her body hang in the air before them. Closed, immobile, his mouth seemed all the more threatening.

"You understand now," Bright Star said to him. "You are the savior."

"Savior?" he questioned softly. "Savior?" He raised his hands from his sides and rose higher into the air. "I am no one's savior." Rush frowned. "I am no one."

"Why do you fight it so much?" The question came in a broken voice. Bright Star's blue gaze lit Rush's face.

"I'm not fighting for anything more than the right to be left alone," Rush told her.

"It's not that simple, Rush, and you know it." Her words, while strong, cracked with her wavering voice. "You can't be left alone. You have a duty."

"I don't," Rush snapped. He raked his hands over his face. "I don't have a duty. I don't have a responsibility."

Bright Star opened her mouth to respond. She closed it again as she considered her next words carefully. "Rush, you have a gift. But this gift is not yours alone. It was given to the world through you. *You* were given to the world. Your power was not meant to be squandered or neglected. It was meant to be used and used for all of our benefits. Your gift surpasses any other's ability. Your gift was meant to shift, change, sculpt, and remake the world. Your gift was meant to save the world. That is your destiny. No denial you make will ever change that. You will save the world and accepting that could save even more lives."

"No, Bright Star," Rush returned. "I will tell you what can save lives. Lives can be saved if you would just ask those people to stop hurting themselves and everyone around them. You can ask them to stop putting themselves in harm's way. Lives can be saved if you just give up this precognitive conjecture. You have to save them. I won't warn you again."

Chapter 24

Maternal Instinct

The pressure was going to kill him.

Jackson sat at his desk with his hands pressed over his eyes. They couldn't go on this way. Not one more day. Not one more minute did he think he could live in that house perpetually being stalked by death. Each moment was a waiting game now to find out how many more Followers would move into their home. What new way would Bright Star use to demand Rush's attention while Jackson hurt each time he saw her and the continual pain she faced. She hadn't tried in months. But that couldn't last.

The pressure was going to kill him.

That morning when he had decided to come back to the SHQ, he witnessed Dr. Randall Sandoval in the observatory talking quietly with the two attendants. He'd greeted them as always, but unlike any other time, he noticed the thin strips of yellow fabric tied around each of their wrists, including Sandoval's. He'd seen it before. He couldn't believe that he was seeing it then.

Followers.

He was speechless. He retreated. He had no answers.

Jackson thought of his mother. He thought of the tape that he had played so many times. That last one she had filmed just for him. For the first time, he considered the fact she had not made such a gesture for Rush. But then, she hadn't had to, had she? Janie would have known that Rush would be able to keep her close to him in a much more significant way.

He thought about not pushing the button, but like every other time in his life when he had been lost, he pushed it anyway. He could feel the familiar tightening in his chest, the swelling at the back of his throat when he saw her. She was smiling, but she still looked sick as all hell. Janie Smothers-Rush. His mother, their mother.

Her curly brown hair hung limp and damp around her face. She swatted at it many times, but it still managed to affix itself to her cheeks and forehead.

The tape started in the middle. It always did. Their dad had been trying to tape something else and ended up clipping the first part. He'd been sorry. He'd apologized profusely. Janie and Jackson had forgiven him for it. "My miracle boy," Janie said, smiling wide. "I didn't know you were coming, didn't even know I could have another child, but I was so happy when I found out about you. Of course, I worried about your father, how he was going to take it. And I worried about Jacob. But I wanted you desperately. I guess I knew that you were going to be special. Remember, there's no surprising me," she kidded. "Well, baby, when it was time for you to come, I was at home with Jacob and no one was answering the phone. Not your dad, not your aunt, not Grampa Ned. No one. So I had to dress your brother, buckle him up and drive us both to the hospital.

"Your brother was so quiet, so calm. It's like he knew, too, that you were going to be special. He was just waiting for you patiently." She paused to take a ragged breath and lie back against her pillows for a moment. Only a moment. Shortly after, she leaned forward again and continued, "When we got to the hospital, the nurses took Jacob away and left me into that awful white room where we were supposed to get ready for you.

"Jack, baby, I barely showed when I had you. You were a tiny, tiny, still thing inside me. I fretted for months and months because I thought something was wrong with you. The doctors wouldn't tell me anything. I think they just saw my… my history, and figured that I couldn't be trusted with any information. They didn't even talk to me. They would only go outside with your Dad and whisper. Sometimes I tried to talk to him, but it made me so tired. But that isn't important. He would always come back in and tell me there was nothing to worry about. I never pressed him. I didn't believe anything could be wrong with my perfect boy."

Jackson could feel the tears starting in his eyes. He was a grown man. He had seen this film so many times before. It wasn't even the last of his mother's video letters, but it was the one he watched every single day he came to work. Never at home because he just didn't know how Rush would react if he ever saw him watching these films. Still, it was bringing tears to his eyes as if it had been the first time.

And in that instant, he thought of Bright Star. She and his mother were so alike and yet so different. They both were devoted to the men in their lives. Janie had been devoted to her miracle boy and so was Bright Star. Bright Star fought for what she believed in no matter what anyone had to say. Bright Star would fight for death, but Jackson knew she would fight for life just as hard.

Jackson wiped his eyes and continued to listen to his mother.

"When it was time for you to come, the doctors just kept shaking their heads. They kept saying you were not helping them. You didn't want to come out. They thought you were going to die, baby. They thought you wouldn't be strong enough. Can you believe that?" She grinned directly at him. "You of all babies. The strongest and most fearless little boy there ever was, and they thought you weren't going to make it.

"I was at my wits' end, you know. Your Dad wouldn't come in the room. He just couldn't take it. He couldn't."

Always an excuse for him, Jackson thought bitterly as he did every time.

"I remember thinking then that if I couldn't have you, then I didn't want to go on living, either." She looked away from the camera. She was embarrassed to admit it. Jackson could never believe that she had. Not when her mental stability had been called into question so very many times. "Then, your brother was there. My little, sad black-haired boy was there. He was screaming as the nurses tried to shoo him away. But he came back. He came back and he hugged me and laid his little cheek and little hand against my stomach. I thought the nurses would stop him, but no, they seemed frozen in shock. He closed his eyes and I knew he felt the same way I did. He didn't want to go on either if you didn't make it.

"But then, sweetie, I felt your tiny body move. Right there inside of me you moved. You moved, and you kicked, and you fought your way out. I remember hearing you cry that first time. I knew any baby who could cry like that would have to have the very healthiest lungs ever. You were only two pounds six ounces when you were born, Jack, but God, you were healthier than any little baby they'd ever seen…"

And she kept talking. But, Jackson was no longer listening. It was unnecessary anyway. He knew each of her next words. What mattered more was that now he knew what those words truly meant. He knew.

* * * *

Jackson swiped his badge against the reader, waited for the light to turn yellow, then spoke a complicated series of letters, numbers, and whole words in three distinctly different, non-derivative languages. He also exerted a controlled amount of High Energy. The light turned green and he opened the door. When he stepped inside the decon cell, short bursts of air puffed at him for 90 full seconds. Then sound waves bounced against him. He could almost hear the very low tones. Then, an inner door opened.

Chapter 25

Sense Dep

Unlike when Destroy and Harm submerged him, Jackson was prepared this time.

Breathing is the most difficult part. First, you have to psych yourself up to even get into the tube. Even though the warm pink jelly is comforting and womb like, the thought of what you have to do makes it almost impossible to get in. Then you have go under. Most guys, even after years in the service, have to be forced under with the sliding lid. It closes over the head, then presses down several inches until all air is one hundred percent displaced. Either breathe in the gel, or panic and die. That first breath of the gelatin makes you swipe at your nose. It gets in your throat and you try to cough but opening your mouth just lets more in. You convulse and bend and snap. You swirl and flail in the near liquid, though your movements seem lethargic and fruitless.

Then you want to die. It's what happens at the start. *Kill me.* That's what the next thought is after you learn to breathe. You want to die immediately. No one knows why or how the depression sets in so quickly, but you want to die. You think about the times when your heart fills for no reason. Like when you're at a stop sign just waiting for the mercy of someone in through traffic to grant you grace. Save your life. And there is eye contact. Quick and serious. Eye contact. And there is a pressing of the brakes that you can't see, but you can feel even before the car begins to slow. She is going to let you pass when she doesn't have to. She is a comrade. She is a grantor of an extended and beautified life. Your heart is stupidly filled. *Whomp!* Stupidly filled. You go back to the idea of breathing and you think that you want to stop breathing. You can't.

Once you start to breathe you can never stop until the squids come. They lie on your chest and spread electrical tentacles. Your chest gets sore as they suck the will to die from within you. They are not squid for everyone. Sometimes they are octopi spiders, leeches, diamond mines and vacuum cleaners. A heart and tubes that sprout from it, stretching and seeking the heart that is nothing without them. The crying is next. Always crying. You still want to die. And you do know why, but you don't know why. You have family. A mother a father and a brother who is dead to you. Dead as he has been given away. He's an orphan... no, he is a soldier sacrifice. The parents give the strong over to the fight. He must protect. He is the placenta that was never ejected from the mother's body and still calls to the child. Then rational thought comes. Sensory Deprivation is an über placebo. No one needs to die. Delirium doesn't need to set in. Five times three is fifteen again. *Envy Defy Envy Defy*. Bionic moving parts and her wet sex. Stupid filled heart. Stupid filled dick. High Energy. Shift. Skateboards eating souls. Free in the street Death will come for you. Stick in her. That's it. Oh God. Oh God. He wants to die again. I want to die again. Sense Dep. Sense Dep. Sense Dep. Sense Dep. Sense Dep.

Black.

Black.

Black.

Primordial. Stamen Pistol. Liver Heart. You understand organ. Organ. You want to get to your liver. You want to look at it from when it is bright burgundy, until it is dark rust blood dead. You want to slice into it and see if it looks the same all the way through. You want to eat it and watch what happens in your opened chest.

Black
Black
Red
Green
Blue
Yellow
Blue
Yellow
Blue

Faulty wiring, the phrase that pays. Ionic. Corinthian. Doric. Doric and Athena. Elements discovered. Heavy viscous. Summer leaves will still die. 36R 4L 12R. Stop me. Kiss the ball. Side pocket. Fly me. Fly me. What more do you want, mother? Why do your eyes come out of your head and follow me home. I'll put them back in. I swear I will. I am seeing red. It is hazy and green.

Have to find it. I know where it is. You have to go with it. No? Then you must die. Never an easier choice.

Precocial. Thunder shakes the room every day, but today the thunder recognizes her. He knows her and knows that she has to come back. He gives her an ultimatum: come back or die.

Bright Star is there in his dream. She is wearing the feathers and palm fronds of a daughter of Destruction. The flowers, leaves and vines curling around her lush, cream white body. She dances for him and she chants. Her song is about Destruction as Creation. Her song is about Guard and how he cannot be lost to her. Her song is about protection and rebirth. Her song is about delivery.

She lowers herself into his lap and wraps long, lithe legs around his hips. The feathered headdress brushes his forehead as she leans toward him. Her body presses to his. She wants to tell him something.

Bright Star blesses Jackson by leaning in even closer until her lips are against his ear. She begins to whisper to him. The words are soft like petals as they brush the inner skin.

It is a narration:

> *You will never know who his father is. We don't even know who his mother was before she gave birth to him. She has no parents. She has no childhood. She has no last name. She is a blank before Rush.*
>
> *When Jacob Rush is born, there is nothing so eventful as torrential rain, lightning, or thunder. His mother does not strain during her pregnancy and she does not strain during the final moments of it. When he is delivered into the world, she is permeated with calm. But it is not only hers. There is a calm that has never been before. An inhale and a sigh that ends a far-reaching suffocation. A worldly suffocation. Not deadly... amniotic. He—Jacob Rush—already belongs to the world.*
>
> *Janie—who never imagined that she would be alone at seventeen with a baby to care for—is trapped in a smoke cloud of despair and responsibility. She wants to love him. She needs to love him, because he is all that she has and she is all that he has.*
>
> *She wants to love him. She does. But every time she looks at him the black-eyed baby looks back at her and she is frightened. Jacob never cries. His eyes just follow her. Janie imagines that he is waiting. He is hoping that one day she will lift him and hold him to her just because*

she wants to and no other reason.

But she can't, and she wonders—not for the first time—what this thing is inside of her that prevents her from being normal, from picking up her baby and loving him like normal. Janie has never been normal. It is why Jacob's father sought her out.

Each day after he is old enough, Janie picks him up from day care. The place is around the corner from the market where she works. Day care is a necessity. That fact helps Janie to feel better about not paying. She can't afford it, but the nice lady who keeps Jacob doesn't know it. She thinks that Janie is the first of the working mothers to pay her every week. Like clockwork, or so she believes.

Janie hates the powers. Not because they make her different, not because she doesn't fully understand them, but because they make her sick. Each time she uses them, she gets pains in her head and saliva pools in her mouth. Her stomach cramps and she wants to vomit. The pain is worse, stronger every time. She starts to double over with it curling into a tight ball on the floor for hours. Janie is a good girl and she doesn't use them for bad reasons. She doesn't know why it still hurts her so much.

It is at the market that she meets Jackson's father. She doesn't remember meeting him, but then, she rarely looks at the people she waits on. She also goes out of her way not to touch them. Janie doesn't like touching people because sometimes her tightly controlled powers break free anyway with the right stimulus. There is just never any telling. Physical contact always gives her visions of their lives and deepest innermost thoughts. Nine times out of ten they walk around functioning every day with an impossible, near unbearable guilt. There is happiness, there is excitement, there is boredom, but there is nothing more powerful than the guilt. And Janie always wants to help them. It's not a desire, it's a need. And whenever she helps, she knows it may kill her. But she does when she can and then, the sickness would come.

With Jackson's father, she feels none of those things.

The first time he touches her, albeit accidentally, she draws back quickly. Startled, she folds her hands together and waits with head bowed for him to place his money on the counter. He does so slowly. She takes it and places his change on the counter as well. He leaves the store. It isn't until he is long gone that she notices she doesn't feel sick. Then she notices that her contact with him does not bring unwanted visions or insight into his psyche. He doesn't make her feel... anything.

He continues to come into the store and always waits in her line. She still isn't sure what he looks like because she can't bring herself to look at him directly. She does know his hands. They are large with broad knuckles and sturdy fingers. They are strong, strong hands.

In three month's time, Janie Rush is her new name. Everett has also wanted to change the boy's name to help eradicate what came before. All anyone has to do is look at Jacob to know that he does not belong to Everett. A fact that Everett himself never forgets. But he still insists on the name change, and the boy with black eyes agrees.

Jacob becomes obsessed with his new name. He says it over and over again. He wants more than to commit it to memory. He wants to commit it to nature. He wants it to become a part of him. No one but Janie knows how much in those early years Jacob wants to belong to Everett. The desire burns in him like acid every day.

He has never asked who is father is, and there has been no sadness about him. Quiet, yes, sadness no. He just doesn't seem to care. But then comes Everett. He's tall and broad and strong and quiet. He's so quiet that Jacob can think of nothing that symbolizes strength more. He strives to be quiet. He strives to quiet his Energy. He strives to control and to blend and to avoid and to fade into the background. A tiger that slinks into the dark recesses of a cage waiting for the fool who one day opens it. He strives to be tall and strong and quiet like Everett. He strives to instill fear with the merest glance like Everett can. To be a man with no Talent other than an uncanny cruelty that intimidated and cowed everyone in its path. No one knows how Rush idolizes him. Another thing he has learned from Everett. No one should ever know what you covet, admire or love. That is as clear as a written and notarized list of the things that can hurt you. He will never admit to anyone the influence that man has over his life.

It is more than simple irony when the grade school kids start to call him Rush. He has been so proud of his name, a gift from Everett, that it becomes his name, and "Jacob" is but a fading star. Everett's family, his mother and aunts and sisters, all of the women who craved a boy for so long, call this one Rush as well. Rush.

And as Bright Star whispered the name, it was as if a rush of air came with it and caused goose bumps to race up Jackson's arms.

He had to get out of the tank. His eyes struggled to come open, but the thick hardened gel wouldn't allow it. He tried to move his arms, but the electrodes and the chemical in his bloodstream wouldn't allow that either.

Jackson didn't permit for more than ten seconds of frustration before he centered his High Energy and caused the water molecules in the tank to expand so quickly that they burst it wide open, flooding the small, dark room. Jackson sat up and brushed his hands quickly over his eyes, nose, and mouth. With a wave of his hands, he was dry, clothed, and ready to go home.

* * * *

"Have you seen my brother?" Rush questioned Point.

The woman who never possessed the audacity to look him in the eye or speak to him directly shook her head.

"Let me rephrase the question. I know what your Talents are, Point. Do you know where my brother is?"

"I… I…" She couldn't get any words out, but she didn't need to. Rush could tell from a quick mental scan that she had not been able to locate his brother either, though she had tried. His face squeezed taut as he tried to untangle the puzzle. Jackson was a strong, Talented Shifter but he did not possess the skill to hide himself from Rush. Rush left her to whatever she was doing and went to seek out Monk. He wouldn't ask Bright Star.

"Monk," Rush barked.

Monk jumped in his seat then pulled off the headphones that had been perched on his head all evening. "Yes, Rush?"

"Have you seen my brother?"

"No," Monk returned. Then for a moment, he thought. "You can't locate him?"

Rush rolled his eyes. "If I could, would I be asking you?"

"Well," Monk smirked, "I wouldn't presume to—"

"You would, and shut up," Rush commanded, irritated. He had always had a bond to his brother. He always knew if he was well or unwell. They were always connected. For the first time in his or Jackson's life, that connection had been broken yesterday.

The last thing he remembered feeling was a great sense of sorrow. He usually felt this when Jackson was at work or anywhere thinking about their mother. And then, that sorrow had seemed to triple to the point where his own heart had started pounding. Then his brother was gone. Just like that. Rush didn't know where Jackson was and he couldn't find him.

Jackson had been gone for four days when he appeared on the front doorstep.

"Where the hell have you been?" Rush roared, stepping into his brother's path.

Jackson didn't answer. Instead, he brushed past Rush and headed to the stairs.

"Answer me!" Rush demanded following.

For two clicks, Jackson didn't answer. He paused on the steps and took two breaths. "Sense Dep," Jackson answered and continued up the stairs.

"That explains four hours," Rush gritted more calm now that his brother was responding to him. He started up the stairs after Jackson. "What about the other ninety-two?"

"I was in Sense Dep for four days."

"What?" Rush whispered. That was impossible. People had been documented to start eating their own flesh after being in the Service Sense Dep after six hours. It was little more than an inescapable torture chamber. "They wouldn't have let you."

"They didn't have a choice," Jackson returned with a yawn and a shrug. He continued up toward his room. "I masked myself when I went in. I kept them out. I didn't give a fuck so I controlled it. For four days. I barely thought I had it in me. Got the idea from those two little bastards, God rest their souls." His voice was wry and cruel.

"You—"

"Learned that from Bright Star," Jackson answered the question before it was posed.

Chapter 26

Parameters of Shift 101

"Why would you have gone in there for that long? What the Hell were you thinking?" Rush questioned his brother with pinched brows. Jackson had slept for two days straight. And even in his dreams, Rush had been unable to penetrate his thoughts, though he tried. When he'd awakened, he went directly down into the kitchen and eaten everything he could find. He'd never been so hungry.

He stood when Rush entered. Felt himself squaring off against his brother. Rush was angry. Jackson was angry.

Jackson said nothing. Instead he gave his brother a long and lethal look. There was a hardness to the gaze that dared Rush to comment on it. It dared him to do anything. Jackson didn't just seem ready to pounce. The Energy rolled like steam or heat waves off of his body into the room.

Emitting.

Undirected High Energy.

It was transparent and only visible in that it warped the very air supporting it.

"Jackson, you're emitting," Rush stated. His words were quiet and measured with little fluctuation in tone. He put his hands up in a declaration of peace.

"Am I?" The words were clear and even. They were menacing.

Parameters of Shift 101: To emit meant to leak concentrated levels of High Energy subconsciously. Emission was as uncontrollable as it was rare. High Energy was not meant to be built and stored. It needed an outlet. It needed to be used. If Jackson didn't use it soon, he would get sick from it.

"You don't have anything to say?" Rush asked his brother quietly.

Jackson grinned unpleasantly. His expression could only be described as insulting. He was daring Rush again.

Rush's eyebrows were raised. His warm face went a dark and splotchy red in the jaw. His neck seemed to darken as well. He gritted his teeth. But then, then he did something he hadn't yet done: he looked at his brother.

Jackson, always hearty and hale and bursting with an optimistic confidence appeared starved and feral. He looked how Violence looked at birth.

Rush considered this, and qualified it. Jackson seemed taller. He had shed some added weight to make his already strong body lean and predatory. His hair was darker though still tipped in dirty blond. His skin had taken on a darker tan.

His eyes were brown.

Rush didn't know how. But Jackson, somehow... Somehow, his brother who had only seemed to be his brother in his heart... Jackson had started to look like him.

"You knew, didn't you?" The voice was deeper, too. Rush had missed the gravelly bass tone before.

"Knew what?" Rush asked.

"Don't play dumb, Jacob," Jackson spat with venom as he called his brother's given name. "You could read my mind. You can see into the future and in the past. You probably already knew this conversation was going to happen. You can take this whole scene away from me if you want to. If it doesn't go to your satisfaction."

Bright Star put her head around the door and looked at them both. Her eyes seemed to widen and blaze when she looked at Jackson. Her mouth lolled open. Sensing the tension, she came in and stood just to the side and back of Rush.

Jackson gritted his teeth.

"I wouldn't do that," Rush mumbled.

"What was that?" Jackson asked with edge.

Rush took a step back. "I wouldn't take your memories away from you again. I shouldn't have done it to begin with, but I thought... I thought..."

"Rush, I know what you thought," Jackson interrupted. "You thought that if anyone found out about you then you would have to go through what I went through. You would be poked and prodded from birth. You would have scientists babysit you—"

"You were a very happy little boy," Rush countered quietly. "You were happy."

Jackson contradicted him outright. "I was alone in this world and you didn't care."

That sounded more like the brother Rush knew. He sighed and took a step forward. "Jackson, grow up and be a little less dramatic," Rush snapped, losing his patience. "You were never alone. I was there. But more importantly, Mom and Dad were always there for you. You were their pride and joy. It's not as if you suffered—"

"So is that what this is all about?" Jackson demanded, his voice rising in pitch. "It's all about the fact that I got their attention when you didn't. They didn't care enough about you to share their love?" The edge was gone and the voice broke. "Is that why you hate me?"

Rush's eyes narrowed. This wasn't making any sense. He tried to slip into Jackson's mind as he always did. He was in for another shock. He could not get into Jackson's mind! Rush couldn't understand any of it. But there wasn't time. He wouldn't think about that. He challenged him gently, "I don't hate you, Jackson. I have never hated you. It didn't matter that Mom and Dad didn't shower all of that attention on me. I wouldn't have been comfortable with it. Besides, what attention they gave you was half what you gave me. You have always been my best friend. You know I don't hate you. Tell me what's wrong."

"Read... my... fucking... mind," Jackson bit out angrily.

One of Rush's eyes blinked, just one. Then, he turned his face away. "Okay," he said finally, then proceeded to try again to do as his brother asked. This time it worked. Rush wasn't foolish enough not to know that this time he only entered his brother's mind by invitation. His eyes widened. His mouth opened but he didn't say anything. He took a defensive step back but found himself pressed against Bright Star. God, he'd forgotten she was there. He immediately separated himself from her again and tried to think of a way for her to avoid witnessing what was coming next. He could send her away, but that would only make her more determined to return and he didn't know if that would be effective.

"*Parameters of Shift 101*," Jackson started without regard for their uninvited guest. "It's one of the first things you learn. What you can and can't do. Who you can and can't be."

Rush could feel her behind him. She was stepping closer. Her ears were straining. Her whole being was compressed and tight like a box spring as she waited anxiously to find out what had caused the discord between the brothers. And what was worse: the High Energy Jackson was still emitting was beginning to reach out to her like air tentacles. The waves caressed her body and disappeared inside of her. Rush held up a hand, palm out, in front of him. The waves started to divert themselves into him.

"Jackson," Rush breathed. "Let's not do this now."

Jackson ignored him, "Stupid of me for never questioning it. I mean, why would I trust that they knew everything there was to know about Shift if I, the Precocial, was a blaring anomaly? But, brother, we know that there are no anomalies."

Rush started to say something then thought better of it. Instead he ran his hands over his face, gave his brother one last glance, and left the room. Jackson hadn't expected that, was surprised really. What didn't surprise him, though, was that Bright Star followed this brother almost immediately out of the room. But as she tripped along behind Jackson, she stole peeps at him over her shoulder. It was almost as if she couldn't help it. She just couldn't seem to keep her eyes off him. If he were any other man…

* * * *

Jackson walked out as well, following them. Following that pair of light cobalt beams. He stopped her in the hallway. "Bright Star," he called.

She turned with a curious look on her face. She had never regarded him with more interest than she did in that moment.

"You understand leakage probably better than anyone."

"Don't do this, Jackson," Rush was nearly begging his brother.

"Energy," she corrected him patiently while smiling invitingly. Rush's hand came out to circle her upper arm, but she didn't seem to heed the warning in that gesture. She didn't even turn away from him to look at his brother.

"The residual affects a powerful shift has on those involved," Jackson offered as a truce. His voice lowered again. Even to his own ears it sounded alluring. "It's not like the excess returning to the Shifter with Perma-Shift. It's like a mist that sinks in to all around."

Bright Star nodded, her succulent lips still slightly parted. Soon Jackson couldn't see her because Rush was standing in front of her again.

"You don't know what you're doing," he pleaded with Jackson. The emotions he usually guarded were open to his brother. There were dark smudges under his eyes and dark grooves in his cheek. His chin and jaw were covered in thick stubble. He looked tired.

"Then make me stop," Jackson smirked, knowing that his brother was too guilty to do any such thing. Aware that Bright Star was still listening intently, he spoke loudly enough for her to hear him and hear him well, "Imagine what kind of affects that could have on a baby."

Even though he couldn't see her, a faint blue was creeping up behind Rush's shoulder. Bright Star was a smart woman. She was getting the picture.

"Imagine if it were an unborn baby that was being saved. A baby with a parent that secretly had High Energy of her own. A baby that one day would have High Energy of his own, that gets the process jumpstarted because his big brother saves his life while he is still in the womb."

Jackson did not look directly at Rush. He knew the pain there would only make him immediately regret what he had just said, what he had just done. He didn't have to avert his gaze for long. Rush vanished. He just went away.

Bright Star's eyes ignited. Her mouth fell open again and the word "*Precocial*" escaped from it. She said it again and again. "Precocial." Her eyes widened and rinsed the room in an azure glow. Rush had known. Jackson had found out only days ago. Now she knew. She had only ever needed one Follower. Only one, and Jackson had ensured that she knew it.

"That is beautiful," she uttered reverently.

Upon hearing those words, Jackson started to shake his head. "Whatever you are thinking, Bright Star, please know that this is a battle you can *not* possibly win."

She left Jackson there in the hallway, then. She had many, many things to do in preparation. Many things to do.

I will kill you. I will find a way, and I will kill you, Rush's voice was so clear and beautiful in her mind that she forgot momentarily her purpose. It came back to her in full force. She continued on her path.

I have always accepted that I might die, was her unashamed response.

Chapter 27

Shattering

Jackson spent the entire next week in his room. He stared incessantly at the poster of the Milky Way that Rush had given him just last year. He thought about how quickly he had become nothing.

Jackson had lived every moment in his life up until the last two years as a special force, as the center of someone's universe. Whether it had been his mother or the folks at the Service, he had always been treated with reverence. But what the hell did he know about reverence? He winced at the thought. He'd been a fool. Their home, a veritable urban palace now, was overgrown with Rush devotees who foolishly scurried for chairs to sit in when he was around because they knew he didn't like them kneeling. They took his brother's clothing and separated it so that each person received a garment to wash. Rush had been near explosion when he found his favorite t-shirt folded and tucked neatly beneath Destroy's pillow.

And Bright Star. She had gone back to referring to Rush as "my world." No, Jackson's world had been some different dimension altogether. It couldn't be possible that Jackson had known what being the center of attention was like.

Jackson recognized his jealousy for what it was. He'd learned to do that in the sensory deprivation chamber. He'd learned to accept all things about him that were true. The facts that he absolutely loved his brother and hated him just a little were now clear. Jackson swallowed. He was thirsty.

In the kitchen, Jackson found a beer with his name marked on it. Literally. It did little to cheer him. Monk must have left it. As if anyone would have taken the beer. He drank it in one long draught. Then he heard Bright Star. His body tightened. He pinpointed her in the house. Her breathing was slow and deep. Her chest was rising up and down, up and down, up and down. She turned over. She turned again. She drew her knees up beneath her until her hands fisted in her sheets and her bottom was in the air. She turned again, this time on her back with a forearm flung over her eyes.

Jackson concentrated for two seconds, and he was there. He didn't even feel the smallest twinge of Perma-Shift. Yet another thing that had changed since he'd gone into Sense Dep.

Jackson appeared on the edge of the bed, his back to her. He felt her move, heard a rustle, then a sigh. Then, warmth stole across his back. He hazarded a glance. Her dark pink lips were parted over white teeth. He could see her red tongue nestled behind them. Her white arm lay across her eyes. Her hair scorched it in a wild fall. A sheet caressed her naked back and thighs. Her bare feet were exposed to view. Small, round toes stroked the bed, then rested. Her breathing was heavy.

Jackson leaned down to press his face close to hers. His lips brushed softly across her silken hair. Her scent was ethereal. He imagined she smelled as Circe had smelled. Beautiful. Undeniable. Disastrous. With lips nestled close to her ear, the words that had haunted him, rattling around in his head for as many months as he had known her slipped from within him to snake their way inside of her, "I hate you."

Jackson stood up. He walked away. He was satisfied that she hadn't heard him. Still, he wanted the words to permeate, to hurt. He wanted her to feel pain. He wanted to be the cause of the pain. He didn't look back. He turned out the light… and was bathed in blue. He stopped.

Flicker.

Flicker.

He turned back. Her eyes were open and radiating; her eyelids flickered as if she were trying to wake but was unable to manage it.

He stood, caught in what had become a tractor beam. He found his way back to her. He stared down and her eyes were wide, but dazed.

Flicker.

Flicker.

Her perfect lips fell open. "Rush," she whispered thickly. Jackson closed his eyes as he stood before her. She thought he was Rush. She wanted Rush.

"Rush," the name was whispered again like an incantation.

Jackson kept his eyes closed against the site of her. He worked his High Energy into a ball that would hopefully propel him from this room, from a cooling Hell. He jumped at the feel of soft hands against his abdomen, a delicate finger delving into his navel and swirling to create an immediate tightening below.

"Rush," she whispered again. Her hands reaching around his hips, drawing him down, down, until he was kneeling on the bed with a knee on either side of her hips. She rolled onto her back and looked up. For a moment, her eyes seemed to focus. Twin beams of royal light piercing Jackson's pupils. He blamed it on panic, on an adrenal and sexual panic. His mind left his body, a body that, in a blink of an eye, had become different, a replica of another's with a face that was stolen as well.

"Rush," she crooned, the word a curse on her lips.

Jackson stretched his stolen body out to lay over her. Her body was trapped between his legs. Her ethereal face with its fine features was cradled within his thick forearms. For a moment, he just studied her. He had wanted her since she had been an orb of light in a puddle of darkening scarlet blood.

"Rush," she cursed him again.

To silence her, Jackson dipped his head and pressed his lips to hers. He was instantly plunged into darkness as the bright eyes closed and mercifully allowed in the darkness of night. Her lips opened to him and the soft, wet inside was too much of an enticement. Jackson slipped his tongue inside, tasting her. She tasted like light. The light poured into him as he sampled, pressing its way through his body, collecting inside him until he believed it would burst out of him. He needed to be closer. He needed to be *inside*. He lowered his weight all the way onto her and squeezed his eyes shut at the exquisite feel of her plump breasts pressed into his chest. Her puckered nipples pricked him as they demanded. He reached between them with one hand and cupped one of the globes, flicking the starved peak with his thumb.

His lips scored her forehead and cheeks. He sucked in one petite earlobe then traced the shell of her ear with his tongue. A soft whimper escaped her lips and her eyes started to open. Quickly, Jackson brushed his lips over them, commanding them to remain shut. If she would just keep them shut… just keep them shut… he would not need to persist in his deception.

He slid down her pliant body, his kisses now adoring her throat. He was encouraged by her soft, warm hands at his nape, and playing over the muscles in his arm and back. Those hands lingered on him, reveling in the way his body felt. They were encouraging him as he lapped at her hot, softly scented skin.

He worked his way down her throat and over her collarbone. He paused for a moment to savor the sight of her extraordinarily pale breasts with the dark circles and large nipples. Her breasts were large and firm and he could feel the tightening in his body just at the first touch. He held them in his hands then pressed them against his cheeks. Lowering his body down to hers—between her parted legs—he held her breasts as he licked their undersides and skimmed his tongue over their peaks. He heard her moan and felt shame but not enough to overtake the primitive male satisfaction at wringing that sound from her. He took one of the stiff nubs into his mouth as he rolled the other between his thumb and forefinger. Beneath him, her legs slid further open and her pelvis tilted up until her sex was against his abdomen. She was drenched. Jackson could feel the cool moisture on his skin. He bit his lower lip and stilled himself. He had to pace himself or he would be finished before he started.

Recognizing he couldn't spend the time on her breasts that he wanted, Jackson continued to kiss his way down her softly rounded belly, pausing to dip his tongue into her navel. She let out a quick yelp and Jackson raised his head, praying that her eyes were still closed. They were. He went back to kissing her until he found the neatly trimmed patch of silken red hair. Below it, he could see her cleft. It was already glistening for him. He licked the cleft. Her body went stiff all over, but her eyes still did not open. He inserted one long finger into her, and her breathing went ragged. He sucked hard and explored with his fingers until a primitive grunt was wrenched from deep within her. Her legs began to quiver; then her entire body began to quake. Her ankles flexed against his shoulders, her toes balled tight against his back. Her feminine mist seeped out against his tongue.

Her legs opened and opened wide. They opened wider as her knees bent and her ankles hooked on the edge of either side of the bed. She arched her back as well so that her head was tilted back and her breasts were offered up to him. She would grant him access to every part of her body.

He squeezed tight to hold off the explosion just waiting to be unleashed. He pressed his head into her glistening cleft. He grimaced with the pleasure of how tight and hot her sex was. Slowly, painstakingly, he eased into her, deeper and deeper. He ground his teeth into the inside of his jaw, fighting the urge to pummel her with his body. The control he exerted was causing sweat to collect on his chin and nose as he strained above her. The perspiration bathed her face and neck and she rubbed it into her skin as if she were being anointed. She let her hands travel to her

Grayson Reyes-Cole

breasts. She touched his chest, then touched her own, rubbing his sweat in there as well. Jackson let out an anguished sigh and slammed into her welcoming heat. Only to find that it wasn't so welcoming. He plowed through the barrier until he was sheathed to the hilt. What should have been pain for her, instead, produced another bone-deep bout of shaking. This time every shudder, every contraction lavished him, milking him until he exploded inside of her. It was an accident.

Jackson had not intended to go this far. He had never intended to spill inside of her. But he had. And it had been wonderful. But he wasn't satisfied. He wasn't done. He was still rock hard inside her and the come from both of them mixed to lubricate and manifest an electric glide. His hips moved in and out, his thick erection moved with unnatural speed with only the most pleasurable friction. She brought her legs up until he grasped the underside of her knees in each hand and pressed them to the sides of her chest. Her body was tilted up to him and vulnerable.

The next stroke ripped a yelp from his throat. He rolled his hips again. This time, the sound came from her. And then, his strokes came faster and deeper until he was wheezing sharply in the night and she sounded as if she were sobbing.

"It's so good," she cried, "so good." When his head dipped down to bite at one nipple then the other, she shrieked. "Please! Please! Please!"

And she did not say his name, but Jackson knew that she knew him, that he was not Rush in her eyes, but Jackson. He dropped one of her legs, to loop his arm under the small of her back to position her for his final earth-shattering thrust. Demanding a kiss, his mouth over hers, he ingested the scream torn from her throat while muffling his own. She returned his kiss then pulled away to nip at his chin. Jackson collapsed on top of her.

Chapter 28

Warning

His chest was on fire. Jackson shot up. His eyes popped open and he found himself gasping for air. One hand clawed at his throat, which felt swollen shut. He could not get oxygen into his lungs. The burning in his chest started to spread to the other parts of his body. His muscles strained. He lashed out, pounding the wall in desperation. That was when he caught sight of Rush and went still.

Rush stood at the edge of the bed with his arms hanging loosely at his sides. His black eyes were intense and unblinking as he watched Jackson. His nostrils were flared. His lips were pressed into an unwavering line. His jaw ticked and ticked again.

It was then that the obstruction in Jackson's throat vanished and he was wracked with coughs. He gulped in air as he rolled, quickly covering his naked body in his sheets. They were damp and still clinging with perspiration. He put up a hand to shield his eyes from the daylight that pierced the blinds. "Rush, what are you doing?" he rasped.

"I would think that was obvious," Rush responded without emotion. Jackson started to cough again.

Jackson massaged his throat with his hand as he continued to cough. "You did this?" he asked in disbelief. Rush did not respond. "But why? Why Rush? What did I—" And then he knew. Every detail came back to him. Every one. He could still smell her on his own body. His body went hot again and his face colored a mottled red from embarrassment. Rush knew, too.

"Yes, Jackson," Rush spoke finally. "That is the question, I think. What did you do?"

"I—I don't know what you mean," Jackson sputtered, amazed that he would lie. Rush already knew. He already knew. That's why he was there. And even if he didn't know before, he could easily peer into Jackson's mind to find out. Rush slipped in and out of his mind with the ease of a permanently invited visitor. There was no point in lying. And yet, he couldn't admit to it, either. He couldn't confess to the betrayal and the depth of that betrayal.

Images of hands came to his mind. His own hands Shifted to look like Rush's. Dark hands grasping soft, creamy flesh. Long fingers flicking her dark rose nipples. Jackson wanted to vomit. Even there in the face of his brother's discovery, even when faced with what he had done, he could feel himself hardening at just the thought of the experience. Rush's eyes were still on him and Jackson was certain, again, that his brother knew exactly what was happening to him.

Rush's hands fisted, defining the veins in his forearms. Still, though Jackson had been sure it was coming, Rush did not call him on the untruth. Instead he stated plainly: "I have never been with her."

Any other day, Jackson would have challenged his brother's words. He had seen them together and he knew that no matter what Rush said, there was a connection between he and Bright Star. And no one could ever deny Bright Star's invariable devotion to his brother. It was why he felt the near unbearable weight of guilt. If Bright Star and Rush did not have that connection, then this would not have been such an unforgivable betrayal. He would not feel like the traitor he was. But Jackson would not challenge his brother's words on this day. He couldn't bring himself to increase the tension in the room. There was no denying that Rush spoke the truth. The blood he'd found had been no suggestion. His head hurt.

"Why are you telling me this?" Jackson asked and for a moment, guiltily, he wanted to believe his brother was telling him that what he'd done was okay. But he wasn't. The stone-faced expression could barely contain the strong emotion simmering beneath the surface. Jackson only wished he could know which emotion his brother was working so hard to hide. He tried reading Rush's eyes but could not. Instead, he found himself averting his haunted, conflicted gaze from Rush's mesmerizing one.

"I wouldn't have been with her even if I wanted to, and I didn't. You will never understand it, Jackson. Never. But—and listen to me carefully—I do not want her."

That, Jackson found impossible to believe. How could any man living not want her? She was pure beauty and unadulterated devotion. Physically, she was undeniable. Emotionally, well, no woman could love a man or commit herself to him in the way Bright Star had committed herself to Rush. Every man wanted that. *Jackson* wanted that.

Rush shook his head slowly. Jackson couldn't help but believe Rush was contradicting his thoughts. And then—it was sudden, so sudden—Jackson realized what that emotion was. It wasn't anger, as he had feared. It was worse. The emotion was pain. "You don't know what you've done—what you've almost done. You have no idea." Those last words were barely more than a broken whisper.

"I didn't—" Jackson cut himself off. There was no point in denying it. Rush knew.

"You didn't even think to ask yourself why she allowed it. You didn't even take one second to find out why she would do it," Rush walked over to the window and peered out.

"You think she made me do this? With Shift?"

"Don't be a fucking idiot, Jackson!" Rush growled. Then his voice softened again, "We both know it wouldn't take Shift to get you to do what you did. Oh, she would have used it if she had to, but she didn't have to. But have you asked yourself? Have you stopped for one single fucking minute to ask yourself?" Rush was screaming and his eyes were glistening, "Why Jackson? You spent all that time in the iso tank figuring out everything. Why are conveniently not understanding this? Why would she have done it?"

Jackson was embarrassed. He tucked his chin to his chest and looked at the floor. He moistened his dry lips with his tongue before he spoke. He had questioned, but he had gotten an answer and accepted it outright. "She thought I was you."

"She knows me. Whether I like it or not, she knows me. She knows me better than anyone, including you. *Including* you, Jackson. She knows every nuance. She knows the sound of my voice. She knows my smell. She knows my Energy. I'm asking you again, why didn't you take one second to wonder why she let you do it?"

"I did!" Jackson fired back, "I told you I—"

"You're not stupid." Rush snapped. His words were sharp but he didn't even mildly raise his voice. "But you wouldn't question it too strongly when you were getting something you wanted for so long."

"What?" Jackson did not understand why he pretended shock. More ingrained than anything. He did not actively try to deceive Rush. No. He actively deceived himself.

"Jackson, you know you can't hide anything from me. You know you can't lie to me. What you don't know is what you've done," Rush admonished as he faced his brother again. His expression had softened. It could have been called mild. "I know your feelings for Bright Star, but they will only bring you misery. You have no idea why she did what she did. And it never occurred to you to ask. Even after you went AWOL in Sense Dep. Even after finding out the truth about Mom, me, and yourself. You didn't figure out why she was doing it. Bright Star is studied, organized, disciplined. She is thoughtful, observant, and she plans. But, above all else—and I say this without ego—she lives and dies for me. She never, never would have made that mistake. I told you, she knows me. You chose to ignore what you knew to be true."

"Well obviously," Jackson countered defensively. "Obviously she was upset with you and the fact that you won't listen to her. And, she needed... she needed..."

Rush did not say anything. There was a look in his eyes. It was like a fire suddenly extinguished. There was no need. He had told Jackson not to try to lie to him. "Jackson why does everyone know it but you? Even after what you experienced in Sense Dep: *Your love can't save her,*" Rush told him baldly. Rush ran a hand over his face. When his eyes were visible again, Jackson could identify the full-on pity in them.

Anger broke like a wave in Jackson's chest. His brows drew together. He wanted to lash out but his nakedness and the undeniable truth of his brother's words kept him in the bed. Dragging his blanket with him, he swung his legs over the side and reached for some jeans lying on the floor. He snatched them on. "No. My love can't save her. It's obvious. The only thing or person that can save her is you!" He pointed his finger accusingly at his brother and breathed heavily as he stared into those dark eyes.

Rush didn't answer. Instead he walked over to his brother and placed his hands on his shoulders. He stared into Jackson's soul. Jackson tried to turn away but found that he could not. Rush held him captive. When he spoke again, his voice was deep and clear and devoid of emotion. "Jackson, your love can't save her. I can't save her, either. No one can save her and in this moment—you won't believe me, I know—she should not be saved. But I can save you. I *will* save you. And I will save—*fuck.* You don't know what you almost did. It would have been the wrong—" Rush bit off his words with a snarl. He jabbed a finger at his brother. "Leave her alone! I've corrected the wrong that was done today. Leave her alone."

Corrected? Jackson thought. "She only thinks of you," Jackson whispered finally.

Rush lost his patience and flung his hand out wide, shattering the windows in the room with Shift. The crash was loud and the glass exploded inward toward them. But before the shards even reached their skin, the glass stopped in midair, then reversed. Each and every shard returned to the place it had been originally and the windows looked as they had just minutes before. The flame in Rush's eyes ignited once more. "How can you be so fucking stupid? How? You have never been this... this... dumb! It doesn't matter who the fuck she thinks about. It doesn't matter whether she loves me or not, loves you or not!" Rush shook his head with a rueful, joyless smile. He started out of the room. "I know what she thinks about, Jackson. If she thought of anything else, we might all escape damnation. Unfortunately, her infatuation is going to completely destroy masses of fucking people. No matter how much of a moron you are, I won't let you be one of us."

Jackson said nothing. There was a stubborn set to his jaw.

"You have to know that I am always going to protect you..."

"You have protected me my whole life, Rush. You think I'm stupid, but I'm not." Jackson told him, feeling emasculated by the cracking in his voice. "I have never done anything, accomplished anything that didn't have you at its heart. You made me!" Jackson was yelling it now and pools of water started to collect in his eyes. "You made me!" he yelled it again. Then, with a sweep of his arms, he overturned his dresser and the heavy wood smashed against the floor. Jackson dropped to his knees. "I am no one. No, not no one. I am your brother."

Rush was silent. Jackson knew the truth of his birth, he knew the truth of it all and there was nothing stronger than the truth. No suggestion would ever repair the damage that had been done by the simple, unerring truth. Jackson was not great. Jackson was not remarkable in any way other than by being Rush's brother. Precocial was a lie... derivative. He reached a hand out to Jackson but knew that Jackson would reject it. The last thing on earth he wanted was Rush's support.

"What did you mean?" a weeping Jackson asked.

"By what?"

"What did you mean when you said that you had corrected the wrong that had been done?"

Rush did not answer right away.

"Did we..." Jackson's jaw dropped. His eyes widened, and he seemed to hold his breath. Rush—correctly—read the look in his brother's eyes as horror. "Did we have a baby?"

Still, Rush was slow to respond. He considered the question as he watched his brother without expression. It was true. He could listen to Jackson's thoughts as well as he could listen to his own. At that very moment, a montage of images were sifting through his brother's mind.

Some of them were shapeless, emotions only. Happiness. Sadness. Humor. Pride. These emotions were intermingled with images of Bright Star and a red haired child with light blue eyes. The child's sex changed from girl to boy and back again as the images flowed. Its age also changed from baby to teenager to adult. So many permutations of the family ran through Jackson's head that Rush was sure this had not been the first time he had considered this as an outcome. Although, this was definitely the first time Jackson had thought of it in the realm of reality. He could have gotten Bright Star pregnant. He could have had that child with her. And maybe, maybe that would be that crucial step in changing her. Maybe this was what could save her.

But none of that would come to pass. Rush had stated plainly that he had "corrected" his and Bright Star's wrong. All of sudden, Jackson felt as if eels were writhing in his stomach. His head was spinning. Saliva started to pool below his tongue. He and Bright Star would have had a child. His brother had done something, perhaps to the child itself to prevent that. His legs seemed rubbery beneath him and he lowered himself to his bed once more. When he looked at his brother again, it was an agonized and tortured plea. He didn't know what would happen if there had actually been a child.

But finally, Jacob Rush, Jackson Rush's big brother, shook his head. He gave a tight and labored upturn of his lips, "You should understand that your child would suffer death after death at the hands of its mother. You should know that your child with Bright Star would change this world forever. I won't let a mistake send us all to Hell. No, Jackson, that wrong was righted long before now."

Jackson accepted these words. He did not believe them, but he did not have any more strength. His stomach quieted, his skin warmed, and his breathing returned to normal.

And Rush tried to be at peace with the lie. This lie that had been his shame for months, years. He'd kept things from his brother, used his brother, betrayed his brother. Then he had sinned. And in days, he knew he would risk the world... For her.

Chapter 29

Night Crawler

The dream was remarkable. Really. Only muted colors: blues violets, roses. There was the smell of spring rain and hot patchouli. His body was writhing in warm satin. Slipping and sliding against the softest material—skin—he'd ever touched. It was everywhere, the scent and the feel. His lips glided smoothly then parted. Others parted slightly on his and he could feel his tongue being suckled gently. His fingers found the cleft of a round bottom and his erection tightened painfully.

"Jacob," her soft voice called to him in his sleep, beckoning him. Rush felt heavy laden. He struggled to wake. When finally, he jerked up in his bed, shaking himself of the honeyed dream of a small brown-haired girl he'd once known, he breathed deep and slow measured breaths. Inhale. Out. Inhale. Out. He needed to calm the raging emotions warring inside of him. He had halfway risen from the bed, but now he flopped back only barely missing Bright Star with one muscular and flailing arm. He stared at the pocked white ceiling wishing for the corrugated slate of the home he'd created for years with Shift.

"What is it, Bright Star?" he asked groggily, turning over to meet her. She had eased closer to him. Reading his thoughts, she changed the fleece blanket to dark satin. The ceiling dripped into the wall. The room looked to be a natural cavern, a deep earth aqueduct. She curled her body up though her only touch was her soft, slender fingers brushing back his hair.

"You do know what day it is, don't you?" she whispered the question. She leaned in to put her lips next to his ear and let the soft satin nightgown she wore fall open over her rounded breasts. The brown-haired girl had had small breasts. She had moved cautiously with eyes that watched furtively. She had been untouched and wary. This woman, while only minimally more experienced, had spent four years concentrating on this moment. She'd fantasized about it. Rush read her thoughts, her history, and saw—half-way experienced—every want, every way that she had imagined taking him into her. And her fantasies, they didn't stop with her own desires. She'd been cautiously, painstakingly slipping into his own mind, stealing his own desires. His fantasies were just as strong inside of her as her own. And they were too strong for an innocent.

Rush considered his own thoughts. Could Bright Star have come to him untouched, untried and been successful? He'd told Jackson any number of times that he didn't want her. He'd believed it, but why did this new path seem to usher in these uncertainties? Rush knew she would go to Jackson again, knew that he would never let her succeed in her horrifying folly. But he had to admit that something inside of him. Some buried morsel of him had wanted her to be incapable of seducing his brother either through her own epiphany or Jackson's.

He watched her. In truth, she had made herself into the very image of Jacob's fantasy. Her body, her skin, her hair, even those radiating eyes. They were all as Jacob would have wanted. But Rush was older. He knew more than Jacob ever could have about nature and future. Bright Star's fingers continued to play over him gently.

He swallowed. Rush was hungry. He was always so very hungry when he woke. She knew it as well as he did. She had to know it. The hunger she felt when she woke was antithetical, complimentary. Her hunger was a palpable force raging, pacing, snarling in the room with them as his was leashed in there, temporarily docile. It growled and whimpered like a trapped beast inside of him. Slowly, deliberately, and with a strength reserved only for his kind, he reached out a hand and ripped the gown from her svelte body. With an irrepressible smile Bright Star rolled further onto Rush's body with one leg thrown over his hip. Her wet sex rubbed against his hard thigh. She brought her lush lips to his jugular and rubbed them there. Then, she softly grazed her teeth over the spot before she lathed it with her tongue. Rush wanted her to nibble at him. She knew it, but she was holding out. With an excruciating slowness, her teeth came again, lightly on his flesh. Saliva pooled in his mouth as he waited and considered clasping her with his teeth as well. He let his head fall back against his pillow and closed his eyes. Finally, she sank her perfect white teeth into his flesh, then sucked gently to ease the minor sting.

Then she slid up and laid a thigh on either side of his hips. She leaned down until her breasts were crushed against his chest. She was nearly nose to nose with him, and then she was still. She waited. Rush knew what he would see when he opened his eyes, and he tried to delay the inevitable. But he opened his eyes. When he did, her tongue slipped into his mouth, then away. She pulled back her red locks with one hand and exposed a creamy sculpted neck. His teeth itched to take playful nips at her. He didn't want to break the skin. He just found it erotic, he would have her clamped her with his teeth as he came inside her. But that would never be.

"No, not today," he whispered to her much as she had whispered to him earlier as she tried to plant her soft suggestion in his head. He pushed her forcefully off him and onto the floor. Then he slipped out from the Shift-made sheets and stood stretching his arms toward the ceiling that was, again, stark and pocked and white. The rest of the Shift faded away as if it had never been, and his body slowly started to cool.

"Rush, don't leave me," she begged as she grabbed the side of the bed and pulled herself up onto it again. Her torn gown fell away from her body as she breathed heavily, lying on the hospital-white sheets with her legs apart and her hands sliding over her own flesh.

Rush watched her. His lips were pressed into a stern and pensive line. Slowly, he neared the bed and slid a warm hand over the soft inside of her thigh. When he cupped her, he could feel her hunger rushing through the veins beneath his palm. High Energy. He knew her hunger could only be slaked, never satisfied through sex. In the end, sex would be the means to an end.

"Bright Star?" he called as she stroked her milky flesh. He had known for moments that she was not Elizabeth.

"Yes, Rush?" Her voice was little more than a purr as she squirmed beneath him. Slowly, she physically transformed. Her hair turning a glistening red.

Rush lowered himself onto the side of the bed. He lay down beside her, his body curling around hers as his fingertips explored her addictive flesh even as it changed before him. He pressed his lips to her ear and asked, "Why aren't the lives I've saved enough?"

He could feel it, actually *feel* something crawl underneath her skin. He looked down, and again it moved. It was like fireworks beneath her skin. Each explosion causing tinted bumps to rise and move, distorting her body. Her naked, raw Energy was a hard thing under her flesh, pushing, cracking, and reshaping her from the inside out. For a moment, he thought of the pain. Only he and the Monk seemed to know. Bright Star suffered extreme pain at all times. All times. Yes, they all saw that she was troubled by the never-healing leg and the scar that nearly bisected her face. But they didn't know this.

He thought of Jackson's Service. How did they ever manage to know everything and nothing at once? Rush was certain they didn't know that High Energy could manifest itself as a physical disease and living entity within a shifter willing to embrace it, allowing it to take over his or her very cells. The incessant pain was, in truth, not the disease, but a symptom of it caused by a voracity for High Energy. It was like a teenager with a growth spurt. All of a sudden, the Energy was doubling and redoubling inside the host and required more High Energy to sustain and stabilize itself.

Rush could only feel for it again as he wondered if Bright Star would ever be in control of it the way he was. Even though it only grew by the years, his physical dependence on it had lessened to almost none. In fact, now his hunger was only sparked by dreams, dreams of her: Elizabeth. She had been dead for years, killed by Bright Star. Bright Star who was now ruining not only his life, but his brother's. He'd told Jackson she would destroy the world one day if she could. He'd done his duty and warned his brother even though he didn't believe it at the time. He hadn't been able to grasp her power. But, as always, his gift had been correct where his natural, mortal self had thought that if she were around and he could keep an eye on her, nothing would happen. That hadn't worked.

"That's what today is," he said aloud as if stunned.

"Yes," Bright Star said, moving one hand to her breast and the other to the moist spot between her legs. Rush's heart beat an irregular staccato, but then remembered what was important about that day. "I'm happy." Bright Star continued, "At least after today, she won't haunt us anymore. You won't hate me because of her."

"How do you know that?" Rush asked, his eyes again drawn to where her hands were making her own breath catch.

"Because even though today is my last on this Earth, Elizabeth will not escape. Even though today is your last on this Earth, you can't send her back," she said, rising up on her knees and pushing her hair back so that she didn't obstruct his view.

Rush didn't even want to ignore his hunger anymore. A flash of a hand moved through the air to latch on to Bright Star's neck. She felt it squeezing, cutting off her breath, freezing delighted words on her lips. The only thing that moved about her were her veins and the beasts of hunger rippling and distending her skin. He stood for a moment just listening to them beat out a rhythm. All in unison her veins were calling to him as he realized that his were doing the same to her. He lifted her from the bed by the throat. He smiled at her, his feral, starving smile that allowed her to see how his hunger had changed him.

But even as he killed her, her body was renewed itself, saving itself. He hadn't saved her from the pipe bisecting her on that train. He hadn't saved her when she drowned beneath the sea. He'd stopped saving her long ago. The only Follower that understood was Monk. Rush had cast off his role as savior months ago. It was Bright Star who perpetuated this madness.

Rush flung her down against the bed. He winced when he saw her head crack against the headboard. He hadn't meant to hurt her. He hadn't meant to use that much strength. She scrambled to get up, struggling with her broken leg.

Frustrated by his own actions, Rush felt his body tense, his fists clench at his sides. "You're strong, Bright Star. Not that strong. You can't give me a suggestion that will overcome my disgust for you." He took a deep breath. "Do you remember how you were—who you were—When I first met you?"

"I…" Her brow crumpled. She seemed to be thinking. "You saved me."

"That is not my question, Bright Star… Elizabeth."

"Don't call me that!" Her eyes flashed as she got to her feet.

"But that's who—"

"No!" her voice was strong and forceful. The one she used to reach all of her Followers. "Elizabeth will die today. For good!"

"You are Elizabeth!"

"I am who you made me!" she raged vehemently.

"Where is she?" he demanded, coming to wrap his hands around her arms. He squeezed tightly until she was lifted from the bed.

Even still she peered at him coyly from beneath her hair. She wasn't listening. Again, the suggestion of sex was clouding his vision and causing him to harden painfully.

He shook his head and continued scornfully, "I see you know you're not pregnant."

Her eyes widened and her mouth dropped open. She gave the appearance of shock.

"You know what I'm talking about," Rush glared at her. He even leaned nearer her to elucidate, "We both know you tried to get pregnant. You used Jackson. And we both know that even though you had him twice, you aren't pregnant. That's the only reason you had the audacity to try what you have tonight."

"Forgive me," she lowered her head.

"I won't," Rush declared. "You know I don't want you, and yet you tried anyway. But—Look at me!" Rush commanded as her head remained down. "Look at me!" He commanded again and this time, she showed him her shame. "I just want you to know. It's not Jackson's fault. No matter what you think. You can't get pregnant."

"What?" Bright Star gasped, pressing her hands to her womb, her completely empty womb. He turned to leave as hot tears started to course from her eyes. She started to shake and utter a low moan.

"Jacob, you had no right to do this to me—"

"I beg to differ. You've told me plenty enough times that you believe whatever I do is right."

"Yes, Rush. Yes, you're right," the tears dripped onto the floor, She sniffed as she wiped the back of her hand across her face. Awkwardly, she flattened the gown around her body. She called again before he closed the door. He didn't want to, but he turned and there before him was skinny, mousy, humble Elizabeth. The very sight of her caused a knot in his chest.

"Bright Star," he bit out. "I hate you."

"You don't hate me," she contradicted in the voice that had haunted him for days... months... years. "You love me," she dared.

The fury started a tightening of his jaw. It grew into a slow burn in his chest. The burn seemed to constrict his lungs so that he could not breathe. He opened his mouth to drag in deep breaths. His eyes began to sting and water. Impulsively, he reached up his hand and pressed two fingers to his throat. For a quick moment, he had believed he was having a heart attack because the pain and confusion were so strong. But he knew... Jacob Rush knew that he wasn't having a heart attack and there was nothing physically wrong with him other than the testosterone, adrenaline and empirical rage building within him. His hands balled into fists and he squeezed and squeezed, trying to get his hands to be still.

Then he struck. Rush hit Bright Star. He didn't slap her. He didn't use his High Energy to hurt her. No, there had been nothing paranormal about his assault. It was a pure and undiluted ferocious man's rage. He hit her with his large and sturdy fist. He connected with her jaw and down she went.

Rush hadn't expected the release and didn't want to feel anything good about hitting a woman. But he couldn't help it. He wanted to hit her again and again until the pain went away... until she would... just... stop.

With a busted lip and gleaming eyes she scrambled to her feet from the floor to face him. "I will never stop," she declared and seemed to raise her cheek to him, waiting for another blow.

Rush's palm itched with the desire to spend his truly physical tension again. He wanted to hit her and hit her and hit her until she could no longer influence his or his brother's lives. The need grew too strong for him to control and he punched her again. This time she did not get up.

"Rush, stop! Don't hit her again!"

The shame was immediate and strong. Rush did not turn to see his brother and Monk coming into the room. It was Jackson's voice he'd heard. Vaguely, in the back of his mind behind the all consuming red haze in his head, he could hear Bright Star addressing Jackson: "He didn't hit me." Her jaw and eye were healing with every breath she took. Redness and bruising faded visibly at a superhuman rate.

"Don't lie, Bright Star," Jackson commanded, though the signs were gone.

She darted around Rush to stand between him and his brother. "Jackson, this isn't any of your business. I'm not hurt. It's none of your business. You should just go."

Jackson was obviously not listening. He stood with his legs apart, his fists clenched, and his eyes never leaving his brother.

Bright Star tried another tack, pleading with the cleric. "Monk, take Jackson and go."

Monk did not take her instruction, either. Instead, his eyes were also trained on Rush. "What did she do to push you this far?" Monk asked in a voice calm beyond suggestion. It soothed the leashed beast trying to break loose in them all. Tension seeped slowly from the room.

Rush placed his hands over his eyes and did not respond. For a long moment he stood there. Though he wanted to, Rush found he could not answer. His tongue was thick in his mouth and he couldn't stop studying his hands. They were large and strong. They seemed larger and stronger in that moment than ever they had been before. He felt like an oaf... A giant staring down, almost disembodied, at the other occupants of the room, even as they studied him.

"Rush—"

Rush silenced his brother with nothing more than a mental shrug, then Shifted himself from the room.

Chapter 30

Revelation

"Why do you think she did it?" Monk dropped down to sit on the ledge of the building, shoulder-to-shoulder with Rush.

The night was cool and crisp. The city that spread to the horizon around them was subdued and dark-metal blue. There were no stars out this night, and Rush missed them fiercely.

Periodically, Rush had been casting himself off the building into the night air. Each time he had returned to the edge of the building. He found comfort in the weightlessness. Released from all pressure, even the downward pressure of gravity, Rush reveled in the void. And then, reluctantly, resentfully, he returned himself to the ledge and allowed himself to be compressed again. He reveled in every worry and expectation until he couldn't take it anymore. And then, he jumped again. And again. That was when Monk found him. Rush returned to his seat and found the cleric there.

"Why do you think she did it?" Monk asked when he didn't get a response.

"I don't know," Rush answered quickly this time.

"I think you do," Monk argued.

"Why are you here? Or is a better question why am I here talking to you, of all people?"

Monk had followed Rush shortly after he disappeared from that room. He'd had to make a choice. Stay and try to prevent the likely disaster brewing between the highly charged couple, Bright Star and Jackson, or try to help Rush make peace with himself and what he had done.

He'd been surprised to find Rush on the roof jumping into the night air. Rush rarely engaged in any recreational activity that one could observe. In those times that he was visible, he was either having a beer and watching television, eating, or performing unimaginable feats of Shift. There was little else. But rather than worry too much over this, Monk decided to focus on the high level of need within Rush. Normally, Rush would protect them all from his feelings. This night he didn't seem to care. His lack of control had already caused brownouts all over the city. White streaks shot frequently through the sky. Even the ground sometimes seemed to recognize Rush's feelings with an almost imperceptible rumble.

Rush looked over at him and gestured towards the ledge. "Again, Monk, what the hell are you doing here? Why do you think I'm going to talk to you?"

"Everyone talks to me," Monk offered slyly, then stood at the edge. He didn't look down. Instead, he slid forward until his toes were over the side. He balanced there, raising his arms out to the side. Then, all of a sudden he lurched forward. He flapped his arms. He missed. "I felt that."

"Of course you did," Rush did not deny the push. "You are, as always, aggravatingly right."

"We've all got to be good at something." Monk grinned. "As it turns out, I'm good at two things. Well, if you ask Point, I'm sure she'd say I'm good at at least five," he waggled his eyebrows. "Anyhow, one of those things is physics. The other, apparently, is being a holy man. Who knew?" Monk sat down again and gave Rush a sidelong glance. "Do you want to talk about it?"

"Not particularly," Rush answered dryly, though he felt his words to be more bravado than anything else.

"You feel bad about hitting her," Monk pressed.

"I don't feel anything."

"Why lie to me now?" Monk asked. "You've haven't lied to this point, so why now?" He didn't truly expect an answer, so he continued, "You do feel something. You feel despair. You feel helpless. And—if I'm not mistaken—you are experiencing a profound grief that I can't for the life of me understand."

Rush gave a wry smirk. Whether Monk believed in him or not. Whether he was really a holy man or not, he had a profound Talent for reading the emotions of others. He had pinpointed Rush's feelings down to the one emotion behind all the others that even Rush had been unable to identify.

"Maybe," was the reluctant acquiescence.

Monk said nothing further. Instead, he reached out and placed a hand on Rush's shoulder. The warmth and acceptance and unconditional forgiveness that radiated from him seeped into Rush, who was surprised to find tears collecting in his eyes. He was alarmed to find this becoming an increasingly frequent habit. He was also alarmed at how much he needed the reassurance and love that came from the holy man.

"This is what you do for all of us," Monk told him. "Every day."

Rush couldn't think about that. He couldn't. It just made him want to fling himself off the roof again, and this time, not return. But he didn't do that. Instead, he opened up. "She was stronger than him," Rush began. Instinctively, he knew Monk would realize he wasn't speaking of Bright Star or Elizabeth. He was silent, still, listening.

"She was stronger," Rush started again, putting his hands over his eyes. "He never knew that all she had to do was think hard enough and his nervous system would shut down. Though she wasn't that powerful, she had the precision of a surgeon with her skill, she did. He never knew that she held his life in her hands."

Monk, again, was silent.

Rush kept his eyes covered as if that would save him from his memories of his tortured mother and of Bright Star. "I can't understand why I did it, why I wanted to do it, why I will probably want to do it again."

"Well…" Monk began. "If you want my honest opinion, which you probably don't…"

"What is it?" Rush lowered his hands and for once looked like a lost little boy.

"I don't think you wanted to do it at all," Monk offered tentatively.

Rush didn't pretend to misunderstand. "Don't think for a minute that I question if she's capable of it. She is capable, and I absolutely would prefer to think it was her fault. But honestly, Monk, do you think I could have fallen to that simple a suggestion?"

"None of us are infallible, Rush," Monk told him. "Not even you. I think that if she were able to key into what can only be a very real fear of yours, then yes, yes you could have fallen to that simple of a suggestion."

"But why? Why that, of all things?" Rush asked with a pained pull of his lips. He was replaying the interchange in his mind. He was testing his body, searching for any residue of the High Energy that may have been used on him. Where his memory failed him, the examination did not. He found the telltale traces of Bright Star's recently spent Energy inside him. "Why would she want me to do this?"

"You know why."

Rush did know why, but he didn't want to think about it. He had no choice. Responsibility. Bright Star had been preaching it from the beginning. He needed to take responsibility for the lives and welfare of not only those around him, but everybody. Additionally, she knew what pain and guilt would come from inciting him to physically lash out at her. She knew the way he would be plagued by memories of his gentle mother. Guilt, in her gamble, had been the dark brother of responsibility. She wanted him to accept this cosmic responsibility, and she had never much cared how she got him to do so.

Rush straightened, "Monk?"

"Yes, Rush?"

"You believe she's crazy?"

"I believe in you," was the answer.

"I know that," Rush accepted with pursed lips. "I know you believe in me. I know that all of the others believe in me. And I know that Bright Star definitely believes in me. That doesn't mean she's not crazy..." He paused. "Or dangerous."

"If you'll recall," Monk said, only half-joking, "I tried to strangle her."

"Yes."

"You stopped me."

Rush rolled his eyes, feeling more relaxed after talking to Monk. "Yes." Then, hesitantly, he added, "You know why."

Monk stared into his palm pensively until a small yellow flame began to build there. The flame slowly turned to green, then to blue, then to purple. "I can never get it to go to red." Monk said.

Rush reached over and placed his hand above the flame. He then opened his mind to the priest. The flame turned red.

Monk's eyes widened and he grinned. But then he noticed Rush was silent once more. "What is it, Rush?"

"She's going to kill you."

Monk swallowed and extinguished the flame in his hands. Then he bent over the edge once more. "I know."

"And your wife. And your child, if but for a moment."

Slowly, Monk acknowledged, "Yes, I know."

"I'm not who you think I am," was the answer.

"You're exactly who I think you are."

"I'm selfish and I don't care like you all want me to care. There are circumstances when I will not save people, even when I have the power to."

"I know." Monk nodded in agreement. "You're not the one. But without you... Without your *selfishness*..."

"No," Rush countered, "Without you."

Monk gave a long shrug. Rush said nothing.

"Do you think she's crazy?" Monk asked, changing the subject.

"Absolutely."

"When you think about it though, it doesn't make sense." He started to stroke his chin.

"What's that?"

"It doesn't make sense," Monk waved his arms. "None of it makes sense, and it should make sense at the very least to me. I am a scientist, you know."

"What doesn't make sense, and what does your being a scientist have to do with it?"

"How can she become stronger and faster? How can every one of her senses be enhanced by your residual Energy except for her goddamned brain? Coriolis pseudoforce—"

"What?"

"Never mind… I can't figure it out. She just continues to follow this… this… path of madness."

"Why do you follow her, then?" Rush asked more casually than either of them felt. The question was one Rush had obviously wanted to ask for some time. He did not like the answer.

Monk grinned. "I don't follow her. All the rest of them follow her, I follow you. And don't think I don't know the difference. Maybe you are not the next savior but you are incredibly powerful and I believe in your power just as strongly as any of them do. I also believe in your goodness." Rush balked. Monk continued, "Yes, your goodness. What I don't understand is…" And in that one, single solitary instant… he did understand. "It *is*." He exhaled.

Rush did not give the gaping Monk his attention. Instead, he continued to stare straight ahead. He appeared to be studying the horizon.

"*It is*," Monk repeated dramatically. "It is helping her mind, isn't it? Physics, biology, chemistry. Motion, cells, and molecules. It's all the same. Our bodies are ruled by static, natural law. Physical, mental, it's all the same. Even those of us that can channel High Energy. Even *you*. *Parameters of Shift 101*, as Jackson says. I didn't understand because it just wasn't possible. It's like Jackson said, there are laws and we are all bound by them. The universe is bound by them. *She* is getting better. It's why she could save herself when you asked that I deliver the bodies from the sea. You thought they were all dead, but they weren't. *She* saved the others, those who were left. The water, it acted as an accelerant for her Energy, just like… God, Rush, do you see what you have done for her? Do you understand? Oh God! *She knows*. I knew you were a… a… but, I didn't know… Oh God." Tears started to course down the Monk's cheeks.

He stood only to sink to his knees before Rush in the same way he had seen Bright Star do it dozens of times before.

Rush reached down and pulled him up until they were eye to eye. "Monk," he said, slightly shaking the other man. "Monk, I told you once before never kneel to me. Never. No matter what you think, I am still a man and only a man. Yes, my Talent can transform others, change others, even grow inside of others. We all know this, but Bright Star has a piece of this power within her… without *me*. And you have a piece, too."

Monk grimaced. His faced crumpled in near grief. "No—"

"The rock, Thaddeus," Rush persisted. "You have the power to transfer High Energy, to transfer a signature, a *life* signature—"

"I—"

"We both know you put your Energy into that rock. You can transfer a life signature, even where there exists one already. You have to help me. I respect you, and you are my friend."

Monk started to shake his head as if being called a friend to Rush was more of an honor than he deserved.

"Listen to me, now," Rush said. "If you want her to live, if you want your daughter to live, then we have to help each other. You have to let me help her. It's the only way."

"You did say you were selfish." A jaw ticked in the Monk's cheek.

Chapter 31

Baby

"Are we cool?"

Jackson regarded his brother under heavily lidded eyes. He didn't answer the question. "She doesn't blame you," was all he said.

Rush visibly tried to contain the desire to shake his brother. "I couldn't care less whether she blames me or not. I'm not asking about her. I'm asking about us, you and me."

"Do you remember when we were little?"

"I remember."

"And Dad—"

"Your Dad," Rush corrected through clenched teeth.

"My Dad," Jackson acknowledged with a quick nod. "You remember what my father's temper was like."

"I don't think I could forget."

"You remembered what would happen between him and Mom."

"There's no way I could forget that."

"Or forgive it?"

"Or forgive it," Rush agreed.

"Then I don't know how you could have done what you did. And, oddly enough, that's not even what I want to know."

Rush gave a pained smile. "You want me to tell you why I never stopped him."

Jackson didn't say anything. He couldn't. His throat had closed over, simply from getting that question out. He had been wanting to ask this for all the days following the incident. Instead, he nodded.

"She wouldn't let me," Rush stated plainly.

"Wouldn't let you—"

"Wouldn't let me," Rush repeated firmly. He neared his brother and stood eye to eye with him. "She didn't want there to be any attention drawn to her Talent or to mine. She didn't want the Talent. Jackson, you couldn't know, she had been in and out of the hospital for it before you were even born. When she met your father, everything changed. He controlled her and somehow, she let him control what was inside of her."

"She could have defended herself," Jackson croaked.

"She could have, but she didn't," Rush returned. "She had no respect for the Talent until you were born. She didn't want it. She felt guilty for having it. But, then you came. And they both loved you. And... and it started to slow down. It happened less and less. the older you got. It happened less and less until they died."

"She died."

"Yes," Rush agreed. "Then he died." The question lay between them, waiting. Jackson would want to know. Rush didn't know whether he wanted to give the truth. In the end, he answered him. "I didn't kill him."

"So he died natur—"

"I didn't kill him. He did die naturally, only a few years later than he should have. She protected him for that last stretch. Without that protection, the disease that was eating him alive had free reign to kill him."

Jackson considered this. "You knew all this."

"Yes."

"You never told me."

"No," Rush answered.

"Why?"

"I don't know, Jackson. I'm protective, I guess. You are my blood. I'd rather deal with it, than have you deal with it."

"You're like her."

Rush did not like the similarity drawn between him and his mother. Though he had loved her a great deal, he didn't want to believe he was that sort of victim. But he couldn't deny the possibility he was exactly that sort of victim. He shook off the thought. "I didn't think you needed or would want to know this."

Jackson did not respond. He ran a broad hand over his face and breathed deeply. His limbs felt like gelatin. He had never known anything. He shook his head, silently disagreeing. With what, he didn't know.

"Jackson," Rush began again. "Are we okay?"

"Yes, Rush, we are okay. But—"

"Leave it at that, Jacks," Rush warned. "Our mother was not defenseless. I'm not defenseless. Bright Star is not defenseless, either."

"That doesn't make it right that you..."

"It doesn't make it right. I never should have done that. I can promise you that I won't ever hit her again, Jackson. I won't use Shift to hurt her either, but mark my words that she will have to be stopped one way or another. She is a danger to everyone around her. Everyone. That includes you and me. She can't be allowed to get away with literal murder. That's no reason to allow her to terrorize these people whether they know they're being terrorized or not. That's no reason for me to allow her to think up and carry out these plans that are more and more dangerous every time. What happens when I can't save them?"

"You mean like when you left them in the ocean to die?"

Rush brought his finger up to tap himself repeatedly on the temple. He continued, and Jackson waited. Rush said nothing. He just tapped.

Jackson knew he shouldn't have said it. It was too late to take it back. There was nothing he could say. He had lashed out because his brother did not believe Bright Star could be saved. He didn't believe she could be reasoned with or passively prevented from her course. But lashing out wouldn't change anything. It didn't change the very real fear that Rush was right.

"Jackson, it is what it is," Rush stated warily and with finality.

"What do you want me to do?" Jackson asked.

Rush measured him with a mental scan. Jackson was serious. Truthfully, Rush replied, "I want you to stay out of the way."

Jackson smiled with only half of his mouth. "I don't know how to do that."

"The other choice is—"

"The other choice," Jackson interrupted, nodding his head, "is for you to tell me what she's going to do. You have to tell me what you have been so afraid of for what is it… Years, now?"

"I can't do that."

"Why not? What will happen if you tell me? Do you think I won't believe you? Do you think that just by telling me what's happening that this catastrophic event will be set into motion rather than averted?"

"Nothing so scripted," Rush replied. "I haven't told you because, honestly, Jackson, I don't think you can handle it."

"Rush, please stop this. I'm an adult. I know how to take care of myself. Don't you understand that you can't put everything you are into being my big brother? You can't protect me for my whole life. Or, hell, even if you can, you shouldn't. You have to stop interfering."

Rush considered his next words carefully. "You're right, Jacks. That's what I've been trying to tell all of the people who live in my house for nearly a year. But I still won't tell you. Knowing what will happen will only generate more questions. If you can't read her yourself, then I can't help but think you still need me."

"So," Jackson said, tilting his head to the side, "What you're saying is that if I can read her, you will trust me enough to talk about this and what you plan to do about it."

"Jackson, if you can read her, there's no need for me to tell you anything," Rush answered.

"Then let's find her," Jackson stated with resignation. He looked at his watch. "The dining hall."

They entered the dining hall. The white room with white tables had stretched, pressed outward until it accommodated table after table after table of Followers. They were all seated in chairs covered in bright yellow satin. Vibrant orange flowers were bundled in the center of each. Heiro's paintings, all giant blocks of yellow, lined up down the white walls.

Rush led Jackson to the only yellow table in the room. It sat in a far corner. No one acknowledged Rush as he passed but behind his back, each of the Followers bowed his head momentarily then turned back to their tables. Rush knew what they did when he didn't watch, but had given up on stopping them. Though they did not express outwardly, he still felt their Energy, their devotion. He sighed.

Bright Star wasn't there yet, so they seated themselves at the table. Rush explained to Jackson, "I hate this place. I still don't know why they do this. I don't know why they must break bread together at the same time every night. At first I believed it was a suggestion…"

"You would have known if it was a suggestion."

"Yes," Rush acknowledged. "It's not a suggestion, but it has become a matter of routine which sometimes is stronger. You learned that, didn't you?"

"*Parameters of Shift 101*," Jackson stated dryly.

"I thought you had thrown that coursework to the dogs." Rush showed a trace of a smile.

"Yeah, I have." Jackson grinned back. "When it suits me, that is."

"Gentlemen," Monk greeted, joining them at the table. "It's a surprise to see you both here."

"Monk," Rush and Jackson greeted him simultaneously.

"You guys worked things out?"

The brothers, who now shared a new and striking resemblance that was undeniable to anyone in that dining room, nodded yes.

"Good," Monk returned, studying them both at length. Then his attention was pulled to the door expectantly.

When Point entered the room the tension seemed to evaporate from Rush's countenance. He smiled and bounded out of his chair to awkwardly come to her side and grab her arm, helping her as she ambled slowly toward them.

Jackson's mouth dropped open. He couldn't have been more surprised to see Rush tripping over himself to assist the lumbering Point. He had even beaten the excited father to her side. He realized quickly that it was the first time he had ever seen his brother in the presence of a pregnant woman.

"Are you sure you're only eight months, Point? You look like you're ready to pop any minute now," Rush teased as Point eased herself into her seat. Monk stood to help but she waved him off.

"I know," she said and continued blushing. "But, I can't be any further along."

"You look amazing!" Rush said, astounding each of the other men at the table. While it was true that Point smiled more every day and her skin, the color of strong tea, shined, they couldn't figure out why Rush noticed.

Once she was settled in her chair, she looked directly down at her plate. She was still uncomfortable around Rush. She was too awed by him. That led to vulnerability and she was not a person comfortable with vulnerability in anyone, let alone herself. But, Jackson noticed, there was something new.

Then Jackson felt the Energy that signaled Bright Star. He could always feel her. He looked up and there she was. She wore a long white dress that moved seductively around her body. Unbidden, the image of a naked Bright Star slipped into his mind. His mouth went dry. Internally, he cursed himself for the desire he felt, but it didn't help. Mercifully, he was distracted by the frown that creased her brow and pursed her lips. She seemed to be concentrating. As she neared them, it became obvious that she was looking at Point.

Absently, she greeted the table, sparing a moment to bow her head in Rush's direction. But her attention went right back to the pregnant woman who had been her right hand for so many months.

Point did not return the regard. But Bright Star couldn't seem to pry her eyes away from her, or rather her protruding belly. Bright Star's glowing eyes were narrowed and focused on Point's tummy. Blue light scanned up and down the belly as if it was x-raying and evaluating the growing life inside. More than once, Jackson had noticed Bright Star's hands rising, testing the air, preparing to reach out to Point, but each time she managed to still them.

Even Jackson had to admit it was unsettling. Bright Star was still watching the mound like she could see inside it. Her mouth worked subtly, saying a soft incantation or talking to the little one inside but wanted no one else to know. Her eyes were predatory. Jackson had the disturbing image of a female jackal—the most vicious sort—licking her chops. He shook his head to clear it. He still could not read her.

"She's coming along well, isn't she?" Bright Star asked Jackson directly as if she knew the direction of his thoughts. Her eyes never lifted to him.

"I don't know," Jackson answered truthfully. "I don't know anything about babies."

Bright Star dismissed him as easily as she had started speaking to him. "Rush," she leveled her gaze at his brother. "Don't you think she's coming along well?"

"Absolutely," Rush remarked with a supportive squeeze to Point's arm. "The baby is strong and beautiful. She will grow to be more special than you can know."

"Yes," Bright Star said absently. "Very special. The baby is very special. Very special. Domina."

"Are you going to eat?" Jackson asked her in hopes of changing the mood of the eerie conversation.

"I'm not hungry," she responded, though her eyes were still predatory, and clearly, clearly she wanted *something*.

"I think you should eat," Jackson returned, trying not to be put off. "You haven't been eating." She stared at him blankly. "You haven't," he insisted. "I've watched you. You're losing weight too quickly and I know I haven't seen you eat in a week."

"That's right," she agreed, nodding. "I'm not eating."

"Why?"

"I'm fasting," she answered with a frail shrug. Jackson was reminded of aged paper, brittle, flaking… losing its important meeting with the unstoppable wave of time.

"Again, I ask why."

"I have asked a question, and I am awaiting the answer." Her voice had gone thin and reedy.

"As if that should make sense," Jackson stated rolling his eyes.

"Don't make fun of me," she told him.

Jackson turned away from her and addressed Monk. "Is fasting some new part of your self-made religion we haven't heard about to this point?"

Monk didn't respond. Instead, he was studying Bright Star. She watched him closely as well with a near hunger in the set to her jaw. Jackson perceived there was a non-verbal exchange between the two of them, but they barred his mental eavesdropping. Whatever the exchange, neither of them appeared pleased about it.

Jackson then remembered his reason for being there. Rush had challenged him to look inside of her. Rush wanted him to prove he didn't need to be protected from this truth that everyone else seemed to know. He swallowed. He swallowed again. He slowed his breathing. He started to count. When he was able, he slowed his heart rate. He looked at her.

He was stunned to realize that she was already looking at him. Her blue eyes flickered light at him and the side of her upper lip curled aggressively. Jackson pushed back in his seat. He expected to hear his startled heart to be racing, but he quickly noticed that it wasn't. Instead, he found that he was still reaching out to her mind. He tried to stop as her eyes continued to heat up and a low groan came from her lips. Jackson started to see himself out of his body and realized he was in her mind, seeing her thoughts. He tried to pull back again, but couldn't. Someone was holding him anchored there. He couldn't tell whether it was Rush or Bright Star herself.

He saw himself and he saw Monk and Point. When the vision shifted to Point, her face was blanked out. It was almost as if her face was blurred, just beyond his reach, but he knew that it wasn't there. Instead, everything about the woman was dim save for a piercing, silvery blue light in her abdomen. Rush's mouth dropped open. And then, then he saw Rush. All went black.

Chapter 32

Prophecy

Bright Star sought Monk out in the temple. He treated the large, ornate room as his home now. He'd explained to any who would listen that he'd only done so because of the space it afforded him in the crowded palace. Bright Star argued each time that he had only accepted his fate as spiritual leader.

When she found him, she let him guide her into an alcove behind the altar. "What is it, Bright Star?"

He sounded exhausted. Bright Star didn't doubt that he was. Point had been sleepless the last two weeks.

"I've come for guidance."

"What kind of guidance could I possibly provide you?"

"I am at a loss, Monk. I don't know what more I can do to get Rush to accept his fate. He's fought me since the beginning. I thought he would stop, but he hasn't. And now, now he's cursed me."

"Cursed you? Come on, Bright Star. There is no such thing as a curse." But there was. In his world it was called the determinism principle which stated that if one knew to an infinite accuracy the state of a system at one point in time, one could predict the state of that system with infinite accuracy at any other time, past or future. Physics. *Parameters of Shift 101*. He couldn't, but a better Shifter could pick any time, good or bad, to rattle off to another. Nothing that Bright Star would ever fall for. She knew the present perfectly, as Rush did.

"I'm cursed!" Bright Star spat angrily, contradicting his thoughts. Her eyes flashed blue fire at him. She brought her hands up to cover her tummy.

Monk's eyes widened. "You're pregnant."

"No," she wailed and rocked back and forth as tears started in her eyes.

"You wanted to get pregnant, but you can't?" Her reply came in the form of a weak nod. Monk wanted to breathe a sigh of relief but realized the dangers that would bring.

"Now it seems I've lost my way." Bright Star moaned. "I don't know what to do."

"Maybe you should do nothing," Monk offered cautiously.

Bright Star only stared blankly at him.

"Yes, Bright Star," he pressed on. "Do nothing. Maybe you should meditate. Breathe. Wait for him to come to you."

"I can't do that," she declared vehemently. She shook her head. "I won't do that. We've already wasted too much time. No. Today is the day. There will not be any waiting. I need to know now what will change him."

"That, I do not know," Monk shook his head wistfully.

"But I believe you do," Bright Star challenged.

Monk's eyes bucked but he remained silent. She knew he was different. He could only hope that she didn't know why.

"Touch me," Bright Star prodded.

"No," Monk refused.

"Touch me." This time it was a demand. She started to ease closer to him, gliding in the air. Her eyes never left his. "I know he's helping you keep me out. But you can't keep me out if you touch me. You have to do it. I know you will be able to tell what path I must take now. I am at a loss. I truly don't know what I must do to get him to realize his potential, to take the mantle of leadership.

"Then search harder inside yourself. Maybe you should go back to that island. Maybe—"

"I will go back, Monk." She assured him in a shrill, fragile voice, "Just not now. I won't go back until I can deliver on the promise I made to those people. I won't go back until I can prove who I am, who he is. I have to give him back to them. I must."

"I won't help you."

"Helping me is not a betrayal, Monk. We believe in the same thing, you and I. Help me."

When Bright Star realized the man would only continue to refuse, she decided to take the matter into her own hands. Literally. With preternatural force and speed, Bright Star grasped the monk's hands in her own. She flew backward with the force of the Energy that jolted from his body into her own. It arced and cracked and caused her skin to contract all over.

She was dazed for a moment only before Monk turned and ran from the room. She dashed out behind him.

Chapter 33

Death of the Holy

"Do you remember anything?" Rush questioned. He sat in a chair near Jackson's bed where he had been lying for two hours.

"I'm not sure," Jackson hedged groggily. "I don't know what's a dream and what's not."

"Let's assume that none of it is a dream."

"How long have I been out?"

"A couple of hours. How do you feel?"

"I feel like I've been hit with more Perma-Shift than any one person can take at a time."

"That would be an appropriate assessment. The only reason you aren't dead is because of your 'special' Talents." Rush put down the book that had been in his lap. "What did you see?"

"I saw the baby," Jackson answered finally.

Surprisingly, Rush grinned. "You saw her?"

Jackson nodded.

"She's wonderful, isn't she?" Rush asked beaming.

Jackson recalled that light. He nodded again in agreement. "I saw you, too."

Rush bowed his head. He seemed tired. He always seemed tired lately. "I know. That's when you blacked out."

"I don't remember what I saw," Jackson stated. "I just know that after the baby, came you."

"You didn't see anyone else?" Rush frowned.

Jackson shook his head. "No."

Rush squeezed his eyes shut for a moment. Then he asked, "You didn't see what she was planning?" The question was asked with hesitance.

"Bright Star?" Jackson raised his eyebrows. "No, I didn't." The voice was tentative. There was more.

"What else did you see, Jacks?"

"Nothing more than what I said. But I felt… I felt so much pain. I have never felt pain like what I felt. I don't know what caused me to black out, if it was that piercing, sharp, throbbing ache or…"

"Or me?" Rush gave a humorless smile.

"Yeah," Jackson admitted slowly, "Or you." Rush's face was expressionless. "But… I don't think it was you."

There was a light, an indefinable flicker in Rush's black eyes. Jackson sensed that the flicker had been relief. "You don't?"

"No. It was her. It was the pain, but not just the pain."

Rush continued to watch him carefully, as if he was waiting for Jackson to make a discovery of some sort.

Jackson pushed up in his bed and leaned his head back against the wall, eyes closed. He had to think. He had to remember. And then it came to him. *Parameters of Shift 101.* He knew that pain, there was only one thing that caused that kind of pain. *Perma-Shift.* Bright Star had given off waves and waves and waves of acute Perma-Shift. But how? She hadn't been in the middle of a Shift and no one, not even Jackson could stand Perma-Shift for any significant period of time. Still, this pain, it wasn't new. It felt as if it had been with her for a very, very long time, and it felt as if it was growing. Yes, Jackson was sure of it. The hurt inside of her had been growing, gathering strength and intensity. He could see it surging, hurtling through her body.

The Perma-Shift was caused by High Energy. Bright Star was harnessing High Energy. His mouth dropped open.

Rush pinched the bridge of his nose between his fingers.

"What is it, Rush? Tell me. What is she going to do with it?"

"Think, Jackson. What could she do with it?"

Jackson went still. Fleeting pictures of Bright Star dying skittered through his mind. He could see the twisted, mangled car of the train she had persuaded the Followers to crash. He could see the phalanx of dead bodies, bloated by ocean water following Monk, then burrowing into the ground. He could see the bodies of Destroy and Harm.

He thought of the barely leashed Energy. Bright Star could do anything. Anything.

"Where is she?"

* * * *

"Where are you going?" Jackson demanded as he watched his brother pull on a loose jacket.

Rush looked over his shoulder at him but did not respond.

"I'm coming, too," he added.

"No, you're not."

"You're going to find her. She's been masking her High Energy since dinner. I know because I've been trying to find her. Whatever she's going to do, she's going to do it now. You know it, so you're going to find Bright Star. You're going to stop her."

Rush said nothing.

Jackson reached out and grabbed his shoulder. "I know you are."

"It's time," Rush answered.

"I have to do something."

"It's too late for you," Rush assured him.

"I have to try."

"It's too late," Rush countered again.

"If I get to the Service…" Jackson's voice trailed off as he remembered the last time he had been there. He remembered that he had been acknowledged as Rush's brother. He remembered the guards whose names had changed, who had started speaking like the parish that inhabited his home.

"It's too late," Rush explained to him again, slowly this time. "It has to be me."

"I should have listened."

"You never would have, Jackson. You couldn't have. This was as much fated as anything could be."

"You don't believe in fate."

"Bright Star," Rush breathed. "Bright Star has a way of making anyone a believer."

"Is this why you have always hated her?"

"I never hated her, Jackson, just like I never hated you. I couldn't. I don't think I can make you understand because I can't understand it." Rush smiled and grimaced at the same time, his eyes spelled irony. "I don't want her. Why would any man want her?" He said the words with a pointed humor. His voice was punctuated by a flashing blaze of his eyes. A yellow light the same as Bright Star's blue one passed quickly over Jackson. Air rushed into Jackson's lungs, he could not head off the surprised reaction. "But whether I like it or not, she is mine—a part of me. She was made for me. She made *herself* for me. So we are parts of the same whole."

A man in a yellow and white robe appeared down the hallway. His identity, or rather his religion, was obvious. Rush called to him. "Monk, come and keep an eye on my brother."

Jackson rolled an exasperated eye. "I don't need him to keep an eye on me. Wherever you're going, I should be going, too. I can help you find her."

Still, before his eyes, Rush disappeared. His body, his mind, his spirit were now just as masked as Bright Star's. Jackson couldn't follow even if he wanted to.

Monk neared Jackson warily, though his first words were congenial and conspiratorial. "All-powerful and yet he runs from us."

"You and your Followers?"

"They aren't my Followers." The monk returned gathering his robes around him. His robes still looked remarkably like stolen hotel sheets. Still, they were startling again his dark skin.

"He isn't running from me. He thinks he's protecting me," Jackson countered.

"He is protecting you, Jackson. I'm glad you finally realize it. He's protecting us all." Jackson knew that he had not imagined the contempt in the monk's voice.

"Do you know what Bright Star is going to do?" Jackson asked. The monk merely closed his eyes in accord. "You have something to say, Monk?" Yet Monk was silent. Jackson huffed out a labored breath. "Why did you stop?"

"Dying?"

"Yes. Dying."

"Before they came for me—Bright Star and Point—I had always known there was something more. Perhaps I had been one of those out there who had that propensity toward High Energy that just never really amounted to much more than passive Talent. You know, a precognitive moment here, an impressive ability to draw a perfect circle there. It was nothing. I could never have affected a Shift back then. Not like you. But they came for me, and it started something inside of me. Even before I was touched by Rush, my High Energy grew solely because I finally understood and accepted what it was. Bright Star was my guide in blindness. She led me to light."

Jackson acknowledged that this was possible. Monk continued, "The first time... that time in the train... I don't know how to describe it. I didn't die that day. No one did. But we came so close. So close. Have you ever been that close to death? Don't answer. We both know you haven't." Monk cleared his throat, then shook his head. "I'm not going to tell you it's exhilarating, because it is not. I had a broken metal rod stuck through my chest. My head was smashed between two seats because I, like a coward, tried to take cover at the last minute during the crash." He took a long breath. "I had never felt that much pain before in my life, and I haven't felt as much since.

"When he came... when Rush came, it was—to sound a little cliché— it was like the sun coming out. The pain subsided to where it was like it was there but inconsequential. And then nothing."

"Nothing?"

"Nothing," Monk repeated. "No pain. No crash. Everything was set right once again as if it had never happened. But it had happened, we all knew it, and somehow, without physical evidence, we could all feel it. I could explain it to you in an equation, a proof. However, to put it simply, the High Energy was left. True, some was used to right our wrong, but the rest seemed to stay inside me. To blend and become part of what was already there, to make me more than I had ever been. I tell you this, but you know it. You may not be able to remember your experience, but it has been a part of you your whole life. Rush has been a part of you."

Jackson didn't respond.

"I don't have to tell you. You know," Monk insisted. "Still, with the enhanced High Energy, I started to see as she saw. I am his child, born of his Talent, but it was Bright Star who made this happen. She led me to the sight."

"And in your sight you lost faith?"

"Faith?" Monk chuckled without humor. "No, in my sight, my faith strengthened. My servitude was complete. I learned something more important than any of those things that Bright Star holds as tenets: *Rush didn't want me to die.*"

Jackson could say nothing. His eyes began to water and he coughed to hide the closing of his throat. Rush didn't want me to die. The words were haunting and pure. He wept silently, failing to comprehend why those words had such a profound impact on him.

"You're crying," Monk remarked. "But you don't know why."

"Everyone reads my mind," Jackson muttered bitterly.

"You may not believe this, Jack..." Monk flashed a quick grin "But half the time, no one has to. You wear your emotions on your sleeve."

"Who is she?"

"I can't tell you who she is. It would be a betrayal to them both."

"Nobody can tell me a fuckin—"

Monk raised a hand and interrupted him. "But I can tell you her nature. She is born of destruction. She struggled with her nature as I struggled against my own nature, as you struggle with the knowledge of your brother's greater power. But in the end, hers is not a struggle she can win.

She knew that once, and tried to set things right. But Rush couldn't let her…"

"You mean the first time they met."

"Yes." Monk nodded. "She tried to end it then, but even then he loved her and couldn't let her do it."

"Rush doesn't love her. He told me."

"Rush doesn't love Bright Star, that's true. But the other…"

"Who?"

Monk ignored this question. Instead, he continued his warning. "I tried to stop her. I tried to keep the truth from her as long as possible, but she is strong. I don't think any of us besides Rush will ever know the true boundary of her power. She sucked the vision from my mind. Jackson, Bright Star has committed murder. She will commit murder. She will never stop committing murder. She will destroy us all, has destroyed us all."

"She is not a force of destruction."

"She is, just as she is a daughter and a sister," the monk snapped. Then, as if in meditation, his eyes closed briefly. When he opened them again, he smiled. He sank to the ground and sat cross-legged before Jackson. "Sit," he instructed.

Jackson dropped to the ground beside him.

"Do you believe the world is in danger?" the monk asked.

"Yes," Jackson answered, a tick in his jaw.

"Do you know what that danger is?"

Jackson's ignorance was a live thing. He shook his head. "Rush wouldn't tell me."

"He didn't want you to try and interfere, even though he's already planted a Shift that will prevent you from leaving this place anyway."

Jackson's eyes widened. Mentally he started to reach outside of the compound as he tested Monk's words. In seconds he found he could not see beyond the walls of his home.

"It doesn't matter." Monk waved his hand. "Since I know you are as powerless as I am, I will tell you what he would not." He measured Jackson with his gaze. "In the simplest terms, she is linking herself to every human being in this world. We are all becoming Followers. We are becoming her as she is becoming us. This includes me. This includes you. And when we are all one, she will do as is her nature."

Jackson's heart ceased to beat in his chest. He felt it stop, seize, fold in on itself. He had to force his veins open wide to save himself. He knew what she was going to do. Perhaps he had known it before this monk had told him. He couldn't breathe, and his right eye started to close involuntarily. "She can't do that," he rasped.

"She will do it."

"No, you don't understand, Monk, she *can't* do it. Even with all of the High Energy she's harnessed. She doesn't have enough of it to affect that kind of Shift."

"You're right," Monk told him. "She needs more, and she needs to focus it."

Chapter 34

High Energy

Bright Star needed High Energy. She needed lots of it. She needed as much as she could take in order for this Shift to bind her, then kill her. Her eyes no longer dimmed, they were constant and near blinding blue beams as she hovered above the city steeped in High Energy. She needed to see the Holy Man again.

* * * *

She dived like a striking eagle through the air. She pierced the ceiling of the temple and stood in front of him. The monk knelt at the altar and she was sure he waited for her. Bright Star crouched beside him like a starved beast waiting to pounce. Her eyes beamed directly into his. Neither Bright Star nor Monk spoke. They didn't even communicate in their common mental path.

"So you understand now?" Monk asked her slowly.

"Yesss," she whispered. Her words were sibilant and her body snaked awkwardly from side to side. Her hands lashed out until she held the Monk's head in her hands, then she leaned forward to kiss him and suck the life from his body, never realizing that he took just a bit from hers.

When she was done, she howled as the High Energy coursed through her. She dropped the body and located the other occupants of the palace. She did not want to hunt them. But she had no choice. She was going to eat them all alive.

One by one, she found them. She lured them to her with a pair of inviting open arms. When they were near, she said the Energy in honor of Monk and their sacrifice. She lured Stream, pressed her lips right to his temple. The she clasped strong fingers to the base of his skill and his High Energy, his very life force, drained from him. He dropped to the ground before she was even finished. Bright Star wavered in the air as her body struggled to hold all of that Energy inside, but she would continue, she had to.

She found all of her children and she ate them all until one and a half remained. Where was Point? Where was the woman who would help her to harness all of this Energy… to focus it? Where was that silver blue star that lived within in her? The star that was second only to Rush with its High Energy. She wouldn't need others, if only she could have that star.

She called to the mother. "Point!" Her voice was loud, ringing, traveling throughout the palace. Point did not come. Then with little Energy, Bright Star reached out to find the most devoted Follower. There was no trace of her. Nothing. But she knew they couldn't be gone. Point couldn't leave. Point wouldn't leave. No. Rush was hiding them somewhere. Hiding them from her.

"Point," she called again, this time adding a powerful suggestion to her voice in hopes of coaxing the expectant mother out of hiding. It didn't work. Bright Star was torn then. She didn't know whether she should go ahead and attempt her Shift while the absorbed Energy was hotly coursing through her, or if she should expend Energy finding Point and the unborn child who now possessed something of hers. The roar that tore from her was deep and low, shaking the walls of the palace.

With a feral and frustrated growl, Bright Star decided to rise through the palace to the roof. She would have to perform this ceremony alone and without Point or the baby's life Energy.

Chapter 35

Wed

Jackson went in search of Monk. The whole compound was eerily empty, and he couldn't stand the waiting alone. He'd tried to walk outside, but Monk had been right, the Shift Rush had used was insurmountable. But Jackson didn't find Monk.

Her copper head was bowed in prayer. Her milky skin was radiant. Bright Star was kneeling in the temple with her hands clasped reverently in front of her. The serenity of her pose only served to underscore the raging Energy pulsing beneath the surface. The passive violence he sensed within her caused him to reach out for Monk. He should have been able to locate him, but just like everyone else, he was just...gone.

"What have you done?" Jackson demanded. His fingers dug into her upper arms as he shook her. She flopped limply like a rag doll. Even as her body was relaxed, he could feel the High Energy and Perma-Shift inside of her coursing strong. His hands started to vibrate painfully from the rapid, pulsing force. It was strong enough to spill around them and cause metallic items to levitate.

"You don't understand," she cried.

"No," Jackson countered, "You don't understand! You will ensure that he saves the world by destroying it yourself. You no longer care about anyone. You are addicted to his thirst for your life. You are destroying him!"

"Rush can't be destroyed."

"All things die."

"He won't," Bright Star challenged. As her words became more forceful, her eyes began to beam blue light at him. The light bathed Jackson's face and he tried to resist the leap it caused in his pants. Still, after all this time he was unsure if the light from her eyes elicited this response. He didn't know if she had some preternatural power over men, or if he simply loved her. No, not quite true. He was certain that he loved her.

She stood and neared him. Her blue eyes turned upward as she approached him to keep him in her thrall. She was so small as she neared him, her copper head thrown back and her beaming eyes holding him. "Haven't you noticed? Can you not see him as I can? He is growing stronger if anything, more unstoppable if anything, more responsible."

"Not more responsible. Quicker only to save you."

"Jackson, you know that's not true," she chided. "He no longer cares to save me. He hates me."

"He doesn't," Jackson argued half-heartedly.

"He does," she insisted with a sure nod. "And he hated the Followers."

Jackson did not fail to note her use of the past tense. *Hated.* "What have you done, Bright Star?"

Instead of answering him, she said simply with a sad shake of her head and in little more than a whisper, "I can't have your High Energy, can I? You are Jackson, The Impervious. I can't take it from you. He won't let me."

"What have you done?" Jackson screamed into her face. He wiped the moisture from his eyes in furious desperation. "Bright Star, what did you do?" He shook her and shook her until he thought he would break her. Then he did.

The suggestion shattered into tiny pieces as he heard the animal growl from the courtyard.

Rush! Rush! Jackson called mentally. He cast a wide net with his mind trying to reach the brother who had shut him out for so many days. *Rush, please tell me where you are. Tell me what's happening.*

The response was distant but strong. His brother was far away, but he was in good health. *Jackson, Bright Star has lost control. She is on a rampage and she will kill everyone with High Energy in her path. She will kill everyone.*

But I—

You are protected. You have been protected since you were born. I thought you had come to terms with that. She can't hurt you. But she will continue to suck the High Energy out of any and everyone she comes across. Don't let her get the baby!

What?

Point and Monk's baby. Protect her with your life, Jackson! You're the only one who can, and she is so important. So important. When the time comes, I won't have the Energy to save her, too.

Grayson Reyes-Cole

Fear was a tangible growing thing expanding to fill Jackson's organs. *Damn it, Rush! What do you mean you won't have the Energy?*

You know I'm the only one who has a chance at stopping her.

A chance? Jackson demanded. *A chance? Rush, stop being so fucking cryptic. I understand now. I understand why you wanted her gone. I understand why you have never given in to her. I understand all of that. I still don't know why you didn't just stop her and why all of a sudden you're the only one with a chance to stop her?* Silence met this question. Then there was more than silence. There was a wall. An implacable, insurmountable wall.

Find Point! The command came and then the wall was back. With an angry grunt, Jackson turned and ran.

He found her by luck and luck alone. She wasn't in the temple. She was, actually, in his bedroom. As he went past the door, he caught a glimpse, just a glimpse of yellow material. It was *that* yellow, the color Monk had called the Rushic yellow. Jackson turned and went into the room, closing the door behind him. His hand on the knob told him why she was in this room. Rush's protective suggestion still lingered within these four walls.

The pregnant woman was lying on the floor, her arms protectively draped over her stomach. Her breathing was shallow.

"Point! Point!" Jackson screamed, slipping an arm under her shoulders to pull her up. Her eyes rolled, then focused on him. Her brow, wet with perspiration, was creased in pain. Jackson wasn't sure yet if it was the physical kind or not. "Point!"

"Jackson," she groaned doggedly. "I can hear you, no need to yell."

Jackson try to smile supportively. "The baby—"

"The baby is fine," she told him. The pain on her face had not lessened. "I am holding her close to me."

"What happened here?"

"The same thing that is happening at the SHQ. The same thing that is happening all over the world where Shifters aggregate."

"Bright Star?"

"Yes, Bright Star."

"Come on," Jackson told her, trying to ease her up. "Maybe if we get you out of the city. Maybe, if I can convince Rush to let us leave here. At least you can be safe until we can figure something out."

"Your brother knows we are as safe as we can be here." In the lull between contractions, Point told him with a grace born of wisdom and patience. "Besides, Jackson, there is no 'outside of the city' anymore."

Jackson considered her words. He eased her back against the wall then frantically beat a path to the window. He looked out and saw the same cityscape he had always seen. This was still his city, his home. In the distance he could see the SHQ. It was pristine as it towered over that section of the city.

It was then that Jackson knew something was wrong. Beyond the SHQ there was nothing but a verdant and abundant forest. There was no forest anywhere near the SHQ. They had been transported. That's when he noticed the bright blue light flickering above the SHQ. Similar blue lights were positioned methodically as far as the eye could see.

"What do you see?" Point asked.

Jackson turned to see her face crumple in a mask of pain. He rushed to her side again. "What's wrong, Point. What hurts?"

"The baby…" she rasped. Jackson paled at the site of her hands clenched over her rounded belly. Then her brow smoothed and the pain had obviously passed. "The baby is coming."

"Oh my God!" Jackson yelped. "Are you sure?"

"Of course I'm sure. That's what my name is. I pinpoint things. I add all the factors together and I pinpoint them." She grimaced. Jackson started to say something but she cut him off. "What did you see out the window?"

"Everything. I saw everything I normally see, but it was different. It's almost as if the city has been carved right out of the ground and transported somewhere else."

"What else?" Point urged grabbing his shirt sleeve.

"I saw blue lights in the sky."

"How many?"

"How many? I don't know." Jackson cast his gaze around looking for something within the room that could help him.

"It doesn't matter," Point stated as she pulled a pillow from his bed and put it behind her. "Nothing can be done now."

Jackson gave up his search and started to use his High Energy to generate a basin of hot water and some towels.

"No," Point shrieked, "No, you use your High Energy now and she will find us. She'll find my baby, even with Rush protecting us. You can't use it."

Jackson stopped gearing his Energy. "I understand. Let me get some supplies. I will have to help you do this," he told her soberly.

She bit her lower lip and closed her eyes. This pain did not come from the baby. Monk should have been there to assist with this birth. But he was dead, and Point was just now allowing the grief to break through.

"He would have wanted you to help," she offered, comforting Jackson even as her anguish struggled to overwhelm her.

"He would have wanted Rush," Jackson returned, surprised to find that he was no longer bitter.

"He would have wanted Rush to do exactly what he is doing now, exactly what he is destined to do."

Chapter 36

Constellation

Bright Star was in eighty-six places at once. She was all over the globe siphoning the High Energy from unsuspecting souls. One in one hundred thousand dropped dead each minute. Her true body was easy for Rush to find. She hovered above the SHQ where the richest of Shifters could be found after all of the Followers had died. She used Sandoval who had always been a focal point and was just as strong as the once loyal Point who had betrayed her.

Souls and High Energy shot into the sky like fireworks. Upward streaks of lightning that struck into Bright Star's body. Her arms were out at her sides as she greedily accepted each sacrifice.

And then, the Energy just stopped. The souls stopped dying and she found she could no longer locate Shifters. She called to them—it was the mental screech of a banshee and eerie longing of a siren—but no one, not one single Shifter responded. Rush.

"You can't stop me, Rush," she roared. "Not yet. You can't stop me yet." But the Energy would not come.

Bright Star pulled all of her replicas together again. Slowly, she lowered herself to the ground. As she did, the white dress she wore faded away. It was replaced by twined vines and flowers. A headdress adorned her head, binding the titian tresses that flowed down her bare back. Her feet were bare, but no matter, they didn't touch the ground as she glided through the trees and up the side of the lush mountain, she inhaled the scent of crisp sea air.

At the top of the mountain, the villagers turned to watch her approach. As they did, Bright Star smiled, until she heard their whispers.

"Burn… Burn… Burn…" They all seemed to be chanting.

"No," she told them. "No. I'm not Burn, I'm Bright Star." But her words went unheeded. They chanted the name anyway. "Bright Star!" she argued. "I will prove it to you. I will prove it to you all. I will bring him back to you. You watch. I will bring him back."

In the center of the village with fury and purpose coursing through her veins, Bright Star raised her arms once more. But she didn't rise. Instead, she sank. The soles of her feet connected with the earth and a soft, shimmering web of translucent blue light began to spread through the rich earth. The translucent veins continued to spread in a circle around her. It reached the trees and began to creep up the bark. It reached the villagers even as they ran and webbed its way up their legs and over their bodies. The threads spread faster and faster, binding everything they touched until they spread to the ocean and scabbed over it to shoot into the horizon.

Even in the compound, Jackson and Point threw back their heads as they experienced the wedding of Bright Star and the world as they knew it. The High Energy and pain of Perma-Shift coursed through them all and the world seemed to cry out for release.

"Elizabeth," Rush called. The word broke into her reverie. She heard even as she grunted but continued to cast her spell.

"Elizabeth." This time when the word was hissed, she felt it was a curse.

"Elizabeth!" This time the word was harsh as it called to her, seeming closer.

"Rush." She turned to see him, her beauty, her love and inspiration, standing before her. His chest was bare and he too was clad in the royal garb of the island.

"You've come to save them. You've come to save everyone."

"I won't need to save them if you stop this right now. Bright Star, you can save the world. *You* can save it, if you would just stop. You have the power. You have the power. If you would just…stop. Bright Star. Stop."

Her eyes narrowed and she bit her lower lip. She was considering his words. "I am not—"

"You can be—"

With a quick and bashful shake of her head, she cast her eyes down. She smiled shyly. "I'm not."

"Bright Star," he pleaded, "Elizabeth… you are more committed than I am. You can get these people to follow you. I can't. You are stronger than I am. Recognize the truth in that. You have long been stronger than me. This is your destiny, not mine. You have always been stronger than me. It's you. It's you."

Her eyes snapped to his. Her mouth dropped open in shock. "Never say that! Never! You are the one. I am a vessel!" And with those screamed words, the binding spurted. The entire earth pulsed with the blue web and then the web disappeared. The merge was complete.

Rush said nothing. He waited. He waited. Then her body, her creamy skin, began to pulse.

Bright Star's limbs started to glow with an inner orange light. Bright Star heard Jacob Rush—Guard—screaming for her, and then she looked up, directly at the sun.

Peculiar thing. The yellow ball was bright and ferocious. Its rim became electric as she watched. She became warm and not only warm. She felt, Gods, she didn't even know what it was she felt, but she knew she was rising. She knew it and embraced it. Around her, the earth was also burning. Volcanoes were erupting. Geysers were spewing sulfur and lava. Electricity shot spontaneously through the air, causing explosions. As her body heated up, so did the core of the earth. If Rush allowed her to die, then they would all die.

Then Jacob was there with her. And there was a faint glow of light around his body, and—she noticed fadingly—a stronger light around her own.

And higher, higher they rose, side by side with their eyes closed now, their arms outstretched. The light that had started out a dim blue glow had grown into a white-hot sphere too bright to look upon. Bright Star could feel Elizabeth down there, the woman who had offended her, the woman who had taken Rush from her and the world. Rush was saving Elizabeth. And like a god on Olympus she struck out. She could see in her mind the child crouched under a low-limbed tree to avoid the affects of the sun. Bright Star could see lank brown locks turning into wild titian curls then becoming flame and her soft brown eyes becoming ash.

Bright Star saw it. In her mind she watched that child disintegrate. In her body she felt the extending of herself as if she were pushing hard against a wall, felt herself send the energy that would destroy that child, and she didn't just feel that. As if he were there holding her hand, pushing beside her and smiling approval, she knew Jacob was helping her, she knew it as well as she knew that child had burned and they had victory. And that is when she opened her eyes.

Those below saw those eyes opening as gaping black holes. From her upturned palms, a red glow started to pulsate and her levitating body rotated to face Jacob Rush. Then her arms came out straight in front of her as she aimed her palms at him. Then his eyes flew open, white-hot light emanating from them. And the light was coming from his nostrils, beams of light shooting from his ears. As if in pain, he bent his head back and arched his back as light escaped through his fingertips his feet, his elbows, and his knees. The light soon overcame him, then just as suddenly, was gone.

Slowly Rush sank to the ground, watching above him as Bright Star's black eyes grew wider. He tried to look into them but could find no characteristic to latch on to, not one single feature in those eyes to let him know what was there. He then watched her ascend even higher with a speed they had not been able to attain together. Still a part of the entity above, the defeated half of this incited High Energy system could shudder with combined ecstasy from the luscious, succulent power coursing through her, and the draining of his own by the second. Jacob watched her rise.

They all watched her rise. Suddenly they were covering their ears as a powerful booming noise from above shook the ground and assaulted their hearing with its thunderous boasting. And then the light surrounding Bright Star was gone and she was hurtling toward the ground faster and faster until she fell, her landing broken by the hard ashes of that little girl. Her skin was covered in gray ash as she flailed, trying to get the scent of charred flesh out of her nose. But she couldn't. She couldn't do anything but swipe at her nose as she grew more and more nauseated and weak. And then the ashes were in her eyes and she was blinded, grappling for a stronghold so that she could stand, though she was being strangled by that very same ash. Clawing into the dirt and moaning, Bright Star felt nothing like she had only moments ago, when she had ascended.

Her fingers soon found flesh, cool flesh as hands reached out to take her. Arms came around her and hot, hot tears coursed down her face. She welcomed them as they washed the ash away and when her coughing subsided. She looked up to find Jacob smiling down at her. He too was covered with ash but Bright Star knew it was his own. She pushed back from him and she heard laughter, she heard the laughter come from all directions as she swiped at her face with the sleeve of her ceremonial robe. She felt hot, sticky sweat all over her face. Though when she looked down at the sleeve she found it drenched crimson. She looked up toward Jacob and found herself faced with him and Elizabeth. They stood side by side, the same benign expression cursing their faces. "I will not burn with you," Elizabeth said. "She will not burn with you," Jacob said as well.

"You can't have her!" Bright Star groaned.

"*You* can't have her," Jacob told her. And, after those words, the spirit that was Elizabeth was gone from his side. "She is free from you. She will be born into the soul of another." They were surrounded by the tribesmen who had persecuted her so many lives before. Those who chanted *Burn! Burn! Burn!* And in unison, like soldiers, they turned and walked away from Bright Star's dying body.

"*Nooo!*" The scream caused a ripple through the ground that ripped the earth open to accept her. Like a geyser, though the soil that had been eagerly awaiting her, spit her from its pursed lip of a ridge. "Jacob!"

In the sky, she saw him. He was physically alone, but she knew. She knew that Elizabeth stood just there over his left shoulder. Elizabeth, the one he had always loved, was no longer a part of her. The only being on earth who wasn't. "Jacob!" She dragged him to her with her High Energy. Elizabeth would never have him. Elizabeth would not stop him from achieving his destiny. "Jacob!" she screamed it again.

As her voice pierced the blackened sky, she could feel rivers swell, drenching valleys and mountains with their shared tears. "Jacob, you have not succeeded in separating us. You cannot separate us." Her words came out of the mouths of each and every witness beneath them. The words came out of the mouths of every individual sleeping, eating, breathing in the world. Every one. Every single one.

The words came, but they were not true.

Jacob lashed out, his Energy sought to insert itself between Bright Star and the subjugated assembly below. It didn't work. They were one. Like a splitting atom, driving a wedge between Bright Star and Earth would only serve to destroy them all. With Herculean effort, he flexed, contracted, squeezed his muscles, his brain, his Energy, until the force he exerted started to work with that of Bright Star's. He could not work against her. He could only use the Energy she expelled, the Energy that doubled and re-doubled itself as it spread through every soul. He could only use its momentum, to help him do what had to be done.

Suddenly, black veins spread in a tainted web over her alabaster skin. Her body began to twist and curl, convulsing and breaking and rebuilding all at once. The scream torn from her body was more than guttural, more than visceral. It sounded like an earthquake and thunder and flooding waters at once. Black tears turned to diamonds as they welled and dropped from beneath her eyelids.

"I am the Prophet and I am the Soul!" Her tortured voice called to them all. She opened her eyes and the entire distance—including the red horizon—glowed blue. Her body began to rise on a watery blue cloud.

Her chest thrust upward, her head flung back. She screamed it again in a voice that was its own accompaniment, a double voice of soft and dark, yet reaching to the edges of the world. "I am the Prophet and I am the Soul." She repeated the words over and over again. She repeated them until the blue light that lived inside her became a beam out of her throat as well as her eyes.

* * * *

Goodbye, Jackson. The voice was stark and emotionless.

It stopped Jackson in the motion of laying a cold compress on Point's forehead. *What are you doing?* Jackson demanded from inside Rush's mind.

You want me to save her, Rush explained as though he were speaking to a frightened child. *But I can't do that. I can't continue saving her. Instead, I'm going to save you. All of you.*

"No!" Panic flared in Jackson's eyes as he called the word aloud. "No, Rush. You don't have to save me. You don't. You've saved me since I was born. You don't have to do this."

Rush sent Jackson a mental embrace, He hugged him fiercely. *I can't fight fate anymore*, he whispered in a calming tone. *I do have to do this. I have to save you, and I must save Domina, and I have to save everyone else.* And then he released the brief embrace and left Jackson only a vision of what was happening miles above him in the sky.

Rush faced the evolving Bright Star once again. The ball of blue light began to pulsate and grow. Heat washed over the assembly as the ball grew hotter, lighter, brighter. Then there was the screaming.

Piercing and deep at once. Blare and echo. Anguish and indignation. The ball was screaming its agony and defiance. The sound was tangible and left no watcher untouched. And then, the world was screaming. Even Jackson and Point threw their heads back and howled their communal pain.

Higher the ball floated into the sky until it gained momentum and hurtled out of the atmosphere. A shooting star in reverse, the assembly watched as the star took its place in the day sky, a smaller, blue sun, as bright as the large yellow ball beside it.

Jackson and Point both stopped their plaintive cries and looked at each other. It was then that Jackson fully understood. When Bright Star bound her fate to that of their universe, she had made herself impervious to earthly catastrophe. She could not die. She was as impervious as he. More so. So she was going to attempt to kill herself with Shift. She was going to kill herself and in that, demand that Rush save her. And she would never stop. Even if Rush saved her this time, she would not stop. She would continue until he could not save her. And she would take the world with her every time.

He couldn't kill her. He could only hold her. Hold her forever. He would have to hold her to him forever. What had she said? *Destined to orbit each other.*

Jackson remembered the day at the observatory. He felt his body go hot and cold at once. Liquid started to collect beneath his tongue and he could feel an acidic burn in his nose. His eyes were raw and his breath was ragged. He fought to find that path, that thread that had bound them together since his birth. *You can't do this*, he pleaded with his brother. He knew what Rush was doing. He understood everything now so well.

Rush didn't answer. *If you do this Rush, I swear I will become the Prophet.* Tears rolled down his dirt-streaked cheeks. *I swear to you that I will die every day just like she did.*

You won't. Domina will not let you, Rush returned, nothing more than a quiet murmur. Then, as Rush rose before Jackson's mind's eye, his body began to radiate red. Much quicker than Bright Star, he became a floating, opaque orange then yellow bubble causing heat and electricity to horrify the assembly.

The new star took less time to achieve its place in the sky. A darkened yellow ball next to the blue one, seated at the horizon.

Chapter 37

Domina

At the moment when two new stars were born into Earth's sky, Point delivered a squalling baby girl into Jackson Rush's waiting arms. The cinnamon-hued baby had a full head of silken, curling sandy hair and soft amber eyes. She had strong lungs. She weighed over eight pounds.

Domina is what she was called. Point did not survive the birth so did not declare it. Jackson hadn't asked. It was her name.

Domina, the second born Precocial, bore a mark high on her tummy, beneath her heart. It was a square patch of skin—no bigger than the head of a cufflink—that looked like three tiny blue stars.

Meet the Author

Grayson Reyes-Cole adores drama, the fantastic, and words. She is intrigued by the relationships people build and what makes them work. Grayson hopes to bring intense and engaging characters to life for her readers along with well-developed, interesting stories.

Splitting her time between Florida and Alabama, Grayson considers herself a quintessential Southerner. She also has a longstanding love affair with travel and speaks two and a half languages (if you count English, a fair amount of French, and the travel Spanish, German, and Tagalog). Grayson never needs her arm twisted to share stories and photos of her adventures across Europe and Asia.

Grayson's homepage: http://www.graysonreyescole.com
Reader email: grayson@graysonreyescole.com